THE RISE OF THE WEST

THE DANCE OF LIGHT: BOOK THREE

Gregory Kontaxis

GK

Translation: Sophia Travlos

Cover Design: Miblart

Interior Illustration: Ömer Burak Önal

Editing: K.E. Andrews

Proofreading: Sue Bavey

PaperBack ISBN: 978-1-0684411-0-3

Ebook ISBN: 978-1-7397294-9-3

Hardcover ISBN: 978-1-0684411-1-0

To all those who love this world

Contents

West Empire/Kerth

Unknown Sea

Moon Bay
Sauris
Sen River
Casir Mountains
Forest of Magic
Roads of Faith
Roads of Faith
Old Mountain
Mirth
Gorin
Cyr River
Death Bay
Bay of Tears

Sea of Men

STORMY ISLANDS

© City

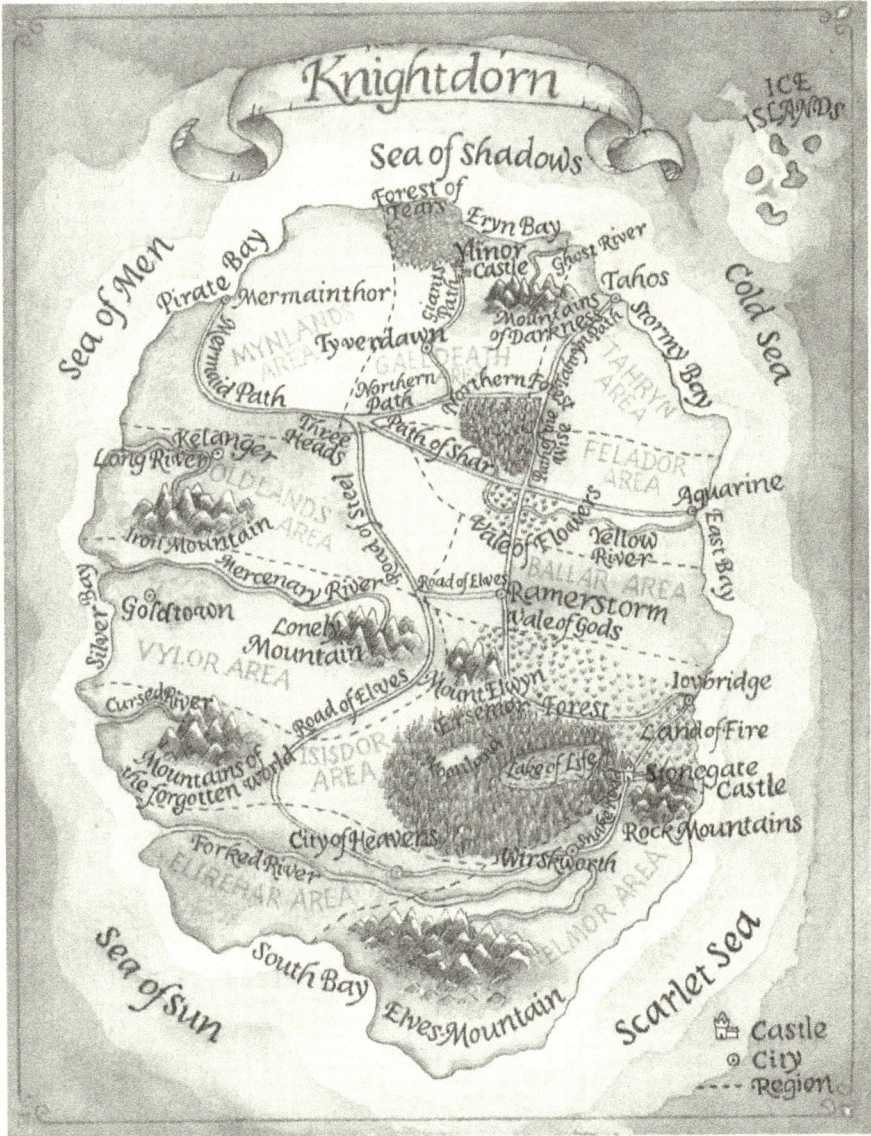

List of Regions, Organizations, and Characters

Kingdom of Knightdorn

King: Walter Thorn
Royal Council/Trinity of Death: Anrai, Rolf Breandan (Short Death), Brian the Sadist
Capital: Iovbridge
Emblem of the Kingdom: Seven swords in a laurel wreath on a white field
Emblem of the queen's House: A white tiger on a red field

Regions of the Kingdom of Knightdorn

Isisdor
Governor / Ruler: Walter Thorn
Capital: Iovbridge
Faith: The Unknown God
Emblem of the region: Seven swords in a laurel wreath on a white field
Emblem of the governor's House: A white tiger on a red field

Elmor
Governor / Ruler: Syrella Endor
Capital: Wirskworth
Faith: The God of Souls

Emblem of the region: A snake on a yellow field
Emblem of the governor's House: A snake on a yellow field

Felador
Governor / Ruler: None
Capital: Aquarine / City of Healers
Faith: The God of Wisdom
Emblem of the region: A golden oak tree on a green field
Emblem of the governor's House: None

Oldlands
Governor / Ruler: Ricard Karford
Capital: Kelanger
Faith: The God of the Sun
Emblem of the region: A hammer and an anvil on a brown field
Emblem of the governor's House: An axe on a brown field

Mynlands
Governor / Ruler: Launus Eymor
Capital: Mermainthor
Faith: The God of Youth
Emblem of the region: A mermaid on a violet field
Emblem of the governor's House: A mermaid on a violet field

Gaeldeath
Governor / Ruler: Walter Thorn
Capital: Tyverdawn
Faith: The God of War
Emblem of the region: A white tiger on a red field
Emblem of the governor's House: A white tiger on a red field

Vylor / Black Vale
Governor / Ruler: Liher Hale
Capital: Goldtown
Faith: The Avaricious God
Emblem of the region: A rusty coin on a black field
Emblem of the governor's House: A rusty coin on a black field

Tahryn
Governor / Ruler: Eric Stone
Capital: Tahos
Faith: The God of Rain
Emblem of the region: An old ship, *The Fairy,* on a white field
Emblem of the Governor's House: The tide of the sea on a green field

Ballar
Governor / Ruler: None
Capital: Ramerstorm / White City
Faith: The Goddess of Nature
Emblem of the region: A white hawk on a black field
Emblem of the governor's House: None

Elirehar
Governor / Ruler: None
Capital: City of Heavens / City of Pegasus
Faith: The God of Life / The God of Light
Emblem of the region: A white pegasus on a light blue field
Emblem of the governor's House: None

Ylinor Castle in the North Beyond the North
Lord of Ylinor: Gereon Thorn
Faith: The God of War
Emblem: A wyvern on a dark green field

Emblem of the Lord's House: A white tiger on a red field

Regions Independent from the Kingdom of Knightdorn

Ice Islands
Leader: Begon the Brave
Faith: The Goddess of the Sea
Emblem: An iceberg in the sea

Stonegate
Guardian Commander: Jarin
Faith: None
Emblem: A red-and-black sun, with spears for rays, on a white field
Emblem of the Guardian Commander's House: None.

Western Empire in the Continent of Kerth
Emperor: Odin Mud
Capital: Mirth
Faith: The God of Justice
Emblem: A red sun, with a white field
Emblem of the emperor's House: A shield, covered in blood, on a white field

Characters

Ador – Deceased. Anrai's father.
Adur – A giant.
Ager Barlow – Deceased. Former King of Tahryn.
Aghyr Barlow – Deceased. Former Governor of Tahryn.
Aiora – A giantess.
Alan Ballard – Deceased. Borin Ballard's son.
Alaric – An elf.

Albous Egercoll – Manhon Egercoll's brother.

Aldus Morell – A lord of Gaeldeath.

Aleron – One of the wisest people of the elwyn race.

Alice Asselin – Deceased. Aymer Asselin's daughter and King Thomas Egercoll's wife.

Althalos Baudry – Deceased. Former Grand Master of Isisdor. He is considered the greatest Grand Master to have ever lived.

Alysia – An elf.

Amelia Reis – Deceased. Lady of Elmor and Sigor Endor's wife.

Andre – One of the Knights of Faith.

Andrian – High Priest and Governor of Felador.

Annora Egercoll – Manhon Egercoll's sister.

Annys – Walter's tiger.

Anrai – Member of the Trinity of Death. His father was a giant and his mother a human.

Anton Loken – Captain of Ballar.

Aremor – Deceased. Aleron's brother.

Areos – Deceased. A former leader of the centaurs. He helped Manhon Egercoll to curse the Elder Races.

Arianna Erilor – Deceased. John Egercoll's wife.

Arne Egercoll – Manhon Egercoll's brother.

Aron – Stonegate's Guardian.

Arthur Endor – Deceased. Syrella Endor's brother and Velhisya's father.

Avery Elford – Deceased. First King of Mynlands.

Aymer Asselin – Deceased. Former Governor of Oldlands who found murdered in his sleep.

Azelor – The God of Light.

Beatrice Egercoll – Deceased. Thomas Egercoll's sister and Queen Sophie's mother.

Begon the Brave – Leader of the Ice Islands.

Bereon – Deceased. Former leader of the Ice Islands. He was the one who forbade piracy in his land.

Bernal Ballard – Deceased. First King of Ballar.

Bert Dilerion – A lord from Felador. Eleanor's brother.

Berta Loers – Ghost Soldier. She is one of the most trusted soldiers of Walter Thorn.

Borin Ballard – Governor of Ballar.

Brian the Sadist – Member of the Trinity of Death.

Brom Endor – Deceased. Lord of Elmor and Syrella Endor's uncle.

Byron the Sturdy – Deceased. Great warrior of the Ice Islands.

Conrad Miller – A lord of Felador.

Daryn Endark – Lord Counsellor of Elmor.

Daw – A guard of the Sharp Swords.

Delia Barlow – Wife of Aghyr Barlow.

Devan – Captain of Oldlands.

Doran Brau – Deceased. Peter Brau's son.

Edgar – Deceased. A former High Priest of Elmor.

Edgar Endor, the Murderer – Deceased. A former King of Elmor.

Edmee Mud – Princess of Kerth and daughter of Odin Mud.

Edmund – High Priest of Elmor.

Edric Egercoll – Manhon Egercoll's brother.

Edward Endor – Deceased. Former Governor of Elmor and father to Syrella, Sigor and Arthur Endor.

Edward Ewing – Man of Isisdor's City Guard.

Egil – A soldier of Gaeldeath.

Egon – A man of the Sharp Swords.

Eimon Asselin – Lord of Oldlands, Aymer Asselin's son and Alice Asselin's brother.

Eira Egercoll – Manhon Egercoll's sister.

Eleanor Dilerion – A lady of Felador. Bert Dilerion's sister. She is one of the most trusted friends of Elliot.

Ellin – Velhisya's mother.

Elliot Egercoll – A young man hailing from a village burdened by his past. He is the last apprentice to have ever been trained by Althalos.

Emery – Captain of Ballar.

Emil – A soldier of Gaeldeath.

Emil Ballard – Deceased. Borin Ballard's son.

Emma Egercoll – Deceased. Thomas Egercoll's sister, Robert Thorn's wife and Walter Thorn's mother.

Emy – Deceased. Anrai's mother.

Eric Stone – Governor of Tahryn.

Erin – An elwyn.

Erneas – Deceased. Grand Master of Gaeldeath.

Eshina – Deceased. Erin's soulmate.

Esme – Deceased. A woman of Kerth. Marin Mud was about to marry her.

Euneas Molor – Deceased. Grand Master of Felador.

Euric – A guard of Goldtown.

Favian Egercoll – Deceased. Thomas Egercoll's brother.

Frederic Abbot – Captain of Isisdor.

Gaius – High Priest in Kerth.

George Thorn – Deceased. First King of Knightdorn and Walter's grandfather.

Gerald Thorn – Deceased. Uncle to George Thorn and former Lord of Ylinor.

Gereon Thorn – Lord of Ylinor. Robert Thorn's brother and Walter's uncle.

Gervin Gerber – Royal Guard of Isisdor.

Girard – Deceased. Grand Master of Oldlands.

Giren Barlow – Slave. Aghyr Barlow's son.

Gregory Egercoll – Deceased. Thomas Egercoll's brother.

Gregory Mollet – Lord Counsellor of Isisdor.

Grelnor Lengyr – Lord Counsellor of Elmor.

Hann – Deceased. Grand Master of Mynlands.

Henry Delamere – Deceased. Former Governor of Felador and Sophie's father.

Henry Endor – Deceased. Sigor Endor's son.

Hereweald Delamere – Deceased. Former Governor of Felador and Henry Delamere's father.

Hugh – Captain of Isisdor.

Hurwig – Elliot's hawk.

Ian – Owner of an inn named Dophin in the Ice Islands.

Ida – A woman of Wirskworth. Her father owns a tavern named Three Arrows

Iren Selin – Deceased. Wife of George Thorn.

Iris Alarie – A lady of Felador.

Ivar – A soldier of Wirskworth.

Jack – A man of the Ice Islands.

Jackin Dilerion – Deceased. Eleanor's father.

Jacob Hewdar – Lord of Elmor.

Jahon – General of Elmor.

James Segar – Deceased. Captain of Iovbridge.

Jarin – Guardian Commander of Stonegate.

Jeanne Karford – Cousin of Reynald and Ricard Karford.

John Egercoll – Deceased. Former Governor of Elirehar. Father to Thomas, Favian, Beatrice, Emma and Gregory Egercoll.

John, the Long Arm – Former Bounty Hunter. He holds a special place of trust in Elliot's circle, being one of the people he relies on the most.

Lain Hale – Deceased. Former Governor of Vylor and Liher's older brother.

Lan – A lad in Iovbridge.

Launus Eymor – Governor of Mynlands.

Laurana Brau – Lady of Isisdor. Peter Brau's wife.

Laurent Mill – Deceased. Lord of Oldlands. He died when Lain Hale attacked to his castle.

Leghor – Leader of the centaurs.

Leonhard Payne – Healer of Felador.

Leuric – High Priest of Iovbridge.

Liher Hale – Governor of Vylor.

Linaria Endor – Captain of Elmor and Syrella Endor's daughter.

Lora Barlow – Sister of Giren Barlow and daughter of Aghyr Barlow.

Loren Elford – Deceased. Former Governor of Mynlands.

Lothar Hale – Liher Hale's younger brother.

Luk – Deceased. A lover of Matt.

Magor the Terrible – Former leader of the giants. He is presumed dead.

Manhon Egercoll – King of Elirehar and brother to Thomyn Egercoll. He was one of the seven riders of the pegasi.

Marin Mud– Prince of Kerth and Son of Odin Mud.

Maris Magon – Deceased. Lord of the Knights and Regent of Elirehar. He served as a regent of Elirehar by the time that Thomas Egercoll became king, and he kept his title after Thomas's death.

Mark – Man of the Ice Islands.

Matt – Prisoner of Liher Hale.

Maygar Asselin – Deceased. Former King of Oldlands.

Mehryn – Deceased. Grand Master of Elmor.

Mengon Barlow – Deceased. First King of Tahryn.

Merhya Endor – Captain of Elmor and Syrella Endor's daughter.

Merick – Captain of Isisdor.

Morys Bardolf – A lord from Wirskworth.

Myren Endor – First King of Elmor.

Odin Mud – Emperor of Kerth.

Odo – A man of the Ice Islands.

Orella – Deceased. Anrai's grandmother

Patrick Degore – Lord Counsellor of Isisdor.

Peter Brau – Lord of the Knights of Isisdor.

Philip Segar – Peter Brau's squire and James Segar's son.

Pip – Guard of Mirth.

Raff – A captain from the Ice Islands.

Rain – An orphan boy in Kerth.

Renier Torin – Deceased. Grand Master of Ballar.

Reyna – Deceased, Morys's sister.

Reynald Karford – Guardian Commander of Stonegate.

Ricard Karford – Governor of Oldlands.

Richard Lamont – Captain of Isisdor. George Thorn made him captain when he resolved a siege by Lain Hale against the castle of Laurent Mill.

Righor – A centaur.

Robb – Man of the Ice Islands.

Robert Thorn – Deceased. Former Governor of Gaeldeath. Father to Walter Thorn and husband to Emma Egercoll.

Robyn – Captain of Isisdor.

Rolf Breandan – Member of the Trinity of Death. He is known as Short Death.

Ronald – A guard of Aquarine.

Sadon Burns – Most powerful lord of Elmor.

Salm – Lord of Kerth.

Saron Gray – Lord of Gaeldeath.

Selwyn Brau – Lord of Isisdor and Peter Brau's son.

Selyn – Elliot Egercoll's sister and lady of Elirehar.

Sermor Burns – Deceased. Sadon Burns' only son.

Shilor Penn – Lord Counsellor of Elmor.

Sigor Endor – Deceased. Syrella Endor's older brother.

Sindel Brau – Deceased. Peter Brau's son.

Solor Balkwall – A lord of Felador.

Sophie Delamere – Queen of Knightdorn.

Sygar Reis – Lord Counsellor of Elmor.

Syrella Endor – Governor of Elmor.

Thindor – The last pegasus of the world. He is presumed dead.

Thomas Egercoll – Deceased. Former King of Knightdorn and Alice Asselin's husband.

Thomyn Egercoll – First King of Elirehar. He was one of the seven riders of the pegasi.

Thorold – Grand Master of Elirehar. He is presumed dead.

Velhisya Endor – Syrella Endor's niece. She is the only known being with an elwyn mother and a human father.

Vyresar Tobley – Guard of the City of Heavens.

Walter Thorn – Governor of Gaeldeath and King of Knightdorn. Currently, he controls Isisdor.

Will – Captain of Ballar.

William – A Defender of the Sharp Swords.

William Osgar – Deceased. Lord of the Knights.

Wymond – Deceased. Grand Master of Tahryn.

Zehir – A centaur.

Zhilor – The God of Death.

The Story So Far

Elliot sets off on his journey to the Mountains of the Forgotten World to find out as much as he can about the ancient curse that has kept the Elder Races imprisoned there. These beings are their only hope of beating Walter since Queen Sophie and Syrella Endor need allies for the upcoming siege. Nevertheless, the Elder Races have suffered at the hands of humans, and it won't be easy to get them to ally with an Egercoll since the House of Pegasus is responsible for the curse that haunts them.

John and Selwyn are trying to expedite the missions Elliot has sent them on so that they can also find soldiers to help them in the battle in Wirskworth. Selwyn hastens to ask for help from Liher Hale, Lord of the Mercenaries, while John travels to the Ice Islands, wishing to build an alliance on Sophie's behalf. At the same time, Eleanor rides away from Elmor to get to Aquarine, her hometown. Elliot has asked her to try to help the kingdom of Felador, which has been without a ruler for seventeen years.

While Walter prepares to attack, Syrella tries to fortify Wirskworth as best she can, and Peter and Sophie are overcome with fear as soon as they hear about the missions Elliot has sent Eleanor and Selwyn on. At the same time, Elliot succeeds in finding the Elder Races but discovers that it will be almost impossible to break the curse that haunts them and set them free. Moreover, his discussions with Aleron, the sage of the elwyn, make it clear to him that these creatures do not trust humans and are unwilling to fight by their side. Additionally, the only two giants left in the world, Adur and Aiora, appear to hate him.

Back in Elmor, Velhisya finds out that Elliot is in the Mountains of the Forgotten World and wonders if he'll manage to break the curse that haunts her mother's race. At the same time, she tries to convince her aunt to allow her to take part in the battle against Walter, but Syrella refuses to let her, because she's not a warrior.

Selwyn seeks an alliance with Liher Hale, who instead decides to imprison him and demand a ransom for his release. Eleanor arrives in Aquarine, where she is received with suspicion, although Andrian, the high priest, appears to like her. Andrian has been chosen by the young lords of Felador to rule the region, though no one in the rest of the kingdom knows about this. In addition, John arrives in the Ice Islands, where he decides that he no longer wants to help Elliot and his allies, as he fears that the war with Walter will cost him his life. So, he decides to live a quiet life in the northern islands, disregarding everything happening elsewhere in the world.

Elliot faces his deepest fears in the Mountains of the Forgotten World. Meanwhile, Alaric, an elf who is very skilled in battle, teaches him how to ward off the fiery blades of the elwyn and elves, which cause a burning sensation on the skin of every other creature, including humans.

At the same time, news of Selwyn's capture reaches Wirskworth and Syrella quarrels with Sophie and Peter about whether they should send an army to free him. He forces Sophie to reveal that she knows Syrella's daughters are Jahon's children and not her dead husband's. Syrella breaks down and admits the truth and decides to truly trust Sophie. In addition, she agrees with the Queen to send a few dozen men with a plan confided to them by Giren Barlow to free Selwyn. Velhisya requests that she lead the mission, and Syrella agrees, even though she fears for her niece's life.

Selwyn is tortured in Goldtown, and the Governor of Vylor's brother helps him during his time in captivity. Lothar Hale wants an alliance with Sophie, and he disagrees with his brother's decisions. A while later, Velhisya and Giren arrive in Goldtown but fail to free Selwyn. Velhisya is taken captive, while Giren and Selwyn get away with Lothar's help.

Walter travels to the Mountains of Darkness with a few thousand select men intent on taming a wyvern. Leonhard Payne, a famous healer, has told him legends which claim that creatures with Orhyn Shadow in their veins can bond with these winged monsters. Walter puts this venom in his veins while simultaneously drinking mermaid blood to give him the strength to live with Orhyn Shadow within him. Leonhard's suspicions are confirmed when a wyvern bonds with Walter. Moreover, one of them rushes to Anrai's side, but Walter prevents their union. Soon after, Thorn orders Anrai to leave his camp and assassinate the remaining giants in the world. Walter's true intention is to distance Anrai from the wyverns since he would be dangerous if one bound itself to him. Anrai accepts the mission but does not intend to carry it out, as he is a half-giant himself. Thus, he takes leave of Walter, no longer devoted to him.

Eleanor shows she has the gift of leadership in Aquarine, and Andrian asks her to take over the area's rulership. She refuses, but the lords of the city swear allegiance to her, so she decides to try. Soon after, Anrai is captured in Felador and confides in Eleanor that he has left Walter once and for all. Despite the opposition of her advisors, Eleanor decides to give him a second chance and allows him to live on her land.

Elliot succeeds in freeing the Elder Races, but just before he does so, Aiora ends her life, unable to stand the torment of the curse any longer. Adur vows to take revenge on Egercoll's successor, while the elwyn and elves decide to fight by Elliot's side.

Soon after, Adur finds Walter and asks to fight for him. Walter accepts the offer and finds out that Anrai has disobeyed his orders and is in Felador. He sends Adur to fight in Wirskworth with half his men and rides on to Aquarine, intent on killing Anrai. Walter and Leonhard believe that if all the giants die, there is hope that all the wyverns in the world will submit to Walter.

Walter's army attacks Wirskworth while Adur, astride his wyvern, destroys the city's gate. It is then that Elliot arrives, along with the

14

elwyn and elves, and they manage to defeat the enemy. Adur loses his life, and some of Walter's men flee. At the same time, Walter arrives in Aquarine and murders anyone in his path, while his wyvern kills Anrai and Eleanor. Then, the world's remaining wyverns bond with him and destroy Aquarine.

The Blasphemous Knights

Marin glanced at Edmee; the woman's face was expressionless. The square around the temple's raised portico swarmed with people. Marin would have preferred to have stayed in his chamber that sunny morning. He didn't want to see what was to follow.

"I want to leave," Marin said.

Edmee turned her head towards him. "No. Father ordered us to be here. Move!" she replied.

The woman made her way through the crowd, heading for the staircase that led to the portico. Two white-cloaked guards saw them approaching and immediately stepped aside. Edmee continued onward in her glittering armour, her straight red hair blowing behind her, while Marin followed, his gaze lowered. They went up the stairs quickly and stood in the portico in front of the temple. Marin looked at the columns that held up the stone ceiling. At the back of the portico was an ornate entrance that led into the Temple of the God of Justice, and in its centre stood three large wooden crosses nailed into the ground.

"Prince Marin, Princess Edmee, sit there," said a soldier approaching them.

Marin saw a dozen men in silk waistcoats and cloaks of gold cloth sitting in wooden chairs. Three chairs remained vacant in the centre of the row. Marin and Edmee took their seats to the right and left of the middle chair.

"I expected you would come sooner, my Prince."

Marin glanced to the right at the old lord with the sardonic smile.

"I'm looking forward to the punishment... I don't want to miss a single moment," the man said.

"Your impatience will be rewarded, Lord Salm," Marin replied.

Lord Salm didn't lose his smile. Marin straightened and looked ahead. The crowd had spread out in all directions around the temple, while the throng reached as far as the Red Palace. He felt a need to disobey his father's order and leave. Marin scratched his chin, deep in thought, as a huge man climbed up to the portico.

The executioner was about thirty years old, the same as Marin, and his smirk indicated that he was looking forward to what was to follow. The man walked slowly towards the wooden crosses and stood beside them where there was a small table covered with all sorts of tools.

Marin leaned towards his sister. "I don't want to see this type of spectacle again," he said under his breath.

Edmee grabbed the arm of the empty chair between them and looked at him, her almond-shaped eyes narrowing. "You're the Prince of Kerth. If you leave, you'll dishonour our father!" she whispered.

His sister may have been five years younger than him, yet she always spoke to him as if she were older. Suddenly, the crowd's jeering grew louder, and Marin looked at the steps that led to the portico. A man in a purple jerkin and black cloak surrounded by four other men was walking with his head held high. A gold crown adorned his bushy, white hair. Emperor Odin Mud climbed up to the portico, greeting the crowd while the jeers grew even louder. Shortly after, the Emperor walked over to the wooden seats, and Marin caught the glance his father cast in his direction before he sat between him and Edmee. Odin's guards remained standing near the wooden crosses, the red sun on the cloaks billowing behind them.

One of the men sitting three seats to Marin's right stood up abruptly. "Bring in the blasphemers! Bring in the renegades!" High Priest Gaius shouted.

Marin saw the priest's black eyes glow with excitement. He would finally get his revenge. The crowd's jeers picked up again, and a few more guards climbed the steps up to the portico. Amongst them, three tattered-looking men walked with stooped postures, their unsteady gait betraying their weakness. A short while later, they arrived in front of the wooden crosses. Marin recognised only one of the prisoners—Andre, who was as pale as death.

Marin watched the guards hoist the three men onto the wooden base of the structures and tie their hands and feet. He could no longer see the prisoners well, as the backs of the crosses blocked his view. He was glad not to see the terror on the men's faces—the terror of what was to follow.

High Priest Gaius walked towards the crosses, and the guards moved away.

"These men admitted to their crimes!" Gaius shouted. "They admitted they dishonoured the Emperor of Kerth and our god. They dishonoured the will of the God of Justice that dwells within our ruler, and now the time has come for justice to punish their deeds."

"We haven't committed any crime!" A voice suddenly shook the air.

Marin couldn't see Andre's face, the man who had called out, but he admired his courage.

"How dare you utter such lies in front of the Emperor!" screamed the High Priest. "You have one last chance, Andre. If you and your followers ask forgiveness for your sins, you'll be granted a swift death. Otherwise, the price of justice will be steep. I'd advise you to watch your final words."

"No god lives inside a man!" Andre shouted again. "No god commands the killing of innocent people, the killing of anyone who disagrees with the will of an emperor! Odin Mud turned us into slaves and built arenas for his slaves to die as gladiators. We, the Knights of Faith, will never bow down to Od—"

The man's voice died with a thump. The executioner had hurried over to the wooden cross and punched him.

"Today, you had the chance to ask for forgiveness... You had the chance to wash away your sins before the God of Justice. Nonetheless, you chose the path of sin. You aren't Knights of Faith, but of *Blasphemy*!"

The High Priest signalled to the executioner, and he stepped closer to the captives, tearing their clothes with a knife.

"Turn the crosses towards me. I want to see the punishment of these blasphemers, these deniers of our god!" Odin suddenly shouted.

Marin hadn't expected to hear those words come from his father's lips. The guards acted immediately and began to turn the crosses. Marin could now see the three naked captives. The crowd began to throw whatever they held in their hands at them.

Tomatoes and carrots hit Andre's face, and the executioner approached again, knife in hand.

"Castrate them!" High Priest Gaius said.

Marin closed his eyes, unable to look any longer. The captives' pained cries pierced his ears. Shortly afterwards he opened his eyes, lowering his gaze. He prayed the men would breathe their last quickly to end their torment. The screams of pain wouldn't stop until the men's voices began to fade as their strength left them.

Marin avoided looking up until he heard the High Priest's voice again. "BURN THEM!"

Before he could stop himself, he raised his head and saw the captives' desecrated bodies. The executioner doused their heads with a thick liquid—oil. Then, a soldier in a white cloak moved towards him, holding a lit torch. The executioner took it and looked at the three men with eyes shining with excitement.

Marin lowered his gaze again while screams filled the air once more. The smell of burning flesh made him nauseous, but he knew that the torment would soon come to an end, and he'd be able to leave this place.

"May the fire purify you of your sins!" yelled the High Priest.

"YOU'LL DIE SOON, GAIUS. YOU, CORRUPT LORDS, AND YOUR EMPEROR WILL ALL DIE BEFORE THE NEXT SUMMER ARRIVES. THE INNOCENT PEOPLE YOU HAVE MUR-

DERED WILL BE WAITING FOR YOU IN THE REALMS OF THE DEAD!"

Marin lifted his head and saw the blazing crosses. The flames engulfed the captives' bodies. He couldn't believe that the voice had come from the mouth of a man whose flesh was burning—or that those words had come from Andre's lips.

His gaze turned to his father. The steely blue eyes of Odin Mud were filled with hatred.

The Messenger of Death

E lliot looked closely at the golden snakes decorating the Governor of Elmor's seat, lost in thought. There was no one in Moonstone's Great Hall that evening. He took a few steps towards the ornate seat and stood in front of it. Then, he promptly kicked it with all his might.

"Fuck!" he cried. The pain had paralyzed his right leg, and it felt like his toes were being torn apart. Nonetheless, he *wanted* to feel pain. Pain was the only thing that subdued the weight in his chest that kept him breathless. Ten days had passed since their victory on the soil of Wirskworth, yet he was no longer certain that they had truly won.

Selwyn was a prisoner of the Governor of Vylor, and no news of Velhisya had reached the city. Elliot bet that she and Giren had been taken captive by Liher Hale's men. *Why did they decide to go to that place?* His anger surged like a bloodthirsty wolf. He knew Velhisya wanted to help free Selwyn, but it was an extremely difficult mission.

"We had to do something. Peter would have secretly escaped the city to save Selwyn if we hadn't sent someone to Vylor." Sophie's words echoed in his mind.

Elliot knew they needed someone with authority to lead such a mission. However, Velhisya didn't have the experience for such an undertaking. *No one could accomplish this mission...* The idea that Velhisya might be suffering at the hands of Liher Hale sickened him to the core. *Maybe she's dead.* The thought was so unbearable that he felt the need to kneel and pray to the gods.

He glanced around. The little light coming through the Hall's windows filled him with unease. Night would soon draw near, and he knew nightmares would accompany his dreams, filling him with fear and anxiety.

Elliot let out a weary breath, and the pain in his leg subsided. He hoped Velhisya and Selwyn were alive and knew he was the only person responsible for what had happened to them. He'd been a fool to send someone to the land of Liher Hale. John had warned him, but he hadn't listened.

Thorold advised you to send emissaries to every place not yet under Walter's orders. His conscience's voice tried to wash away his guilt in vain. Thorold had told Elliot what he had to do to win the war, but he should have considered what his choices would cost. As if that weren't enough, he'd received no news from either John or Eleanor and had received no word from Reynald in days. It was the first time Hurwig, his hawk, had taken so long to return.

Maybe they're all dead, just like Morys, because they followed my commands.

Elliot kicked the stone seat again. His bones cracked as pain spread throughout his leg. He screamed. He had achieved the impossible—setting the Elder Races free—while failing to save so many people he loved. What had become of all of his companions was unknown, and Velhisya had also paid the price for his decisions.

He thought of the battle they'd won against a large army and a giant. Even though they'd won, Elliot felt like they had lost. *Where is Walter?* he asked himself for the umpteenth time. They'd sent scouts all over Elmor without discovering Walter's whereabouts or learning about his movements.

Elliot tried to piece together the events once again to find what was missing. Syrella had told him a scout had reported the arrival of the giant in Walter's camp a few days before the battle, but no one else had confirmed this piece of information. So, the Scarred Queen had decided to ignore it.

Syrella should have listened. Elliot had heard that the enemy army had set up watches throughout the land, preventing Elmor's scouts from gathering information about its movements. Moreover, there were reports that thousands of Walter's men had retreated some time ago, but these had not seemed convincing enough to be believed. Syrella and Sophie had assumed that Thorn was trying to mislead them before besieging the city.

Elliot continued to rack his brain, and flashbacks of the dead soldiers' empty gaze came to him. He and a few of Elmor's guards had looked for surviving men on the battlefield in an attempt to find out where the rest of Walter's soldiers had gone. The images were seared into his mind—lifeless eyes staring at him while the soil turned red with blood. He might have been skilled with a sword, but if he could, he'd never fight again in his life. No one should have to witness so much death. Elliot hadn't found any of the enemy's troops alive but had heard some soldiers calling to him. He'd run to their side and had found a lad with a spear stuck in his thigh, groaning.

"Where are the rest of the men? Where's Walter?" Elliot had asked.

The lad had spat blood onto the ground before he spoke. *"I don't know."*

Elliot had crouched by his side. *"I know you were devoted to Walter Thorn, but all he did for you was to send you to your death... He sent you here to die and then made a run for it... Tell me where he went."*

The soldier had lifted his head to look Elliot in the eye. *"I don't know. The giant arrived at our camp a few days ago and spoke to the officers and governors,"* he gasped. *"We heard Walter asked for half his men to meet him in another place, but we never found out where. Only the commanders and the governors knew... All I heard was that they were travelling northeast—towards White City."*

"Were the governors not shocked by the new orders?"

"They didn't believe the giant, but he had a letter from Walter. They obeyed. The giant gave the new orders and flew away. He didn't want to

be seen by Elmor's scouts in order to keep the element of surprise. He also advised us to increase the guards around our camp so that you wouldn't find out that half our forces were to depart. Some men whispered that even the giant wasn't pleased that our army was to be broken up, but he maintained that Walter had to fight two battles," the lad gasped, running out of breath.

"I'd have thought that the governors who stayed back to fight would have reacted to the order. It'd be far more difficult to win with half the number of men."

A smile formed on the bloodstained lips of the young man. *"Nobody disobeys Walter if he wants to keep his life. I could have sworn that even the giant was afrai..."*

The soldier hadn't managed to finish his sentence before his gaze went blank, staring into nothing. They had tried to find other survivors amongst the enemy troops in vain.

In a swift motion, Elliot drew his sword and slammed it against the stone seat. For a moment, he saw his angry face reflected in the blade.

"I think you should calm down. I don't think Syrella will be pleased to find out you ruined her seat."

Elliot turned and saw Aleron standing at the entrance of the Great Hall. "How long have you been there?" he asked.

"Long enough... I'm glad the city guards didn't hear your cries," Aleron replied.

"Why didn't you speak up?"

"Anger such as that must be given vent to sometimes..."

Elliot avoided the elwyn's gaze. "I'm to blame for everything."

Aleron took a few steps towards him, his green cloak fluttering behind him. "You can't take responsibility for everything that happens in the world, Elliot."

"I sent my companions—my friends—to their death."

"A few days ago, you wanted to die. You wanted to take that sword and drive it into your heart." Aleron's gaze landed on the Sword of Light in Elliot's right hand. "However, you weren't responsible for the curse caused by one of your ancestors hundreds of years before you were born."

"I may not have been responsible for that... But I sent—"

"Every being in this world has the gift of free will. I'm sure you didn't force your friends to travel to the places they went to. They chose to do so—they chose to help."

"They trusted me... They trusted me and I—"

"They knew the risks," Aleron interjected again. "They knew they might die on their journeys, but they still decided to go. You cannot protect everyone, Elliot. Nobody has that power. If your friends became one with the power of Light, make sure their sacrifice wasn't for nothing. It's all you can do... Nevertheless, we can't be sure what has happened to them."

As wise as Aleron's words sounded, Elliot couldn't shake his guilt. "Thorold told me that we needed new allies, that we would have no hope without help. He advised me to send an emissary to every land in the kingdom that hadn't yet submitted to Walter, and I obeyed. Syrella told me that Liher Hale would never agree to an alliance with us. Thorold was wrong!"

"The repercussions of our actions are complicated, my lad. Thorold gave you a piece of advice, and you chose to follow it. He didn't order you to fulfil his wish on pain of death, and the same applies to your friends."

"Even Velhisya..." Elliot didn't want to finish his sentence.

"She tried to fight for all that was of value to her."

Elliot looked Aleron in the eyes. A good-natured smile played on his lips.

"We have to find Walter. We need to find out what has happened."

"This is truly a mystery. However, I believe we will hear from him soon," Aleron said.

"Here you are! I've been looking everywhere for you," came a voice.

Elliot and Aleron turned towards Jahon as he entered the hall. "Why were you looking for me?" Elliot asked, looking at Jahon.

"A lord from Aquarine and five more men have arrived in the city," the man replied breathlessly.

Elliot almost choked. "Have you heard what news they bring?"

"Not yet. Syrella and Sophie will be in the Great Hall soon, but the news isn't good." Jahon's gaze was sullen.

Elliot felt the room shrink around him. "Why? Tell me what you know!" His voice echoed off the hall's high ceiling.

Jahon's gaze fell to the ground. "The lord said that the words he brings are only words of death."

The Winged Monsters

Elliot's body tensed with impatience. Beside him, Aleron looked worried, too. Minutes passed, and Elliot's eyes darted to Jahon, who waited a few feet away, next to the Governor of Elmor's stone seat. The moon had made its appearance and could be seen in the sky through the Great Hall's windows, and a few torches illuminated the room. Footsteps echoed from the entrance to the Great Hall, and Elliot held his breath as he prayed that Eleanor was okay.

Syrella entered the hall accompanied by her daughters and two guards. Her gaze shifted between Jahon and Elliot. "Where is the messenger?" she asked.

"I told the City Guard to keep him at the gate for a while. I wanted to have the news sent to you and Sophie before they brought him to the castle," Jahon said.

The sound of more hurried footsteps drew closer, and Sophie entered the room, clearly agitated. Peter, the Lord of the Knights, followed beside her, along with three guards and Master Thorold.

"I heard an envoy from Aquarine has arrived," Sophie said, worry written on her face.

Syrella turned to her. "He's being held at the gate and will be here soon."

With these words, Syrella moved towards Jahon. She reached her seat, but she didn't sit. Syrella turned her head as Sophie approached her and nodded curtly. Sophie sat on the stone chair reserved for the Governor of Elmor. Syrella's daughters, Master Thorold, and Peter approached Elliot.

The guards spread out around the hall.

As they waited, the atmosphere became reminiscent of a funeral, and Elliot looked towards the entrance of the Great Hall again. He could have sworn he heard people approaching. The sound grew louder until a few figures crossed the threshold. Two soldiers in yellow-black cloaks strode in while a man of medium height walked between them. The messenger was young with black hair and a stocky build.

The guards and the messenger stopped a few feet away from the stone seat, and Sophie rose with a jolt.

"Who are you?" she asked.

"My name is Solor Balkwall. I am a lord of Felador," the messenger replied. His clothes were dirty, and his face seemed tired.

"What brings you to Wirskworth, Solor? Did Eleanor send you?"

Elliot could have sworn the newcomer's eyes flashed with sorrow.

"Lady Dilerion is dead."

Elliot's legs went numb. Sophie looked as if she was about to lose her balance. Peter quickly moved to the Queen's side, holding her by the shoulders to keep her upright. Sophie gave him a curt nod, and he stepped back.

"How?" was the only word that left the Queen's lips.

"Walter Thorn attacked Aquarine."

Silence spread around the room.

"Why?" Elliot knew he should leave the questions to Sophie, but he wasn't able to restrain himself.

"I don't know—nobody knows. The Governor arranged a feast in the gardens of the city. On the day of the celebration, a few thousand men attacked Aquarine."

"The Governor? Did Eleanor take over the rulership of Felador?" Sophie asked.

Solor nodded.

"Didn't you realise that an enemy army was approaching the city?" Syrella asked.

"We weren't expecting an attack. The enemy was on horseback and approached Aquarine quickly. The villagers had no hope of sending news before the attack began," Solor replied.

"How did you escape?" Elliot took a step towards Solor.

"At the time of the feast, I was a few miles away from Aquarine, inspecting some plots that belong to me, or should I say, belonged to me," the man replied with a sad face.

"How come a lord of the city chose not to attend a feast thrown by the Governor of Felador?" Elliot asked.

"Certain decisions made by the Governor didn't sit well with me, and I decided not to attend the celebration."

Elliot drew the Sword of Light, enraged. "Did you betray Eleanor?" The blade touched Solor's neck.

"Elliot!" Aleron's voice echoed through the hall.

Elliot turned to the elwyn whose starry blue eyes reflected his anger.

"Elliot Egercoll," came Solor's voice. "From what I've heard about you from Lady Eleanor, I was sure you'd be a hothead."

Returning the sword to its sheath, Elliot repeated sharply, "Did you betray Eleanor?"

"No. The fact that I disagreed with some of her decisions doesn't mean that I wanted her dead, nor did I want Walter to kill every person in my homeland. Even my fiancée is dead," Solor said, looking at him dispassionately. "I didn't betray Eleanor. However, I don't know whether anyone else in the city did."

Elliot knew he shouldn't have let his anger get the better of him. The man before him had lost everything.

"How do you know that Eleanor is dead? You said you weren't in the city at the time of the attack," Peter said for the first time.

"No one survived. Walter attacked with thousands of men astride a winged monster. I had never seen a creature like that one. It must have been a wyvern. His men burnt the city. No one could have survived the attack."

Elliot's mouth went dry. He recalled Reynald's letter telling him that a wyvern had bonded with Walter, and he'd informed Syrella and Sophie about it. They should all have been prepared. Even now, the thought of Thorn on the back of one of those monsters filled him with dread.

Syrella approached Solor. "You said you don't know if someone else betrayed Eleanor. Why do you believe that someone may have wanted to betray her? If she wasn't well-liked in Felador, why did you give her the governance of the region?"

Solor sighed wearily. "Andrian believed she could help our land."

"Andrian? Is High Priest Andrian alive?" Syrella asked.

"He was, up until Walter's attack," Solor told her. "Andrian was the Governor of Felador until he convinced us that we had to give the title to Eleanor."

Despite her sorrow, Sophie appeared surprised. "Who made him governor?"

"The lords of the region. After the death Walter brought to our land seventeen years ago, Felador remained without a leader for a long time. Our noblemen, officers, and ruler were all dead. The only lords left were some children who survived the massacre, myself amongst them. When we grew up, we decided to sell our crops to rebuild our ruined city, and the people of Aquarine allowed us to appoint Andrian as Governor of Felador while we acted as his advisors."

"And did Andrian choose to give his title to Eleanor as soon as she arrived in your land?" Elliot asked.

"Not in the beginning. Eleanor arrived at our doorstep with a letter and told Andrian that Queen Sophie and Elliot Egercoll believed that Felador needed a ruler. She told him that she was capable of helping our land. Lady Dilerion didn't know that we already had a ruler, and no one would have been appointed Governor of Felador because of a letter..." Solor's gaze shifted to Elliot. "However, after the incident with this lord of Gaeldeath, Andrian changed his mind."

"What incident?" Sophie asked as she moved closer to Solor.

"A lord of Gaeldeath, Aldus Morell, had been stealing our crops for years. We couldn't stop him without getting embroiled with Walter. So, we decided to cultivate different plots of land in places no one knew about. However, Morell always appeared just before a bountiful harvest. We wondered how he found our fields until we caught him talking to one of Aquarine's lords. Our guards attempted to bring the treacherous lord into the city to be punished, but Morell tried to protect him. Nevertheless, he didn't have many soldiers with him, so the guards of Aquarine surrounded him and his men and brought them before Andrian." Solor paused for a moment.

"Most of the lords, myself included, asked that the traitor be punished by death and intended to let Morell go free. If we had killed him, Walter would have punished us. However, Morell said that if we killed the traitor, he'd make sure Thorn would kill us all. He wanted us to let him leave with the traitor."

"What does all this have to do with Eleanor?" Sophie's face tightened.

"Eleanor insisted we not kill the traitor because that would make us as bad as Walter. She also offered Morell a deal. If he accepted, we would freely give up a large proportion of our harvests without his having to search for them any longer. In return, he would protect Felador from the rest of the thieves who stole from our land. At the same time, the traitor would be imprisoned in our city, and his life would be spared. That way, we would also keep some of the harvest, and we'd be safe.'"

Elliot felt proud of Eleanor. "And did Morell accept?"

Solor nodded. "He decided that it was in his favour to sacrifice a traitor to get the most valuable crops in the kingdom for free. Now, he no longer needed spies. Just a few men would be sufficient to help us guard our land from other thieves and mercenaries."

"I assume that when Morell accepted the deal, Andrian decided Eleanor was able to rule Felador," Aleron said.

Many of the people present turned to look at him.

"Exactly," Solor replied. "Andrian told the lords that he belonged to the past, and Eleanor was the future of our land. He also told us that she was prudent and clever and she knew that violence is only needed when no other solution is available."

"Andrian was wise," Aleron said.

"Indeed. Still, the incident with Morell proved that there was at least one traitor in Aquarine. Perhaps there were others... Perhaps one of them betrayed Eleanor and her agreement with Morell. I'm sure Walter wouldn't have been happy to hear that one of his lords had made such a deal with us," Solor spoke.

"Walter wouldn't change his plans for a greedy lord!" Elliot snapped. He had to put aside the pain burning in his soul and find out the truth. "Walter was to march his troops to Elmor to kill his enemies. Did he change his plans to destroy a city without an army to punish a lord? Thorn would never have left the last battle for the kingdom for such a reason."

"Walter may have come to Felador because of the giant..." Solor seemed troubled as well.

"What giant?" Aleron's voice took on a sharp edge.

"A few days before Walter's arrival, Anrai, the man of the Trinity of Death, was caught on Felador's land."

"What was Anrai doing there?" Elliot asked with bated breath.

"Our men caught him and brought him before the Governor. He told us that he'd decided to leave his King for good. He claimed that Walter had ordered him to go to the Mountains of the Forgotten World and kill the remaining giants. Anrai couldn't do what he had asked, so he rode to our land, looking for somewhere to rest for a few days. Eleanor decided to allow him to remain in the city and forgave him for everything he'd done at Thorn's behest."

Elliot's brow furrowed. "And did Anrai remain in Aquarine?"

"Yes. He seemed to believe that Eleanor was the ruler he'd been looking for all his life. However, I and a few other lords disagreed with the Governor's decision. We didn't trust Anrai and knew that he was very dangerous. We were also afraid that Walter would find out about him and perhaps attack our city to punish the traitor of the Trinity of Death. A single lord might not have mattered, but Anrai's betrayal would enrage Thorn. Eleanor commanded us to withhold the information, but news like that rarely remains secret."

"Do you think this reached Walter's ears, and that's why he rode to Aquarine?" asked the Queen.

Elliot looked at Sophie. She seemed desperate to find out why Eleanor had died, as if being able to explain events would ease her pain.

"Perhaps... I'm sure Walter wanted to kill the giant," Solor told her.

"None of this makes any sense." Elliot's anger mounted again. "Walter wasted half of his army on the battlefields of Elmor. All his remaining enemies were here. Were he to kill them, he would remain king forever. And he chose to leave all that behind him for one man? He could have killed Anrai later."

"I don't know. However, there is something else... Something I can't explain." Solor lowered his gaze. "I don't know if it's important, but I've been thinking about it all the way here."

"Tell us what you know," Elliot insisted.

The lord lifted his eyes, his forehead creasing. "I didn't run away from Felador's land immediately when I saw Walter's soldiers attacking. I and the men who had accompanied me watched the attack from a distance. We wondered if there was any way we could help. Shortly after, the gate fell, and we heard screams of death as the winged monster destroyed everything in its way. I stood there, incapacitated, just watching the attack. When my men insisted that we go far away, I saw something else in the skies."

"What did you see?" Elliot pressed.

"Black shadows among the clouds... A dozen winged monsters like the one Walter rode filled the sky above Aquarine and soon after, they too attacked the city."

Elliot instinctively turned to Aleron, and what he saw frightened him more than anything else that night. It was the first time he had seen Aleron look scared.

The Price of Victory

Walter made himself comfortable on the throne and looked around the room, lit up with the rays of the morning sun. The Royal Hall in the Palace of the Dawn looked more beautiful than ever. He remembered the moment he'd first sat on the throne—the moment he'd been defeated on the soil of Elmor, his enemies having slaughtered his soldiers in the White City. Now, things had changed. This time he sat on the throne, feeling victorious, like everyone in the kingdom would finally submit to his will.

His eyes fell on the clipped wings jutting out on the right and left of his seat. It seemed laughable how Thomas Egercoll had asked for two pegasus wings to be carved on his throne. Walter had ordered the craftsmen of the city to cut them and leave only a small part. This served to remind him that it was he who had clipped the wings of the pegasi, destroying the House of Egercoll once and for all.

I lost half my army for this. He hated that thought. It was the only thing that made him bitter now, yet it had been a necessary evil. There had been no other way. The price of gaining the wyverns' loyalty—the price of victory—was heavy. Walter assumed that none of his men who had fought in Elmor had survived. He had flown amongst the clouds above Wirskworth astride his wyvern a few days ago and realised that his forces hadn't taken over the city. He knew that Adur was dead and since the giant had fallen, it would have been difficult for the rest of his men to have succeeded. He wanted to find out what had happened in the battle, but there was no one left alive whom he could ask.

"Your Majesty," came a voice.

Walter looked down as the aged figure of Leonhard Payne approached the throne. "I didn't realise you'd come into the hall," Walter said.

The old man wore a frown. "Ricard Karford has arrived in the city. He's alive," Leonhard told him.

A wave of surprise flooded Walter. It was as if the God of War had heard his thoughts and decided to send him the answers. "Bring him to me."

"I've already ordered the guards to escort him here, but I wanted to let you know first."

Walter stared at his most valuable ally. This healer with the sun-dried, wrinkled face and gaunt body, the man who looked like the living dead, had given him more than any other ally he'd ever had. He wouldn't have achieved many of the things he had without this man's help.

Footsteps came from the entrance to the Hall, and Walter saw a man approaching the raised throne. Ricard strode in quickly.

"I'm glad you survived, my old friend," Walter said.

"Really?" Ricard stopped and met Walter's stare, anger etched onto his face.

Rage stirred within Walter. He didn't like to be looked at in anger, only in fear. "What do you mean, Ricard?"

The Governor of Oldlands seemed to squirm, hearing the threat in Walter's voice. "You ordered half your men off the battlefield! We were slaughtered by Elmor's army!"

"If I'm not mistaken, the enemy's soldiers numbered fewer than twenty-five thousand. I left thirty thousand men for the battle, and I sent a giant on a wyvern's back to help—the only giant who ever fought on the side of humans.

"Elmor had more soldiers!" Ricard insisted. "At first, we thought we were about to win the battle when the giant managed to ram Wirskworth's gate, but a new army attacked us."

"I ordered Adur to tell you that that scumbag, Thomas's son, might arrive on the battlefield with the elwyn and the elves. I advised him to set up archers around the men and to kill those creatures before they got close to you. They had no horses... I thought it would be easy to—"

"They had horses! All of them!" Ricard raised his voice, and a fearful frown appeared on his face. He seemed to regret shouting.

"Were the elwyn and elves on horseback?" Walter asked.

"Yes!"

"Strange," Walter remembered Adur saying that the Elder Races didn't have horses in the Mountains of the Forgotten World.

"They flanked us, and it was very difficult to shield ourselves from their swords. The light on their blades burned the men's hands—"

"I know," Walter interjected. "Was the giant not able to help you?"

"He tried," Ricard admitted. "However, the light emitted by those swords struck the wyvern over and over again, and the monster struggled to escape the rays. It seemed to be wounded by them. Adur attacked and injured some elwyn and elves until he saw Elliot on the battlefield. I had never seen the boy before, but I heard the giant cry, 'You're going to die, Egercoll!'"

"And what happened?"

"That's when I decided to retreat... Most of our men were fighting at the wrecked gate of Wirskworth, trying to enter the city, and the elwyn, the elves, and the Guardians of the South surrounded them. I was sure we would lose, so I ordered some men to retreat."

"Didn't you see what happened to the boy and the giant?" Walter asked.

Ricard tilted his head. "I think the wyvern chased Elliot in an attempt to bite him. Soon after, a sound shook everything. If I saw correctly, the boy lured the monster towards the city and, along with the giant, crashed into the wall."

Damn, the giant was a fool, Walter thought, gritting his teeth. "Did Elmor's men not go after you?" he asked.

"No. They may not have realised I was retreating at the time. I left with three thousand mounted men. I thought we'd be more useful to you alive than dead since the battle was lost."

"How many elwyn and elves were there? The giant told me about five thousand of them were able to fight," Walter went on.

"I think Adur was right," Ricard told him.

"It wouldn't have been possible for them to find five thousand horses on their way, and the giant told me there were no horses in the Mountains of the Forgotten World." Walter turned to Leonhard. He was usually the one who had answers when no one else did. However, the man stood silent with a furrowed brow as if he couldn't explain the mystery.

"They would have had no hope of winning had we all fought together. Why didn't you come to the battlefield? Why did you order the men from Tahos and Gaeldeath to retreat?" Ricard said.

"There was another battle I had to win. A battle that was more important than anything else."

"What battle?"

"Have you heard that a wyvern bonded with me?"

Ricard's eyes narrowed, making him seem troubled. "The giant told the Governors and the officers, but many were doubtful. We didn't know if he was right in his mind. Adur didn't talk much. All he said was that he wanted to kill the Egercolls. He told us that he would destroy Elliot Egercoll in your name, in the name of the only human to ever tame a wyvern, but no one knew whether what he said was true."

"It was!" Walter snapped.

Ricard flinched. "Since you managed to tame a wyvern, what other battle did you have to win?" he asked hesitantly.

"One wyvern wasn't enough. I wanted all of them to follow me—all that were left in the world... And I succeeded."

Ricard stared at him, his eyes wide. "I thought humans couldn't tame wyverns. How were you able to bond with all of them? Even giants can't—"

"This was the battle I had to fight."

"With whom?"

"With Anrai."

"With Anrai?" Ricard repeated.

"Leonhard discovered that if all the giants died, the wyverns would only obey one master." Walter was careful how he worded his reply. He couldn't say anything more. No one was to know about the mermaids and Orhyn's Shadow that lived in his body.

Ricard's expression grew confused. "And when you discovered this secret, did you kill Anrai?"

Walter got up and slowly walked down the steps from the throne. "Not right away. At first, I ordered him to go to the Mountains of the Forgotten World and kill the remaining giants. It wouldn't have been wise to assassinate a member of the Trinity in front of my soldiers just before the battle with my enemies. It would have created turmoil and questions."

Walter walked towards Ricard. "You see, I wanted to send someone to the Mountains of the Forgotten World who would be accepted, someone whom the creatures living there wouldn't have considered an enemy. I knew that if I flew there on the back of my wyvern, I would have had no hope against the Elder Races. However, Anrai could have succeeded, and he would have got the giants out of the way. Even if he hadn't succeeded, my goal was for them to kill each other and for me to kill whoever was left."

Walter stood in front of Ricard. "Anrai disobeyed my order and decided to leave me. I thought he was devoted to me, but I was wrong... When I asked him to kill his kind, the kind that had raped his mother, he turned on me. I found out by chance from a merchant that he was in Aquarine."

Ricard tried to speak, but Walter cut him off. "I got news about Anrai the moment Adur arrived at my camp astride a wyvern. The giant told me that Elliot had freed the Elder Races but that he would fight on my side. He was the only giant left, and he wanted to take revenge on the

Egercolls—the humans who had unleashed the curse."

"The legends about the curse are true..." Ricard whispered. "How did Elliot break the—"

"That's of no significance!" Walter was incensed whenever he considered the fact that the boy had succeeded in breaking this curse. "Adur wasn't to know that I wanted him dead. He wasn't to speak to Anrai. So, I ordered him to fly to Elmor and give you new orders while I and the rest of the men rode to Aquarine to kill Anrai."

Ricard's eyes widened. "You sent Adur to Elmor to die! You knew we would lose without all our forces, but you wanted him dead so that you could tame the wyverns!"

Walter smirked. "I wasn't sure you'd lose. I assumed the giant might die if thousands of elwyn and elves attacked him; it would be difficult to face them alone. However, it would have been foolish of me not to have used him against my enemies."

"And what if he hadn't died? If we'd succeeded in Elmor?" Ricard asked.

"Then, my enemies would have all been dead, and it wouldn't have mattered if I won the devotion of all the wyverns. I'd have killed Adur after the battle, and there would have been no rival left in the kingdom."

"You sacrificed half your men to tame the wyverns! You sacrificed the entire army of Oldlands!" Ricard took a step forward. "We'd agreed that we would attack with sixty thousand men, drenching our blades with Orhyn Shadow. None of that happened!"

Walter could feel Ricard's rage. However, the Governor didn't dare unleash all his fury. He knew that if he did, his head would leave his shoulders. "There was no time to send you the poison. I did what had to be done to win the war, Ricard... What does it matter if I sacrificed thirty thousand men? What are thirty thousand lives worth compared to the peace that my reign will bring to this kingdom?"

Ricard's face turned red. "Why didn't you kill Adur the moment he found you? You could have executed the giant and ordered us to wait. If you then rode to Aquarine and killed Anrai, we could have all attacked Elmor together—sixty thousand men alongside all the wyverns in the world."

Walter frowned and looked down at the short man. "It wouldn't have been easy to kill Adur then. He may have wanted to fight by my side, but he didn't trust me. If I'd tried to assassinate him and had failed, he would have killed any number of my men, and his wyvern might have wounded mine. I couldn't risk that until I'd done away with my enemies. Moreover, countless supplies would have been needed to have you set up camp for so long."

"But—"

"I did what I thought best," Walter snapped. "Adur never found out where I intended to go. I told him I had to win another battle to destroy the Egercolls while insisting that I couldn't divulge any details. If he was successful in Elmor, he would gain my trust, and then I would explain it all to him. At first, he was disbelieving, and he wanted us to fight together, but I managed to convince him to follow my orders."

Walter pushed back his long hair. "Adur couldn't stay in my camp since I didn't intend to kill him at that moment. It was too dangerous. He found out at the same time as me where Anrai was. I told him that I'd ordered him to go to the Mountains of the Forgotten World to seek an alliance with the giants and that he'd disobeyed me without my knowledge. I also told him that he may have hated the giants because his mother had been raped by one of them. I insisted that I'd been disappointed, but that I'd spare him his life. Adur wasn't to know my true plan. If he suspected anything at all, he might have sought Anrai out, and together, they could have ridden two wyverns and attacked me. The safest thing was to have him go away by giving him a mission."

Ricard didn't seem convinced. "But Adur failed in Elmor. We lost thirty thousand men, and our enemies survived."

"I'm sure our enemies lost quite a few men, too. Even with the Elder Races by their side, they were outnumbered. Meanwhile, I now have

41

sixteen wyverns ready to fight for me!" Walter's voice echoed through the hall.

"I hope they can take care of the Elder Races. The light from the swords of the elwyn and elves seemed to weaken Adur's wyvern quite a bit."

Interesting. Walter had considered attacking his remaining enemies once he'd tamed the wyverns, however, his instincts had told him to wait. He didn't know whether sixteen of those monsters would be enough to take on the elwyn and elves. "Did the Elder Races defeat the wyvern easily?" he asked.

Ricard sighed, putting his hands on his hips. "The light repelled it again and again, yet it turned in the air and lashed out with its tail. Nevertheless, I think it was only a matter of time before it would have been defeated. One wyvern wasn't enough to dispatch so many of those creatures. Perhaps you could attack Wirskworth alongside your wyverns and destroy Elliot and Delamere once and for all. They don't know you have sixteen of these monsters or even that you've managed to tame one! They won't be expecting an attack like this. You could catch them unawares."

Walter smirked. "I won't attack a city full of creatures that can hurt my wyverns, not alone," he said.

Richard's face fell. "So be it... Whenever you attack, you'll have the element of surprise on your side. They won't be expecting to see wyverns fighting with you now that the giant is dead."

"News like this never remains secret," Walter said. "I'm sure everyone in the kingdom will soon hear what happened in Felador. Many saw the wyverns tearing through the skies by my side. Did you see any pegasi on the battlefield?" He had saved the most important question for last.

Ricard blinked. "A pegasus? Are there any living pegasi?"

So, the boy hasn't managed to ride Thindor yet, Walter thought. *I still have the upper hand.*

"There may be one... However, we'll deal with him when the time comes, if necessary," Leonhard said, breaking his silence.

"Now, leave me, Ricard. There are a few things I need to discuss with Leonhard," Walter said and turned back to the throne.

"I wondered why you kept Anrai by your side all these years. After all, you sought the downfall of the giants..." Ricard told him. "Why didn't you send him to the Mountains of the Forgotten World earlier?"

The question made Walter stop. "I didn't know that the giants had to die for me to gain the devotion of all the wyverns," he replied and turned around. "I heard this legend only a short time ago, but I didn't intend to kill Anrai right away. I didn't know how many wyverns were still alive, nor whether Anrai could bond with one of them. Anrai's nature was also human, and I thought he might not have been endowed with that gift. When we reached the Mountains of Darkness, I found out the truth, and it was then that I decided he had to die. I wish things had been different... Anrai was a powerful ally. However, I had to tame the wyverns—only then would I be invincible." With those words, Walter cast a brief look at Ricard. "It's time you left."

Ricard swallowed, straightening as he summoned his courage. Instead of leaving, he asked, "Why didn't you let the men from Tahryn fight in Wirskworth? Why did you order them to return to Iovbridge, though you sacrificed the men from Mynlands and Oldlands?"

Walter sneered and returned to the throne. "If I'd lost the battle, I didn't want to lose all my soldiers, Ricard. I would have expected you to find that logical."

"I meant, why hold back Tahryn's men and not mine?"

Walter didn't lose his smile as he climbed the steps. "Because Tahryn has ships, and I suspect Elliot sent an emissary to the Ice Islands. I believe he has sent a messenger to every place with an army that isn't under my command. The Mercenaries would never fight for him, but the Ice Islands could attack and take Tahryn. Then, if they had sailed to Iovbridge, I would have had to fight on two fronts. I needed Tahryn."

"My men were more devoted to you than any from Tahryn will ever be!" Ricard said, his voice coloured with anger.

"You're being short-sighted, my friend," Walter said and sat on the throne. If the man didn't leave quickly, he would kill him. He stared down Ricard until the man walked hurriedly towards the exit.

"One more thing."

Ricard stopped dead in his tracks and turned to face Walter again.

"Reynald betrayed me. He was Elliot's spy the moment he set foot in Iovbridge."

"What?" Ricard exclaimed. "Reynald would never do such—"

"Don't interrupt me." Red crept back into Ricard's face, but he kept his mouth shut. "For years, I'd suspected that your brother was in love with that traitress, Alice Asselin. When I killed her, he asked to leave the Trinity of Death and go to Stonegate. He tried to convince me to spare her life. I found no proof of my suspicions, but a few days ago, I became convinced that I was right. The moment Reynald found out who Elliot was, he chose to spy on his behalf."

"Are you sure?"

"He confessed before I killed him," Walter said.

A beat of silence passed before Ricard bowed deeply. "I apologise for my brother's betrayal, Your Majesty. I'll dedicate my life to washing this shame from my House."

Walter smiled. "Very well. I hope you won't betray me either, Ricard. If you do, I will put the head of every man with Karford blood on a spike."

Walter nodded curtly, and Ricard hurried out of the hall as fast as he could.

The White Angel

E lliot had no more tears to shed. Solor's words whirled in his head over and over. Eleanor was dead. Her soul had travelled to the realms of the dead, to the place where Morys's soul was, too. Elliot had never envisioned the number of losses he would contend with to defeat Walter Thorn. He wiped his eyes, slowly, thinking back to the time of his training when all he sought was revenge.

Althalos had tried to warn him. Now, he'd learned the hard way that no victory came without sacrifices, while the lust for revenge brought only death and more pain. For a moment, Aleron's words found their way into his thoughts.

"Every being in this world has the gift of free will. I'm sure you didn't force your friends to travel to the places they went to. They chose to do so. They chose to help."

He knew it was true, but he didn't care. He should have thought things through and come up with a plan that would have protected his friends. *I should have sent Hurwig to Eleanor, Selwyn, and John. If I'd told them that Walter had bonded with a wyvern, they might have been more careful.* He knew in his heart of hearts that even if he had, nothing would have changed. No one could have anticipated that Walter would attack Aquarine.

Elliot had thought of sending the white hawk to his friends many times. Nevertheless, his desire to discover Thorn's plans had overshadowed all other thoughts. Elliot presumed Hurwig was dead, and sorrow filled his heart. It had been a long time since he'd last sent him to find

Reynald, and he hadn't returned. He wondered who could have killed him.

He glanced out his chamber window. It would soon be night. A whole day had gone by since he'd heard about Eleanor, and he never wanted to leave this room again. He wanted to be left alone while the pain tore through his core. Elliot remembered the way he had felt in the Great Hall when Solor had told them the news. It was as if the room had shrunk around him, and the walls were crushing his bones.

Elliot thought of talking to Sophie, but he couldn't gather the courage. The Queen had lost everything, and he couldn't face her. He sighed wearily and interlaced his fingers. He knew the pain would never truly leave his soul.

Why should the world be a place filled with so much hate and death? Elliot cupped his face in his hands. Eleanor had been murdered, Selwyn and Velhisya were captured or dead, and he had no idea where Long Arm was.

He could no longer feel anger over what had happened, only sorrow. He glanced at the walls of the small chamber in the Tower of the Sharp Swords. He'd experienced some of the worst moments of his life in Moonstone. The only thing that gave him joy was that the elwyn and elves hadn't suffered great losses in the battle. The creatures that weren't capable of fighting had remained in hiding and had marched into the city after their victory, finding a new home after a whole three hundred years.

Elliot got up from his chair and walked around the chamber. His legs had gone numb from being still so long. Pacing, he thought of Aleron. The man had looked surprised when he heard that a dozen wyverns had rushed into Aquarine. If Walter had succeeded in taming all those monsters, it meant there were many secrets they had to uncover before it was too late.

I must speak to Aleron. We're running out of time. Elliot needed to find the strength to put the pain of the past aside and focus on the present, yet it was impossible. At any other time, the idea of Walter controlling dozens of wyverns would have terrified him, but now he didn't feel the slightest thing. Eleanor's death had numbed all other feelings.

A strange knocking noise made him jump. *What the hell?* Elliot searched for where the noise was coming from until his eyes landed on the chamber window. His heart raced. A creature was tapping on the glass with its beak—a creature he thought he'd never see again.

———◦———

Elliot ran down dark corridors with Hurwig in his arms. The hawk's right wing was injured, with missing feathers and an open wound, and his breathing was weak. Elliot searched for the chamber where Thorold would be. Hurwig appeared to be getting ever weaker in Elliot's clutches, and he quickened his pace until he saw a familiar door. He pushed it open, and his eyes fell upon Aleron and Thorold. They looked at him in surprise, not expecting anyone to interrupt their conversation.

"Hurwig has returned... He's hurt," Elliot said.

The men moved quickly towards him, and Thorold took the bird gently.

"Something sharp cut his wing. I'd say it was a knife," the Master said as he examined the hawk.

"When did he find you?" Aleron asked.

"Just a little bit ago. I heard him knocking on my window."

Thorold put the white hawk on a wooden table next to a small bed and walked briskly to the corner of the room. A few candles lit the chamber, while countless vials glistened like pearls on the shelves across the room. A shudder moved down Elliot's spine. This was the chamber in which Morys had passed away. Moments later, Thorold returned to Hurwig's side, holding a vial with a gold-looking liquid in it. Carefully, the Master poured a few drops onto the wounded wing and Elliot hoped that the hawk wouldn't meet with the same fate as Morys.

"This will help," Thorold said.

"Will he live?" Elliot asked, his throat tight.

"Yes." The Master nodded. "It's a miracle he managed to fly here with such a wound. This creature is truly hardy."

Elliot neared the wooden table and stroked Hurwig gently on his small head. The hawk closed his eyes as he touched him. "I wonder how he always manages to find me while also being able to find anyone I want. It's like he reads my mind," he said.

"Naturally... This hawk is a White Angel," Aleron said.

"White Angel?" Elliot had never heard that name before.

A smile formed on the elwyn's lips. "No other bird but a White Angel can either find whomever you ask for or find you wherever you may be..."

"I don't understand."

"White Angels are beings that many believe are endowed with magical powers. Some legends say that their kind was created by centaurs."

"By centaurs?" Elliot repeated.

Aleron nodded. "Legend has it that centaurs used an ancient magic and endowed two common hawks with unique powers. These hawks were the first White Angels. There used to be more of them, but today most of them have disappeared."

"I've heard that hundreds of years ago—before humans and centaurs set foot in Knightdorn—White Angels were the messengers of Kerth," the Master added, pouring a few more drops of the golden liquid onto Hurwig's wing. "At that time humans and centaurs were banded together, so the centaurs had given some of those hawks to the humans. These very same legends say that centaurs have even endowed some human men and women with magic powers, however, this has never been confirmed." "Nobody can be sure about any of this. The only certainty is that White Angels have a special wisdom whose origins no one knows," Aleron said.

"I was so committed to the battle against Walter that I never asked myself about this... The first time I thought I should send a letter to Sophie, Hurwig found me and held out his leg. I never thought how..."

Elliot muttered, lost in thought. "Syrella saw me tie a letter to Hurwig's leg, and Eleanor and Selwyn didn't seem surprised when I told them about it. They knew..."

"But of course!" said Thorold. "White Angels and their talents are very well-known, even though these creatures are rare nowadays. I haven't heard of any other human having such a hawk under their command, yet I'm sure your friends knew what Hurwig was. A White Angel is Ballar's coat of arms."

"Althalos never told me about this." A familiar anger rose in Elliot's chest. It broke through the numbing pain of Eleanor's death.

"What matters is that our friend gets well," Thorold replied.

"It's also safe to assume that Reynald is dead," Aleron said.

Elliot turned to him. "How do you kno—"

"Reynald had many opportunities to harm Hurwig. I believe Walter found out the truth and tried to kill them both."

"Reynald may have been using us. He may not have been faithful." Elliot didn't really believe what he'd blurted out.

"I doubt it... He saved your life when you were at his mercy," Thorold told him. "I think Walter had caught on. He wanted to use him to lure you into some sort of trap. However, when he decided to go to Aquarine, he was forced to kill him... He wouldn't be able to keep that from Reynald. He feared Reynald might tell you where he intended to go."

Elliot looked at the aged Master. He was the only one who had known about Reynald's mission from the start. "Why would he keep it secret? Even if I'd found out, I wouldn't have been able to change anything. Aquarine is hundreds of miles awa—"

"I'm sure Walter found out a whole lot from Adur—things he's been ignorant about all his life," Aleron said, cutting him off. "Now he knows a pegasus is alive... He may have been afraid you'd go to Aquarine on Thindor's back to save Eleanor. Then, Anrai would have found out about Walter's plans and might have run away from the city. Adur couldn't be sure whether Thindor had bonded with you, and Walter knows little about pegasi. I think Thorn wanted to make sure nothing would stand in his way of killing Anrai. He has no idea whether Thindor is stronger than his wyvern. Of course, this is all speculation," the man seemed pensive.

"If all this is true, I feel sorry about Reynald's fate..." One more death weighed on Elliot's conscience. The pain was unbearable.

"I'm sorry, Elliot, but you need to clear your head. If you wallow in grief, the last battle with Walter will send us all to our death." Aleron told him.

"Do you believe Solor's words? Do you think dozens of wyverns rushed to bond with Thorn?" Elliot asked. Thorold turned and looked at Aleron strangely. Elliot could have sworn the two men had known each other for a long time, but he didn't ask his question.

"Yes," Aleron said after a few moments.

"How is that possible?"

"There's an ancient myth—one that I never paid much attention to. I remember some giants saying that if every one of their kind died, then all the wyverns would submit to the last of them. To the only creature alive with Orhyn Shadow in their veins," Aleron murmured. "You told me that Walter has Leonhard Payne at his side. The healer probably knew about that legend. This explains why Walter would have ignored the battle and hastened to kill Anrai in Aquarine. He wanted to try and tame all the wyverns in the world, and I believe he succeeded." The man's starry blue eyes turned to Elliot.

"But Walter's not a giant! He doesn't have Orhyn Shadow in his veins!" Elliot exclaimed.

"He must have found a way of inserting the poison into his body. It's the only logical explanation." Aleron stared off into space.

"Walter would never have left the final battle if it wasn't absolutely necessary. He sacrificed half his men because he believed he would gain something new—something that would make him invincible," Thorold added. "Otherwise, he could have used Adur and Anrai to defeat his enemies and get them out of the way later. I believe he killed Anrai and sent Adur to the battle to die. One giant wasn't enough to win the war. In the unlikely event that Adur had survived, Walter would have dealt with him later. But Anrai was dangerous. I'm certain he knew too much about his old master's plans."

"I can't believe Walter changed all his plans based on a legend. Most legends are pure nonsense!" Elliot snapped.

"A man with such arrogance and delusions of grandeur thinks he's special. He believes he can achieve what no one else has ever achieved," Aleron said.

"He may indeed be special... He managed to get all the—" Elliot stopped short, suddenly growing weary. He wanted to return to his chamber and mourn over the loss of Eleanor. He no longer had the strength to talk. "If I'm to have any hope of defeating Walter, I need Thindor. Wyverns fear pegasi," Elliot said, remembering Alysia and Alaric's words.

"I've told you before to forget about Thindor!" Aleron raised his voice. "That creature is in greater danger than ever before now that Walter knows of his existence. Don't tell anyone about him unless it's necessary. The fewer who know, the better. If he wishes it, Thindor will be by your side. Until then, stop thinking about him! Elliot, you need to clear your head and let go of your pain and anger if you want us to succeed. Don't forget that after the last battle, the elwyn and elves are Walter's enemies, too. If we fail, we'll all die. We need you. The people of this city have their hopes resting on you."

Elliot felt that familiar weight on his shoulders—the weight of responsibility. "I'd like to be alone," he said suddenly. He couldn't help anyone anymore. He just wanted to grieve.

The two men looked at him in silence and nodded. Elliot turned to leave, but Hurwig cried softly. He stopped and met the hawk's small eyes. "You will be well soon," he said, then faced Thorold. "Let me know as soon as Hurwig is well again."

With that, he left the room and walked back to his chamber as fast as he could.

The Fear of Power

Walter took a hurried look at the Scarlet Sea as he walked on the pier beside Leonhard, the gentle breeze caressing his face. He watched the moonlight reflecting off the small waves. The landscape filled him with a strange sense of serenity—the serenity that came with power. He may have lost thousands of men, but now the throne was his, and all the while, the most powerful creatures in the world had submitted to him. Iovbridge had started to grow on him. Gaeldeath may have been his ancestral land—a place imbued with the power of the gods—but now, the royal capital symbolised all that he'd achieved in recent years.

The wyvern may not be able to beat a pegasus.

Sometimes, he hated his thoughts, even though they were what kept him alert. He tried to calm his mind, but the war wasn't yet over.

"Do you believe a pegasus could beat the wyverns?" Walter asked out loud.

Leonhard didn't lift his head. "I don't know. However, there is only one pegasus, and you have sixteen of those monsters," he replied.

"When Manhon Egercoll cursed the Elder Races, only one pegasus remained in the world." The aged healer remained silent. "Before the curse, there were thousands of giants and hundreds of wyverns. How did Manhon manage to imprison the Elder Races? Why didn't the giants kill him riding high on their wyverns?" Walter asked.

"Nobody but the Elder Races have the answers to all of this," Leonhard said.

"Adur said wyverns are afraid of pegasi," Walter insisted.

Leonhard looked up. "At the time when Manhon cursed the giants, they'd been decimated in the battle against the elves, and thousands of wyverns had been slain. I'm also sure the Elder Races didn't know exactly what Manhon was about to do. They didn't expect to be cursed. Had they known, they might have fought hard and defeated Egercoll."

Walter frowned. "Legend has it that Manhon attacked with the centaurs and his army. He forced the Elder Races to give him the Sword of Light and then unleashed the curse. The Elder Races must have known he was going there for a battle. If the legends are true, that means neither the giants nor the wyverns could stop him."

"The centaurs may have pushed the wyverns back. I've heard that some of their race have magical pow—"

"Centaurs cannot create the light that burns the wyverns' body!" Walter cut him off. "As for their magic, Reynald, a human, managed to slaughter them with a few thousand men a few years ago." Anger overwhelmed his soul. Leonhard didn't understand how important what they were discussing was.

The old man grimaced. "I don't know how Manhon did it. No one would share those secrets with us. I've heard that the elwyn always tried to settle their differences peacefully. Perhaps it was they who convinced the giants not to fight."

"Adur seemed certain the wyverns were afraid—"

"Adur may have been right." Leonhard was one of a few men who dared to interrupt Walter. "Wyverns may fear pegasi. However, every creature whose nature it is to be tamed by a master has as much courage as its master does."

"What do you mean?"

Leonhard smirked. "No giant has ever been as powerful as you. Their bodies may be larger by nature, but there have been none with powers like yours. You're the only human to have tamed a wyvern—the only man in the history of the world to have gained the devotion of all these monsters." He stopped walking and looked Walter in the eye.

"What I'm trying to say is that the giants who were still alive at that time may have been ravaged by the battle against the elves and lost their courage. But you were never a coward! You don't fear anything. The wyverns that have bonded with you won't cower in the face of a pegasus. Thindor, like the wyverns, is a creature whose nature commands him to submit to a master. Elliot will never become as powerful a master as you are. So Thindor will not be able to beat the wyverns"

The man's words assuaged Walter's fears. "The boy hasn't succeeded in bonding with the pegasus yet. Perhaps he never will..."

"Even if he does, he'll be defeated. Just like Adur said, the First Kings killed six pegasi and had no wyverns by their side."

True... If the First Kings killed six pegasi, I could easily kill one. I'm more powerful than them. "I wonder... I wonder how the boy managed to break the curse. Althalos used to say that only an almighty—"

"Althalos was weak," Leonhard cut in again. "He saw strength only hand in hand with honesty and *love*. I don't know how the boy succeeded... However, what I do know is that others before Elliot have tamed a pegasus, but no human has ever tamed a wyvern."

Walter smiled for the first time that night. "I'll kill the boy. He'll die such a torturous death that he'll wish Althalos had never trained him. Nevertheless, we must be careful... Ricard said that the elwyn and elves had no trouble dealing with Adur and his wyvern. I mustn't attack unless I'm sure I'll win."

"I agree," Leonhard replied.

"We now have about as many men as Elliot, and the elves know how to guard Wirskworth against my wyverns better than anyone else. I need more soldiers," Walter said.

"Moreover, news of our defeat in Elmor, combined with the fact that Thomas Egercoll's son has freed the Elder Races, may sow discord amongst our men. Of course, the wyverns flying over the city skies will convince them who is truly the most powerful force in this war."

Walter knew what he meant. The soldiers from Gaeldeath showed blind devotion to him, but the same couldn't be said of the men from Tahos. Tahryn may have belonged to the north, but he had dishonourably killed its former ruler, along with many of the region's noblemen. "I'll speak to Eric Stone and make sure every man in Tahos knows that if he doesn't fight for me, he'll become a meal for the wyverns."

"Fear is a useful ally," Leonhard said approvingly.

Walter studied him a little closer. His bony frame seemed to be breathing with difficulty. "Are you alright?"

Leonhard's eyes shone under the moonlight. "I'm ill."

Walter stopped abruptly, bewildered. He hadn't got wind of this before. "Ill?"

The old man nodded. "I've seen this illness before. It's rare, and no one can know how much time I have left."

"Perhaps if you drank a little mermaid blood, it would help."

A smile formed on Leonhard's aged face. "Even if the pain went away, I don't want to live much longer in this miserable body. The blood is useful for young men who can keep their youth forever. My own body, whether with the blood or without it, is now useless."

Walter frowned. He didn't want to lose Leonhard. This man was truly valuable. "You're the only one I'd trust to drink a little of that blood, the only one who would never try to put Orhyn Shadow into his veins and take my wyverns... You've never revealed any secret of mine, and I was never afraid you would. I've never thought you wanted to gain power for yourself." Walter paused. "Why not?" he asked after a moment.

The smile didn't leave Leonhard's lips. "I never wanted power... All I ever wanted in life was the *truth*. I wanted to solve mysteries and find all the answers to this strange world. However, people fear the truth, and they're afraid of discovering the secrets around us!" His tone grew angry as he uttered his final words.

"Henry Delamere ousted me from Felador when he heard I was experimenting on dying soldiers and bastard babies. Those babies helped me find the antidotes to dozens of diseases that have saved countless children today. No one could fathom the magnitude of what I had discovered! It was then that I decided I would never waste my knowledge on a weakling again." He turned to Walter. "You never held me back, and you never hesitated to make sacrifices to tame all the powers of this world. You didn't even hesitate to change your very nature. I would never have been able to conquer the world, so I wanted to offer my knowledge to someone who would make use of it. I don't care how many you kill to become the Ruler of Knightdorn or how many creatures die so you can live eternally. The only thing I'm interested in is finding answers that no one else has yet discovered."

Walter felt invincible; he loved being held in awe for his mettle. Leonhard's words filled him with a sense of power, the same power he'd felt when Adur had rushed to find him to fight on his side.

"I don't know how much time I have left... I want you to swear to me that you'll crush all the cowards who are trying to destroy what we've built," the old man said.

Suddenly, an idea formed in Walter's mind. It was one of those moments when he felt that the gods had endowed him with all their virtues and thus, no matter how many obstacles came his way, none would ultimately stand in the way of his destiny.

"I swear. I'll do everything possible so that you might see the end of our enemies and that you can leave this world knowing that we won."

Unbearable Pain

S ophie watched as people hurried by, the tightness in her chest becoming a painful knot. She glanced at the moon as she walked. The sunlight hadn't completely faded from the evening sky, yet the full moon had made an early appearance, turning orange in the dying light. It had been a while since she'd seen such a full moon. She stood still with her gaze fixed on the sky for a few moments, searching for anything that could take her mind off her dark thoughts.

She continued down Wirskworth's cobbled lane. Merchants gathered their wares while peasants and artisans headed home. Sophie walked the city for hours until her legs stiffened in pain. She wanted her weariness to be so unbearable that when her body touched her bed, she would be enveloped in a veil of dreams immediately.

Many people had wanted to talk to her during the past few days, but she didn't care. She wanted to be alone. Battles, Walter, and politics no longer mattered to her. Her parents had been murdered, her life partner had died, and now the only woman she loved as a sister had also passed away. Her sorrow over Eleanor was so strong that it numbed her body. The pain had taken root inside of her and would never go away, accompanying her until her own soul journeyed to the realms of the dead.

She turned into a narrow, deserted alley with a few houses sprung up here and there. She noticed the smoking chimneys as a black bird flew overhead, squawking. Her legs ached, and her lungs gasped for air. She liked the feeling. The fatigue brought a strange serenity to her soul.

Her gaze fell upon her right hand where three parallel cuts decorated her wrist. The sight of them filled her with dark memories. Sophie hadn't managed to get a minute's sleep from the moment she'd heard what Solor had told them two days earlier. She remembered the words of a healer who had visited Iovbridge long ago in an attempt to save Bert. That man had told her that the pain caused by a momentary cut is so strong that it could tame a tortured mind. So, when the last dawn had appeared, she'd taken a small knife and cut the skin above her wrist.

Since then, she'd cut her wrist three times, and the pain each time had given her some relief. Her thoughts had finally quieted, and she managed to fall asleep. But the moment she woke up, she'd remember the intense emotions. It was what she'd felt way back when Eleanor's brother, the only man she'd ever loved, had passed away. It felt like a knife had been thrust into her insides over and over, and no matter how hard she tried, she couldn't get it out.

Sophie heard someone giggling and saw a young woman walking beside a tall man returning from one of the inns. The man made a sudden move and grabbed the girl's buttocks while she smiled at him beguilingly. A moment later, the couple passed her, their laughter ringing in her ears. She couldn't understand how people had a zest for life. Eleanor was dead and would never be back. Sophie wanted time to stand still, for people to cry over what had happened in Aquarine. And yet, nothing had changed.

Of late, Sophie often wondered why she deserved this fate. Why did she deserve to lose every person she loved? Why did she deserve to bear the weight of the responsibility to rule? Suddenly, she remembered Peter knocking on her chamber door the day before. She hadn't replied, and he had shouted that he would come again.

Peter knows how you feel, a voice in her head said.

She sighed wearily. Peter had lost everything in the war against Walter, and now there was little chance of Selwyn's being alive. The lad had been murdered at the hands of Liher Hale, and Velhisya and Giren must have died, too. She couldn't stand her grief.

"What happened to Eleanor isn't your fault."

Sophie turned and saw Elliot standing behind her. "How did you find me?" she asked.

"That's not important," he replied.

"Have you been following me?"

Elliot shook his head.

Her anger flared up. She didn't like not getting straight answers. "I don't want to speak to anyone. I please ask you to leave."

"You cannot change what has already happened, Your Majesty."

Sophie looked him in the eyes, feeling momentary hatred, the very same hatred she'd felt when she'd ordered her men to kill the hostages who had survived Peter's attack in White City. "You're right... I can't change a thing," she said and stepped toward. "But I told you that it was very dangerous for Eleanor to leave Iovbridge! I'd already told you that she meant the world to me, and you took her with you to Stonegate! You risked her life, and when you eventually managed to bring her to Elmor, you commanded her to travel to Aquarine. Eleanor hadn't left Iovbridge for years! She knew nothing of the world. The journey to Aquarine was dangerous, and yet you sent her there. You're to blame for her death!"

Elliot's eyes looked tear-filled under the moonlight, yet Sophie felt no remorse.

"Why did you ask her to go to that place? Why didn't you let her stay here in the strongest city in the world?" Sophie went on.

Elliot remained silent, his eyes reflecting the immeasurable guilt he felt. "When we managed to get Walter and his horsemen to flee, I spoke to Thorold and realised we had no hope of defeating Thorn without allies," he said a few moments later. "I don't have many friends in the kingdom... So, I decided to send John and Selwyn to the only places where we might have been able to gain soldiers. I tried to free the Elder Races, and I thought that Eleanor would find peace in Aquarine."

Sophie was furious. "Peace? Why would she find peace in the place where her parents were murdered?" she snapped.

"Everyone in the kingdom knows that Aquarine has no army. Walter wouldn't have attacked there, and so that was a place where Eleanor could have lived far from misery and death. I sent her there because I thought she could live a beautiful life and also help Felador. A virtuous leader can bring life to a place filled with pain."

"Felador had a ruler!" Sophie said, raising her voice.

Elliot frowned, sighing heavily. "I didn't know. But even the High Priest also saw what I saw in Eleanor. He recognised that she was the future of Felador. If Eleanor had found out that John, Selwyn, and I were going away in an attempt to build new alliances, she wouldn't have sat idly by. She would have insisted on helping. I couldn't send her to the Black Vale. Hale would never have respected a woman. Moreover, the trip to the Ice Islands would have been too difficult for her. I thought about taking her with me, but I didn't know what kind of a reception I'd have got in the Mountains of the Forgotten World. So, I decided to give her a mission that would have helped the people of Felador and provided her with a peaceful life."

"You should have made her stay here!" Sophie insisted.

Elliot looked up at the sky. "She wouldn't have listened to me! Not as long as her friends risked their lives to find our allies. Eleanor couldn't stand this place. She didn't want to stay in the city where Morys had died. It was also dangerous in Wirskworth. Without the Elder Races, we would all have died in battle."

Sophie had discovered that Eleanor had fallen in love with Morys during her stay in Wirskworth, which had puzzled her. However, none of that mattered now. "Your plan was brilliant... Now we've all lost our loved ones except you! You haven't lost anything!"

"Have I not lost a thing?" The sorrow on Elliot's face was gone, rage taking its place as his voice bounced off the alley. "I grew up an orphan in a village, trying to get trained—trying to kill the man who robbed me of everything I should have had! I lived in hardship, learning to kill before I even learned how to walk... No child deserves this fate. I tried to help you... and in doing so, I lost two people I loved. I've been carrying the burden of saving the kingdom on my shoulders from the moment I was born!"

Pangs of guilt broke through her fury. She was about to speak, but Elliot cut her off.

"On my journey to Elmor, I happened to be in the City of Heavens, and there I met a young woman I remembered from when I was still a child. My twin sister. When Walter found out from his informants that Thorold was alive, he stormed the City of Heavens, and so I rushed to save her but didn't make it. Selyn had taken her life for fear of falling into the hands of Walter's men."

Sophie just stood there open-mouthed. "Your twin sister?" she asked. "I thought... I thought you wanted to save Thorold... I thought you wanted to save him because he was Althalos' friend."

Elliot looked at her, pain and anger warring on his face. "Althalos separated me from my sister when I was a baby to train me. He believed that if I stayed near her, my will to protect her would have distracted me from my true purpose—the salvation of Knightdorn. Naturally, he never bothered to ask what I wanted... He just believed that I was the chosen one. The boy who would set the Elder Races free, the boy who would save the kingdom. He, along with Thorold, believed in some legends and decided to deprive me of everything! Neither of them expected me to remember her, and yet, as soon as I saw her, I remembered everything."

"I'm sorry, Elliot." Sophie's already wounded heart broke a little more. "I'm truly sorry..."

He looked away. "Few people know the truth about my sister. My former companions, Thorold and Aleron, are the only ones who know... I don't want anyone else to find out about this. In your veins runs the blood of the Egercolls. You had to know."

"I'm sorry about what I said," she said. Sophie had been searching for someone to blame for Eleanor's death, wanting to punish those responsible for her murder. She had been so blinded by her pain that she hadn't considered Elliot's suffering. Walter had ruined his life from the moment he was born.

Sophie folded Elliot in her arms. "I'm so sorry," she whispered in his ear. Elliot returned her embrace before he gently pushed away.

"Eleanor's death wasn't in vain," Elliot said, sniffling. "She died fighting for a better future, and we have to carry on. We have to carry on until we either succeed or die. If we get lost in sorrow and don't do the best we can, we'll defile her memory."

Tears welled up in Sophie's eyes.

"We have to try. Eleanor would have done the same," Elliot added.

Sophie touched his hand. "I swear I'll try. I swear upon her memory."

A faint smile formed on his lips. "Aleron wants to talk to us in the Tower of Poisons."

Sophie didn't want a council that night. She wasn't ready yet. A faint image of Eleanor flashed before her. The girl was struggling to learn how to duel in the yard in Iovbridge. Eleanor never stopped trying. She took a deep breath and nodded curtly.

When Sophie and Elliot arrived at the Tower of Poisons, they found Syrella and her daughters sitting at the head of a large table near a fireplace, while Peter, Jahon and Aleron were next to Thorold. At the other end of the table sat two elves, Alaric and Alysia. She'd heard they were great warriors whose opinions carried weight among their tribe. Near them was another man, a man she hadn't seen for a long time. Borin Ballard, the former Governor of Ballar, didn't depart his chambers often.

Sophie remained standing, and Elliot moved to her right. She wanted the council to finish quickly.

"I brought you here because we need to talk," said Syrella, and she stood, staring at Sophie and Elliot. "We may have defeated Walter's army a few days ago, but we lost thousands of men. Now, there are only about twenty thousand of our soldiers in the city who can fight, while Walter must have about thirty-five thousand men. As if that weren't enough, we've heard that dozens of wyverns may have bonded with him."

"I still don't understand how such a thing is possible!" Peter exclaimed.

Aleron rose from his seat. "There's a legend... A tale that I heard years ago."

Sophie listened carefully as Aleron told her the legend. "But how can Walter be the last being with Orhyn Shadow in his veins?" she asked, bewildered.

Aleron let out a weary sigh and looked away. "I don't know. No one knows," he said.

"The most logical answer is that he found a way of putting the poison into his blood without it causing him pain. How he did that is difficult to answer," Alaric told them.

"And how did Walter find out that Anrai was in Aquarine?" Linaria asked. Syrella's daughter had abandoned her armour and was dressed in brown leather trousers and a linen jerkin.

"I've asked Solor over and over, but he has no answers," Elliot responded.

"If Walter wanted the wyverns, why didn't he kill Anrai before?" Linaria continued.

"He may not have known about the legend... He may have heard about it recently," said Thorold. The white sleeves of his robes pooled on the table as he rested his hands on the wood. "Moreover, Anrai was only half-giant. Walter may have hoped that the wyverns wouldn't submit to a creature like him, but he realised that he was mistaken."

"None of that is important," Merhya, Linaria's twin sister, said as she stood. "Walter will attack again soon, and this time, we won't get off so easily."

Elliot took a step towards her, pensive. "I agree. It will be difficult to win this time, but I don't think Walter will attack anytime soon," he told her.

"Why not?" Merhya asked.

"He's already lost two battles. His men are exhausted from travelling. I'm sure he'll wait a while until he marches into a new battle."

"He may attack us with just the wyverns. If he has a dozen of them, he can kill us all," Linaria said, her face grim.

"No!" a new voice exclaimed.

Sophie turned to Alysia. The elf's features had hardened. "I haven't met this man, but I've heard that he's clever and cunning. He won't attack a city that has elwyn and elves on its side with just wyverns. If he does, he'll be defeated. We've fought giants riding on the backs of wyverns before when there were thousands of them, and I'm sure he's heard the stories about that battle."

"What matters is that we need more men!" Jahon snapped. "If Walter attacks with thirty thousand soldiers and wyverns, he'll charge the gate with ease and kill us all."

"If we fight smartly, we may be successful with the men we have left!" Linaria said.

"I don't think so," Elliot said, shaking his head. "However, there's no one who can help us... Liher Hale has shown his intentions, and I have no news from Long Arm. I don't know whether he got to the Ice Islands and what reception awaited him. I may send Hurwig there when he's recovered." He had now revealed to those present where John was.

Sophie turned to Elliot, her eyes wide. "Hurwig? Your hawk?"

Elliot nodded. "He came back yesterday. The last mission I sent him on was to find Reynald Karford. Hurwig came back wounded. I believe Walter realised Reynald was spying for me and killed him while wounding Hurwig."

Sophie was dumbfounded. "Was Reynald spying on Walter on your behalf?" she asked.

Elliot nodded. "I revealed this secret to everyone a few hours ago, but I didn't want to disturb you, Your Majesty," he said.

Sophie was mad, she couldn't believe what she'd just heard. "Reynald killed thousands—"

"Reynald loved my mother." Elliot cut her short. "He left Walter and went to Stonegate when Thorn killed her, hoping never to meet him again. When I was at his mercy, he saved my life, and I decided to entrust him with this mission. He sent word to me with Hurwig for some time until I stopped hearing from him."

Sophie tried to digest this information, but she struggled to understand Elliot's choice. No one should have trusted a man like Reynald.

"Enough." Syrella's voice cut through the air. "The Ice Islands don't have enough men to tip the balance in the war. We need stronger allies, and we need to send an army to Vylor. I need to know what happened to my niece and find out if Selwyn might still be alive."

"If we send an army to Vylor, there will be no one left to defend Elmor when Walter attacks. We can't fight two battles if we don't find more soldiers," Jahon said in a raised voice.

Syrella and her daughters turned on him, furious. "Our cousin is there! She may have been captured, she may not be dea—" Linaria couldn't finish her sentence, swallowing and clenching her fists. "If she's alive, we have to save her."

"We have no men! I also want to kill Hale, but if we're not careful how we act, we'll all die," Jahon insisted.

"Will the Guardians of the South fight against Walter on our side again?" Elliot asked.

"The Guardian Commander told me they were going back to Stonegate. They can't leave off guarding the castle now that Walter has Iovbridge. If he tries to take the castle, they'll delay him and retreat to Elmor," replied Syrella, still looking at Jahon with eyes narrowed and a frown etched onto her face.

"This is nonsense!" Thorold snapped, and many heads turned to him. "Walter has the wyverns on his side. If he attacks Stonegate, he'll destroy it. The Guardian Commander must bring his soldiers and his people to Elmor, otherwise, they'll all die."

"I agree," Aleron said.

"I'll speak to the Guardian Commander at first light," Sophie replied. "However, there's no one else to help us. We can't attack Liher Hale and deal with Walter at the same time. Already our men aren't enough to—"

"There is someone else," Syrella interjected. "Someone else who may be able to help us."

"Someone else?" Sophie repeated. She could see hesitation on the Governor's face.

"I heard that the Emperor of Kerth wanted to have you marry his son." Syrella's words were like a blunt knife.

Sophie flushed with rage. "Do you want me to marry that bastard's son?" she didn't expect this betrayal from Syrella.

"I've spoken to several merchants who trade with men from Kerth in Silver Bay. The Western Empire has about forty thousand men, and they have over seven hundred ships. If they decided to fight with us, we could even take Tahos," Jahon said.

"Tahryn's fleet is the best the world has ever seen," Peter spoke. "Only the Ice Islands may have fitter men for a naval battle, but their ships are few compared to those of Tahos. The Western Empire has ships only for trade, and rumour has it that its men aren't good at sea battles."

That's of no importance!" Syrella snapped. "They have ships to transport their army here, and their forty thousand men will be enough to defeat Walter and his wyverns."

"Even if I agreed, I doubt the *Emperor* still wants this marriage! He asked me to wed his son when I sat on the throne of Knightdorn. Now I'm just a..." Sophie didn't know how to continue.

"You're the Queen of Knightdorn! If we beat Walter, you'll sit on the throne again, and your son will become King," Syrella insisted.

"How do you know he still wants this marriage?" Sophie asked.

"As soon as Elliot's hawk gets better, we'll send a letter to the Emperor with Hurwig," Syrella replied.

"A letter? Do you think he'll be convinced by a letter that he receives from a bird's leg? We have to send an emissary!" Sophie hated the idea. She would rather die than marry that man.

"That would take too long... Walter may delay his attack, but we don't have much time. We'll send Hurwig, and if he doesn't come back with a positive answer, we'll drop this plan," Syrella said.

Sophie's gaze met Peter's. The man's face was inscrutable. She didn't want to agree to this plan. She had never wanted to marry anyone but Bert, and at the same time, she didn't like the rumours about the Emperor. He had once killed all his enemies at a feast.

"If Kerth fights with us, we'll have as many men as we need, and we'll be able to send an army to Liher Hale's doorstep without fearing losses," Syrella went on.

"If we lose our army, we'll be dependent on the Emperor! That man is cunning. He's capable of killing us all if he realises that we have no hope without him," Sophie said. This frightened her more than the marriage itself.

"I can't leave Velhisya in Vylor!" Syrella shouted.

Sophie looked at Elliot. His eyes seemed to beg her to agree. He was worried about Velhisya, too. She felt an overwhelming pressure resting on her shoulders, pushing down on her spine. She wanted to go back to her chamber to be alone and mourn Eleanor's loss. "Lord Borin... What are your thoughts on all of this?" she asked the old man, who hadn't said a word during the discussion.

"I don't know, my dear Queen. The truth is, I've long since stopped plotting against Walter Thorn," Borin replied. "The last time I did, I lost my children... I lost my sons. The heirs to my House are dead, and I wish I were, too."

Sophie felt compassion for the man. She'd wondered why he had accepted the invitation and come to the council.

Suddenly, a knocking came from the door.

"Come in," Syrella called.

A man from the Sharp Swords entered the room. He had been standing watch outside the chamber's entrance. "I've just been informed by a lad that we have visitors to our city," said the guard.

"Who?" Sophie had spoken before Syrella.

"Selwyn Brau and Giren Barlow have returned to Wirskworth."

The Fall of Humans

Velhisya had lost all sense of time, and the wavering light given off by a few torches was her only company in the dungeons of Goldtown Castle. She didn't know how long she'd been there. She thought months had gone by, but she wasn't sure. She felt dirty, after wearing the same clothes for weeks, and she could smell a rank odour in her hair. For a moment, the image of her aunt came to mind. She knew Syrella would sacrifice every man in Elmor to save her, but she wasn't sure whether she was still alive. She'd tried to find out from the guards whether Walter had attacked Elmor but to no avail.

Her legs creaked as she attempted to stand, and her breath quickened. Her stomach ached from hunger while thirst burned her throat. For a moment, she wished she had been endowed with her mother's powers, the abilities of the elwyn race. Her father had told her that elwyn couldn't feel hunger or thirst and that they were immune to countless things that killed and afflicted humans. He had told her all this just a few days before he left the world forever.

Some years ago, Velhisya had tried to test whether the powers of the elwyn resided within her. However, that had resulted in one of the greatest disappointments in her life. She remembered the fire burning her fingers and almost drowning when she had dunked her head in a tub of water. As if that weren't enough, she'd discovered that hunger and thirst affected her. At that time, she'd even tried taking poisons that numbed her limbs and caused pain. She knew the elwyn were immune to these poisons, yet all of them had harmed her body. She had been so disappointed. Her mother may have been elwyn, but Velhisya didn't seem to have inherited the elwyn traits from her.

Suddenly, she felt a shiver of hope. The moment she had tried piercing her body with Orhyn Shadow filled her with courage. She remembered how fearful she had been, knowing that every poison she'd put into her body had hurt and that Orhyn Shadow would tear through her insides. However, this poison was the only one that had caused her no pain at all. She took a few steps and touched the ice-cold bars of her cell door.

Velhisya had never been able to explain why. She'd also tried to light the blade of her mother's Aznarin sword. That wasn't a pleasant memory. No matter how many times she tried, the blade only lit up for a few moments.

The Light of Life is weak within me, she'd thought countless times. However, there was another thing, too... Another thing about the elwyn that terrified her.

Elliot's image came to mind. Velhisya remembered feeling a whirlwind of emotions the last time she'd come face to face with him. She knew that the elwyn could bond their souls with their mates, and if her soul had bonded with his, her life would end when he left the world. However, even if she'd been born with the curse of being able to bond her soul with someone, she hadn't slept with Elliot. Her father had told her that the union of souls was only achieved through the union of flesh. Even so, she wondered what had happened in that moment with Elliot. Velhisya wished she had every elwyn power but that one. That *gift* seemed like a curse in her eyes.

"The union of souls is the greatest power the elwyn have." An unseen voice whispered her father's words to her.

She didn't agree. The thought of handing over her soul to someone who could tear it to pieces at any moment was terrifying.

Another rumble moved in her belly. She wished again she couldn't feel the pangs of hunger. However, she was lucky. She'd heard from the guards that Selwyn had endured much worse torture than she had. She wondered whether she would be tortured more. She'd rather have her hands and feet cut off than be raped by Liher Hale.

A wave of anger made her shiver. Liher had tried to take her to his chamber over and over, but Lothar always appeared out of nowhere and stood in his brother's way. Velhisya suspected that Lothar was trying to put in place guards who were loyal to him, but Liher had learned his lesson. After Selwyn and Giren's escape, he always had his loyal guards at the entrance to the dungeons. She believed it was a matter of time before she'd fall into Liher's hands. He was the Governor of Vylor, and sooner or later, he'd find a way of getting his brother out of the way.

He doesn't want to hurt me and torture me so that I can be pretty when he rapes me. The thought filled her soul with poison. She hated Liher more than she'd ever hated anything or anyone in her life, and at the same time, she was afraid. *If Liher rapes me, perhaps my soul will bond with his.* She felt the need to pull her hair out, to inflict pain on herself—to find her path to redemption. *If Liher is to rape me, I pray that mine and Elliot's souls have been united*, she thought.

Humans are the most fallen race in the world. She knew that her own nature was half-human, yet she couldn't help but feel disgusted at the actions of that race.

A loud sound snapped her out of her thoughts, and she backed away from the cell door.

"Move aside," a deep voice said.

Her heart started pounding. She knew who the voice belonged to.

"I've been waiting for this moment a long time," Liher said.

Velhisya heard quick footsteps and saw a shadow on the wall across the way from her cell. A few moments later, the figure of the hated man appeared before her.

"Good evening, my dear," Liher said with a sardonic smile. He stuck a key in the door and forced it open. "Tonight, we shall dine together in my chamber. I'm sure you're hungry."

"My aunt will give you plenty of gold in exchange for me," Velhisya said, pressing her body against the wall to move as far away from him as she could.

"Your aunt is dead."

"What? How do you know?" The ground felt like it had disappeared beneath her feet.

"Walter was going to attack Wirskworth, my dear. I don't know if Syrella is already dead, but even if she isn't, her death won't be long in coming."

"But if she defeats Walter, she'll put your head on a spike if you dare to touch me."

Liher laughed. "Nobody can beat Walter. But let's not worry about any of that." He took a step towards her and took her hand. Velhisya pulled away forcefully. "I know you're hungry. I promise we'll have a great time."

"Leave her alone, Liher."

Velhisya saw another man at the entrance to the cell. Liher turned around in anger. "What are you doing here? Who told you I'd come to the dungeons?"

"No one," Lothar said.

"I'll kill the guards!" Liher was furious.

"No guard came to find me, brother. I expected you'd once again try to rape this woman. After what happened with Selwyn Brau, anyone who knows you would expect that you'd kill anyone you could get your hands on from the Delamere camp. The only reason you're keeping this woman alive is to rape her."

"I might want to ask for plenty of gold, you fool."

"Gold?" Lothar took a step forward. "Do you want to ask for gold from a governor you consider dead? If Walter takes Elmor, nobody will give you gold in exchange for this woman."

"Get out of here."

"I've told you this before. I won't let you rape her."

Liher advanced on his brother. "Why do you want to protect her? You

73

said you were afraid of the consequences... You said that if Syrella stays alive, she'll kill us all if we harm her niece, and you want to *save* the people of Vylor." Sarcasm coated his voice. "Nevertheless, you know that Syrella Endor hasn't a hope in hell of defeating Thorn. She may even be dead already. Why then do you want to save her?"

Lothar didn't reply.

"Dozens of women are raped in the city every day, and I've never seen you bat an eyelid. Why do you care about this woman?" Lothar remained expressionless. "TALK!" Liher was now enraged. "I know why you're doing this. You're jealous. You want to be the one to fuck this whore." Velhisya felt the urge to punch Liher in the face. "Or have you perhaps fallen in love with her? Tell the truth, my little brother."

Lothar brought his face to his brother's. "No one knows whether Syrella Endor is dead. No one knows whether you'll be sentencing all of Vylor to death by harming this woman. Even if the Ruler of Elmor is dead, prisoners deserve respect, Liher. You, too, may perhaps find yourself in a cell. The two of us may be held captive one day. Would you like to be tortured? Would you like to be raped and castrated?"

Liher didn't say a word.

"I want to treat this woman with respect, just as I chose to treat Selwyn Brau with respect. I wish you were a wiser ruler!"

"How dare you talk to me like that?" Liher's voice was oddly calm, a calm that concealed the threat of death. "I'm the Governor of Vylor, and you're nothing. You helped those cunts escape and now you want to protect a whore because you think you're an honest and virtuous man. You're nothing, Lothar, and you'll be punished. Your name won't be enough to save you again."

"You can punish me, but you won't rape her. Only when I'm dead will you be able to do that."

"You'll die soon."

Lothar smiled. "Do it. Order your men to kill me, and then you'll soon find out what's been said about you in Vylor all these years. Our people still whisper behind your back about your decision to fight alongside the man who killed your brother. Kill me, Liher, and I swear you'll die at the hands of your own people."

Liher laughed again. "You've always been a fool. All the men of Vylor want is gold, whores, and wine. No one in this land would ever devote themselves to you—an idiot who only cares about honour and hopes it will save him. Your end will soon come, and then you'll find out what the price of honour is."

Liher turned and looked at Velhisya with eyes that dripped with malice. "We'll meet again soon." He took another look at Lothar and left the cell. His footsteps echoed in Velhisya's ears until they died away.

"He'll kill you…" she whispered.

"He won't dare," Lothar said angrily.

"He'll do it, and then he'll get what he wants. You'll die in vain!" Velhisya insisted.

"Don't shout. I don't want the guards to hear us." Lothar stepped towards her. "I promised Selwyn I would help you, and I'll honour my promise."

"Why are you helping me?" Velhisya looked him in the eyes. "Your brother is right… My aunt may be dead. Even Selwyn may well be dead. You know there isn't much hope of a man like Walter being defeated…" She paused for a moment. "I've seen how you look at me—I know that look. Men have been looking at me with lust for as long as I can remember. Is your brother, right? Do you want to help me because you want me for yourself?" Velhisya knew that her words were full of self-conceit, dishonouring the man who'd done all he could to save her from the most hideous torment. Still, she wanted to know.

Lothar's face was inscrutable. "I spoke the truth. I want to help you, just like I helped Selwyn."

Velhisya moved closer to the cell bars. "Do you not want anything else from me?" she whispered.

"It doesn't matter what I want!" Lothar's eyes flashed. "All that mat-

75

ters is that this land may one day cease to be the kingdom of greed—the place where even the First King chose to attack, the place famed for rape, bastards and deceit. I believe this land deserves something more, and I want to fight for that."

Velhisya admired his words. "If Walter defeats his enemies, the whole kingdom will become the same as Vylor."

"I know... I know I may die because of everything I believe in. I don't care, and I expect nothing in return for what I'm doing for you." Lothar looked away from her.

Velhisya took his hand. She could feel how he lusted for her. The way he looked at her had betrayed him. That was her only hope. She had to succeed. "Liher will kill you, and he'll rape me. I'm sorry, but you can't protect me."

Lothar frowned. "I told you I wouldn't—"

"He'll do it! Liher won't rest unless he gets what he wants. Men like him love a challenge—the power play. He'll find some way of getting you out of the way, and then he'll defile me until there's nothing left of me."

"What do you want from me? I can't set you free. Liher has his trusted men in the dungeons all the time," he said softly.

"I want you to kill me, Lothar," Velhisya whispered, squeezing his hand.

Lothar jerked out of her grasp. "I could never kill a defenceless woman. I'm not—"

"I know! I'm asking you to deliver me from this hell. I'm asking you to help! I'd rather die than lie with your brother. Please, I beg of you, help me." Her voice cracked, lips dry.

The man's gaze was lost in thought for a few moments, and Velhisya prayed he'd listen to her plea.

"No." Lothar's voice was harsh. "I can't."

Lothar turned away without looking at her and walked out of the cell towards the guards at the entrance to the dungeons. Velhisya heard the sound of his boots as he walked.

"Lock the cell," she heard him order the guards.

Velhisya heard a guard approach. Soon after, he locked the door and disappeared from sight. *It was worth a try.* She knew she would fail, but she'd had to take a chance. She'd hoped that perhaps her beauty could have been of real help for the first time.

She sat on the ice-cold stone floor, filled with sorrow, and her eyes fell upon the torchlight once again. *If there are more humans like Lothar, there may be hope. Humans may perhaps be able to escape their sins one day.*

A Wise Leader

Syrella paced back and forth in the chamber of the Tower of Poisons, her breath shallow with anticipation for the arrival of Selwyn and Giren. A few feet away, Sophie tapped her foot impatiently, though there was a hint of relief on both the Queen's and Peter's faces. Selwyn was alive.

Minutes passed in silence as everyone waited. Aleron, Elliot, the two elves, Jahon, and Borin sat frowning while Thorold and Syrella's daughters stood as if unable to believe that Selwyn had survived. Suddenly, a knock came from the entrance.

"Come in," Syrella called, and the door opened. A handful of men entered the room, though they weren't the ones they had been expecting. "What are you doing here?" Syrella looked at Sadon Burns, who stood next to a few other lords.

"Lord Burns decided to celebrate his nameday at an inn and invited us to the feast," said Sygar Reis, a pockmarked, white-haired lord with a thick moustache.

"And how did my councillors find their way there?" Sophie asked.

"Lord Burns was kind enough to invite us to the feast as well," replied Richard Lamont, a captain in the Queen's council.

"And why did you leave the celebration and come here?" Syrella asked.

"We heard that Selwyn Brau had returned to the city, and we found out that he would be coming to this chamber to see you, my lady. We wanted to know what happened," Sadon said.

Syrella took a step in his direction. "I wonder who informed you about this. The news only reached my ears a while ago."

"A guard," Sadon told her.

Syrella shot the old lord a pointed look. She didn't like him ordering men from the City Guard to bring him information. Sadon's actions had been infuriating her of late. "I'd advise you to stop looking for informants among Wirskworth's guard. The men are subordinate only to me."

Sadon turned red. Syrella glanced at the aged lord, whose eyes had narrowed. "I thought you were against Thomas's decrees... I thought that the lords in Elmor kept their men and only, when necessary, granted them to the rul—"

"I've never made you pay taxes, and I've allowed you to keep command over your men, even if you left your castles and came to Wirskworth," Syrella interjected and took another step towards him. "I ignored Thomas and Sophie's decrees and stayed by your side! However, I expected to be kept informed about the orders you would give the soldiers to show some appreciation for my decisions. The fact that city guards are bringing news to you at the same time that I, the Ruler of Elmor, am being informed is intolerable. I didn't call you here, and no one should have told you where I am. If I find the man who gave you this information, I'll have his head on a spike to make an example of him.

"We humbly apologise, my lady. I insisted that we shouldn't have come here since we hadn't received an invitation from you," said Lord Reis.

"I thought you kept no secrets from your council. The news Lord Brau brings is particularly important, and I thought we should come—"

"I'll share whatever I want, when I want, with the council, Lord Burns. I hope you remember that," Syrella said.

The flabby lord's breath came out sharply, his gaze cold. She used to appreciate Sadon, but of late, his actions seemed to undermine her authority. For a moment, Walter's traitor came to mind. *That's out of the question*, she thought. *The only reason he'd betray me would be if he believed the rumours about me and Jahon. If he did, he would have said something by now.*

There was a knock on the door again, snapping her out of her thoughts. "Come in."

Two men accompanied by a guard entered the hall.

"Selwyn!" Peter rushed over to his son.

Syrella was delighted to see Selwyn throw himself into Peter's arms. A little further off, Giren was scowling. Brau's son had grown a beard and lost weight, his clothes were stained with dirt.

"Where's Velhisya?" Syrella had no more patience. She had to find out.

Selwyn broke free of his father's arms and walked over to Giren's side. "Liher has her," he said in a steady voice.

Syrella's hands went numb, while her forehead was sweating. "What happened?"

"I managed to convince a guard to take me to the dungeons of Gold-town Castle, and just as I was waiting for him to drink the poisoned wine I'd offered him, he hit me on the head. He'd caught on to me," Giren told her.

"Liher's men suspected there were other soldiers and found your men outside the city. All of them are dead, and Velhisya was taken prisoner," Selwyn added.

"And how did you get away?" came Elliot's voice. He approached Selwyn, his eyes filled with angst.

Giren took a deep breath. "Liher's brother, Lothar Hale, helped us. He's hated Walter ever since he killed their elder brother, so he wanted Vylor to ally with Elmor."

A gasp escaped Sophie's lips. "Liher captured Selwyn and Velhisya, and his brother hopes to ally with us?"

"He hopes he'll get Liher to change his mind. If that fails and Vylor finds itself at our mercy one day, he'd like us to show compassion to those who haven't done us any harm," Selwyn said.

"Why didn't he help Velhisya escape, too?" Syrella felt a mixture of fear and rage, but she tried to keep calm.

"He couldn't. Liher was holding her somewhere in his castle... Nevertheless, he swore he'd protect her."

"The oaths of a Hale are worth less than dung!" shouted Sadon Burns.

Selwyn turned on him angrily. "Lothar Hale saved my life. I'd still be tied to a chair with the Heretic's Fork around my neck if it weren't for him."

Syrella felt herself shudder. "Did they torture you?" She couldn't see any wounds on his face.

The man nodded.

"At first light, I'll order my men to get ready. Elmor's army will march onto Vylor and destroy everything in its way. They won't dare torture Velhisya!" Syrella shouted, unable to contain her rage any longer.

"And how shall we deal with Walter when he arrives in Wirskworth?" Richard asked, looking first at Syrella and then at Sophie.

"I heard on my way to Elmor you defeated some of Thorn's men. You fought them and forced them to retreat. Rumour has it that Walter got away but that a large number of his men died. I saw the shattered gate as soon as I got to Wirskworth but couldn't be sure how much of that was true," Selwyn said.

"Walter sent half of his men to attack us. He didn't ride into Elmor, and the rest of his soldiers pulled back. We won the battle, but not the war," Syrella replied.

"Why did Walter—" the younger Brau started.

"You'll be filled in later, Lord Brau," Richard cut in. "What's important now is that we discuss how we'll deal with Walter when he attacks again if we send an army to Vylor."

"The Royal Army will stay here, and my men will return quickly. Thorn won't march into Wirskworth anytime soon. He has been in many battles recently. He needs all his men if he's to make certain that he'll win the last battle, and they need to rest before they head for Elmor," Syrella said, remembering what Elliot had said earlier. She wouldn't accept any objections.

"Our cousin needs our help." Linaria raised her voice.

"Our men could delay in returning! We cannot defeat Walter with the Royal Army alone," Lord Reis said.

"Our men belong to the Governor. If she wants to attack Vylor, we can only obey," Sadon told them.

Syrella couldn't believe that those words had come out of Sadon's mouth. "I didn't expect you to support me in my decisions again."

"I would do the same for my son," Sadon replied, fixing his gaze upon her.

Syrella nodded.

"I apologise for intervening, but the Queen of Knightdorn is the one who must agree to the tactics for the battle," Richard said.

Sophie looked at her captain sternly as if to say he should remain silent. "I understand you want to save your niece," she said, turning to Syrella, "but we'll need thousands of men to lay siege to Vylor."

"Liher might give us Velhisya as soon as he sees our army at his doorstep," said Elliot.

"I doubt it... That man is ruthless." Syrella crossed her arms. "A few days ago, you asked me to send an army to save Selwyn. You explained how important he was to Peter," she told Sophie. "I have to do the same for Velhisya."

"We only sent twenty men. If we now send all of Elmor's army, even if we free Velhisya, she will die a few days later when Walter attacks us. We will lose countless soldiers," Peter insisted.

"We sent twenty men, and the plan failed. We can't save Velhisya without taking Goldtown!" Syrella snapped.

"I am sure we can do something to save her!" Elliot said.

"How do you even know she's alive? Liher may well have killed her. I'm sure he must have been furious after Selwyn's escape, and he knows that Walter will attack us soon. He's certainly not going to get any gold from Elmor," Peter went on.

Rage welled up in the pit of Syrella's stomach. What he'd said was logical, but she refused to believe that her niece was dead. "She's alive! I can feel it. We'll do what—"

"Syrella." Sophie stepped in front of her. "Like you said, Liher is ruthless. Even if he sees your army outside his gates and knows that his end has come, if Velhisya is still alive, he's liable to kill her out of hatred alone. He'll do it before he dies to take revenge on you."

"So, are you suggesting we do nothing?" Linaria asked and moved to Syrella's side, rage contorting her features.

"I don't know what we can do, but if we lose the battle with Walter, we'll all die!" Sophie retorted.

"I feel sorry for Velhisya, but the Queen is right," Aleron said, his voice cutting through the noise.

Syrella turned to the elwyn. She'd learned to appreciate the man's wisdom, but she couldn't leave Velhisya defenceless. "My niece was the one who offered to save Selwyn! She was the first to volunteer to help Giren and lead the mission. After all she's done, are we going to leave her to die alone in Vylor?"

Sophie frowned. "Her mission proved that twenty men aren't enough, and there's no way we can get her out of Hale's castle. Perhaps Lothar will help her escape when he gets the chance. He swore to Selwyn that he'd protect—"

"I don't trust the promises of a Hale!" Syrella's words rang out through the chamber. "My men will take Vylor's capital and will return before Thorn arrives."

"We can't waste so many men!" Sophie cried.

"If you accept what I've told you, we can find new soldiers!" Syrella spat.

"New soldiers?" Sadon repeated, brow furrowing.

The Queen's lips became a thin line. It was clear that she wasn't in agreement about an alliance with the Emperor through marriage. Syrella swore Sophie didn't want her councillors to find out about that plan.

"Where will we get new soldiers from?" Sadon asked again.

"Forget those words, Lord Burns," Sophie told him without taking her eyes off Syrella.

"Sophie is the Queen. We're obliged to do as she wishes," Richard said and moved closer to Sophie.

"Don't forget who hosts you in their city, Captain," Sadon replied angrily. "The Governor has the right to use her men as she wishes to save her niece."

"And then we'll all die! And so will Velhisya *if* we manage to save her," Peter interjected.

Syrella's anger bubbled over as arguing spread between the room's occupants. All that mattered was that they save her niece.

"Enough!" To Syrella's surprise, Aleron's shout had brought about silence. "Elwyn blood runs through the veins of Velhisya Endor. I'm duty-bound to help her with all my power, but if that means the end of my people, I cannot do it, as much as it pains me. A wise leader must put what's best for his people above one person's life. How many will cry for their children, their husbands, and their loved ones if we are defeated by Walter?"

Silence spread through the chamber.

"I agree, even though I would like Velhisya to be saved," Thorold said.

"Me, too," Elliot said, his voice cracking.

Syrella glanced at him. His eyes seemed wet. She felt as if the room were shrinking around her. Suddenly, Sophie took her hand.

"You know what you have to do. If we could take Vylor quickly, without losing any soldiers, I wouldn't hesitate in giving up all my men to you. You know I speak the truth," the Queen said, meeting Syrella's gaze with sadness in her eyes.

Syrella felt an overwhelming pressure weighing down on her. She couldn't sit idly by.

"Perhaps there's a way of entering Vylor's capital without laying siege to it," Selwyn said.

All faces turned to him. His eyes were wide as if he was surprised at himself for not having thought of it sooner. He raised his hand, holding an object between his fingers. Syrella stared at the rusty key, trying to understand its meaning, until a flutter of hope flickered in her heart.

A Gulp of Serenity

John threw the coin, and it hit the goblet with a clink, making it wobble. He groaned inwardly as the goblet fell and spilt its contents onto the wooden table. The men around him had erupted into squeals of joy.

Damn. This isn't my lucky night.

"I told you this gold coin belongs to me, Long Arm!" Ian yelled.

John turned sheepishly towards him. "We're not done yet."

"Do you think you'll win?" Ian laughed, revealing a set of rotten teeth.

"I'd say you should give him the coin now," said another man. John didn't know his name, and his clothes were tattered and dirty, as were those of most people in the inn.

"It's time this gold became mine." Ian walked to the other end of the table, picked up the goblet, and took the wine-stained coin.

John's eyes wandered. The men in the Dolphin Inn had formed a circle around them, looking at the spectacle. The game was simple. Whoever got the gold coin inside the cup three times would be the winner. John hadn't yet managed to do so even once, while Ian had already hit the target twice.

"I have a suggestion," John said amid the cheers of the surrounding men.

Ian laughed again as he walked back towards John. He wore black clothes made of cheap cloth, and a pointed beard protruded from his tiny face. "A suggestion? No suggestion will save you now."

John smiled back. "What do you say we double the bet?"

The man's eyes widened. "You're the most addicted man to gambling that I've ever met, Long Arm, but you're also a fool! Do you want to lose even more gold?"

"I thought you'd only care about how much gold ends up in your pockets."

Ian frowned. "So be it... If I manage once more, I'll get two gold coins instead of one!" he said.

"Not so fast. I won't double the bet if the rules don't change."

"What do you mean?" Ian took on a hostile tone now.

"We begin again, and whoever puts the coin in the cup first wins."

"Fuck you, John! Did you think you were going to trick me with that ploy?" Ian shouted.

John took a step towards him. "I thought you were the best at this game. Actually, you're just a coward!" He glanced at the men around them quickly. They had stopped shouting for a few moments.

"COWARD!" shouted John.

"COWARD!" one of the patrons echoed.

John sneered as the jeers of the men in the inn grew louder than before.

"COWARD! COWARD! COWARD."

"SHUT UP!" Ian screamed.

"COWARD! COWARD! COWARD."

The man's face had gone red. "I won't accept that bet. If I lose, I can't pay two gold coins!"

"I thought no one could beat you," John said mockingly.

"You have to be prepared for the worst." Ian tried to be heard over the cat-calling that filled the air.

If nothing else, at least he's prudent, John thought. *That's rare in the Ice Islands.* "If you haven't got two gold coins, then if you lose, I'll be drinking for free in your inn for a year!" John declared.

The shouting died down while Ian pursed his lips, thinking. John wondered whether he'd accept; the Dolphin was his favourite inn on Grand Island, so, if he won, he'd be drinking night and day in this rathole.

"Agreed," Ian said with sudden confidence. "Who gets to throw first?"

John extended his hand. "Give me the coin."

A furrow appeared on Ian's forehead. "I haven't agreed that you should throw first."

"I'll hide it in one of my hands. If you find it, you'll go first, otherwise, I'll go first."

Ian sighed angrily, but he put the coin in his hand with a sudden move. John put his hands behind his back and immediately extended them. Ian's face had hardened as he tried to decide, the faint light of the candles making his bald head shine. He touched John's right hand.

"I'm sorry," John said, smiling. He unclenched his empty palm and raised the other with the coin to his opponent's eye level.

"Throw first, then, Long Arm... You won't succeed!" Ian snapped.

The men's shouts grew louder again, and John turned his head towards the goblet on the wooden table. He raised his hand and readied himself to take his shot when a figure caught his attention. A man in his fifties sitting at the other end of the inn was smiling at him. A black cloth covered one of his eyes.

"What are you waiting for?! Ian shouted. "Throw!"

"THROW! THROW! THROW!" the men around them clamoured.

John glanced at the cup once more. *Gods of pleasure and debauchery, help me!* With a flick of his wrist, the coin left his hand and headed towards the cup. It was as if time stopped, and the shouting ceased. The coin hit the edge of the cup, flipped up into the air, and immediately landed inside the goblet.

A thunderous din engulfed the inn as dozens of men grabbed John and lifted him into the air. "LONG ARM! LONG ARM! LONG ARM!"

John laughed as the men lowered him back down to the ground. "I'd like two cups of your best wine," he said, turning to Ian.

The man cursed his luck. "I should never have accepted this bet!"

"And your father shouldn't have knocked up your mother. Bring on my wine!"

Ian cursed again and moved to the wooden bench at the end of the inn. John turned to the one-eyed man he'd seen earlier. He was still there, and as soon as he saw him, he raised his cup, laughing.

"Here you are," came a voice, and John turned around. Ian held two mugs in his hands.

John took them and lifted them slightly. "Cheers, my friend," he said, drinking the sweet wine in the first mug in a single gulp. "I'll need more soon."

John handed Ian the empty mug, ignoring the inn owner's angry glare, and headed towards the one-eyed man.

"Good evening, Jack."

"Great way to spend your nights, Long Arm," the man said.

"I just won free wine for a year... Can't call that a waste of time," John responded.

Jack heaved a sigh, shaking his head. "You'll never change."

"I'd say your life is duller than mine. Gambling is somewhat more interesting than fishing," John said and sat beside him. He had met Jack years ago when he'd visited the Ice Islands for the first time. He loved talking to Jack; the man was headstrong but also sharp.

"Fishing ain't that boring these days." Jack took a sip of wine.

"What do you mean?"

"Fishing boats haven't been coming back lately." Jack's voice took on a forlorn tone.

Strange. "Is someone attacking the fishermen of the Ice Islands?" John asked, licking the remnants of his drink from his lips. He couldn't think of any reason for someone to attack the men of the Ice Islands.

Jack frowned. "I don't know... Begon wants to solve the mystery. He wants to know what happened to these men. At first, he thought they were unskilled sailors whose boats had been sunk by squalls. But quite a few have failed to return in the last two months."

John pushed his hair back. "The men of these islands are the best sailors the world has ever known. It was Begon's folly to believe that his fishermen couldn't deal with the waves... The Leader of the Ice Islands should know the strengths of his own men."

"I agree."

John took a few sips of his wine. "Even so, gambling is better... I prefer it to risking my life just to catch a few fish," he said, breaking the silence.

"The problem is that you wouldn't risk your life for anything. What's the point of life if you don't want to risk it for anything?" Jack asked, staring into space.

"Great words..." John said sarcastically.

"I'm really curious. Didn't you ever want to fight for a cause? Something worth risking your life for?"

"No!" John snapped, Elliot's image flashing in his mind before he pushed it away. "And you?"

"Only once," Jack mumbled.

"When was that?" John leaned in, waiting for Jack's reply.

The man sipped a little more of his drink. "When Begon swore he'd fight by Thomas Egercoll's side. I remember the Second King. For years, the rulers of Knightdorn sneered at us and our land. They taunted us because our islands didn't belong to the kingdom, but Thomas showed us respect. I'd seen him walking with Begon in the harbour and had heard a few of his words. He'd said, '*I never thought that in this little place, I would find greater prudence and reason than in the whole of Knightdorn.*'"

"I know he respected this place," John said.

Jack nodded. "We soon learned that he admired our politics and traditions and wanted to bring them to his kingdom." His eye lit up with excitement. "It was the only time I, too, wanted the Ice Islands to join Knightdorn. It was worth being under that king."

"And when Walter rebelled, did you want to die for Thomas?"

"I did."

John found his words foolish. "Why? Why die for a king in a place hundreds of miles away? The Ice Islands had good fortune away from Knightdorn for centuries... It wasn't worth dying for a kingdom and a ruler that meant nothing to you and your land."

"Wise words..." Jack said, the irony evident in his voice. "I'd die for the only king I believed could build a better world. Nevertheless, I didn't fight and nor did any of us."

"It was the right decision."

"Walter will soon take the throne. If the new king gets bored, he might kill every man in my land just for fun," Jack told him.

"I doubt it, but even if that does happen, you'll find somewhere else to go," John replied.

Jack shook his head disapprovingly. "For some, the homeland means everything, Long Arm. To have no home, country or purpose is a miserable life..."

John snorted. "All those who died for a country or a cause—all those young lads sent to their death for the land and riches of various rulers—are the ones who lived a miserable life. I like you, Jack. You're one of the few men I respect in this place, but you won't get me to change my mind."

Jack looked away. "There are some things worth dying for."

John didn't answer as his eyes fell upon a beautiful young woman who had entered the inn. His gaze followed her across the room, his focus drifting away from Jack.

"That boy, Thomas's son, he may have deserved your help," Jack added.

John grew angry and stared at the ceiling in exasperation. He shouldn't have told him about that.

"I've known you for many years, John... The only time you spoke of someone with respect was when you told me about Elliot."

John motioned for him to lower his voice. "Nobody must find out about that!" He liked Jack, but he was loud.

"At some point, they will find out. Such news will even reach the Ice

Islands."

"They'll find out when it's too late to do anything," John whispered.

"Regrettably," Jack muttered.

"Do you believe Begon would choose to fight? Would he disregard his treaty with Walter? If he'd wanted to do that, he could have fought for Sophie. I told him the Queen wanted his help," John said.

Jack frowned. "If he'd wanted to fight for Sophie, he would have done so years ago... However, Thomas's son might make him change his min—" He stopped mid-sentence. "I don't know what he'd do. I've never understood why Begon complied with the treaty with Walter."

John looked at him in bewilderment. "I never thought you went for heroics, Jack. Walter came here with thousands of men. If Begon hadn't accepted, you would have all died."

"You've got me wrong. I said I never understood why he kept to the treaty, not why he did it."

"Begon has honour."

Jack snorted. "Honour is due only to those who are virtuous. Begon shouldn't have abided by this treaty. He should have fought by Sophie's side when Walter left our land. There is no honour for a perverted man like Thorn."

"You'd all have died!" John repeated.

"We would have died for an ideal—for a free kingdom and a free world. Now, if the new king decides to attack us, we'll all die like cowards, or do you think Walter will care a damn about our treaty?"

John didn't want to talk about it anymore. "I don't know what Begon would do if he found out about Elliot, but I've made up my mind. The boy may already be dead." That weighed heavily on his chest. He had to push his feelings aside. He knew better than anyone that caring was a weakness, not a strength.

"It's been a while since I last saw you, Long Arm," came a voice to their right.

John saw a man he didn't want to see. "Good evening, Raff."

"Watch this bugger, Jack. He asked me to bring him here a few weeks ago to deliver a letter to Begon, and as soon as he found himself before him, he said he'd lost it," Raff said. His clothes were black and thick.

"Get out of here," John retorted.

"I thought you liked my company, Long Arm." Raff was smiling.

"If you want payment for the trip, I'll give you a gold coin."

"Keep your gold and give the Queen's letter to Begon."

"I've told you this before, I've lost it!"

"Liar!" Raff raised his voice.

"I told your ruler what the Queen wants, and he chose to stay away from the war. If you have any reservations about his decisions, ask for an audience with him!" John snapped.

Raff turned red. "You told him in your own words, without a letter! No one can be sure whether you're telling the truth. I'm sure if he'd seen the letter, he might have given it some thought, and I think there's more to this. There are things you didn't want Begon to know! You wanted us to stay out of the war so you could stay here and save your life."

"Even if that were the case, I did you a favour. You wouldn't want to set sail with your ship to fight against Walter," John said, annoyed.

"For years, the northerners have considered us trash and have mocked us. Soon one of Thorn's allies will attack us and then..." Raff looked at Jack as he trailed off. "Have your drink, Long Arm, and think about where you'll go if this land is conquered by Thorn one day." With that, the man walked away.

"Damn it," John muttered.

"He's right," Jack told him.

"Enough. I've just won a bet, I have gold in my pockets and free wine for a year. I'll speak no more of wars and battles."

"So be it." Jack gave him a weary look.

John brought his goblet to his mouth and took a sip of wine. "I've never asked you how you lost your eye." He'd wanted to know for years but had never found the courage to ask.

Jack smirked. "I was wondering when you'd ask..." He said and drank from his cup. "I lost it when I was a pirate."

"I assumed so," John replied with a nod. "Did you lose it in a battle while trying to rob merchants?"

Jack shook his head. "My father was a pirate, too, and we were on a ship together when it happened."

"Your family honoured the life of a thief!" John laughed.

Jack's face remained sombre. "My father believed that the traditions of our land were our most valuable asset—even more valuable than gold. The first pirates on the continent of Knightdorn centuries ago were men from the Ice Islands. However, Bereon, one of our old leaders, decided to put a stop to them. We would soon be attacked, as the merchants had lost their patience. Then piracy was banned, and those who opposed Bereon were exiled. Many left, arguing that a pirate's life was a tradition in our land." Jack paused for a moment, frowning.

John had heard that the fathers of all pirates were the men from the Ice Islands.

"My father found out that one of our ancestors was the most illustrious pirate there ever was, so he decided to follow suit and lead the life of a pirate away from the Islands. My mother was pregnant with me at the time, and my father was only seventeen years old."

"Begon exiled my father and forbade him from ever returning to the Ice Islands. When I grew up, I tried to find him without anyone knowing. One day, I located him, and he gladly accepted me on his ship. He'd become a captain. After that, we started robbing merchant ships together. One day, his crew rebelled against him. They wanted a bigger share of the spoils, and my father refused."

"Did you try to fight, and that's when you lost your eye?" John asked.

"Not exactly. They caught my father and were about to throw him into the sea. I begged them to spare his life. They told me they would, but in exchange, I had to give them my eye. This would be payment for what my father had stolen from them over the years."

John was stupefied. "And you did so?"

Jack nodded and touched the spot where his eye had been. "As soon as I'd plucked my eye out and thrown it at them, they threw my father into the sea, laughing. My father paid for his choices... He paid for his desire to live without rules, honouring the traditions of our ancestors."

John was horrified. "How did you survive?"

"I was lucky. One of the crew members knew how to treat wounds, and he liked me. He kept me alive, and the new captain dropped me off on land in Knightdorn. My father's death was enough for him. I made my way back to the Ice Islands from there."

"Did you ever take revenge on them?"

The man shook his head. "I left my past behind when I got off that ship."

"I'm sorry," John said.

Jack was lost in thought for a few moments. "Why did you become a pirate before becoming a bounty hunter? Was your father a pirate, too?"

John scoffed. "My father knocked up a whore, and when I was born, he asked her to sell me to a pair of nobles who couldn't bear children in exchange for gold. He was greedy, and he loved to drink."

"And they sold you?"

John nodded. "My mother agreed. She shared his love of wine and already had enough children to feed. At least, that's what my new parents told me."

"I would never have thought that you grew up in a noble house," Jack remarked.

"I didn't... I detested the life of a lord. My new parents tried to teach me how to eat, stand, and speak, to show off my noble heritage, but all I wanted was wine. I wanted to know what the liquid that made my parents sell me off was all about. So, I ran away at the age of thirteen and became a pirate. I liked a life without rules until I eventually got sick of the sea and started catching those with bounties on their heads."

He saw Jack looking at him out of his one eye with a strange expression as if he pitied him.

"Cheers, Long Arm," said Jack, raising his mug.

John took another gulp, feeling the familiar numbness settle in. The clink of the mugs echoed in his ears as he let the wine wash over him. It was a fleeting peace, the kind that dulled the memories, even if just for a moment. He'd always felt detached from his past, but in this silence, with the wine in his veins, it was as if everything—his parents, his origins—faded into the distance. The cruel irony was that this peace, this escape, was only possible because of the very thing that had torn him from his parents in the first place.

Dead Fear

Selwyn felt Peter's hand touch the back of his neck.

"I'm so glad you're back," Peter said as they walked down the dark corridors of Moonstone. A few torches lit up the hallways, while a handful of stars were visible in the sky through the windows to their right.

"Me too, Father." Selwyn was glad to have escaped Liher Hale's clutches, yet he felt an emptiness within him. Velhisya was still imprisoned in the land of the Mercenaries, and that tormented his soul.

"I need to tell you something," Peter said, his brows furrowed.

Selwyn felt uneasy. He knew that look. "Is Mother well?"

Peter frowned and touched his blue silk outfit nervously. "Your mother is fine. I'm sure she's asleep at such a late hour, but we'll wake her. She'll be overjoyed to hear you're back safe and sound."

"What do you want to tell me?" Selwyn stopped, waiting for his father to speak.

His father lowered his gaze. "Eleanor—"

Selwyn felt his palms sweat. "Eleanor?"

"She's dead."

"What?" Selwyn's voice echoed in the corridor.

"Walter attacked Aquarine and killed her."

Selwyn thought he had misheard his father. "I don't understand! Why did Walter go to Aquarine and not attack Wirskworth?"

Peter told him everything, and Selwyn felt rage and sadness upon hearing about what had happened. "Has Walter bonded with a wyvern?"

he suddenly interjected. His father nodded sharply. "How?"

"Nobody knows."

Peter continued with the rest of the grim tale, and Selwyn seethed, his anger boiling over until he was left stunned. "Are the giants dead? Does Walter now have all the wyverns at his command?"

His father nodded again.

Selwyn cupped his face in his hands. "Are you sure Eleanor is dead?" he asked in a whisper.

Peter looked away again, sorrow in his eyes. "That Aquarine lord was certain that no one survived the attack on Felador."

Selwyn screamed and punched the wall. "Be damned, Walter Thorn! I'll kill you with my bare hands!" he said, feeling pain shoot through his fist.

"No one expected him to attack there, and no one could ever imagine a wyvern—"

"I saw an elwyn and two elf-like creatures in the chamber we were in before. Elliot freed the Elder Races... I would have expected they would have been able to explain how Walter—"

"They don't know. They suspect he tried to get Orhyn Shadow into his blood," Peter told him.

"But that's impossible. The poison would have caused him unimaginable pain," replied Selwyn. "Why do the elwyn and elves think this would win over the wyvern?"

"Orhyn Shadow is what binds the giants to the wyverns. Without it, no one could bond with them. Nonetheless, we don't know how Walter got it into his blood."

Selwyn sighed angrily. A flame burned in his chest. He wanted revenge for the loss of Eleanor.

"You've changed," his father said. "The Selwyn I knew used to look frightened when he heard such dreadful news."

"I no longer fear anything. My fear died out in Liher Hale's cell. I will avenge Eleanor's death and save Velhisya."

Peter looked bemused. "If we send an army to Vylor, it will only be Elmor's men."

"Velhisya led the mission to rescue me. It's my duty to help."

"The Queen's men will stay here!"

"Then, let the Queen try and stop me!" Selwyn snapped.

Peter seemed angry. "This is a betrayal of your ruler—"

"I went alone to Liher Hale's doorstep to ask for an alliance in the Queen's name!" Selwyn cut him off. "If Sophie thinks I'm a traitor, let her execute me. You won't hold me back any longer, Father. I'll do what I think is right."

A new furrow formed in Peter's brow. "Lothar Hale knows you left clutching a key to that secret passage in the dungeons of Goldtown Castle... He may tell his brother, and they'll change the lock or set traps. This plan is very dangerous. It could cost us our army before the final battle with Walter! You mustn't go to Goldtown again," he insisted.

"Why didn't you share those thoughts with Syrella?" Selwyn asked.

"She won't listen to me! I need to speak to Sophie. She's the only one who can make the Scarred Queen think straight," Peter said, his eyes narrowing.

"I don't believe the plan will fail. No one will expect us to return to Vylor now. Everyone will know that we'll soon be fighting the last battle against Walter and the wyverns on his side."

"Liher might be expecting an atta—"

"No. He won't be expecting us to attack him. Liher only cares about gold—nothing else is on his mind. Lothar won't expect us to travel to their land now, either. No locks will be changed."

"And if you're mistaken?"

"Then we may lose... We may die. Velhisya deserves my life after what she did for me," Selwyn said decisively.

"While the Queen does not?"

"She'll have the men of Iovbridge by her side."

Peter's face reddened.

Selwyn took him by the shoulder. "All my life, you've tried to protect me. You've got to let me make my own decisions now."

Peter swallowed, staring at his son. "If you fall into Liher's hands again, you'll be subjected to a torturous death," he said.

"I can't be a coward—not this time." *No matter what he says, he won't change my mind.*

"If we defeat Walter, I swear I will lead the assault on Vylor," Peter said.

Selwyn frowned. "We can't wait that long! Even at this very moment, Velhisya may be suffering torture. She needs our help."

"She may already be dead!" Peter snapped.

"I don't think so. Lothar told me he would protect her."

"He has no power against the Governor of Vylor!"

"If that were true, I wouldn't be here."

Peter shook his hands, nervously. "Think about it. Liher won't allow anyone to escape from under his nose again, and he'll take revenge on any captive from the Queen's camp that falls into his hands. He'll want to avenge himself for what happened!"

"You're right," Selwyn said. "Nevertheless, Velhisya is a woman... A beautiful woman. Knowing how Liher spends his nights with naked girls dancing in front of him at dinner time, I'm sure he'll want to rape Velhisya. He won't kill her quickly. We have to move fast to rescue her."

Peter closed his eyes, sighing heavily. "Perhaps... However, no one could refute Aleron's words. A wise leader must put the interests of his people above all, even those of a beloved person. If the trick with the key and the secret passage fails, we'll lose countless men to defeat Liher, and then we'll be defeated by Walter without question."

"Tell Sophie to talk to Syrella, to let her know that if the plan with the key fails, we'll try to free Velhisya by laying siege to Goldtown. If we don't succeed in two or three days, we'll turn back. The Mercenaries won't chase us beyond their walls," Selwyn said.

Peter looked very worried. "If Walter finds out about our plan, he may pursue our men out in the open with his wyverns!"

"No one in the kingdom will expect us to be there. This news won't get to Thorn. I swear I won't do anything foolish, but I have to try to save this woman. If I die, know that I died proud that I overcame my fears." Selwyn's words came out more decisively than ever before.

A tear rolled down his father's cheek. "I'm proud that you're my son."

Selwyn smiled and hugged his father tighter than he'd ever hugged him before. He had longed to return to his parents for so long, and now that he was finally home, he had decided to leave again.

Selwyn sat on his bed in his chamber, overcome with exhaustion. His body ached all over. He raised a hand to his jaw and chest, tracing the spots where the Heretic's Fork had dug into his flesh. There were scars, but the skin had healed.

His mind wandered to his parents. His mother couldn't believe he'd come back alive when he and his father went to see her. Despite how much he had missed his parents, Selwyn wasn't going to stay with them for long. He had to fight for Velhisya.

I won't let you be murdered like Eleanor. The thought of Eleanor brought tears to his eyes. She and Morys had died, engulfing his soul in pain. *Is Long Arm still alive?*

A knock on the door made him jump. "Come in."

The door opened with a hissing noise, and Elliot entered. "I can't believe you're alive. I thought I'd lost you," he said, looking at Selwyn sadly as his voice cracked. "I shouldn't have sent you to that place."

Selwyn stepped towards him and hugged him. "We needed allies... No one expected Liher to capture and torture a mere messenger," he said.

"I should have expected he would!" Elliot choked out once he was free from Selwyn's embrace.

"It's not your fault... I agreed to go there and do everything I could to help you. I was thinking about you while I was imprisoned," Selwyn said.

"I'm sorry... I hope you didn't hate me."

Selwyn smiled. "I kept on thinking that you would have found a way to escape, and I tried to imagine what you would have done. I also was sure that I'd make it out of that cell and that by your side, we would overthrow Walter."

"I'm honoured by your words—"

"When I travelled with you to Elmor, I was a coward," Selwyn went on.

"You were never a coward," Elliot said firmly.

"I was! I was afraid of death, and I didn't dare admit it. That day when we saw Thorn's men throwing corpses into the Forked River, you too saw the fear in my eyes."

"There were ten soldiers, and there were only five of us. Anyone would have been afraid."

"You don't need to find excuses for me." Selwyn shook his head. "I know I was more frightened than all of you. And yet I, the coward, survived, while Morys and Eleanor are dead."

"I wanted to tell you what happened..." Elliot couldn't finish his sentence, his eyes watering.

"Forget your guilty feelings, Elliot. No one expected Walter to attack Aquarine. Nevertheless, I'm sure Eleanor would have sacrificed her life for you and your cause. I'm sure she never regretted helping you."

"No one should have to die for me!" Elliot's voice rose, and his hands clenched at his sides "I shouldn't have taken a young woman who had never fought in battle before to Elmor. I shouldn't have sent her to Aquarine! I made mistakes, and I have her death and that of Morys on my shoulders!" Elliot seemed very angry with himself. "As if that weren't enough, I sent you to a place where it was almost certain that we wouldn't gain any soldiers, and now Velhisya is being held hostage! You don't understand what it's like... You can't know—"

"You can't win a war without using the people you trust to help you.

It would be impossible not to lose anyone. There was no other way," Selwyn told him.

"There was a way! We defeated Walter's men twice in this city. If I hadn't sent you far away, Eleanor would have—"

"Walter attacked with half his forces, and we were almost defeated. We needed allies, and we still do."

"But—"

"Listen to me. No war was ever won without sacrifices." Selwyn raised his voice. "I lost my brothers, and you lost your parents. Eleanor lost her entire family, as did the Queen. Nothing will change unless we kill Thorn and the rulers who support him. We need to rid the kingdom of men like Walter and Liher, and you're our best chance! Morys and Eleanor made their choice. If you don't fight with all your heart so that we might win, it will be disrespectful to them. It was an honour for us to be entrusted with these missions. It was our choice to try to carry them out. Put your guilt aside. We must save Velhisya and kill Walter because of everything he's done to all of us over the years."

Elliot's face darkened upon hearing Velhisya's name. Selwyn had seen them dance together at the Dance of Blood. He'd realised that the lad had feelings for her.

"I wanted to lead the mission to save Velhisya the moment I heard what happened to her. But Aleron was right. We couldn't risk everything for one person. Now that we have the key, we will succeed..." Elliot said. "I should have never sent you to that place... If I hadn't, Velhisya would..."

"It was my choice to go there, and her choice to try to rescue me. You can't be responsible for everything in this world."

Selwyn's words reminded Elliot of an old man who had said something similar a few days ago. "Aleron will like you," Elliot said after a while.

"How did you manage to set the Elder Races free?" Selwyn asked. "I've been gone so long, and I've missed so much."

"That's a long story. I'll let you rest up and tell you everything in the morning." Elliot tried to leave, but Selwyn grabbed his hand to stop him.

"Syrella said we might be able to gain new allies. What did she mean?"

Elliot sighed, his shoulders slumping. "She suggested Sophie consider marrying Odin Mud's son."

Selwyn snorted. *Sophie would never accept such a thing.* "If the Queen had wanted this alliance, she would have married his son years ago."

"I agree. Now, try to rest."

Selwyn didn't let go of his hand. "Is John alive?"

Elliot frowned, seeming worried. "I don't know. I'll soon send Hurwig to find him. I'm sure he didn't succeed in building an alliance with the Ice Islands, otherwise, they would have come to Elmor by now."

"My father told me all about Reynald Karford. He also told me that he's dead and that Walter wounded your hawk," Selwyn said quietly.

Elliot stood expressionless. "I'm sorry I didn't tell you where I'd sent Reynald. He'd asked me to swear that I'd keep it secret. When Hurwig returned wounded, we assumed Walter had caught wind of him and had killed him."

"I understand why you didn't reveal that secret. But why didn't you send your hawk to us earlier on? It would have been useful for you to get news from us, just like from Reynald," Selwyn told him. "Hurwig wouldn't have been able to find me in Goldtown's dungeons, but he would have reached John and Eleanor."

"I wanted to find out as much as I could about Walter's movements... So—"

"I see," Selwyn muttered and let Elliot go. "I hope John is alive."

"Me too. If he has survived, I don't want to ask him to do anything else for me."

"I've told you before that—"

"John didn't want to fight," Elliot interrupted. "One day, I asked him to stay by my side, and he accepted, but I felt he wasn't sure about the decision he'd made. He just didn't want to let me down. Maybe we haven't heard from him because he's decided to follow a different path.

If his wish is to live a quiet life in the Ice Islands, I don't want to force him to fight for me. I don't want to lose anyone else."

Has John made such a decision? Knowing his character, it wouldn't be unlikely, Selwyn thought. "Send him a letter asking if he's well, and let him write you whatever he wants. If he doesn't want to fight, he'll only send you his best wishes. Hurwig will manage to find him if he's alive..." *I hope he is alive,* he thought.

"I agree," Elliot said.

"I think Syrella will convince Sophie to send an army to Vylor," Selwyn told him after a few moments. "Now that they know about the key that leads to Liher's castle, the Scarred Queen will be more persistent than ever. I told my father that I would march with Elmor's soldiers as soon as they were ready to start."

Elliot nodded, arms crossed over his chest. "I agree. Syrella isn't going to sit idly by. I'll ask the Queen to let me lead the Royal Army. We'll speak again at first light."

Elliot was about to turn and leave when Selwyn said, "We will win. We'll defeat Walter together!"

"You've changed," Elliot said, turning to him with a faint smile.

Selwyn grinned. "I know. I may hate Liher Hale, but I'm indebted to him for killing my fears."

Elliot's worn expression softened. "Fear is useful as long as it doesn't make you a coward," he said quietly. "Don't let revenge get the better of you, my friend. If you do, there will come a day when you'll be worse than everyone you're trying to overturn."

The New Member of the Trinity

Walter looked at those present in the Royal Hall. He noted the bowed heads of the kneeling figures before him illuminated by the rays of the morning sun streaming into the hall. "Is this everyone?" he asked the guard standing a few feet away.

The man nodded.

"I'll give you one chance," he said to those kneeling.

The heads remained bowed, and some seemed to tremble. He enjoyed seeing wrinkled figures cowering in fear before him. If nothing else, these people deserved their fate. He'd ordered his men to inspect every house in Iovbridge and bring him anyone who owned items adorned with the Egercoll coat of arms. Anyone who dared speak up for Sophie Delamere was murdered on the spot.

"If you swear allegiance to me, pronouncing me the one and only king, I'll spare your lives. If even one of you refuses to swear allegiance to me, you'll all die." No one spoke. Walter could hear their sharp, fearful breaths. "Will you swear allegiance to me?"

"Long live the new king! Long live Walter Thorn!" said one man.

"Long live the new king! Long live the new king," came other voices.

Walter walked among the kneeling people as the voices grew louder and louder.

"I'll never swear allegiance to you."

Walter froze. The beast had awakened in his chest, ready to devour everything in its path. He slowly looked to the right at an old man who had raised his head and looked Walter in the eyes. "You've just sentenced all these people to death," he said.

"Why should we die? The rest of us have sworn allegiance to you, Your Majesty," a man protested.

"Please, Your Majesty, I beg you. I have two small children," a woman pleaded with tears in her eyes.

"Your children will be raised with the right principles under my reign even if you die," Walter said, paying no heed to her tears. "It's not my fault you're not the right mother for them. No man or woman who paid homage to the usurper should have children."

"I made a mistake, Your Majesty, but now I've sworn allegiance to you!" the woman sobbed.

"We all swore allegiance to you! Why should we die because of one fool?" repeated the man who had spoken earlier. He was young with black hair.

"You have something in common... You all betrayed me for the usurper and the House of Egercoll. All of you needed to repent for me to grant you your life. It isn't my fault that this old man has condemned you to death."

"Please, my King!" the woman screamed, her voice drowned out by several others. The guards took a few steps towards the kneeling people.

"Silence!" Walter shouted, and the voices died down abruptly. He regarded the old man who had refused to bend the knee to him. "If you apologise for what you said, you'll save the lives of about sixty people. It's your last chance."

The old man stared at him with cloudy brown eyes. "Very well. I pledge eternal loyalty to you, Your Majesty," he said, kneeling and bowing his head.

Walter took a few steps towards him. "You look quite old. Were you in the city when my grandfather, the First King, ruled?" he asked.

The old man remained hunched over. "Yes, Your Majesty."

"Did you admire his reign?"

"Yes."

"And when Thomas rebelled against my grandfather, did you fight by his side?"

"I never fought for anyone, Your Majesty. All my life I sold bread and spices... If I'd fought, I would have brought more trouble than help."

"You had the Egercoll coat of arms in your house and didn't fight for George Thorn, your true King. I've changed my mind! Kill them all!" Walter yelled at the guards.

Screams filled the air as swords were unsheathed. The floor of the Royal Hall turned red. Walter loved the sight. The screams continued to echo in his ears until a hand touched his boot.

"Please, Your Majesty. I'll do whatever you ask of me," the woman who had begged him earlier had approached him. Her blonde hair cascaded down her shoulders, and her blue eyes were filled with tears.

Walter drew the Blade of Power and cut off her head. He wiped the blood off the sword on his crimson cloak and walked among the corpses.

"Leave the hall and find Brian, Rolf, and Berta. Tell them to meet me here now," Walter told the guards, and they hastened to carry out his orders.

"For a moment, I thought you were going to spare their lives," came a voice.

Walter turned to Leonhard. He'd forgotten he was there. "They didn't deserve the life the gods gave them."

"It was kind of you not to kill their children, too," the man snapped.

Walter frowned. He tried to avoid killing children. Nonetheless, sometimes his anger was so fierce that he couldn't restrain himself. He remembered his attack on the City of Heaven not too long ago. That day—the day he'd found out that Thorold and Althalos had been alive for years and that there was a living descendant of Thomas—he'd been unable to tame his rage.

"We've been going from battle to battle lately and have neglected certain things," Leonhard said.

"Such as?"

"I imagine you'll restore the male line of succession now that you are King."

Walter scoffed. "I'm immortal, Leonhard. I don't care about succession."

"Nobody knows, nor can they find out. We don't want people wondering about our secret. When years have passed, you'll spread the word that the gods have spoken to you and given you immortality. Then, you'll inspire even more awe and fear," Leonhard said.

"I agree," Walter said.

"However, I think it would be good to change some of Thomas Egercoll's decrees, the ones you promised your lord-allies would change as soon as you sat on the throne. This will ensure their allegiance."

"I'll announce the restoration of the male line of succession," Walter said with a hint of indifference.

"And for the governors? You promised that if you took the throne, you'd restore the male line of succession for their offices as well."

Walter waved his hand as if trying to shoo away a pesky fly. "I don't like that idea. If one of them betrays me, I don't want his descendants to take his title."

Leonhard seemed thoughtful. "Tell them that you'll restore the male line of succession and that they can only lose their title through death. However, if they betray you, the punishment will be death by hanging. Moreover, the law will ensure that their Houses are eradicated. If ever you wish to get rid of one of them, you'll claim that he betrayed you."

"I like that idea," Walter replied with a nod and cast a look at the bodies scattered around the hall.

"At the time of the First King, rulers could abdicate and appoint a new successor. Perhaps you could bring back that law, too, and use it if you want to get rid of some governor." Leonhard's eyes brightened as he spoke.

"No. I'd rather they lose their title only through death, and if they betray me, they and their families will die. Such laws will bring stability to the kingdom," Walter said sharply.

"You also need to choose councillors," Leonhard told him. "You don't need to change anything for them. The current law states that they can lose their office through death, but also through treason."

"I don't need councillors! You and the Trinity of Death are all I need!"

Leonhard shook his head disapprovingly. "You can use us to discuss anything important. However, you must bestow this honour on the governors and lords who supported you. You need only announce your decisions to them. This will give the impression that you want to rule fairly and honour your promises."

"So be it."

"There's another thing. At the beginning of your rebellion, you promised to allow the lords to return to their old castles, taking up to a thousand soldiers, without paying taxes. Now that you've become king, you must honour—"

"No one will take men from me and the governors! It will be difficult to control the soldiers if they owe allegiance to hundreds of lords," Walter snapped, his temper flaring.

"I agree. However, we need loyalty. If you try to rule through fear alone, thousands of plots will be hatched against you over the years," Leonhard insisted.

"And what hope will they have pitted against immortality and my wyverns?"

Leonhard frowned. "You don't want the lords to conspire against you. You can't control the whole kingdom without keeping a few of your allies happy."

"If they want to return to their castles, let them do so. But they will not take soldiers from the regional capitals!" Walter said sharply.

"Spread the word that after so many years, this would hurt their trade. They will think you are doing it for them. Perhaps in return, you can relieve them of certain taxes in the first year of your reign," Leonhard suggested.

Walter was tired of their conversation. "I don't want to talk about these things anymore," he said.

Leonhard scoffed. "All your life you've fought to conquer the kingdom, but being a king is a more boring job, though it requires attention."

Walter didn't like that idea. He wouldn't spend his time on such boring matters. "We still have a lot of work to do. When all our enemies are dead, I'll deal with those issues... I dream that this kingdom will spread over the entire world and that I'll become the greatest ruler ever to be born. The Western Empire, the Mercenaries, and the Ice Islands will all submit to my will. There will be no land beyond my kingdom," Walter said.

"I agree. Nevertheless, announce what we discussed. To conquer the whole world and keep it under your command, you must use other methods besides fear. Trust me."

"So be it," Walter replied. "We need to discuss something far more important than all of this... We need more soldiers to make sure Elliot meets his father this time."

Leonhard looked at him wordlessly as footsteps came from the hall entrance. Walter saw Rolf and Brian walking towards him with Berta by their side. Their eyes fell on the dead, whose bodies were still pooling blood.

"These traitors had to be punished," Brian said, smiling.

"Wise words," Walter said approvingly and approached the newcomers. "The Trinity of Death needs a new member."

"Every man in the kingdom would want such an honour, Your Majesty. We'll find the best warrior in Iovbridge," Rolf 'Short Death' said with eyes that glinted.

"I'm sure you would have liked such a mission. I have, however, already found the third member of the Trinity."

"That's fantastic news. Who will it be?" Brian asked.

Walter's eyes fell upon Berta. "I know you've wanted it for years," he said.

The woman fell to her knees, and the blood of the dead splattered on her black leather trousers. "Thank you, Your Majesty. I swear I'll be your most faithful servant, and we'll destroy every single one of your enemies," she said, her eyes filling with tears.

"I'm sure you'll keep your every vow," Walter said.

"I respect your decision, Your Majesty. However, this will make a bad impression on our allies. Only the weak entrust powerful titles to women!" Brian snapped, eyes narrowing at Berta.

Brian, the Sadist, Walter thought with a smile. *A fitting nickname for him.* "Two men of the Trinity betrayed me. I trusted Anrai and Reynald, and they paid me back with treason! I know that you find women weak and think they don't have the courage to do what is needed. However, there's no other woman like Berta. I know she'll never betray me and won't hesitate to kill my enemies."

Berta rose swiftly. "I swear to you that one day I'll castrate Elliot Egercoll and feed his balls to Delamere," she said, turning to Brian. "If you think I'm weak, draw your sword and fight me."

"That's enough!" Walter shouted, and all the members of the Trinity immediately bowed to him. "You're my most able warriors, and you owe allegiance to me and to each other."

"I apologise for questioning your decision, Your Majesty," Brian said, keeping his gaze on the floor.

Walter nodded tersely and turned his back on Brian. He took a few steps to the end of the hall and picked up the Sword of Destiny from the floor. Then, he moved closer to the Trinity and Leonhard, who watched him in silence.

"This sword belongs to you," he said and extended his weapon to Short Death.

Rolf looked puzzled and bowed down before him again. "I never expected this highest honour, Your Majesty."

"You've been with me longer than any other member of the Trinity, and you've served me faithfully. The time has come for this sword to go into the hands of someone who deserves it. Make sure you make good use of it." Short Death bowed down once more. "Enough with all of that," Walter told him. "I've told all of you that we need more soldiers. This time, there's no room for failure. We must destroy our enemies!"

No one spoke, their silence as dead as the corpses around them.

They have no answers... It'll be hard to find new men. Walter walked among the dead, his boots echoing around the hall. He knew what he had to do; it was the only solution. Nevertheless, it wouldn't be easy.

"Keep thinking and order the slaves to clean up the hall," he said, looking at the Trinity. Then, he turned and left the room, lost in thought.

The Ruthless Queen

Sophie looked at the tall black tree in front of her with disgust. She remembered the first time she'd laid eyes on a Night Tree. Its trunk was full of knobs, and its branches looked diseased. She reached out to touch the trunk. She knew that every part of this tree was particularly sharp and that Orhyn Shadow was to be found throughout it. Sweat ran down her forehead as she prepared to touch it.

"What are you doing?"

Sophie pulled her hand away and turned around suddenly. Elliot stared at her, wide-eyed. He wore brown leather trousers and a lemon-coloured woollen jerkin. "I wanted to... It's of no importance," she muttered.

"Did you want to suffer?" he asked.

Sophie looked up at the bright sky. The sun's rays were warm that morning.

"You don't deserve to suffer," Elliot went on.

Sophie glanced back at her cousin. "Have you heard what I did when Peter defeated Walter's men in White City?"

Elliot took a step towards her. "I found out a few days ago."

Sophie sighed. "The only time enemy men found themselves at my mercy, I chose to kill them. I didn't grant anyone their life."

"Your Maj—"

"I heard that Syrella also wanted to kill the prisoners from the battle against Walter—the battle in which Thorn himself was present in Elmor," Sophie interrupted. "You asked her not to kill them—to show

114

mercy—and she listened to you."

Elliot nodded. "You've lost everything because of Walter. It's logical that—"

"You've lost everything, too! Peter and Syrella have also lost many of their loved ones because of Thorn."

Elliot frowned. "We all make mistakes. On my journey to Elmor, I found myself in the Centaurs-Land, and my rage blinded me. I told them they should have helped my father and demanded they fight for me, honouring their oaths. It was a miracle they didn't attack me."

Sophie had not heard that before, but it no longer mattered. "You didn't kill anyone," she told him, looking at the beautiful view the poisonous forest near Moonstone offered them.

"I've killed many men on the battlefield," Elliot insisted.

"It's not the same. I'm sure you would never kill unarmed prisoners, no matter how enraged you might have been."

"I can't be sure," Elliot murmured. There was a deepening silence between them. "Why are you here?"

Sophie straightened. "I've always found it strange that the Endors had a small forest full of poisonous plants near their castle. I like coming here," she admitted.

"I know quite a few who spend their time here," Elliot said with a smile. "Why did you want to touch the tree? I'm sure you know it's laced with poison, and it's particularly sharp." His face took on a serious expression.

Sophie didn't answer, and she felt the cuts on her wrist tingling. She'd harmed herself again the night before.

"Do you think you deserve to suffer because you killed those men?"

"Maybe!" Sophie snapped.

"You've already suffered enough, so don't torture yourself more. No one can always do the right thing in a life filled with pain and death."

Sophie put her hand on her hip. "All this time, I never thought about those men. They died before my eyes, screaming for mercy, and I don't even remember their faces." Her cheeks flushed. "Ever since I heard about Eleanor, their screams have been playing in my mind over and over. Perhaps the gods knew what I am really like, and that's why they gave me a life full of pain. They knew I deserved to suffer."

Elliot's eyes widened. "If that were true, Walter must have suffered the most out of all of us for everything he's done. You can't believe something like that."

Sophie pushed her hair out of her eyes. "I don't know if the self-proclaimed Emperor still wants to have me marry his son. However, if he consents, I'll do so," she said grimly.

"Why? I thought you would never accept such a plan."

"Do you know what I feel when I think of the death of those men? The prisoners I murdered?"

Elliot's face was inscrutable. "No."

"Nothing. I know that I showed no mercy—that I was merciless. Nevertheless, I feel neither regret nor guilt."

"That's because you're hurting." His expression softened. "Your pain for Eleanor won't allow you to feel anything else."

"I'm seething and incensed. I feel that if I could, I'd kill all of Walter's soldiers!" she shouted, her voice echoing through the poisoned trees. "I remember feeling remorse the day after killing those captives, but soon after that went away, and I never thought about those men again until now. Now, whenever they come to mind, I feel calm. I feel a sense of justice. If it weren't for men like them, my loved ones would all be alive. I want to kill more of Walter's soldiers!"

Elliot frowned. "I've felt rage all my life, and I've wanted to kill Walter. I still want to, but hate isn't the answer. For us to build a better world, compassion is needed."

Sophie laughed. "I used to believe all that, too, but I don't believe any of it anymore."

"Everything you feel will pass. You won't feel pain and rage forever," Elliot told her.

Sophie considered his words for a few moments. "You asked why I've decided to agree to this marriage." Elliot nodded. "For so many years I've tried to have honour, to be better than Walter, and to help my subjects. Now, I've learned that no one can win a war by playing fair. I'll marry the Emperor's son, use his soldiers, and if I succeed, kill Thorn with my own hands. I'll do anything to get revenge for Eleanor's death! And if I'm unhappy in this marriage, I'll kill my husband, too, when I don't need him anymore."

Elliot grimaced. "Althalos always said that you must fight to protect those you love. If you do it only for revenge, you'll send even more people to their deaths."

"Althalos gave a lot of advice during his lifetime. Nevertheless, he was the one who trained Walter. If he hadn't, thousands of people would be alive today," Sophie said, every word spiked with anger. "Furthermore, he asked me to sit on the throne and deprived me of everything!"

"He made a mistake," Elliot said in a low voice.

"He made thousands of mistakes! He kept you away from your sis—"

"I know what Althalos did," Elliot cut in. "Nevertheless, that doesn't mean all his words were mistakes."

"It makes no difference now. All I want is to see Walter Thorn's corpse lying in front of me, and I'll do everything in my power to succeed. My honour died along with Eleanor."

"Listen to me." Elliot walked up to her and took her hand. "If you take that path, your decisions will lead other people to their death, and then you'll feel even more pain. Trust me."

She looked into his green eyes. He was seventeen—almost still a boy—and life had burdened him with more suffering than most people who had ever lived. Sophie knew his words revealed the weight of his burden. He had felt hatred himself. He had sought revenge and believed that his hatred had led his friends to their deaths.

"You may be right, but I don't care anymore. I'd rather go down in history as a ruthless queen than be remembered as a weak woman who lost everything. As for the people, my decisions may send to their death... Now, no death can hurt me," she said without lowering her gaze. "Eleanor is dead, Bert is dead, my parents are dead. I have nobody. When you've lost everything, nothing else can hurt you."

She pulled her hand away gently and began to walk away.

"You have me. You may not have loved me like Eleanor, but I'm also your family," Elliot called after her.

Sophie stopped and turned back to him. "Caring makes you weak. We've both learned our lesson the hard way. I'd rather not have any family any longer. I don't want to love anyone else and lose them. I'd advise you to put aside your feelings, too, and perhaps then we may win this war. Inform everyone else of my decision, and as soon as the hawk is healed, I'll give you a letter for the Emperor."

She headed towards Moonstone, more determined than ever before.

Elliot carefully tied the letter to Hurwig's leg and patted his little head. The hawk closed his eyes at Elliot's touch. He still couldn't believe that Hurwig's wing had healed in just three days.

"I want you to be careful," he whispered to the bird. "I don't want to lose you, too."

Hurwig opened his black eyes, seeming to understand Elliot's words. The cool breeze blew against Elliot's face in Moonstone's courtyard. The autumnal evening was neither cold nor warm. Sophie's image popped into his mind. Deep down, he believed she hadn't meant the words she'd said to him a few hours earlier, that they were only words of pain. For a moment, he thought about the captives Sophie had ordered killed. He knew Syrella would have done the same if he hadn't stopped her, yet it had surprised him that Sophie had defied Peter.

The memory of a bloodied man begging for mercy arose. It was one of Walter's soldiers who had attacked him at Forked River. Elliot had felt his rage boiling over when he'd seen Thorn's men throw the corpses of the people they'd tortured into the river in an attempt to contaminate Wirskworth's water. He and his companions had killed them all, except one man. He was only an unarmed captive, and yet Elliot had mercifully finished him off without a second thought.

We've all made mistakes. This war is so brutal that it's impossible to keep your anger contained at all times. Elliot didn't believe Sophie felt no guilt over the murder of the prisoners. If that were true, she wouldn't have been thinking about the incident again. The reason she kept bringing it to mind was the guilt and desperation she didn't want to admit she felt. People always tried to understand their fate when bad things happened to them and inevitably became crueller, allowing their anger to overwhelm them.

Sophie may have truly changed. Eleanor's death may have changed her for good, a voice inside him whispered. He remembered Althalos saying there was an invisible threshold—a point of no return when pain could make a person change. That was necessary for one to bear the pain and survive. He hoped Sophie hadn't reached that point. If she had become like Walter, their battle would have been in vain.

"If you decide to fight for revenge and hatred, there will come a day when you'll be worse than those you're trying to overturn."

He remembered Aleron's words in the Mountains of the Forgotten World. He remembered the rage and hatred he'd felt all his life, trying to become the best warrior ever. Nonetheless, his prowess in fighting had never brought him any joy.

He looked up at the dark sky, lost in thought, and the happiest moment of his life came to him. The Sword of Light was about to be thrust into his chest, and Thindor had torn the skies apart as he flew towards him. Elliot had become the master of the sword and broken a curse that no one else had been able to break before him. Those images gave him strength when he tried to forget his hardship. He remembered the emotions he'd felt when Thindor had rushed to find him. Rage, hatred, revenge... Nothing mattered except for the pain—pain caused by the fate of the Elder Races. He wanted to free them and atone for the sins of his ancestors whose blood flowed in his veins. He hadn't feared death at all. The idea had seemed like redemption, a catharsis that would bring him peace. It was one of the most selfless moments of his life.

I'll protect you from hatred, Sophie, he thought. Now, he knew that strength and peace weren't found in hatred, nor in thirst for revenge.

Hurwig let out a nasal purr, and another face popped into Elliot's head. Sophie wasn't the only one who seemed to have changed lately. Selwyn had been more determined than ever during their last meeting, and that familiar fear Elliot remembered seeing in his eyes had now vanished.

Suddenly, a sharp ache tore through Elliot's insides. He tried not to think of Selwyn when he was alone, as it reminded him of Velhisya, making it impossible to control his emotions. None of them knew whether Velhisya had travelled to the realms of the dead. Elliot had wanted to scream that they should head for Vylor at first light the moment he'd heard that she had fallen into Liher's hands. But Aleron was right. They couldn't risk the lives of countless people for their loved ones. They had to be careful. The key to Goldtown's secret passage that Selwyn held gave him hope that they might yet be able to save her.

A tear ran down his cheek. He was afraid Liher would rape Velhisya, and the thought made him want to vomit. He wished he could turn back the clock and kiss her at the Dance of Blood. She flooded his thoughts more than any other woman did. There was so much that connected them. Both had grown up as orphans, were courageous, and willing to die to protect their dear ones.

His tears welled up even more. The fact that Velhisya had rushed to Selwyn's rescue moved him more than ever before. He wanted to get a horse, sneak out of the city, and ride to Vylor. Liher Hale deserved to get beheaded for everything he'd done. The thought drove him to a familiar hatred; no matter how hard he tried, he couldn't contain it.

He knew he wouldn't be able to sleep that night, either. Something gently pinched his palm, and he saw Hurwig looking at him with a sad expression. It was as if he could feel everything that was tormenting Elliot.

"It's time you went," he whispered.

The hawk stroked Elliot's arm with his wing and launched into the air. Elliot watched the white raptor in the sky until it disappeared. Now, he could only discern the stars, but they brought him even more pain. The stars reminded him of Velhisya's eyes.

Rage sparked in his very core. As much as he wanted to leave the path of revenge and hatred behind him, he knew that if Liher Hale were ever at his mercy, he would depart for the realms of the dead without his eyes, tongue, and limbs.

The Forgotten Memory

John ogled the buxom woman's naked body with satisfaction. Her breasts were large and round, her lips rosy red, and her eyes were as blue as the sea. He loved those traits, which he didn't often find in prostitutes.

"Where are you from, my lord?" she asked.

John scoffed. "I'm not a lord." He was tired of being taken for a nobleman.

The woman looked surprised. "You come here often, and I assumed you were. You've got a lot of gold."

"You don't have to be a lord to be rich."

The prostitute smiled. "Did you make your fortune in Knightdorn?"

John grasped his goblet from the wooden bedside table and drank some wine. "Yes," he told her.

She kept watching him, her dark hair falling over her eyes with a casual elegance he hadn't seen in years.

"But you haven't told me where you're from," she said.

"From the Galleon Villages," John responded.

"I've never heard of such a place before."

"There are three villages near Mermainthor, the capital of Mynlands. However, I haven't been back there for many years."

"Why not?"

"There was nothing there for me."

The woman turned her naked body towards him on the bed. "Are your parents still there?"

John frowned. "I haven't seen my real parents since I was a baby. I was given to another couple, who raised me in a small castle near Mermainthor."

"If you grew up in a castle, that means you're a lord!"

"The people who raised me were lords—not me," John said, eyeing the woman's bare breasts.

He took a few more sips of wine and felt his body grow cold. With his left hand, he pulled the sheet over his naked body while his gaze wandered to the window. An enormous moon lit up the sky.

"Remind me your name," he said.

"Elenna."

"I'm glad I'll be spending this night with you, Elenna."

The woman inched closer to him and bit his ear while her hand fondled him between the legs. He felt the heat awaken within him, and he set his wine down. He threw off the sheet and moved her onto her back. John cupped her breasts and thrust into her. The girl moaned, her blue eyes fixed on him. Their coupling continued for some time, their groans growing ever louder until John pulled out of her and came on her belly.

A smile appeared on Elenna's lips as she lay in bed. "I haven't met many men your age with such an appetite," she said breathlessly.

John smiled back and lay down next to her. *You abandoned Elliot to his fate to spend your life with whores and wine. Your father would have been proud.* John closed his eyes wearily. He hated the voice of his conscience and had to push it away once again.

"Are you alright?" the woman asked. "You look like something's bothering you."

"Yes!" John snapped, frowning. "If someone needed your help to change the world, would you give it to them if you knew it might mean the end of you?"

Elenna's face took on a strange expression as if that was the strangest and most surprising question she'd ever heard. "I don't know. I've never thought about something like that because I wouldn't be able to help anyone change the world."

"How did you end up keeping company with men for gold?"

"It's better than carrying water home or ploughing fields."

John was lost in thought for a few moments. "If you could do anything, what would you like to do?"

"I would travel to Mirth."

John didn't expect such an answer. "Why?"

"I've heard there's a forest there—the Forest of Magic. My mother would tell me that centaurs lived there before they left Mirth for Knightdorn. It's said to be the most beautiful forest in the world. I'd like to live there with a man and have a family, far from this cold and inhospitable island."

"At least there's no war on the Ice Islands. If you lived in Knightdorn, you'd only encounter murder and death."

"You're right about that," the woman said, her face unreadable. "Who needs your help?" she asked after a while.

"Forget what I said!" John snapped. He had to get Elliot out of his mind.

"How would you like us to spend the rest of the night?" Elenna asked.

John lifted his goblet again and drank its contents in one gulp. "We'll drink wine and make love until we fall asleep," he replied.

Elenna took his left hand and placed it between her breasts. "This is the first time I've ever slept with a man who could change the world," she whispered with a smile.

John felt angry. *I shouldn't have told her that.* Thoughts began to poison his mind again, but the softness of the woman's breasts made him relax. He was going to spend the night in the brothel, and the following morning, all thought of Elliot would have vanished, or so he hoped.

"You're beautiful. I'm surprised you haven't managed to seduce a man. If I were younger, I'd take you to the Forest of Magic myself to spend the rest of our lives together."

She smiled. "You're a liar."

John frowned. "Why do you say that, my dear?"

Elenna had taken on a playful tone. "Men like you are never happy with one woman. You wouldn't be able to stand spending the rest of your life with just me."

"That depends on how often you'd let me touch these breasts," John said and stroked her nipple.

Elenna drew him close and kissed him on the mouth. "Has there never been anyone you wanted to spend the rest of your life with?" she asked as their lips parted.

"Not yet," John muttered.

Elenna seemed surprised. "I can't believe no woman has stolen your heart all these years."

A memory flashed before John's eyes. A memory he had buried in the deepest corner of his mind. John's body shuddered. He hadn't felt such panic in years. "I'd like to spend the rest of the evening alone," he said bluntly, pulling his hand away.

Elenna looked bewildered. "Why? Did I do something to offend you, my lord?"

"I just want to be left alone. Here." He grabbed a gold coin from the bedside table and handed it to her.

Elenna looked him over one more time before taking the coin and leaving the bed. She picked up her clothes off the floor and dressed quickly. Soon after, she left the chamber without so much as a backward glance.

John's body trembled. He'd shut out this memory for years. The image of Nemesis' lifeless eyes staring at him made his heart pound. He'd decided to forget her. Her memory brought him pain he couldn't handle.

You wasted your life on wine and whores, he heard Nemesis' voice say in his mind. John felt helpless. He grabbed a jug of wine off the floor and drank its contents as fast as he could. He lowered the jug a few inches and took a deep breath. The wine had to numb his mind—he had to bury that memory in a place where he'd never be able to find it again.

You never avenged me. You forgot me. You forgot the fate Walter sent me. John brought the jug to his lips again, to pass out and wipe out his memories. He couldn't stand this torment.

Help Elliot beat Walter. You owe it to me but also to yourself, Nemesis' voice whispered again.

Tears flowed from his eyes. He knew he was a coward. Much as he wanted to help Elliot, he would never risk his life. He feared death, preferring to spend a meaningless life full of gold, whores, and wine than cross its threshold.

Time passed and he felt his heartbeat calming, while his mind was already numb from the wine. He lay his head down on the mattress, ready to be engulfed in the maelstrom of dreams, when he heard what sounded like voices.

What's happening? John listened hard, but the sound had vanished. *The wine has clouded my brain.* He caught sight of the moon dominating the sky through the small window. He'd heard stories that said the full moon brought the tides to Tahos and the continent of Kerth, but he had no idea if that was true.

He fumbled for the jug on the floor, and when he found it, he took a few more sips of wine. A soft belch escaped his lips. If he drank any more, he would throw up. He set the jug on the floor and turned onto his back on the bed. His thoughts had settled, and his eyes began to close.

Golden-blue seas floated around him under a clear sky teeming with multicoloured birds. He was on a ship, and a woman with black eyes and chestnut brown hair stood at its helm. He had to get out of the dream. He tried to fly away and then he saw some figures standing on a cliff before jumping into the void. *No. No!*

A sound jolted John from his sleep, and he jumped up, the images in his dream still in his mind. The door had been flung open noisily.

"So here you are, Long Arm." Three men entered his room. One smiled as he looked at John's naked body.

"Who are you? What do you want from me?" John asked.

"Begon commanded that we find you and take you to him."

The Missing Fishermen

J ohn followed the men uneasily to the tower of the Leader of the Islands, having no other choice after they had forced him to dress. The three men had surrounded him, and there wasn't a soul in the alleys of the Grand Island. John knew he had no hope of escaping. All three of his escorts were tall and stocky, and large swords hung from their belts. He was drunk from the wine, yet the memories of his dreams still haunted him. The full moon lit up the sky as the cold wind made him shiver under his woollen clothes.

What could Begon want of me? John racked his brain for an answer as he tried to walk straight, and there was only one thing it could be.

They walked for a while until the imposing tower appeared before them. He'd never thought that the day would come when Begon the Brave would ask to speak to him in the middle of the night.

Begon the Brave, John thought and smiled momentarily.

He had no idea why the man had that nickname. He couldn't recall hearing about any of his brave deeds over the years. Nevertheless, the leaders of the Ice Islands always had nicknames, and some whispered that Begon had made many brave decisions throughout his life. John wasn't aware of what those might be, but he had never tried to find out.

Suddenly, John lost his balance and was about to fall to the ground when the man behind him grabbed him by the shoulder.

"Careful, you fool! Keep moving!" the man snapped, propping John up on his feet. "I wonder why Begon wants to talk to this drunk," he added to his two companions.

They didn't seem to have a clue.

The dark cloaks of his escorts fluttered in the strong wind, and John wished he was still in the brothel. He dreaded the meeting that was to come. *Begon has found out about everything I hid from him.* That's the only reason these men are dragging me through the street in the middle of the night.

The tower grew larger, and banners with an iceberg in the middle of a stormy sea—the emblem of the Ice Islands—could be seen hanging from it.

They reached the entrance to the tower, and two guards stepped aside as soon as they saw them. John walked into the building with the three men, examining its interior. The tower was nothing like the manor houses of the large cities of Knightdorn. The decor was bare and the corridors were cold and dim. Moonlight crept through some windows to his right, while large torches lit up the space.

They passed dozens of doors, and John wondered when they would reach the hall where Begon awaited. The men led him through the building, and John couldn't keep track of all the turns. After a while, the group came to a double-leafed wooden door, and one of the guards pushed it forcefully, revealing a large room. John made out dozens of rugs on the floor while a fire burned in a huge fireplace at one end of the chamber.

"At last," came a voice, and John spotted a man sitting in a chair at the back of the room.

"We brought him here as quickly as we could, my lord," one of the men said.

Begon stood and walked over to John. He wore a purple robe, and his white hair was dishevelled, his age resting heavily on his face. The Leader of the Ice Islands stopped in front of him and looked at him with his amber-coloured eyes.

"Are you sure you lost that letter you were carrying for me?" Begon asked.

John swallowed hard, his mouth dry and the wine souring on his tongue. "Of course," he said.

"I know everything, Long Arm!" the old man shouted, his voice echoing in the chamber. "You told me Sophie wanted my help with the last battle in Iovbridge! However, you omitted to tell me a lot more that you knew about."

"My lord—"

"Silence!"

John lowered his eyes.

"Walter has taken the throne of Knightdorn, and the Queen has retreated to Elmor... I assume Sophie wanted me to travel there to help her."

"Yes." John knew there was no point in lying anymore. "I didn't think the location of the battle made any difference to you."

The old man's eyes flashed, and his nose wrinkled at the smell of wine rolling off John. "But what might have perhaps made a difference was that Thomas Egercoll's son is fighting at the Queen's side!" John couldn't look Begon in the eye. "How could you have hidden such a thing from me?"

John wondered how the man would react if he found out that it was actually Elliot who had sent him to the Ice Islands.

"Look at me!" John looked up timidly. "Why did you hide the truth?"

"Because I wanted to live in a place that was far away from the wars of Knightdorn. I didn't want to—"

"You hid the existence of a descendant of Thomas Egercoll out of cowardice!" Begon yelled. "You wanted to live a life of whoring and drunkenness in my land, and you decided to lie to me! Where is Sophie's letter?"

"I never had a letter from Sophie," John reiterated.

"Stop lying to—"

"Sophie ordered me to take Elliot Egercoll to Elmor to forge a new alliance with Syrella Endor. Walter found out that the Scarred Queen might go to war again and decided to attack her in Wirskworth before she could join forces with Sophie. Elliot wanted to lure Walter to Elmor, and he did so. Syrella succeeded in driving the enemy into a retreat. Elliot then asked messengers to take the news to the areas not yet under Walter's rule, looking for alliances. He knew Thorn wouldn't wait long before attacking Elmor again, and he needed more soldiers. So, he sent me here. Sophie hadn't yet arrived in Wirskworth when I left for the Ice Islands, so Syrella wrote a letter on her behalf."

"So, it was Elliot who sent you to my land! You got to know him; you led him to Elmor, and when you left for my islands, you betrayed him."

John felt that Begon would kill him soon. "Yes," he said. No lie could save him now.

"Have you got Syrella's letter?"

"I burned it. It contained all you now know."

Begon frowned. "It would appear that Syrella, Sophie, and Elliot won the second battle without my help, too."

John almost choked. "What?"

The aged man looked at him disapprovingly. "I heard Walter's men were defeated twice in Elmor."

"So, is Walter dead?" John asked with bated breath.

Begon shook his head. "No. Rumour has it he wasn't in the second battle. Only some of his men fought."

John didn't understand. "Are you sure of your sources, my lord? Why would Walter—"

"I don't know! However, the merchants who brought me the news rarely make mistakes. There are many strange rumours."

"What rumours?"

Begon turned his back and paced around the chamber. "I heard that Elliot fought alongside elwyn and elves in Elmor and that amongst the enemy soldiers was a giant that was killed along with his wyvern."

"Elliot freed the Elder Races!" John exclaimed, speaking more to himself than to anyone else. He never thought the boy would succeed in doing such a thing.

"I've never paid much attention to the legends surrounding the Elder Races, but I know they never fought on the side of a human before," Begon said. "The elwyn and elves threw themselves into the fray on Elliot's side, and the giants took Thorn's side."

John felt a tingling in his chest. He never wanted to find himself up against a giant on the back of a wyvern. Nonetheless, the legends said that elves and elwyn knew better than anyone how to deal with giants. "I still don't understand. Why didn't Walter fight?" John asked.

Begon's face was inscrutable. "I told you before, I don't know. I've heard he attacked Aquarine with thousands of men, but this information seems odd even to me."

John's heart pounded, and his hands grew sweaty. "In Aquarine?"

Begon nodded, and John remembered Eleanor's mission. Is *she dead?* He felt a strange pain in his stomach. He was sure that if he hadn't had so much to drink, he would have crumpled at the news.

"There's another thing the merchants confided in me," Begon said, and John remained silent. "When Walter attacked Aquarine, he did so astride a wyvern. Not long after, several of them could be seen above the city skies."

John's senses were numbed by the news, but this revelation hit him like a bolt of lightning. *If the Elder Races and the wyverns are now fighting in this war, I did well to run away. I no longer have anything in the least to offer Elliot.* Suddenly, the image of a mermaid that had appeared before him on the shore a few days ago came to mind. *The mermaids may fight as well against whoever imprisoned their sisters!* Nevertheless, something didn't seem right. "How did Walter ride a wyvern? Those monsters only obey giants."

Begon threw his hands up with an exasperated sigh.

"If anything, you found out a lot more information than I was supposed to bring you," John said. The aged man shot him a steely glare. "Will you fight by Elliot's side?"

Now, Begon looked furious. "Are you afraid of losing your comforts, Long Arm? I'd wager that the gold you're wasting on my land was a gift from Syrella Endor for your journey. I still cannot fathom the magnitude of your betrayal."

John took a step forward. "When Elliot asked me to take him to Elmor, I told him I wouldn't fight for him. I told him I'd help him until he got to Syrella's doorstep, and then I'd be free to leave. He never denied my request!"

"And when you left Wirskworth with gold and a letter for me, had you confided your intentions about what would happen once you got here?" Begon asked. John choked back the words he was going to say. "You betrayed those who believed in you!"

"Those of us who helped Elliot get to Elmor almost died! One of us is dead, and two more may be dead." John didn't know whether either Selwyn or Eleanor were alive, although the news about the latter wasn't promising. "I decided to live!"

"And now it's time for you to be punished for your decisions. We don't tolerate lies on the Ice Islands. If you'd wanted to, you could have told me the truth and made it clear to me that you wouldn't fight, no matter what decision I made."

John knew that under different circumstances, he would have panicked by now, but the night's events had drained him of all emotion. "Will you fight for Elliot and Sophie?" he heard himself asking again.

Begon frowned. "I know I should never have capitulated to a man like Walter, but I put the good of my people above honour and courage. If I break the treaty, it could mean the end of this land. The Ice Islands don't have many men. What have I to offer Elliot Egercoll against thousands of men, giants, and wyverns?" John didn't answer. "A wise leader must think of his people above all."

"I agree," John said, and the old man glared at him. "I'm not saying this because I want to stay here... The Ice Islands could only help in a naval battle, and Walter isn't intent on having a battle at sea." Begon didn't answer but looked thoughtful. "All you could offer Elliot would be to take Tahryn now that most of its men are on Walter's side."

A gasp escaped Begon's lips. "And what wouldn't I give to kill this blackguard, Eric Stone? Since Walter lost the second battle at Elmor, there may not be many men left in Tahos. But if I attack this land, it will be as if I was declaring war on Walter, and I don't want to see a wyvern sowing death in the Ice Islands."

John's mind drifted to the winged monsters for a few moments. If the giants had taken Walter's side, it made sense that some wyverns would have fought for him. Nonetheless, he couldn't fathom how Thorn himself had tamed a wyvern. He'd never heard about a human having succeeded in doing so before.

Perhaps this information is just nonsense.

"So be it," Begon said. "What I do with my men is my business. Now, you're on my land, and you must pay for the lies you uttered."

"If you want to kill me, do it." John was surprised by his response. It was as if the fear of death had vanished. There were so many things that tormented his mind that an eternal sleep seemed like a blessing.

"I won't kill you... You'll do something for me. But if you try to get away, you'll die," Begon told him.

"What can you possibly want with me?" John asked, surprised.

A smile formed on Begon's lips. "In recent years, the fish have vanished from the Cold Sea. So, my men sail their ships to the Sea of Shadows near Mermainthor. There's a small island north of Knightdorn, and my fishermen had been getting the best catch there for years until something strange began to happen."

John recalled Jack's words at the inn some days ago about the sailors going missing.

"My captains, who are the best in the world, haven't been coming back the last three months. I thought that Mermainthor's men may have been attacking my fishermen, but I have no proof..." Begon looked angry and troubled at the same time. "If I send a fleet north of Mermainthor, they'll think I want to attack them. I don't want them to assume such a thing, and I'm not yet ready for battle. I won't attack a territory under Walter unless I'm sure he's violated our treaty and killed my men."

"Why would Walter attack your men for just a few fish?" John asked, brow furrowing.

"That's what I thought, too," Begon said, frowning. "Those seas have enough fish for everyone. No one would have any reason to attack my fishermen."

"What do you want of me?"

"I heard from Captain Raff that you're Jack's friend. Jack hasn't been fishing in the area, but in a few days, as soon as the storms calm down, he will sail to that small island in an attempt to find out what's going on. Since you were a pirate, you'll be able to help him."

Fuck! John would have wished for any other punishment but that. He'd decided that he no longer liked spending his time on ships and at sea. "What makes you think Jack will come back?" he asked.

"He's our best captain. If he fails too, I'll send a fleet there! I want to know what has happened to my men." Begon's voice was steady, indicating he wouldn't rest until he found out what had happened to the missing ships.

"If Mermainthor's men have been attacking your fishermen, you'll be sentencing Jack and me to death," protested John.

"It won't be easy for them to sink a ship with Jack at the helm." John snorted, and Begon gave him a sharp look. "If you try to escape, I'll order my men to tie you up and take you to Syrella Endor to stand before her. They'll deliver a letter from me into her hands, describing how you spent her gold and betrayed her trust. I don't know whether Elliot will forgive you, but the Scarred Queen will place you in the front line of the next battle if she hears this news."

I can't believe this... John stared at the chamber ceiling in dismay. He'd never understood how he'd got embroiled in so much trouble and had managed to stay alive.

A Tournament of Death

Walter watched the duel disinterestedly. One of the two duellists raised his sword to parry a blow aimed at his head. Soon after, he countered with a jeer. His opponent pulled to the side, and the sword cut through the air. *Fools.* It was the most boring tournament he'd ever watched. The sunlight shone onto the crowded courtyard as the two duellists carried on attacking each other clumsily.

"I'm tired of watching these idiots!" he snapped at Leonhard, who sat next to him.

The old man frowned. "I thought there was perhaps a capable soldier in Iovbridge... Someone who, with a little training, could join the Ghost Army. A tournament is the best way to find such men."

"Good thing you didn't make them fight on horses... They're so useless, they'd accidentally hurt them, and we'd have laid them to waste," Walter said.

"It was worth a try," Leonhard said, glancing at the courtyard where the two men fought. He and Walter sat on a raised platform.

Walter was about to rise from his seat, but Leonhard took him by the arm. "What are you doing?" Walter asked angrily and yanked his arm back. He didn't like being touched.

"The courtyard is full of people. They've come to see you," Leonhard whispered.

"They've seen enough of me, I have more important things to—"

"You're the new king," the man hissed. "A king who has been portrayed as a tyrant for decades. You need feasts and tournaments to distract the crowd from all the hardship, and they need to see you. To be in awe of you. You must make the people of Iovbridge believe that you're the king they've always wanted, that under your rule they will become rich, and that their land will gain honour and glory. Feasts always fill the minds of ordinary people with hope, while your presence creates the illusion that you care about this city and its people."

"I don't care about the people of Iovbridge... They'll be subservient to me forever, and anyone who dares to rebel will have his head adorn the city square," Walter said nonchalantly.

Leonhard pursed his lips. "I told you before. Fear alone isn't enough to rule. Sometimes, worship and awe are stronger than fear. It's better to have the immature lads of this city fight for you because they worship you than out of fear. They'll betray you the first chance they get if they aren't loyal to you."

"And what can the lads in Iovbridge offer me?" Once again, Walter's eyes fell upon the two duellists who were now fighting even more clumsily than before.

"We need every man who can hold a sword... Delamere's men are no better than these." Leonhard watched the fighters. "These lads didn't want to leave the city and so they stayed here. I'm sure that while Delamere sat on the throne, men like these belonged to the Royal Army."

Walter snorted contemptuously. "I can't believe that it took me so many years to defeat the usurper and her army."

"We can train some of these lads. As you said, we need more men to be sure that we'll defeat our enemies once and for all this time," said Leonhard.

"Tell the Trinity of Death to find a Ghost to train them. I cannot bear to watch such a spectacle any longer."

"MERCY! HAVE MERCY!"

Walter turned to face the duellists. One had dropped his opponent to the ground, raised his sword, and was on the verge of finishing him off.

"MERCY!" the fallen man cried out once more.

The winner of the duel lowered his sword and took a few steps towards Walter. As soon as he got near him, he bowed deeply.

"Why did you grant him his life?" Walter asked.

"He begged for mercy, and I decided to show him some, Your Majesty. I've proven that I can beat him."

Walter rose from his seat. "To have pity is a great virtue... However, in a true battle, no one has any pity. All your enemies want is your head." The young man didn't say a word and bowed down again. "I've been watching the duels, and the losers constantly ask for mercy, but in a battle, there is no mercy." Walter turned to face the crowd that had gathered around the courtyard. "From this moment on, the winner will take the life of the loser. There will be no more mercy in this tournament. Only then will I understand who has the strength of a true warrior."

Walter saw the young lad turn around suddenly and advance towards the fallen man.

"NO! NO! MERCY!"

The sword separated the man's head from his body, and the young winner bowed down before Walter from afar.

"Let the next pair of duellists come through," a man standing near the courtyard shouted, and the crowd erupted into loud cheering.

Walter returned to his seat and turned to Leonhard with a smile. "Maybe now we'll finally see which of these wretches deserve to be trained by my Ghosts."

The old man's face displayed puzzlement. "Do you think those who dare to take a life make better soldiers?" he asked.

Walter shook his head. "These boys enter the arena knowing that even if they lose, their lives will be spared. The only way to see a man's true face is when he fears for his life. Only then is it revealed who has the courage of a soldier and who doesn't."

"You're the most skilled warrior in the world. However, you don't fear for your life. You're immort—"

"Every battle I've fought to date, I fight as if it's my last, Leonhard,"

Walter told him. "I keep thinking that if I'm defeated, my enemies will find a way to take my life, that the name of my House will die, and the usurpers and the weak will rule my grandfather's kingdom, the kingdom of the Thorns. I'll never allow such a thing. The idea of what will happen if one day I fail makes me the most powerful warrior in the world."

Leonhard remained silent.

"Moreover, knowing that no one will die renders these combats dull and wearisome for the crowds. Listen to their jeering... Now this tournament has true value."

"I have more wisdom than you when it comes to what it takes to rule. However, you know about war better than anyone else," Leonhard said and settled back into his seat.

Walter saw the two new duellists charge at each other in a frenzy. It was obvious that things had changed. He knew full well what the feeling of fear could do in battle. That fear unleashed the wildest and darkest instincts, and the weak-minded quickly lost their lives. Walter had never feared that someone was more capable than he, yet the idea that if he lost to his enemies one day, the name of his House would be treated with disrespect by the weak aroused fear and rage in him.

I'll never allow such a thing to happen.

One of the two duellists lost his sword, and his enemy was about to finish him off when the lad threw dirt into his eyes. Just then, he punched his opponent in the face. The man's scream drowned out the jeering of the crowd as the lad picked up his sword again and plunged it into his opponent's throat.

Walter smiled. *Finally, some real action.*

"I'd like to speak to you, Your Majesty."

Walter turned to his left and saw Ricard Karford standing next to him. He seemed enraged, yet fear kept him from unleashing this fury.

"I saw Rolf holding the Sword of Destiny," Ricard said curtly.

"Of course. Rolf deserves this gift after so many years of devotion," Walter responded.

"And me?"

"And you?"

"I fought for you all these years! I've never once refused any of your commands. I sacrificed almost all my men in the last battle in Elmor for you, and I've been one of your most loyal allies." His voice was loud, but no one could hear him over the jeering of the crowd.

Walter looked him in the eyes, curious to see how he would continue.

"I believe that the sword of my House should return to me for the dedication and loyalty I have shown all these years."

"Bold words, Ricard," Walter said, folding his arms across his chest. "However, you forget that you owe me your dedication. I was the one who gave you Oldlands—the one who got the Asselins out of the way and gave you the title of governor after decades. You tried to marry your cousin off to the traitor Thomas Egercoll in the hope of gaining his support and getting rulership over your region. You were a coward, and I showed you the true path to getting what you wanted. I showed you the way of the sword and of blood. I gave you what you craved, and your brother was bestowed with the honour of joining the Trinity. I gave everything to your House. You owed me dedication, and your brother betrayed me. If I were you, I'd be happy I still had my head."

Ricard's expression had changed, and his lower lip quivered. He'd been overcome with fear. "Thank you for all you've done for me, Your Majesty," he said and bowed deeply.

"I heard you wanted to talk to me," came a new voice, and Walter saw Eric Stone, the Governor of Tahryn, standing behind Ricard.

Walter gestured sharply to Ricard, who left with a bow. "Sit," Walter said, and Eric sat in the empty chair to his left.

A scream rang across the courtyard, and Walter glanced at the fighters. One had a dagger stuck in his opponent's eye while the crowd's screams erupted louder than ever. "What did you think of the winner?" he asked Leonhard.

"He's quite able!" snapped the healer.

"Send him for training with the Ghosts," Walter said and turned back to Eric Stone. "I want you to go back to Tahryn with some soldiers."

The Governor seemed taken aback at his words. "Why?" he asked.

"I suspect Thomas' son sent an emissary to every region that isn't under my command in Knightdorn. If old man Begon decides to fight, he may attack your land. There aren't any soldiers left in Tahos."

A furrow appeared on Eric's forehead. He was just over forty years old, yet he looked much younger. His thick, short, black hair covered almost all his forehead, and his black eyes seemed ruthless. "Do you think Begon will jump into the fray for Elliot? He's never fought all these years... Will he do so now? He is so old that the mere idea of battle might upset him."

Walter frowned. "Begon has always wanted to fight for Thomas and Sophie, but he chose not to out of fear for his people. However, the revelation that Thomas' son is alive, along with the fact that there's the last battle for the kingdom soon to be fought, may cause him to break our treaty. I'm not certain whether he'll take part in the war, but in the unlikely event that he does, I don't want the ships of Tahos falling into his hands."

"He doesn't have many men!" Eric said.

"The men of the Ice Islands are among the best in the kingdom at sailing. If they take Tahos, even with only a few men, they could seize nearly all your ships and attack Iovbridge while I'm battling in Wirskworth"

"And if they do, you'll crush them with your wyverns," Eric said amidst the clash of swords.

"I don't know how many wyverns will be left after the battle with the elwyn and elves. I don't want a battle on two fronts. Take five thousand mounted men and return to Tahos. That will be enough with which to face Begon if he attacks with his small number of ships."

"Don't you want me at the battle in Wirskworth?"

Walter could tell that Eric wanted to be there when he was about to kill the last of his enemies. He could sense his devotion. "I won't set off for Elmor yet. My men need rest. As soon as I'm ready to march, I'll mount my wyvern and come to Tahos to inform you. If Begon hasn't attacked by then, I don't think he'll do so at the last moment. You'll be able to catch up with us before the battle."

Eric nodded. Walter was satisfied with his decision to give him Tahryn after the murder of Aghyr Barlow. That region was deeply devoted to the Barlows and therefore needed a ruler that would root out the loyalties to that House. He'd heard that Eric punished anyone who resisted his rule harshly and that he'd managed to increase the number of soldiers in Tahryn.

"I've always wondered why you didn't kill Begon when you got to his land," Eric suddenly said.

Walter scoffed. "If I'd killed a leader of the Ice Islands, the men in that land would have continuously rebelled against whomever I'd have left there to govern. When I know that it's impossible to control a region, I prefer to either keep it out of the war or to kill every one of its people."

"You should have killed them all!" Eric said, gripping the arms of his chair.

"I don't disagree. Nevertheless, at that time, I'd just killed Thomas. Many in the kingdom were outraged by my actions, and I didn't have enough allies. I didn't need another genocide."

"So be it," Eric answered.

"Leave at first light tomorrow," Walter told him, and the man nodded, moving to rise. "One more thing. I heard that Aldus Morell cut a deal with the trash that governed Felador. He promised to protect her land in exchange for their harvests. As soon as you go north, send a few men to take his head. My men take what they want from my enemies by force, not with alliances."

Eric nodded brusquely as he rose from his seat and left the courtyard. Walter turned back to the fighting men. A tall, robust lad fought against the skinniest man Walter had ever seen. Nevertheless, the skinny fighter was so fast that his opponent's sword couldn't strike him.

"Not so long ago, I wondered why you'd chosen to sacrifice the men of Oldlands and Mynlands in Elmor and to keep those of Tahryn." Leonhard leaned towards him. "Now I know."

"I had no choice... I had to keep the region's army with the largest fleet in the kingdom intact. No one knows what Begon might do," Walter said, propping his elbow on the arm of his chair.

"You did the right thing," the old man agreed.

Walter scratched his chin and watched the duel. "I'm sure many of Ricard's men were more devoted to the Asselins than to him. After the death of Alice Asselin and her father, many in Oldlands hated me, and everyone knows they still do. But I've needed them all these years. They're excellent armourers, and they're second to none when it comes to sieges. Nevertheless, it was an easy choice to sacrifice the army of Oldlands a few days ago. Since I've tamed a wyvern, they are no longer necessary. However, from the northern regions, I'd rather have the men of Mynlands around me than those of Tahryn. I'm sure that in Tahryn, their loyalty still lies with the Barlows, and I was the one who destroyed that House. Eric may have the presence of a ruler, inspiring fear and preventing rebellions, but in Mynlands, there were always more who were loyal to my name."

"I've heard that in Mynlands, they were angry with Loren Elford for not taking your side when you rebelled against Thomas," Leonhard said.

"That's true... When I arrived with my army in the regional capital and beat Loren's champion in exchange for Mynlands, I was received with cheering. Most people wanted Launus Eymor to be the new ruler. That's why I would have preferred their army above that of Tahryn. In Mynlands, they've always supported the Thorns."

"You had no other choice. You had to sacrifice Mynlands' men... However, Launus Eymor will be furious when he finds out that he's lost his army."

Walter shrugged. "The only fury that matters is my own."

The crowd started jeering again, and Walter saw the thin man's head fall to the ground as the other man bowed. Walter clapped, and for a moment, the image of Elliot flashed through his mind. The winner of the duel looked a little like him. Walter felt enraged whenever he thought of Elliot, the boy who threatened to tear down everything he'd fought for over decades. Walter wouldn't allow such a thing. Thomas' son would follow his father to the grave sooner or later. Adur's words echoed in Walter's ears. The giant had told him that Thindor had been hiding in Ersemor for hundreds of years. He'd considered taking his wyverns and rushing to the forest of centaurs to kill the last living pegasus, but he knew this would be foolish. It wouldn't be easy to find him or kill him. Adur had told him that a pegasus could fly faster than a wyvern, and so it was Thindor who would have to choose to go to battle for Walter to murder him.

"I was thinking of something else, too," Leonhard said. "Kings must always have a queen by their side—a strong woman who exudes authority."

"Delamere sat on the throne for years without marrying!" Walter abhorred such silly traditions.

"Delamere was weak and foolish. You could perhaps marry Berta Loers. She comes from a noble house in Gaeldeath. This would make you a prestigious leader while further glorifying Gaeldeath throughout the kingdom."

"Gaeldeath doesn't need a wedding to be glorified. I'll make sure they all honour its name for the rest of their lives," Walter said with disdain in his voice.

Berta's face came to mind. Her broad cheekbones, full lips, and cold eyes had entranced him for years. However, this wasn't what made him want to get inside her every chance he got. What set Berta apart was her adoration of him and the fact that she was also the most skilled female warrior he'd ever met. She had made every effort to get his attention for years, to show him that her loyalty wasn't all she had to offer him, and she'd succeeded. Walter respected her for that. He knew that it was very difficult for a woman to shine amongst so many men. He didn't care whether he had women or men as his sworn allies, so long as they could bring death to his enemies.

"Even your grandfather wedded a noblewoman from Gaeldeath." Leonhard's voice drew him back to the present.

Walter huffed sullenly. "Berta told me the same foolish things one day. She even told me that she could give me an heir," he said, waving his hand dismissively. He liked Berta, but he had no desire to wed her—marriage wasn't one of his priorities.

"Princes and weddings are great ways to distract people from war and famine. All people care about is the gossip about the royal family, and they give no thought to whether they have food on their plate or not."

Walter turned to him, his jaw clenched. "I don't need an heir. It's my destiny to live forever. I also told Berta that I am endowed with the power of the gods. A god doesn't need an heir."

"Nonetheless, you could perhaps be wedded," Leonhard insisted.

"Perhaps. However, I won't waste my time on such foolishness until I defeat my enemies."

"You need every crop in the city for the soldiers! Famine will wreak havoc on Iovbridge by the time we're victorious, and the battles have depleted our supplies. You need some distractions until the war is over. Soon, there will be no more battles, and all the riches in the kingdom will be in our hands. Then, the people will praise you as a god. You'll make it known that you've brought the famine to an end and have killed the usurper; you'll spread the word that the people of Knightdorn will never go hungry again while you sit on the throne."

Walter was tired of listening to Leonhard's thoughts on ruling the kingdom. In his opinion, fear was sufficient.

"Do as you please, but stop talking. You brought me here to find potential soldiers," Walter said.

"Of course, Your Majesty," Leonhard replied, bowing his head.

Walter watched the duellists, but his mind drifted. He wasn't sure how he'd find the new soldiers he needed. With a few thousand more men, he would finally be able to destroy Wirskworth and end the war once and for all. The solution he'd thought of a few days ago was on his mind, but he wasn't at all sure that such a thing would be successful.

"Good evening, Your Majesty."

Walter saw Berta, dressed in brown leather, bowing before him. "Sit by my side," he said, and she sat in the chair on his right.

"What do you think of the duellists, Your Majesty?" she whispered.

"Amateurs," Walter responded. "However, after I said the loser would leave his last breath in the courtyard, the battles are a little more interesting." Berta laughed, her brown hair falling into her eyes.

"Your Majesty," came a shout from the courtyard, and Walter tore his gaze away from Berta. "It would be an honour to join the Ghost Army." A young lad who wasn't dressed in armour faced Walter while his opponent stood nearby, his sword raised for battle.

"What's your name?" Walter asked.

"Lan."

"You seem very sure about your abilities, Lan. You're the only one who has decided to fight without any armour."

"I'm sure, Your Majesty."

"Show me what you're worth, and I'll think about it," Walter said. The young man bowed and turned to face his opponent, smiling. *Arrogance and incompetence—a bad combination.*

Lan's opponent lifted his sword and brought it down with force, and Walter flinched. *Impressive,* he thought. Lan had dodged the blow and cut his enemy's head in half. The corpse fell to the ground, and blood poured from its mouth while the rest of its face lay a few feet away. The clamour of the cheering crowd shook the air.

Lan wiped his blade on his woollen cloak and bowed again.

"Where did you learn to fight?" Walter shouted, and the cheering died down momentarily.

"I'm self-taught, Your Majesty."

"Your request has been accepted. You'll be trained by my Ghosts, and you'll become one of them."

"Thank you, Your Majesty. I want you to know that there still are capable men in Iovbridge. We're devoted to you, and you can use us in battle. You don't need to rely on women to defeat your enemies."

Walter raised his hand, and the cheering in the courtyard came to a sudden halt. "What do you mean?"

The lad took a step closer. "I heard that the woman sitting next to you has become the new member of the Trinity of Death. A man with your power doesn't need women for such titles. You can find men who deserve such an honour and can offer you more when up against your enemies."

Walter stood. "I appreciate your devotion, Lan." The lad bowed down again. "However, you should know that no one has the right to insult the members of the Trinity of Death. This is the greatest insult to my person."

"Forgive me, Your Majesty." Lan's stance changed, his confidence wilting.

"Do you believe that you would beat Berta in single combat?"

Lan didn't say a word and seemed to have regretted the words he'd uttered. "I don't know," he said after a while.

"Since you decided to question my judgement about the new member of the Trinity, you'll have to fight Berta. If you win, I swear here and now, before all these people, that I'll give you her place immediately."

"Very well." Lan seemed to have regained his courage.

Walter turned to Berta and nodded. She stood without batting an eye. There was only pure fury in her gaze.

Berta faced Lan in the courtyard. The lad smiled and raised his sword, and she mirrored the movement. Walter didn't even see Berta's blade as it tore through the air. The crowd fell silent, and a croak of death escaped Lan's mouth. Berta's sword was stuck between his legs, and the red liquid soaked his pants.

Walter smiled at the spectacle. Berta withdrew her sword and caught Lan by the shoulder as he breathed his last. "Tell everyone in the realms of the dead that it was a woman who took your manhood, Lan. Tell them it was Berta Loers—the only woman ever to join the Trinity of Death."

The Emperor's Decision

Elliot wandered through the alleys of Wirskworth, taking in his surroundings. He enjoyed walking through the city to clear his mind. It was a cloudy morning, and birds flew low over the roofs of the city towers. Several days had passed since Sophie had sent a letter to the Emperor, and everyone anxiously awaited some news. The Emperor's response would determine many of their plans for the future, and with each passing day, the chances that Velhisya was alive grew ever slimmer.

"I want to lead the mission to save Velhisya," he had told the Queen and Syrella a few days ago when he'd found out they'd agreed to send an army to Vylor.

"Your place is by my side," Sophie had said. *"If the Emperor accepts this marriage, I want you to accompany me to Kerth."*

Elliot thought he'd misheard. *"But—"*

"I thought you'd sworn allegiance to me." Sophie's blue eyes had been alight with anger.

"Of course, Your Majesty. However, how do you know that Odin will wish to have the wedding take place in his land?"

Sophie had laughed. *"The Emperor thinks so highly of himself and also of his land. He won't agree to the wedding taking place in Elmor. If Odin agrees to have me marry his son, I'll have to travel to Kerth without an army. We have neither time nor ships to take the Royal Army to the Western Empire. I'll have to trust the Emperor and risk a trip to his land with very few soldiers. I want you to accompany me there."*

Elliot was dumbfounded.

"My soldiers will carry out the plan to free my niece," Syrella had added. *"Nevertheless, they aren't yet ready to travel after the last battle against Thorn's men. They'll need about two weeks."*

"If the Emperor doesn't agree to this marriage, we'll discuss our plans again. Until we get his answer, no one is to leave Wirskworth," Sophie had said.

Elliot played the scene over in his head. If they didn't hear back soon, they'd have to assume this wedding was never going to happen and decide on their move. He carried on walking through the alleys until he found himself in one he didn't remember seeing before. The alley was deserted, and small stone buildings stood out along his path.

"Where are you heading, lad?"

The unexpected voice made him jump. He turned and saw a young woman with blonde hair and green eyes peering at him from behind a half-open door. She wore a white dress patched in several places.

"What do you mean?" Elliot asked.

"The men who come by here are only looking for one thing, and you seem in a hurry."

Elliot took a closer look at her and then realised where he was. Long Arm had often spoken to him about the alley with the best brothels in Wirskworth. He thought about leaving quickly, but something kept him rooted in place.

"Come in with me," the woman said, holding out her hand.

A voice in his head yelled at him to leave. However, there had been so much tormenting Elliot lately that a small part of him wanted to follow her instruction. Perhaps he'd forget about his hardships for a while in the little house.

He took the woman's hand, and she gently pulled him inside the house. The place was dark, and a handful of candles lit the space. He saw a few more young women in the interior of the brothel, all of them looking at him ravenously.

The woman pulled him to the right, towards a wooden door. She

150

pushed it open and led him into a small room, where a red curtain covered the window. Elliot noticed a narrow bed in the centre of the chamber. His heart pounded nervously.

"What's your name?" the woman asked him.

"Elliot. You?"

"Amy."

The woman directed him towards the bed. "I'm lucky I found you first. All the women were looking at you as soon as we entered the brothel," she said.

"Why were they looking at me? I should think that hundreds of young men come to this place," Elliot blurted.

Amy laughed. "Actually, no. Ageing lords and one or two ugly merchants usually visit us. There are some young lads with enough gold to come here, but few are as handsome as you are."

Elliot felt uneasy. "I don't have any gold, just a few bronze coins," he said, meeting her green eyes. She was beautiful and young.

Amy continued smiling. "For such a handsome lad as yourself, gold isn't necessary—bronze coins are sufficient," she said and pushed him onto the bed.

Elliot fell back onto the hard mattress, and Amy climbed onto him while removing her dress. Soon after, she took his hands and placed them on her rounded breasts. Heat flushed through his body.

"How do you want to have me, Elliot?"

"I don't know," he remarked, fondling her breasts. Her skin was incredibly soft.

"Tell me what you like."

"I don't know. I've never slept with a woman before." His heart pounded faster.

Amy gripped his hands. "What do you mean?"

"Well... I haven't..."

"Do you like men?"

"No!"

"Are you a virgin?"

He nodded and felt a strange sense of shame under Amy's gaze. They were about the same age, yet she was far more experienced than him.

Suddenly, the woman started laughing. "It's my lucky day. Who would have thought that I would be teaching the secrets of love to such a handsome young lad like you?" Her green eyes looked at him full of lust, and she put his hands on her breasts again. Elliot looked at her face and then, two starry blue eyes flashed in his mind. Amy leaned in to kiss him, but he pulled away abruptly.

"Are you alright, Elliot?" she asked, a worried expression crossing her face.

"I'm sorry, Amy, but I have to go."

"But why, my lord? I promise you'll never forget this day," she said, sliding her hand into his pants, between his legs.

Elliot pulled away again. "No. I have to go." The image of Velhisya's eyes lingered in his mind. He had no idea if she was still alive, but he wanted her to be his first.

He jumped off the bed and opened the bedroom door without looking back. He rushed outside, ignoring the stares of the rest of the women. Clouds still adorned Wirskworth's morning sky. He was about to turn down the alley when he felt something sharp grip his shoulder before a familiar weight landed on him. He turned and saw a white hawk that filled him with relief.

Elliot paced up and down his chamber impatiently as he watched the sun setting in the sky through a small window. It had been some time since he had given the Emperor's letter to the Queen, but no one had requested his presence. He'd heard that Sophie had asked to speak to Syrella as soon as she'd received the letter, but he had no clue what they'd discussed. Elliot was eager to hear the news. Had Odin Mud accepted to wed Sophie to his son?

Time passed excruciatingly slowly until a knock came from the chamber door. Elliot pulled it open and saw a guard standing in the hallway.

"Queen Sophie requests your presence."

About time. "Where?" Elliot asked.

"In the Great Hall," the guard told him.

Elliot nodded and left the room. It was now dark, and the torches on the walls lit Moonstone's deserted corridors. When he arrived at the entrance to the Hall, he found the doors open. A dozen people stood in its centre. He saw Thorold and Aleron next to Sophie and Syrella, their faces devoid of expression. Sophie's lilac dress made her look like a fairy, while her tousled hair hid her shoulders. A little farther off, the Governor's daughters stood with folded arms while Alaric and Alysia were scowling. Peter stood tall behind Selwyn as Jahon stared into space a few feet away from them. It was obvious that Elliot was the last to arrive at this council.

"Well? What news from the Emperor?" he asked as he approached them.

Sophie's face had hardened. "Odin Mud has agreed to have me marry his son." Her stiff voice revealed no joy.

"Are you sure you want to do this?" Elliot asked.

"It doesn't matter what I want... I must do what is necessary." A spark of anger flared up in Sophie's eyes as she spoke. "Once we've united our Houses, the Emperor will grant us his army to reclaim the throne from Walter Thorn. However, he didn't agree to the wedding taking place in Elmor. He wants me to go to his land for the ceremony, as he believes that his empire is the most prestigious place in the world. Once I marry his son, he'll set sail with his men for Knightdorn so we can retake Iovbridge."

Elliot pondered her words. Everything had gone according to plan, and they'd anticipated Odin's insistence on the wedding being held in his land.

"After this news, I conferred with the Queen, and we've decided what our next move will be," Syrella said, and everyone turned to her. "Sophie will travel to Kerth with three hundred men of the Royal Army, and Elliot and Peter will be amongst her escort." The Scarred Queen's gaze shifted from him to Peter.

"As you know, we have neither the ships nor the time to transport the Royal Army to Kerth. You'll accompany the Queen along with a select few men and will vigilantly protect her. The voyage will be undertaken on a merchant ship that I own. The captain knows these seas, having traded with Odin's land for decades. As soon as the wedding is over, you'll return to Elmor with the Emperor's army," Syrella went on without taking her eyes off them.

"This could be a trap. Odin will be able to do Sophie harm if he so chooses in his land," Thorold said.

"The Emperor has no reason to want my undoing!" Sophie snapped.

"He may get you out of the way on Walter's behest," the aged Master continued.

The Queen smiled. "Odin wants to spread his rule to Knightdorn and expand his empire across the world. Walter would never give him sovereignty over his kingdom... The Emperor needs me to get what he wants. He would gain nothing from my death right now."

"Nevertheless, we must be careful," Peter told her.

"I agree," Elliot said. "I wanted to head the mission to free Velhisya, but if Her Majesty wants me at her side, I'll travel to Kerth." Elliot felt invisible thorns pricking his body. He wanted to be both at Sophie's side as well as part of the mission to free Velhisya. The fact that he had to choose between the two caused him painful sadness.

"The Royal Army, along with Elmor's soldiers, will go to free my niece, and my daughters will head the mission. Moreover, Aleron and Alaric will accompany our soldiers along with their most skilled warriors. Most of the elwyn and elves will follow them, too, since they don't want to get separated," Syrella announced.

Elliot wasn't expecting those words. "I thought only Elmor's army would march into Goldtown."

Jahon seemed taken aback as well, though Alaric and Aleron did not look surprised by the information.

"Syrella and I have gone over this again and again," Sophie replied. "If it were certain that we would have to besiege Goldtown, I would insist that the Royal Army remain in Wirskworth. We shouldn't have to risk losing all our men in a prolonged siege. However, we have a key that will secretly get us into the city of Liher Hale, and we'll be getting new soldiers through my marriage. By sending all our forces to Vylor, we'll liberate Velhisya safely. The Mercenaries won't dare pursue so many soldiers outside their walls. If we only send Elmor's men, Liher's soldiers may attack them in the open as soon as they start making their way back.

"I don't find this decision to be wise, Your Majesty," Elliot said, his hands on his hips. "Even if we secure Odin Mud's army, those men will never be loyal to you, only to the Emperor and his son. If something goes wrong in Vylor, we'll be surrounded by soldiers who could betray us at any point in time."

"We won't lose our men in Vylor," Syrella told him.

"If Liher changes the locks to the secret passage, we'll lose the element of surp—"

"We believe he won't. No one in the kingdom expects us to send an army to that place," Syrella cut in.

Elliot saw holes in this plan. He didn't want to have to remind the Governor of her failure at the Forked River, but he had to make her understand the risk. "Walter's informants are to be found in Wirskworth. No secret is safe."

"Perhaps!" Syrella snapped. "Nevertheless, Walter doesn't care about Liher Hale and Vylor. I see no reason why his informants would rush to break the news to the Mercenaries. No one leaves Wirskworth without my permission, and Linaria and Merhya will see to it that none of our soldiers leave camp until they reach Goldtown."

Elliot wasn't convinced.

"If the plan works, the soldiers will easily free Velhisya if she's ali..." Syrella stopped short, her mouth twisting.

Sophie moved to the centre of the group. "If Liher has changed the lock to the secret passage, our men will only besiege the city for three days. If they fail to bring down the gate, they'll return to Wirskworth. We've agreed that no one will stay in Vylor for more than three days, even if that means we don't save Veli... the Queen stuttered. "We'll do what we can without risking countless lives."

"Furthermore, as Sophie mentioned, the Mercenaries won't dare chase after our men outside their walls if we send such a large army," Syrella added.

Elliot approached Sophie. "A few days ago, you thought it was crazy to send only Elmor's men to Vylor! Now you want to risk our whole army?"

"I didn't know about the key," the Queen said bluntly. "Furthermore, Syrella promised me that no one would stay on Liher's land longer than agreed. Our men number about twenty thousand, while Vylor's army numbers no more than ten thousand soldiers. Whether we succeed in taking Goldtown or retreat, there aren't enough of them to harm our army significantly."

Elliot turned to Aleron. "Do you agree with this plan?" he asked.

The old man's eyes were bright. "Yes. I also believe that we'll manage to save Velhisya and return before Walter attacks," he replied.

"I thought you didn't agree with risking the lives of our people to save our loved ones." Elliot would have been the first to make a rash decision to save Velhisya, but now he felt that everyone's suggestions were risky, and thus, he had to be the one to restore some sanity.

"It's a fact that a leader shouldn't risk countless lives to save a single loved one. However, the news brought by Selwyn Brau made me reconsider, and I've changed my mind about Velhisya. Now, I agree with Sophie and Syrella's decisions. I believe the plan with the secret tunnel will succeed. I also think it will take Walter some time to march his armies back here, so we won't be in any significant danger until we return. Of course, he could attack us with the wyverns alone, but I'm sure he won't attack without soldiers. He knows the elwyn and elves can deal with these creatures. A large army will be safer than a smaller one when it comes to journeying to Vylor."

"On the other hand, if you have to besiege the city for a few days, many soldiers will die," Elliot said.

Aleron's brow furrowed in thought. "My warriors are prepared to give their lives for the only being born of an elwyn woman in three centuries. It's their choice, and I hope it won't be necessary."

His words moved Elliot, but he feared it could all go wrong. "Walter might ally with Liher, and they'll then attack our men together."

"No one expects us to attack Vylor, and Liher and Walter drew apart years ago. They hate each other, if you want my honest opinion. Even if Walter's informants in my city scramble to send information to the new king, that will take quite some time. My men will already be on their way back, and I'm sure Thorn won't throw his wyverns into battle without the rest of his army," Syrella said, her chin raised high.

"So be it," Elliot sighed, shaking his head.

"Two thousand of Elmor's men will remain here for my protection. Jahon will be their commander," Syrella continued.

That is to be expected, Elliot thought.

"Alysia will also stay here, along with a few elwyn and elves to fortify the city as best they can against Walter's impending attack. Selwyn and Giren will stay in Wirskworth as well and help Alysia and Jahon with anything they need."

"No!" Selwyn shouted.

Elliot turned towards him, and several stares snapped in his direction. Peter's look told his son to keep quiet.

"Velhisya tried to save me. It's my duty to—"

"It's *our* duty to save our cousin as well, and we need your help," Linaria cut him off and uncrossed her arms. "My sister and I want this mission, and Wirskworth will be without any captains during our absence. You're the only one we trust to help Jahon command the men while we're gone. Alysia might also need your help in fortifying the city. You and Giren have to help us."

Elliot knew it was a huge honour for Selwyn, and he bet that Syrella Endor had never entrusted a stranger in her land with anything like it. Selwyn's gaze met his, and Elliot gave him a nod. He was moved by Selwyn's fervour, but now he had to obey.

"Thank you for this mission and for the honour you do me in trusting me, Lady Endor. I will do as you and the Queen command of me." Selwyn bowed sharply without further protest.

"Very well. It's time we ended this council and made preparations for what's to come," said Syrella.

"I have a question," Selwyn said again as he straightened. "I don't know if the ploy with the key will succeed in Goldtown. However, I'd like to know what will become of Liher Hale if we manage to sneak inside the city or take it. Is there any plan for his murder?"

Syrella looked at Sophie and then at her daughters. "If we sneak into the city, our soldiers will free Velhisya and make their way back as quickly as possible, without a fight. If Velhisya is alive and we need to lay siege to Goldtown, Liher will die if our men get through the gate."

"And Lothar?" Selwyn asked.

Elliot frowned. It was obvious that the man had gained the loyalty of the younger Brau.

Syrella paused a moment before she replied, "I don't trust any Hale, and I believe that the people of Vylor are so corrupt that if they were ruled by a virtuous leader, they'd kill him."

"But—"

"Nevertheless," Syrella continued, "I respect that he helped you and Giren, and he may have helped my niece, too. If my men take Liher's life, and the Mercenaries surrender, we'll let the rest of the soldiers in Vylor live on condition that they swear allegiance to Lothar and appoint him ruler of their land."

Selwyn bowed sharply upon hearing her last words.

"Swear to me that your men will abide by everything you've said. The elwyn have never fought and killed before in their history. We've decided to help Elliot against Walter Thorn, however, we will not participate in the slaughter of innocent people for revenge," Aleron said.

Sophie and Syrella turned to face the old elwyn.

"I swear we'll keep our word." Sophie's expression matched the sincerity of her words.

Elliot's eyes stayed on Syrella. "I swear, too," the Scarred Queen echoed, the scar on her cheek tightening as she spoke.

Silence settled over the room as Elliot processed everything that had transpired in the Great Hall. Doubt and hope warred within him. He had seen too many plans unravel, too many promises broken. Yet, he wished with all his heart that this time, their plans would not fail.

The Bridge to the Other World

S elwyn stared at the small bridge opposite him again. He'd never seen a bridge within a castle before, and he had no idea where it led. Its surface glistened in the torchlight. A sigh escaped his lips, and he put his hands on his hips, unhappy about what had happened in the Great Hall. He was sure he wouldn't be able to sleep that night. Selwyn desperately wanted to disobey Sophie and Syrella's orders and go to rescue Velhisya, but he knew he shouldn't. If nothing else, the Governor of Elmor had bestowed the highest honour upon him by leaving him in Linaria and Merhya's stead until they returned.

Selwyn scratched his chin. He felt he'd won the confidence of quite a few people, but he knew that he wasn't admired for his skill in battle. If he were a warrior like Elliot, they would never have chosen to leave him behind in Wirskworth instead of sending him into battle against Liher Hale.

Jahon will also remain in the city, and he's a skilled swordsman, he thought. Selwyn couldn't explain why he so wanted to return to Vylor. Now that fear had left his soul, he felt a flame burning in his chest—the urge to fight to bring justice and to punish all who deserved it.

The image of Velhisya being tortured at the hands of Liher Hale haunted him, and the Heretic's Fork poisoned his dreams. Selwyn want-ed revenge. Liher Hale was a brutal sadist who lacked honour, and such men had no place in this world. He'd imagined countless ways of mur-dering the man, and each of them filled his soul with joy but also with a strange desire.

Don't let revenge get the better of you, my friend. If you do, there will come a day when you'll be worse than everyone you're trying to overturn.

Elliot's words rang in his ears, but he felt no need to curb his thirst for revenge. He had learned that men like Liher and Walter deserved a torturer's death.

"I didn't expect to find you here."

Selwyn turned to see his father standing a few feet away. "I was just passing by and stopped to admire the bridge," he said, glancing at it again.

Peter smiled. "It's called the Bridge to the Other World," he told his son.

"Why?"

"Hundreds of years ago, Edgar the Murdered, an old king of Elmor, used to torture countless men and women in this city. It's said that he'd lost his mind and saw enemies trying to take his throne everywhere."

"Was Edgar from the House of Endor?" Peter nodded. "I've never heard of him before. I thought the House of Endor always produced honest and noble rulers."

"No House has only had noble people," Peter said softly.

"What's all of this got to do with the name of the bridge?" Selwyn asked.

"This bridge leads to a staircase, at the end of which are the dungeons where Edgar tortured his enemies. In his time, no one came out of this place alive, so this bridge became known as "the Bridge to the Other World." All the prisoners who crossed its threshold never returned to our world."

Selwyn surveyed the bridge, and for a moment, he wondered how many people had walked along its length on their way to their death. "Why are so many men brutal? It seems that the gods who gave us life wanted our world to be filled with torture and death."

His father's expression became sorrowful. "One day, this kingdom may perhaps become peaceful."

Selwyn shook his head. "I thought about it countless times while I was

161

in Liher Hale's cells. As long as power and gold exist, there will be men prepared to do whatever it takes to get both."

"Power and gold will always exist," Peter muttered.

"Exactly... That's why I believe the gods only want war for this world."

"The elwyn and the elves have never fought for land and riches."

"Nevertheless, they too were blinded by greed for the Egercolls' power to tame the pegasi."

Peter sighed and held his arms out wide. "All we can do is fight in the hope of building a better world."

Selwyn remained silent.

"I know you wanted to travel to Vylor and fight to free Velhisya. However, the tasks that Sophie and Syrella have assigned to you indicate their appreciation of—"

"I know!" Selwyn snapped.

His father stood beside him. "I know how you feel."

"No one knows how I feel."

Peter laughed. "Do you think you're the only one who's ever felt a thirst for revenge? Do you know how many times I've wanted to challenge Walter to single combat? To try to avenge your brothers? I've dreamed of killing that man more times than I can count." Selwyn turned to face him, his eyes widening. He hadn't expected to hear those words. "I know that a part of you died inside that cell while another was born. However, a life of hatred and revenge is a miserable life, filled with anguish and torment. You don't deserve such a life, son."

Selwyn felt strange, unable to find a response.

"You may not be fighting in Vylor, but soon Walter will try to kill us all, and then you'll get what you desire. But remember, death and war will not help you find peace. If you leave everything that happened behind and find peace within yourself, you will live a happy life."

His father patted him gently on the shoulder and walked away. Selwyn's gaze wandered over to the Bridge to the Other World while Peter's words ran through his mind. *Will I ever be able to leave behind everything that has happened in my short life, or am I doomed to live forever consumed by misery, rage, and revenge?*

Laurana's hand drifted across Peter's chest. His wife was half asleep by his side, but he was sure that he would remain awake. The journey of their armies to Vylor, the Queen's wedding, and Selwyn's change in personality—they all plagued his mind, preventing him from calming down.

He glanced at the smouldering fire at the other end of the chamber and contemplated the dark sky outside. In recent years, experience had taught him in the cruellest way that grand plans rarely succeeded, and now they were risking so much that it would be impossible for something not to go wrong. Peter didn't trust Odin Mud, and Sophie and Syrella's decision to march all their soldiers to Liher Hale's land was far too risky. If there was one thing that brought him some comfort, it was that Selwyn would remain in Wirskworth. He knew that the city had spies devoted to Walter, and Thorn himself would soon lay siege to it for the third time. Still, Elmor's capital was safer than the destinations the rest of them would be heading to.

Peter caressed his wife's bare shoulder as she rested her head on his chest. *Selwyn has changed,* he thought. He'd realised the moment he'd laid eyes on his son after his time in the dungeons of Goldtown Castle.

He remembered Selwyn asking him to travel with Elliot to Elmor not long ago. That memory seemed so distant, and yet only a few weeks had passed. Peter knew his son well. He may have said that he wanted to avenge his brothers' deaths, and he might have demanded to travel with Elliot, but in reality, Peter could tell that he was afraid of dying. Peter had spent dozens of years in battle and could discern when there was fear in a man's face. He knew all too well that the fear of death bred cowardice, and cowardice kept young men from becoming great warriors.

The truth was that in the past, he'd rejoiced in Selwyn's fear. He didn't care whether his son was a coward if that was what saved his life. Nevertheless, things had changed. Selwyn had thrown off his fear into the carnage of the past, and it would never return. Peter had seen that transformation several times during his years of war in many people, and he knew that the addiction to revenge was so sweet that few could resist it.

Selwyn's brothers hadn't feared death. That was what scared him. Selwyn now reminded him of his brothers—just as reckless. Peter knew better than anyone that revenge and recklessness was a combination that had sent countless young men to the realms of the dead.

Have you forgotten your revenge? Have you forgotten the pain Walter gave you? A voice inside him asked.

He knew the pain would never go away. However, the existence of Selwyn, his last son, gave meaning to his world, and that meaning overshadowed his grief. If Selwyn were to die, he'd be plunged into the never-ending dance of revenge, too, and he'd then be capable of anything. A man who had nothing left to lose was unhappy but also dangerous.

"I'm glad Selwyn is staying with me. I've missed him so much," Laurana murmured in her sleep.

Peter stroked her back gently, the warmth of her body enveloping his. His thoughts turned to the upcoming trip to Kerth once more. He was well aware that he had to be careful there and that the Queen would be vulnerable without an army in the land of the Emperor.

Suddenly, a memory came to him, and he covered his face with his hands. As much as he tried to put them behind him, the images had haunted him for decades. No matter what he did for Sophie, it wasn't enough to block out his regrets. Peter had tried to speak to the Queen about his betrayal countless times but had never found the courage to do so. Many a time, he felt that the death of his two sons was the price for his treason. Nevertheless, if that were true, the gods had behaved more cruelly towards him than he could have ever imagined.

Peter wrestled with his memories until his eyelids grew heavy. A tall, brawny soldier found his way into his dreams, a smiling man, departing on the mission he'd decided to accomplish. He wanted to stop him, but he couldn't find a way to do it.

The Poisonous Touch

T ime seemed to stand still in the dungeons of Goldtown Castle. Velhisya no longer knew how many days she'd spent in the cell, and her instincts told her that her end was near. Quite some time had gone by without her having to face the Governor of Vylor again, and nor had she seen Lothar Hale. Neither of them had visited her cell, and the guards who brought her food were the only people she had seen.

Perhaps you'll survive somehow. A solution might be found, just like with Giren and Selwyn. An inner voice tried to give her courage but in vain. Velhisya knew that even if she was freed from her prison, it would be nearly impossible to remain unscathed, and if Liher Hale laid his hands on her, it would be as if she'd died.

She bent forward and put her right hand on her waist as she sat in a corner of the cell. She rubbed her skin hard, trying to ease the pain. Sleeping on the hard floor hurt her bones. Footsteps broke the silence, and she sat up. She'd been brought food a while earlier, so it seemed strange that someone was hurrying to visit her. Shadows appeared on the wall opposite her cell, and Velhisya saw three figures in the dim torchlight. A tall, burly man stuck a key in the cell door and forced it open. Soon after, she saw two petite figures approaching her—two women dressed in brown clothes. One of them extended their hand towards her. She had a square face with a large nose and small eyes, and a big mole dominated her chin.

Velhisya pulled away from her. "What do you want?" she asked.

"To take care of you, my lady," she said. The two women shared the

166

same dark hair.

"Who sent you?"

"Lord Lothar Hale."

Velhisya was suspicious. She looked at the two newcomers more closely. They were past their prime and looked like maids from the castle. "Has Lothar sent two women to look after me without the Governor's consent?"

"Lord Liher agreed with his brother that you need a bath and some new clothes," said the woman who had spoken earlier.

"Where will you take me?" she asked after a while.

"To a chamber with a bathtub. We'll wash you there and give you new clothes."

"And then are you going to bring me back to the cell?"

The woman shook her head. "You'll stay in the chamber."

Velhisya knew this was all too good to be true. "I don't believe it," she said.

"What is it that you don't believe, my lady?" the woman asked, narrowing her eyes.

"Liher Hale would never agree to all of this."

"I don't know what to tell you, my lady. That's all I know."

Velhisya examined the woman's words for a trap. "I want to speak to Lothar," she said.

"Lord Lothar will meet you later in your new chamber!" the woman snapped.

"And what if I refuse to leave the cell?"

"I don't believe you have the option to refuse, my lady," the strange woman said again.

"Be quick," the guard waiting at the entrance of the cell told them.

All her instincts told her not to give in, but she knew that if she resisted, they'd haul her to the chamber. She hoped Lothar had made his brother change his mind, but she couldn't imagine a world in which Liher would stop being a sadist.

Velhisya rose slowly, and the two women walked out of the cell. She followed them, and as soon as she stepped out of the steel entrance, the guard locked it again with a bored look. They continued walking towards the dungeon's exit, the bones in her legs creaking. She felt so weak as they emerged from the dungeons and climbed a circular stone staircase.

Velhisya struggled to see in the dim light. As she reached for a torch mounted on the wall to her right, a hand seized her shoulder.

"What are you doing?" asked the guard who had been following her and the two women all this time.

"I can't see!" Velhisya snapped angrily and pulled away from his hand.

She felt invisible nails digging into her calves, her lower back aching as she pushed herself up the stairs, her lungs burning. Just as she reached the ground floor, a new light flickered into view. There was a window in front of her, and she could see white moonlight glinting through the clouds. Velhisya had thought that she might never see the sun or moon again.

A hand touched her shoulder again, and she looked back to see that the guard wore an angry expression. The women in front kept walking while Velhisya stopped to catch her breath. She started moving again, her gaze fixed on the beautiful moon. Velhisya continued through the deserted corridors, and another staircase appeared before her. She wished to reach the chamber quickly because her knees couldn't bear any more steps.

Velhisya finally reached the top of the stairs, lagging behind the two women. The new corridor was lined with windows and appeared more well-kept than the others. The walls were lined with tapestries and statues, and the smell of damp no longer reached her nostrils. Suddenly, the women in front of her stopped short, and she nearly ran into them.

"Here it is," the woman who had spoken to her in the cell said, pushing open a door on the right.

The women entered the room and Velhisya followed them while the guard closed the door behind them, remaining outside. The chamber was decorated with many rugs and cloths, and a few dozen candles were spread around it. Her gaze fell upon a large wooden table with two chairs and then to a four-poster bed at the other end of the chamber.

"This way, my lady," one of the women said, and Velhisya saw a low wall to the left which hid part of the room. She walked behind the maid and, a moment later, saw a large wooden tub steaming behind the wall. She wanted to throw off her dirty clothes as fast as she could and get in. Nevertheless, there was one more thing she had to do before her bath.

Velhisya turned and headed towards the table. In the middle of it, she spotted a plate and felt as if she might pass out from hunger. On the plate were slices of bread, cheese, and a handful of figs. Velhisya grabbed a slice of bread and ate greedily until she felt a touch on her waist.

"You'll dine later, my lady. Lord Lothar has arranged for a sumptuous meal to be brought to you."

Velhisya gave the woman a sceptical look. She didn't like her sharp tone, and her words sounded like commands.

"I'll eat whenever I please," she said.

"But my lady—"

"If you don't like it, take me back to the cell."

The woman sighed, closing her eyes for a moment. "Once you're done, come to the tub!" she snapped and walked away.

Velhisya carried on eating bread and cheese. With each bite, she felt strengthened. The food wasn't plentiful, but it was better than nothing. Velhisya wiped her lips on her sleeve and turned towards the wall that hid the wooden tub. She moved closer and saw the two women pouring oils into the steaming water.

"Get in, my lady," the woman with the mole said once more.

Her manner made Velhisya want to refuse, but she couldn't find the strength to react. She threw off her dirty clothes and put her feet into the hot water. The warmth enveloped her as she sat in the tub, relieving the pain in her back. Her heart began to beat faster.

She felt hands on her back and, out of the corner of her eye, saw the woman who hadn't spoken a word all that time rubbing her body with a cloth. Velhisya didn't pull away while the second maid began to brush her hair.

She'd lost track of time with the hot water soothing her senses when a voice snapped her out of her slumber.

"Get out so that we can dry you, my lady," the woman with the mole said in her familiar sharp tone.

Velhisya looked at her.

"Your dinner will arrive in a moment," added the maid, unsuccessfully trying to sound good-natured.

Velhisya wanted to stay in the bath, but her fingers had wrinkled, and her stomach still ached with hunger. She rested her hands on the tub and lifted herself out of the water. The two women wiped her down with long white cloths, and a moment later, the maid with the mole picked something up off the ground. Velhisya saw a yellow linen gown in her hands that appeared to have been sewn from expensive material.

For a moment, she felt a hint of suspicion. She may have felt relaxed after all the hardship, but it seemed odd that Liher Hale had allowed his brother to give her such lavish gifts. *My aunt may still be alive... She may have promised him all of Elmor's gold after all.* The thought didn't seem realistic, yet she couldn't find any other explanation.

Velhisya put on the robe, and the maids bowed to her.

"Your dinner will be here soon, my lady," said the ugly woman.

Velhisya stared at the door for some time, waiting. No one entered, and suspicion crept in. She took a few steps towards the large bed and examined the mattress. She wanted to wait longer for Lothar, but her body was exhausted. Pushing the canopy's fabric aside, she lay down. The mattress was so soft that she thought she'd fall asleep immediately, when a sound startled her.

"Not so fast, my dear. I'd say we shouldn't lie down before dinner."

Velhisya jerked upright and saw Liher Hale standing in the doorway, smiling. The man walked towards her, his purple cloak touching the ground as he got closer.

"What are you doing here?" Velhisya snapped. Sweat dripped down her forehead, and her fingers went numb.

"What do you think I'm doing?"

"Where's Lothar?"

Liher laughed. "Did you really believe that my foolish brother would stand in the way of our fate? The gods wanted us to sleep together, my dear, and so they sent you into my arms." Liher stood before her and looked at her lustfully. "You smell wonderful."

It all made sense now. The repulsive Governor wanted her to be clean before he raped her. She was a fool not to have realised what was happening sooner.

"Where's Lothar?" Velhisya asked again, trembling as she tried to step backwards.

"When I spend the night with beautiful women, I prefer them to be without my brother," Liher snapped and reached for her.

Velhisya punched him in the face, and he let out a cry of pain. Rage hardened his features, and she prepared herself for his blow.

"Whatever you do, you won't escape fate tonight. If I were you, I'd choose to comply, otherwise, I'll tie you to the bed, and once I'm done with you, I'll order every guard in the castle to fuck you."

"One day, my aunt will hang your headless body on the gate of this city," Velhisya spat.

Liher laughed again. "Your aunt is dead," he said between his guffaws. "Did you believe she would defeat Walter Thorn? You're all doomed."

Velhisya felt terror. "Have you heard that Wirskworth has fallen?" she asked, her heartbeat catching in her throat.

"Not yet... Nevertheless, it's just a matter of time. Nobody can defeat Walter."

Where is Lothar? Please god! Please help me! "One day, Thorn will kill you, too," she told him.

The man was out of breath from laughter. "Walter doesn't give a damn about me, stupid girl."

It was Velhisya's turn to smile. "You're the stupid one," she said, taking another step back. "As soon as Walter destroys his enemies, he'll punish all those who didn't stand by him all these years. You're a dead man, Liher Hale."

The smile faded from the Governor's face. "So be it... I may be a dead man, but until then, you'll be my whore," he replied and strode menacingly towards her.

Velhisya tried to escape his grasp. "Lothar will kill you if he finds out you raped me. He told you he would start a rebellion against you if you did! Where is he?" she cried.

Liher sniggered. "My little brother is more worthless than dung, and he can't do anything in the least to me. The people of this land are devoted to me. He won't bother us."'

"Have you killed him?"

"That wasn't necessary. A few herbs in his evening wine were enough to induce a pleasant sleep... When he wakes up, you can tell him what has happened if he visits you. I'd like to see him try to have me overthrown!"

Velhisya tried to dart past him and run to the door, but Liher grabbed her by the shoulders and pulled her back hard. She struggled, thrashing against his grip, but he shoved her towards the bed. She swung at him, desperate to break free, but he overpowered her, pinning her to the mattress

"Calm down, and you'll enjoy it more than you think. I've sown countless bastards over the years. I promise that if you fall pregnant, I'll recognise yours and make you a true princess in my land."

Velhisya sank her teeth into his right hand, and Liher screamed before he slapped her across the face. Stunned by the blow, Velhisya couldn't stop his hand from moving to her thighs under her robe. She had to do something; she had to defend herself. The man grabbed her breast, and then she felt his other hand between her legs.

NO! NO! The image of her dying father flashed before her, and soon after, her mother appeared in her mind. *I love you, Velhisya.*

"NO!" Her scream shook everything around them, and Liher jumped back in pain, letting out a piercing cry.

"What was that?! What did you do to me?" The man was frightened and looked at his limbs. He gave her an angry look, stood up, and tried to climb onto her again with his heavy body.

Velhisya grabbed his face in her hands, feeling a powerful force envelop her body. Liher screamed as if he was on fire until his voice died away, and she pushed him back off her. The man's body fell onto the floor beside the bed, lifeless and unmoving. The door to the chamber opened with a loud thud.

"What has happened?!" The guard who had brought her from her cell looked at Liher before staring wide-eyed at her, stunned.

Stormy Secrets

Elliot had never travelled on a ship before. The air on deck whipped his face, and the swaying caused by the swell of the waves made him nauseous. He took a few clumsy steps towards the ship's interior, struggling to walk through the swirling wind while sailors ran around him and shouted to each other.

I hope the captain knows what he's doing. He remembered the short, fat man who reeked of wine, telling them that the autumnal storms weren't that strong in the sea leading to Mirth, the capital of Kerth.

Elliot managed to get below deck and saw a large wooden table between some chairs. The great cabin was deserted, and he sat in a chair, trying to keep himself from vomiting. The ship continued to rock, and Elliot wished he hadn't eaten that morning. It had only been a few hours since they'd set off on their trip, and he wondered how long he'd last until they reached their destination.

"I'd say sea voyages don't suit you." Sophie appeared in the cabin out of nowhere. She wore a woollen dress while a black cloak adorned her shoulders.

"I've never been on a ship before," Elliot responded.

"Neither have I," Sophie said and sat beside him.

The Queen looked composed, unaffected by the ship's movement. "Where were you?" Elliot didn't understand how she had entered the cabin without him knowing.

"There's a small staircase at the back of the room. From there, you can go to the rest of the cabins. I wanted to see them."

"What are they like?" Elliot wanted to talk about anything to forget the nauseating seasickness.

"Nothing special. However, the captain has given me his cabin, which is the largest after this one." Sophie looked around the space. "You and Peter can have the ones adjacent to it."

"And our men?"

"They'll be sleeping with the crew on the lower decks of the ship. Unfortunately, there's no other option."

Elliot looked around him. "This is a huge cabin. It could make for a very spacious chamber," he said.

"On the old ships, this place would have been the captain's cabin. On the new ones, it's a gathering place for the crew when discussions need to be held, and at all other times, it's where the captain dines."

"I hope he doesn't leave the helm to dine tonight," Elliot said, fearing what would become of the ship if it were left without someone to steer it.

"Don't worry. It may seem scary, but the sailors are used to storms."

Elliot hoped this was true.

"I wanted to ask you something." The Queen's voice was hesitant. Elliot looked at her, waiting for her to continue. "Did Thorold tell you that young woman was your sister?"

Elliot nodded and lowered his gaze. That was the only subject he didn't want to talk about.

"Your sister was very brave," Sophie murmured, her tone mournful.

"Why do you say that?" he asked.

"A woman who dares to end her life to avoid torture is more courageous than a lot of men."

Elliot's eyes grew wet.

"I realise that talking about this brings you much pain."

He looked up. "Why do you want to talk about this? I thought that caring made you weak and that we should suppress our feelings to win the war. One might say that such a conversation would only be had by two people who care for each other. If you're asking just to make conversation, then I don't want to talk about my sister."

Sophie's lips quivered. "This war has changed me. I've often thought about what I should have done differently to avoid everything that has happened, and I always conclude that it would be better if I didn't care about anything. I would have no one to love, and therefore no one to lose."

"And then you'd have lived a meaningless life. Even if you won the war, you'd be alone."

"And now that I have lost everyone that I loved, what meaning does my life have?"

Elliot scoffed. "Pain and loss are a part of life. If we didn't have loved ones to lose, we wouldn't be who we are. People who don't care about anyone end up like Walter."

"Is that what you thought when you found your sister dead?" the Queen asked in a calm voice.

Her words stirred up unpleasant memories, and he tried to push them away. "No," he admitted.

"Maybe the only way to be happy in this world is to be like Walter."

"No." This time, Elliot's voice was firm. "Men like him always want more. No matter who or what they conquer, even if they conquer the world, it's never enough. They live in fear that they'll lose everything they've acquired, and they know that without the weapon of fear, no one would give a damn about them. I can't imagine a more miserable life."

For a moment, he felt as if the spirit of Althalos had come to life within him. He couldn't remember ever sounding like his old Master before. He stared at Sophie. Her face was stupefied and her eyes wide.

"I'm sorry about your sister, Elliot. I'm still grieving over Bert, my parents, and Eleanor. As much as it hurts, I know that if I had the chance to live again, I wouldn't change my love for them. Now, I won't let anything distract me from my goal. I'll start caring about people again when Walter is dead." Sophie said.

"If Peter or I die, won't you care?" Elliot asked.

Sophie frowned. "I cannot banish all my feelings, but I won't live in fear of people dying. I have to defeat Walter, and until I do, nothing else matters anymore."

Elliot didn't know if he believed her. It all seemed to be a shield against the pain she'd felt for years. "Why did you ask me about my sister?" he asked.

Sophie smiled for the first time in days. "It's obvious you don't want to talk about her... I felt the same way about Eleanor. However, sometimes talking about those we've lost helps us come to terms with their death."

The Queen rose from her seat, heading to the staircase that led to the ship's cabins. Elliot remained where he was, Selyn's face flooding his thoughts. After a while, John's face appeared in his mind. Elliot hoped he was still alive. He couldn't bear another death on his conscience. He stood and headed for the deck again. The time had come to send Hurwig to find his old friend.

Peter held onto his cloak tightly, fearing the wind would blow it away. Clouds hid the moon, and the cold air on deck was bitter. The sailors quickly tied ropes, and the captain didn't let go of the ship's helm for a moment as the storm raged.

"Hey, you." The sailor turned to him—Peter couldn't recall his name. "Who'll steer the ship if the captain falls asleep? I don't imagine we'll be able to drop anchor in these waters."

The sailor laughed. "It would be impossible to drop anchor at such a depth, but with waves like these, the anchor wouldn't even hold us in the shallows," he said. "The second captain will replace him."

Peter nodded, and the sailor left. Having never spent time on a ship before, Peter didn't have the faintest idea about the duties of its crew. He felt tired and headed for his cabin. Elliot and Sophie must have already gone to sleep, as he hadn't come across them for some time.

The wind froze his forehead as he pushed open the door of the great cabin under the quarterdeck. A few candles burned slowly, and a gentle warmth enveloped him. He was sure he'd fall asleep as soon as he fell onto his bed. He moved towards the staircase leading to his chamber and descended the steps. Suddenly, the ship lurched so violently that he lost his footing, and his body tumbled down the wooden stairs, crashing onto the landing.

"What the hell?!" Pain shot through his back. He reached through his clothes and touched something wet. Blood was gushing from his torn skin.

"Are you alright?" Sophie ran from her room, her light blue night-gown fluttering as she moved. Her hair was tousled and unkempt from sleep.

"I slipped on the stairs," Peter muttered as the pain wracked his body.

"Let me see." Sophie bent down and tried to lift his cloak and woollen jerkin.

"No, Your Majesty. I'm okay. You shouldn't trouble yourself with my wounds."

"Stand still." Sophie raised her voice, and Peter felt his clothes being raised. "I have to stitch this wound."

"That is no job for you, Your Majesty."

"Come into my cabin. That's an order."

Peter sighed wearily, got up, and followed her, taking slow steps. He entered her cabin, where a small flame burned from a half-melted candle on the table.

"Sit on the bed," she told him.

Peter wanted to leave and go to his cabin, but he couldn't disobey. He sat down on the hard mattress, and Sophie lifted his clothes, which were now soaked in blood. The Queen looked at the wound and hurried to one end of the cabin. She bent down and rummaged through a leather sack. Sophie raised her right hand, and a small needle glinted under the faint light of the candles. She looked at it closely before she picked up a spool of thread. Sophie stood and moved towards Peter.

The Queen placed the end of the needle in the candle's flame. She sat down next to Peter. He expected to feel the hot metal piercing his flesh, but something cold touched him instead.

"What's that?" he asked, noticing blood seeping into Sophie's sheets.

"I have to clean the wound. I'll use some wine."

Peter craned his neck to see her holding a wet washcloth that had turned red with blood. Next to Sophie was a small cup filled with wine. He nodded stiffly, and she rubbed his wound, the pain numbing his senses. Peter felt his eyelids drooping when the needle pierced his skin, making him jump.

"I didn't expect you to know how to do this," he told her, teeth gritted against the pain.

Sophie didn't respond straightaway. "I thought I'd told you that when I was young, my dream was to become one of the healers in Knightdorn."

"Yes, but I didn't know you'd had any training."

"I haven't. My mother taught me to sew up wounds when I was a child, and I've never forgotten."

"Have you ever needed to do this before?" He felt the thread tugging the wound closed.

A laugh escaped the Queen's lips. "I often sewed up Eleanor's shoulders after her battles in the courtyards of Iovbridge."

Peter smiled. "I'm sorry, Sophie—I'm sorry about everything," he said softly. Sophie didn't respond. "Do you think Odin's son will be a good husband?"

"No," the Queen said bluntly.

"Then you shouldn't have agreed to this plan," Peter replied.

"We have no other choice. Besides, no one can harm me more than I've already been subjected to."

"I won't let him harm you, Your Majesty. If he hurts you, we'll leave as fast as we can."

"I'll be fine. The kingdom has always depended on my misery," Sophie said in a strained tone.

As the needle pierced his flesh, the urge to finally confess the truth gnawed at him—to reveal his past, to admit his betrayal. But he couldn't. He wasn't brave enough.

"I'm done," Sophie told him. "We'll have a healer look at the wound when we arrive in Mirth. Unfortunately, there's no healer on this ship."

Peter lowered his cloak and jerkin and stood. "Thank you, Your Majesty," he said, bowing slightly as the stitches pulled at his skin, sending a sharp twinge of pain through him.

"Don't bend!" the Queen said, her blue eyes sparkling. Her fingers were stained with blood.

Peter nodded. "I hope the crew is coping," he said, feeling lucky that the ship was now steady.

"I think those lurches are routine for the sailors."

Peter smiled. "Good night," he said.

He turned and strode out of the room. He walked a little further and pushed open the door to his cabin a few feet away from the Queen's. Once inside, he rested his head against the wooden wall and breathed heavily. He knew he could never reveal his secret—the secret of his betrayal that he had kept from Sophie all these years. If he did, it would shatter the heart of a woman already tormented by too much pain.

A Trip to Freedom

S ophie couldn't sleep. The sound of Peter crashing to the floor earlier had woken her abruptly. She looked around her bare cabin, the room cold and inhospitable. She stood and moved to the round window. The stormy waters looked black that night, and there was little light. Clouds had often covered the sky over the past few days as it grew colder. The captain had told them before they left that winter would soon arrive, and then it would be very hard to travel to Kerth. She knew that in these seas, winter brought the worst winds, which surprised her because in the northeastern part of Knightdorn, the worst storms occurred in autumn.

She continued staring out at the sea until something passed the window. Sophie saw the white wings of a bird until darkness swallowed its outline. *How can birds fly against such wind?*

Sophie tore her gaze away from the window and walked into her small cabin. She often mulled over her prospective marriage to the son of the self-proclaimed Emperor. She was sure the man would be vicious and arrogant, just like his father, yet a small part of her was glad to be travelling to Kerth. It was the first time in her life that she had left Knightdorn—the first time the war in the kingdom felt like it was a world away. She might have been travelling to another continent just to gain more soldiers. She might have known she would soon return to the kingdom she never wanted. Yet, despite that, the mere thought of being far from Knightdorn offered her a sliver of peace.

If Odin Mud were honourable, I could stay in Kerth forever.

A continent removed from war and death seemed like a lifeline after

181

the suffering of the past. But Sophie knew from the rumours that Odin was a cunning man who had no honour. Kerth, the Western Empire, had three major cities, and there had been three rulers for years. Odin Mud had organised a jousting tournament and had killed the other two leaders there without any cause. He'd organised a feast in his city, Mirth, just to get his rivals for the rule of Kerth out of the way.

Odin had ruled the continent for years, refusing to submit to the ruler of Knightdorn. His son's marriage to Sophie was an attempt to expand his empire across the entire world. Moreover, he wouldn't hesitate to kill her once he'd taken the throne he sought. However, having this knowledge was also to Sophie's advantage. The Emperor would do her no harm until his son sat on the throne, and if they succeeded, she was prepared to get their party out of the way before they had time to murder her.

Tired of her cabin, Sophie slipped a cloak over her gown and headed for the deck. The wind howled in her ears as she reached the door. Bracing herself, she pushed hard against it, fighting the force of the gale. Sophie stepped out onto the deck. When the strong wind beat against her forehead, she felt a sense of freedom. She couldn't make out a single star in the dark sky through the clouds. A few men were working around the great white sails. She turned back on them to look towards the high point where the captain steered the ship.

The man behind the helm was not the one she knew; she'd assumed there was a second captain for the nights. She got a closer look at the man and saw him turning the ship's wheel repeatedly as the waves ensnared the ship in their dance.

Sophie walked to the edge of the starboard side of the deck, bracing herself against the wooden railing of the ship, and looked down. She loved the wildness of the sea. It looked like a woman who would vent her anger on anyone who dared to touch her.

She stared at the waves, lost in thought until her mind drifted to Elliot. She knew the words she'd said to him were harsh. The boy had endured a lot in his short life and had tried to help her as much as he could. Nonetheless, Sophie didn't want to get close to him. The war wasn't over, and she couldn't bear to mourn the loss of yet another loved one.

If Elliot dies, you'll be hurt. You'll regret everything you said when he was close to you. She'd decided to ignore her conscience. The past had shown her that those who didn't care about anyone were powerful in war.

I don't want to become like Walter... Perhaps I'm more like him than I like to think... That could be why I killed those captives, she told herself. *No. I have nothing in common with that man.* Sophie turned her attention back to the waves.

"Your Majesty, what are you doing here?"

Sophie looked back and saw the captain who had been steering the ship all morning. "I just wanted to get some air," she told him. He was fat with grey hair and a big chin.

"It's very cold. You'd better get back to your cabin."

"I want to stay a while longer," she said tersely, hoping to be left alone.

"What's troubling you, Your Majesty?"

"Why do you think something is troubling me?"

The man laughed, and Sophie watched him closely. "I've never seen anyone so deep in thought as you. I may just be a mere captain, but even I can read that look."

"What's your name?"

"Ronald, Your Majesty."

"Do you like life at sea, Ronald?"

The man silently approached her. "More than anything. I've been captain of this ship for twenty years, and it feels like yesterday was the first time I sailed on the open sea. Every time I leave the harbour and cross the ocean, I feel free, as if an invisible force commands me to stay young forever. I'll only give it up when I can't set sail on the seas anymore."

"Have you ever wanted to become captain of a warship?"

"No..." the man said. "I've never wanted to fight. The only thing I adore is the sea—carrying merchandise is a safer job than being the captain of a fleet. Why do you ask?"

"I envy you," Sophie said.

The captain laughed once more. "A Queen envies a mere captain?"

Sophie nodded. "I'd give anything to live a life doing only that which I really want. To feel free."

"Perhaps one day you'll change your mind, Your Majesty. Life is complicated. Nonetheless, you can enjoy the freedom of the sea for a few more days." The captain bowed awkwardly and headed for the ship's helm with ungainly steps.

Sophie stared back at the waves, and then a flash caught her attention. The light of the moon shone dimly through a small cloud. She often wondered if her parents, Bert and Eleanor, could see her from high up in the heavens. She hoped the legends about life after death were true. The idea that her loved ones watched over her from another distant world made her feel less alone.

Suddenly, two wings passed in front of her, and again, she saw a white bird flying above the ship. She wondered if it was the bird she'd seen earlier. The bird tore through the air as it headed towards the moon. She followed its path for a while until Elliot's face reappeared in her head again.

"How did you free the Elder Races?" she remembered asking him.

"I had to cast the past aside and find the truest part of myself. When I put my rage behind me and felt true compassion for the suffering of those creatures, I was stronger than ever. It was then that I succeeded."

"I don't understand," Sophie had said.

"I can say no more. However, if one day, you feel what I felt, you'll understand what I mean."

Sophie glanced at the moon once more. She knew that the rage and pain that accompanied her throughout life would never abate until she died. Perhaps she would never feel the power Elliot had spoken of, but she had come to accept that this was her fate.

A Helping Hand

John brought the cup to his mouth, sipping wine as he gazed out at the stormy sea. Waves didn't use to reach as far as Merynhor, the harbour of the Grand Island, since its walls prevented the winds from gaining entrance. Nevertheless, the wind was very strong that night.

John had spent the last week in taverns, drinking and laughing his heart out to try and clear his mind from everything the future held in store for him. Soon, the storms would subside, even just a little, and then he'd have to travel to the island Begon had commanded him to go to. He didn't want to think about the trip, and instinct told him that he wouldn't be able to save his life this time. The Ice Islands were renowned for the seamanship of their men. The fact that the fishermen hadn't returned from that islet for months was a very bad omen.

He continued watching the waves and then remembered the mermaid who had spoken to him a while ago. He was sure there was some connection to what he'd heard over the past few days, but he couldn't figure out what it was. A mermaid had told him that someone had taken her sisters, and Begon had sound information that Walter had tamed a wyvern. He remembered the time he'd seen a wyvern tear through the skies when he was still young. At the time, he had just decided to abandon the life of a pirate and become a bounty hunter. A merchant had asked him to catch someone who owed him money, and that scoundrel had discovered that John was on his tail. John had headed for the Mountains of Darkness and had spent days there trying to catch him. He remembered the night when a huge creature had filled the sky above his head. The spines on its body were enormous, and it was a blessing it hadn't seen him. The idea that those huge monsters were fighting against Elliot was terrifying. Nevertheless, none of that explained how such a creature had bonded with Walter—a human.

John suspected that the disappearance of the mermaids might have played a part in Thorn's feat, but he couldn't find the connection. The answer kept slipping through his fingers. The north belonged to Walter, and no man of sound mind would dare to capture creatures like the mermaids. John had seen some of them destroy a pirate ship years ago, and the vessel he was on had managed to sail away from the attack in time. He'd heard that the mermaids had attacked that ship because a pirate on its crew had tried to take one of their sisters captive out of love. John wondered how he'd managed to survive so many adventures. A little later, the mysterious questions that tormented him came back. *Why had the northerners captured mermaids? How had Walter tamed a wyvern?* The simplest explanation was that some mermaids had died of unknown causes, their sisters had wrongly blamed humans, and what was being said about Thorn was just a rumour. John knew there were just too many unbelievable elements for all of the rumours to be true.

He took a few more sips of his drink, and a sigh escaped his lips. As the years went by, everything seemed to get more and more complicated. *If the northerners attacked mermaids, perhaps their attacks were related to the disappearance of the Islands' fishermen.* Still, he couldn't explain how. As if all that wasn't enough, he felt immense sadness over the loss of Eleanor. He'd asked some merchants, and all of them had heard that Felador had proclaimed a new ruler—a woman who was murdered during Walter's attack. Eleanor had managed to take rulership of the region, only to be killed. He wished the news weren't true, but his instincts told him that Eleanor was dead. She was one of the few people he'd ever felt the need to protect, and her death gave rise to yet another question: Why had Thorn left the battle in Elmor to attack Aquarine? The city had been forsaken by the whole kingdom, and it had no army...

John now felt angry. He didn't like mysteries, and lately, they'd been popping out of every corner like shadows. It had been many years since he'd allowed himself to truly care about someone, and now that he had, pain had ripped through his very core. Morys and Eleanor had wrongfully passed away, just like so many others during the years of war. He wondered how Selwyn fared in Liher Hale's city, and he knew that Elliot's future would be just as bleak. A battle against giants, wyverns, and a massive army under Walter's command didn't bode well.

Elliot freed the Elder Races. He's special. He may succeed. But... How did he free them? John hadn't believed in the legend of the curse for years, but the meeting with that elwyn, Aleron, in Ersemor, had changed his view.

"How come an elwyn is far from the Mountains of the Forgotten World? I thought the elwyn were cursed," Morys had asked.

"Human curses hold no sway over me, young man! I'm the wisest of the glorious elwyn race! No curse is worse than the existence of your kind," Aleron had replied.

John wondered whether the news of Elliot's feat would have been enough to make Begon change his mind and decide to throw himself into battle at the boy's side. He didn't believe it would, and none of them knew where the last battle between Walter and the son of Thomas Egercoll would take place. Logic said that Elliot and Sophie would be waiting for Thorn again in Wirskworth, but he wasn't entirely sure about that. John didn't want to have to think anymore.

A woman's scream snapped him out of his thoughts. John turned sharply, the cup slipping from his hand. He jumped up and started running along the shore, his heart pounding. He couldn't see anything through the clouded night, and now the sound could be heard no more. He walked up the road that led to the coast.

"Leave me alone!"

John changed course and headed for the coastline where the harbour of the Grand Island began. He became out of breath, and his body grew sweaty under his thick woollen clothes. He stopped and looked for the source of the sound again.

"I told you to get lost!" someone shouted.

John saw two figures near the shoreline. He ran in their direction until he saw a man pulling a woman by her wrists.

"What's going on here?" John asked breathlessly.

The man turned to him. He was tall and well-built, with thick black hair, and his eyes had narrowed. "Mind your own business!" he snapped.

"Assaulting defenceless women is a serious crime in this land."

"I know the laws."

"Then leave this woman alone," John said, looking at her. She had wild, tufted red hair, and her big eyes were filled with fear.

"This whore robbed me!" the man shouted. "She asked me for gold in some inn to sleep with me, and when I went to get some wine, she ran away. She isn't defenceless, and theft is severely punished too in the Ice Islands." He didn't release his grip on the young woman's wrists.

"If that's true, you can ask Begon for a hearing. If you're vindicated, this woman will be forced to return your gold, and your leader will decide her punishment," John said.

"I want my gold now."

"You don't have the right to decide her punishment."

The woman bit the man's hand, and he screamed in pain. She was about to escape when he slapped her, knocking her to the ground.

John drew the small sword hanging from his belt. It was one of the few times he'd decided to take it with him. "The men of the Ice Islands don't treat women like that. Let her go," he said.

The man laughed. "What are you going to do to stop me, Long Arm?"

John didn't expect him to know who he was.

"I know who you are!" the man snapped as if reading his thoughts. "A stranger who came to our land to drink himself into a stupor, betraying his Queen. News travels in these islands. I won't take orders from a foolish drunkard like you, and if you take another step, that sword will find itself in your mouth."

"Leave her alone."

"Call yourself a virtuous man?" the man asked, laughing. "If she gives me my gold, I will do so."

"I don't have your gold. It was stolen from me," the woman said, hauling herself to her knees.

"Liar!" The man grabbed her by the hair, and John took a step towards him. "One more step, Long Arm, and you'll meet with a worse fate than hers."

"Leave her alone, Odo," came a voice.

John turned to see Jack standing a few feet away, holding a torch ablaze with fire.

"This whore robbed me!" Odo protested.

"Is it true that you took this man's gold?" Jack asked, looking at the fallen woman. Now, Odo had taken his hands off her.

"Yes," she admitted in a whisper.

"Why?"

"He visited the brothel I work at yesterday and hit one of the women... He hit her because she didn't lie with him a second time, even though he'd only paid for her to do so once! None of us could stop him, so I decided to take revenge on him."

"The bitch is lying! Her friend took my gold and didn't stick to her side of the bargain!" Odo protested.

"Go to the brothel. The women will confirm my side of the story," the woman said again.

Odo whirled around. "Shut up!"

Odo lifted his hand, about to hit her, but Jack raised his voice. "If you so much as dare to hit this woman again, I'll see to it that you're castrated."

"How dare you threaten me?" Odo's voice betrayed his fear and hesitation.

"Women who work in brothels don't have any lesser rights than any woman in our land. If these charges are confirmed, you'll suffer severe consequences. I suggest you leave this woman and get out of my sight as quickly as possible, and I'll overlook it this time. If I hear such accusations against you ever again, you will not get away with it," Jack said.

Odo stood still, like he was trying to come to a decision. "Very well," he said. He took one last look at the fallen woman and walked away.

Once Odo was gone, the woman stood and stumbled, struggling to remain upright. John moved to her side to help, but she raised a hand, signalling him to stay away. After regaining her balance, she began making her way back to town.

"If someone does what Odo did again, don't try to get revenge by stealing from them," Jack told her. "Another crime is not the way to avenge yourself for a crime. Speak to Begon's guards, and they'll help."

The woman nodded. "Thank you," she mumbled.

"Go now. Spend the gold you stole to eat something and take care of the woman Odo hit."

The young woman nodded again and hurried off. John sheathed his sword. Silence fell between them until the one-eyed man turned to John.

"I was right about your having a good heart after all, Long Arm. Few would have rushed to save a strange woman," Jack said.

John remained silent. He'd avoided meeting Jack since discovering he'd be sailing with him on Begon's mission. He knew Jack wasn't to blame, but if he talked to him, the one-eyed man would tell him about his plan, and John just wanted to forget the mission until they left the Ice Islands.

"Why did you let him go?" John asked after a while.

Jack frowned. "We don't have many builders in these Islands, and Odo is one of the best. He is also well loved by many. I didn't have the jurisdiction to punish him, and that woman did admit that she had robbed him."

"Such men shouldn't get away with crimes."

Jack laughed. "As I said, you have—"

"Shut up!" John snapped.

The man's smile didn't leave his face. "Are you happy to finally be travelling with me to unknown waters, living an adventure?"

John felt revulsion. "No."

"Meet me in the harbour tomorrow after sunset. I'm sure that what I show you will fill you with more enthusiasm for our trip."

Jack turned and left while John silently cursed his poor luck. He swore he must have lived other lives that were hopelessly boring. Only that could explain why, in this life, he never managed to find a moment's peace from trouble and misadventure.

The Frightened Prisoner

V elhisya's eyelids grew heavy. She hadn't managed to get a moment's sleep the night before, and the scene in Liher's chamber had replayed in her mind. She closed her eyes as she sat on the cold cell floor, and the image of fat hands on her body invaded her thoughts again, making her shiver. Liher's disgusting body had pinned her down as his hands fondled her until he was flung backward. She remembered a strange power spreading through her—a power more distinctive than she'd ever felt before.

Whatever that power may have been, it arose inside me at the right moment!

Velhisya had gone over everything her father had told her about the unique gifts of the elwyn, but what had happened didn't match anything she remembered. Liher seemed to have burnt at her touch, while she'd felt a maelstrom coursing through her veins. She remembered the image she had seen in her mind before the power had been unleashed—her mother looking at her with tearful eyes, her lips parted.

"I love you, Velhisya."

The memory brought tears to her eyes. It was the only memory she had of her mother. Velhisya had had no picture of her until her aunt had let her leave Wirskworth to free Selwyn. That day, her mother's face had found its way into her mind clearer than ever. She knew that it was the moment of her birth, the first image she'd ever had of her mother, and she wondered how such a distant memory had remained hidden in the depths of her mind all these years.

Nevertheless, none of that explained what had happened in the chamber where Liher had tried to rape her. Velhisya thought she'd killed him, but when the guards lifted his unconscious body, Liher had started coughing. He was immediately taken to a healer while a guard seized her and returned her to the dungeons. It felt like several hours had passed since the incident, yet no one had spoken to her, and the guards had brought her no food.

Perhaps Liher died shortly after what happened, she thought. That would have caused turmoil, and so far, no one had come for her. If the Governor were still alive, he would have sent men to punish her for what had happened.

No matter how hard she tried, she could make no sense of it. Velhisya wondered whether Lothar was alive. Liher had said he'd added herbs to his drink, but she was sure he'd killed him.

The sound of footsteps broke through her thoughts, and her heart started beating quickly. Whoever it was that was coming for her, it wouldn't be good. A man appeared in front of the barred gate leading to her cell.

"I thought I'd never see you again," Velhisya said as Lothar appeared. He hadn't visited her since that time she had asked him to kill her and save her from the fate that awaited her. She felt relief that he was alive.

"What happened? Are you alright?" Lothar asked from outside the cell, his face pale.

"Your brother tried to—" It was so heinous that she couldn't even say it. Velhisya was still wearing the dress Liher's maids had given her. She wanted to remove it, to tear it apart, but being naked in the cell would only bring more trouble. "He tried to rape me and then something strange happened," she said after a moment.

"I heard... The bastard put some herbs in my drink, and I passed out. Some of my loyal men were alarmed because they hadn't seen me for hours, and they found me unconscious in my chamber. They managed to get me right, and I raced to see if Liher had harmed you. That's when

I found him lying down, weak, and the healer told me that something like an invisible fire had struck his body. It's the first time I've ever seen my brother like that. He was babbling. What did you do to him?"

"I don't know. Such a thing has never happened to me before," Velhisya told him.

"You indeed have elwyn heritage," Lothar muttered.

"Why do you say that?"

"Whatever happened came from the elwyn blood that runs through your veins. Humans don't have such powers."

Velhisya had also considered that but couldn't figure out which elwyn power would do such a thing. "Your brother will kill me for what I did to him. He'll feel that I humiliated him in front of his men."

"As soon as he came to, he demanded that you be hanged," Lothar said.

Velhisya felt invisible nails being driven into her body, yet an optimistic thought found its way into her mind. "I'd rather die than lie with that disgusting man," she said.

"You won't die," Lothar told her.

"What do you mean?"

"I told my brother that I won't allow him to kill you. We had a heated argument once again, but as I've told you, Liher can't get me out of the way that easily. There's anger in Vylor about his deeds, and many men are loyal to me instead of to him."

"That didn't stop him from trying to rape me..."

Lothar sighed. "Liher is reckless and stupid. He didn't believe I would start a rebellion against him if he raped you. But I promise you that he won't try to sleep with you again. After what happened, he's afraid of you; I saw it in his eyes. Also, he won't kill you. He'd be a fool to do so until he knows for sure that your aunt is dead. Otherwise, she might attack him if she survives. I'll have a few of my men keep watch on the dungeons. If he tries to harm you again, I'll know immediately."

"Maybe next time he'll just put a deadly poison in your drink. He'll claim your death was an accident," Velhisya replied.

Lothar frowned. "No one will believe him. If I'm found dead in my sleep, everyone will be sure Liher was behind it. My brother won't admit it, but he's afraid of the riots that might break out if he does something like that. Our people might not have given a damn whether Liher raped you, but they won't sit idly by if I'm murdered. The Mercenaries may not be honourable, but they honour the men of my House. They still begrudge the fact that a Hale asked them to fight for a conqueror who murdered his brother."

Velhisya was tired of finding counter-arguments for his words. She felt exhausted and had no idea what would happen to her.

"There's more news that just reached the city."

Velhisya rose from the ground. "Have you heard about my aunt? Is she dead?" Velhisya asked, feeling a knot in her chest.

"No."

Velhisya breathed a sigh of relief. "Didn't Walter attack Wirskworth?" she asked.

"The news is strange," Lothar said.

"What do you mean?"

"We heard that part of Thorn's army attacked Wirskworth where they were defeated."

Velhisya felt a flutter of hope in her heart, yet something didn't make sense. "*A part* of Thorn's army?" she repeated.

Lothar nodded. "We don't know why Walter and the rest of his men didn't fight. It's rumoured by some that he attacked Aquarine while others say that he returned to Iovbridge."

"None of this makes any sense. Why would Walter attack a forgotten place like Aquarine? It doesn't add up that he returned to Iovbridge while his men were fighting the last of their enemies in Elmor."

"I know," Lothar said. "There are other rumours as well. Word's going around that elwyn and elves fought alongside Syrella and Elliot Egercoll, while giants riding wyverns were on Walter's side." Velhisya's heart stopped for a moment. If all that was true, it meant that Elliot had succeeded in setting the Elder Races free. His face flickered in her mind for a few moments. "Are you sure?" she asked.

"No. However, I have heard all of this from various merchants. It seems strange to me that everyone would make up the same false stories."

"I agree," Velhisya said. "And did my aunt defeat Walter's men while giants fought alongside them?"

"So, I heard. Even Liher seemed astonished by the news. He never expected Syrella to win a second battle against Thorn's men, let alone with giants riding wyverns at their side."

"I've never seen a wyvern before," Velhisya muttered, lost in thought.

"Me neither. In fact, until recently, I believed that the Elder Races and the wyverns were creatures of ancient times that no longer existed."

"I know that the rumours about me and my mother have spread throughout the kingdom. Did you also think that what was being said was a lie?"

"Yes, until I saw you for the first time... Then I began to change my mind," the man said.

"What changed when you saw me?"

Lothar smiled. "I've never seen a woman who looks like you. It's obvious that you're not fully human," he said, lowering his gaze. The man seemed lost for words for a few moments until he raised his head again. "There's one more rumour that has reached my ears. The men who claimed Walter attacked Aquarine reported that he did so astride a wyvern."

"Himself?" The man nodded. "That's impossible."

Lothar's brow furrowed as if he didn't know what to believe. "I, too, have heard that only giants could ride these monsters. Now, there are reports that they've been seen in the kingdom again and that one of them bonded with a human... It's all very strange."

"I imagine Liher is now truly perturbed about whether he needs my aunt's favour or that of Walter. No one knows who will prevail. Thorn has suffered two defeats for the first time in history, but there are still rumours that giants and wyverns are following his orders."

Lothar nodded. "Perhaps that's why he didn't insist on killing you even though you sullied his honour..." Lothar looked over his shoulder. "I have to be going now. I'll be sure to find out more about all this." He was about to leave, but he immediately turned back to her. "I'm sorry you're here again... Is there anything you need?"

"Food and new clothes," Velhisya said.

"I'll take care of it," Lothar said, and, with one last look, walked out of sight.

Velhisya sat back down on the ground, trying to process the information Lothar had told her. Elliot's image whirled through her mind, bringing her a sense of hope. If the rumours were true, he was the one who had put an end to the torment that had plagued her mother's race for centuries. She wished she could hug him.

The sound of footsteps reached her ears again. *What could Lothar have forgotten?*

Velhisya listened in silence when a voice pierced her eardrums.

"Throw him in here!" said a man while shadows danced in the torchlight on the wall opposite her cell.

She heard the door of the cell next to hers open, followed immediately by a thud. The door closed, and the footsteps faded into the dark dungeons. It was the first time she'd seen another prisoner brought into the cells since she'd been captured. In Vylor, it was more common for people to be punished by death than be imprisoned.

Velhisya got up again and approached the wall that separated her cell from the one next to it. "Is anyone there?" she asked in a low voice.

She didn't hear a thing until a sound that seemed like breathing reached her ears. "Who are you?" came a loud male voice. His tone betrayed his youth, and she guessed he was her age.

"Don't raise your voice! The guards will hear us!" Velhisya whispered, eyes darting to the cell door.

"Are you imprisoned here, too?" the voice asked in a lower tone. Velhisya could hear the man's shallow breath behind the wall that separated them.

"Yes. Why were you imprisoned?"

"My father is a rich merchant from Kerth." His voice trailed off for a few seconds. "Three Mercenaries who happen to be guards in Goldtown claim that the last goods he sold them were bad... They demanded that they get their gold back, but my father refused. Then, just before he set sail for Kerth, they caught me and brought me here. I believe they didn't kill me because they want to ask for ransom. They told me that Liher Hale himself had found out about my father's fraud and had asked for him to be punished for the wrongdoing he'd done to his men," the lad continued, breathing heavily.

Velhisya felt sorry for him. Even if the Mercenaries' accusations were true, the merchant's son shouldn't have to pay for it.

"Why are you here?" asked the man.

"My aunt sent a messenger here. Liher held him captive and demanded a ransom for his release, and then my aunt sent me to free him. The plan failed, and the men who accompanied me died while I was taken prisoner."

"Who is your aunt?"

"Syrella Endor."

"The Ruler of Elmor?" His tone of voice revealed his astonishment.

"Yes," Velhisya replied. She hadn't expected her aunt to be held in esteem by a man from Kerth.

"What's your name?"

"Velhisya. Yours?"

"Matt."

They remained silent for a while until Matt's voice came again in a faint whisper. "I fear what they'll do to me if my father doesn't pay. I'm truly afraid, Velhisya."

Velhisya touched the cold stone of the wall. "Fate has sent both of us to this place so that we can overcome our fears, Matt. Together, we'll succeed."

A Dead Man

Syrella stared at the two golden snakes twined around her seat. Lately, she'd been spending more time in the Great Hall of Moonstone. She felt that the room reminded her of who she really was and gave her strength for everything she had to do. The morning sun's rays danced on the Hall walls while Syrella sat lost in thought.

I mustn't lose heart... I am Syrella of the House of Endor. Those who paid me with treachery will get what they deserve. She repeated those words to herself, and as she looked around the Great Hall, all her ancestors who had ruled within the castle passed before her eyes. The Endors had ruled Elmor since the era of the First Kings, and alongside the Egercolls, they'd brought glory to the south. Walter Thorn may have hurt her House, but she was still alive and had to send a message. She had to remind everyone that the Endors weren't cowardly and would do anything to punish those who showed their House any disrespect.

"Excuse me, my lady."

Syrella turned in the chair to see Jahon watching her. He wore a white jerkin, and his yellow-black cloak touched the ground. "I didn't notice you coming into the hall," she said.

"You seemed deep in thought," the man said and closed the door.

"I was," she responded tersely.

Syrella had been angry with him the past few days. He had said they shouldn't risk sending their army to Vylor at one of their council meetings debating Velhisya's future. Jahon knew full well how important her niece was to her, yet he hadn't supported her.

"How much longer will you ignore me?" Jahon asked, raising his voice.

"I don't understand what you're getting at."

"You know what I mean."

Syrella sighed and gave him a deadly look. "Do you have something you want to say?"

He took a step towards her. "I know you're angry because I didn't support your plan to save Velhisya." Syrella folded her arms across her chest, waiting for him to continue. "I was afraid... I don't want what happened at the Forked River to ever happen again. I remember how sure you were that nobody would anticipate our plan at the time."

Syrella frowned. "I'm trying to remember how many times I've told you that Velhisya is all that remains of my brother. All the people of my House, apart from her and my daughters, are dead!"

"I know—"

"You know nothing! How can I sit, arms folded, when Velhisya is being held hostage by Liher Hale? Each night I close my eyes, I see his disgusting body touching her—torturing her!"

"He might not hurt her."

"Are you an idiot?!" Syrella shouted and slammed a fist on the arm of her chair. "The Mercenaries have raped and sown bastards through-out their history. I only met Liher once before he even became ruler of Vylor... I asked him why they'd never sought to bring the tradition of marriage to their land. Do you know what he said?" Jahon didn't respond, looking puzzled. "*Even if a marriage brought me gold and valuable alliances, I'd rather have dozens of women in my bed. Whichever bride I took would hate me and the alliances would be lost as soon as she saw the whores strolling into our chamber every night*."

Jahon seemed stupefied.

"Do you think Liher wouldn't rape a woman as beautiful as Velhisya? He won't believe his luck that we sent her into his arms."

"I don't want Velhisya to come to any harm," Jahon said in a low voice.

"However, if we all die, none of it will matter! I was trying to find the best solution." Syrella looked away, rage eating away at her insides. "We need as many soldiers as possible to deal with Thorn! If we free Velhisya and in a few weeks Walter takes the city, what could happen to her in Vylor will happen to her here. Merhya, Linaria, you will all fall into the hands of the enemy!"

"BE QUIET!" Syrella screamed and jumped to her feet. His words had evoked pictures in her mind she didn't want to imagine.

"Do you believe that your rage will stand in Walter's way?"

Her cheeks burned while hatred boiled up inside her like lava. She knew Jahon was trying to help, but she couldn't control herself. Her House had lost its power, and not only was it in danger of being destroyed, but its remaining members were also in grave danger of leaving the world dishonourably.

"Our army will march on to Vylor despite my apprehensions. We've agreed on what to do, and we have to prepare for the battle against Thorn. We must be united. Anger won't help us," Jahon went on.

"Until the war is over, you won't come to my chamber again," Syrella told him.

His eyes widened. "Do you still want to punish me?"

"You're a fool!" Syrella snapped and sat back down again. "You tell me that we have to defeat Walter, that we must do everything in our power to avoid falling into the hands of his men... If anyone sees us together, if our secret leaks out, there'll be friction in the city. It's the last thing we need just before the last battle."

"A few days ago, you insisted that Elmor was devoted to you! You told me that nothing would happen as long as you were the ruler of this land, and you were afraid that after your death, our daughters would be the ones who would pay for our sins if our secret got out."

"That's all true."

"Then why are you afraid of the discord our relationship might sow now?"

Syrella was furious. "I never expected I would have to face wyverns in my city. One of those monsters was enough to destroy the gate. The morale of the men is hanging by a thread! I don't want anything to distract them!"

Jahon sighed heavily. "Nobody has seen us since—"

"Everybody has suspected the truth. They simply don't dare to believe it," Syrella said. "For someone as clever as Sophie, it only took a few days for her to realise it... Imagine if the rumours begin to spread like wildfire just before the battle against Walter... Sadon Burns, my dead husband's father and the lord with the most soldiers devoted to him, has been turning against me lately. If he believes the rumours to be true, he might cause trouble for me. You talk about how dangerous it is to attack Vylor, but you haven't given a moment's thought to *this* danger."

"I remember you saying that Sadon's power is insignificant compared to yours and your House."

"And I was right! However, this is no simple battle. Elwyn, elves, wyverns... I don't want anything else to distract my men now." Syrella was angry with him. He cared only about himself.

Jahon seemed unconvinced. "Even if someone were to see us, no one would know how long we've been sleeping together. Your husband died a long time ago. It isn't a crime if you found someone after his death," he said.

"Do you think it would be wise to have something like this leak out now?"

Jahon frowned. "If you keep shouting, everybody will learn our secret today," he said. "No... We'll do as you wish," he added firmly after a few moments, tearing his gaze away from her.

The door of the Great Hall burst open with a thud. "Lady Endor! Lady Endor!" A bedraggled guard rushed inside and ran towards her.

"What's going on?" Syrella asked, sitting up straight.

"We have a new emissary from Vylor," the guard said breathlessly.

Syrella shivered. "Bring him here immediately," she said. "Send word to my daughters and Selwyn Brau to come here." *Liher dared to send a messenger to my city again!* She thought angrily.

The guard nodded curtly and left the Great Hall.

Once the doors closed, Syrella jumped up and began pacing up and down, clenching her fists. "That damned Hale wants to ask for my gold again..."

"I didn't expect him to send a messenger again since the last one didn't return," Jahon said pensively.

"He knows that my relationship with the Queen isn't good. I'm sure he expected I wouldn't give all my gold for Selwyn Brau. He sent an emissary to say those words to sow discord. I'm certain he was laughing at the thought of our faces upon hearing his demands. Nevertheless, things are different now. He suspects I'd do anything for my niece."

Jahon's frown deepened. *What should I do?* Syrella pondered. She sat in her seat again, and her eyes fell upon the yellow and black banners decorating the corners of the hall. The sunlight made them glisten while the hunting trophies hanging on the walls took on a red hue.

"I didn't think you'd summon Brau's son here." Jahon broke the silence.

"Since the day he set foot in the city, he's wanted to free Velhisya. He deserves to be the first to hear the news," Syrella replied.

Her legs twitched in anticipation until she saw figures begin entering the hall. Her daughters were armoured with yellow and black cloaks fluttering behind them, long swords hanging from their belts.

"Did Liher send another emissary?" Merhya asked as she approached. Syrella nodded stiffly.

"I imagine he'll meet the same fate as the previous one," Linaria said, and then Selwyn entered the hall. He wore his navy blue jerkin and brown leather pants as he walked towards her.

"Where is the messenger?" Selwyn asked.

"He'll be here soon," Jahon said. Selwyn's eyes revealed his eagerness.

"You seem excited," Syrella remarked pointedly.

"Of course! The fact that Liher sent an emissary means that Velhisya is alive and that he wants to negotiate her release," Selwyn replied.

Syrella felt foolish. She'd been so wrapped up in her worry and frustration for days that she could no longer think clearly. Selwyn was right, and she wondered why neither Jahon nor her daughters mentioned that fact.

Selwyn met her gaze. "I'm sure Liher won't harm Velhisya for a few days. He'll wait until his emissary returns. That means if we arrive at his land around the time he'd be expecting his messenger, she—"

"My niece will remain alive," Syrella said. The younger Brau's words were so obvious, she couldn't believe she hadn't realised it sooner. She felt a glimmer of hope, having almost forgotten what that felt like over the past few days.

Three men appeared at the Great Hall's open doors. A short, thin young man with red hair and black clothes walked ahead of two armoured city guards.

"What news does Liher send me this time?" Syrella asked before the messenger had got near, her voice carrying through the Hall.

The messenger sized her up for a few moments. "The Governor of Vylor sent me to negotiate the terms of the release of Velhisya Endor," he said.

Silence spread in the hall for a few moments.

"Do you have some sort of letter from Liher?" Syrella asked.

The man shook his head. "My lord told me that you sent Velhisya to his land. You know that she's there, so there's no reason for you to doubt my words."

"I'm curious about something," Jahon said, and the messenger turned to face him, bewildered. "Everyone in the kingdom knew we were expecting an attack from Walter by now, and most thought we'd be defeated... We may have won the battle, but news takes days to travel the kingdom. For you to be here so soon, I think you left for Elmor before the news had reached Liher. Did he expect us to have won the battle?"

The lad smiled. "You're right, my lord... The news hadn't reached Liher when he ordered me to ride to Wirskworth. He asked me to find out what had happened and if you'd survived, to bring you his message."

"That man is cunning. He wanted you to be prepared to ask for gold even if he didn't think we'd win!" Jahon scoffed.

"And here we are," the messenger retorted.

"What is Liher asking for to free my niece?" Syrella asked.

"The same as he asked for the release of Selwyn Brau. My Ruler wants all the gold in this region. Every piece of gold that belongs to you, as well as to your lords, will need to be delivered into his hands."

Naturally... One day I will castrate that scumbag, Syrella thought, hatred bubbling up. "And if I refuse?"

"Then, Velhisya Endor will hang," the young man said.

"You're brave to come here. I imagine you know what happened to the last messenger who uttered such words to me." She could have sworn she saw a glint of fear in the young man's eyes.

"If I don't return, Velhisya Endor will die," the messenger said in a steady voice.

"How do I know she isn't already dead?"

"What would my ruler have to gain from that?"

Syrella put her hands on the arms of her chair. "Selwyn escaped from Goldtown a few days ago." Her gaze fell on the younger Brau, and the emissary looked at him in surprise. "When he arrived in my city, he told me that he'd been tortured at the hands of your ruler. Has my niece been tortured, too?"

"I don't know anything about that," the young man replied bluntly.

"I'd reconsider that answer," Syrella said, her tone hinting at a threat.

"I've spoken the truth. I don't know—"

"Do you know you're a dead man?" Syrella snapped, and the lad gulped, growing pale. "When you left your land to come here, Liher knew he was sending a dead man to my city. He knew that the words you brought would be punishable by death—that's why he didn't give you any soldiers for this trip. Nonetheless, if you tell me all I want to know, you'll meet with a better death than what awaits you currently."

Out of the corner of her eye, she saw Selwyn looking at her strangely, as if he wanted to say something.

"Whatever I might say would be a lie. They sent me here to bring you the conditions for the release of Velhisya Endor. I don't know anything else." The young emissary's voice was now filled with palpable fear.

"Very well. Undress him and bring me his manhood," Syrella said, looking at Merhya.

Her daughter drew her sword and advanced towards the messenger while the city guards held him down.

"I don't know anything! I'm telling the truth!" he shouted.

"So, you're useless to me. Liher sent you here to insult me, to threaten me that if I don't give him all the gold in my land, he'll spill my blood. You should have thought more wisely before coming here. You should have run away and never returned to Vylor. Those who bring such words to me are punished by death, even if they are mere messengers."

Merhya grabbed the emissary by the shoulder and brought her sword between his legs.

"No!" came Selwyn's voice.

Syrella's head snapped in his direction, eyes narrowing. "Lord Brau, I brought you here out of respect as I know you care for my niece. Know your place!" she said.

"Velhisya is worth Elmor's gold," Selwyn told her.

"Are you suggesting I give all the gold in my land to Liher?" The truth was that, if it were up to her, she wouldn't hesitate to give the Lord of Vylor whatever he asked for, but she couldn't.

"Yes," Selwyn insisted.

If he doesn't hold his tongue, I'll throw him out of the room. "I'd really like to, Lord Brau," Syrella said. "However, if I do, my councillors and every lord in my land will be irate. I don't want any discord, especially since Walter will soon be at our doorstep."

"The lords will obey their ruler. Send this man back to Vylor to bring the news to his Governor—to tell him that if he harms Velhisya, the deal is off and that we will deliver the gold in about three weeks."

Merhya left the messenger and waited for orders while Syrella stared into space. Selwyn was a genius... Her men needed about twenty days to reach Liher's land. The return of the messenger offered them a chance to arrive in Goldtown and strike under the guise of delivering the gold to him.

"The lords of Elmor are compelled to accept your demands," Selwyn added.

Syrella turned to the young emissary. "Very well. I should have considered your words more carefully, Lord Brau," she said, casting a glance at Selwyn. He bowed.

"Go back to your Governor and tell him that he'll get his gold in approximately twenty days. I'll be sending a few dozen men to deliver it. However, if I find out that he has so much as harmed a hair on my niece's head, the deal's off."

The emissary nodded fearfully without taking his eyes off Merhya's sword still pointed at his manhood. "I'd like a letter for my Governor," he whispered in a trembling voice.

Syrella scoffed. "Of course. Hold this man at the castle entrance until I write the letter, and then you will escort him out of the city," she told the guards.

They pushed the young man towards the exit, and Merhya sheathed her sword.

Syrella turned to the left where Selwyn stood, renewed hope welling up inside her. "I should have had you on my council years ago, Selwyn Brau."

Liquid Fire

John looked around, but he couldn't find the part of the coast he was searching for. The wind was strong, and soon it would be dark. He would have preferred to have been in some inn drinking wine, but he was, nevertheless, looking for the place where he'd agreed to meet Jack. The one-eyed man had told him to find him in the old harbour of the Grand Island, which nobody used these days.

"Why do you want to meet in an abandoned port?" he'd asked.

"I want to show you some things away from prying eyes," Jack had answered with a smile.

Damn. John had regretted having agreed to meet him. He moved up the hill along a rugged path near the coastline, and the rocks hindered him from moving quickly. Suddenly, the wind picked up and gripped at his jerkin tightly, and his pace slowed. He lifted his head and looked out to sea, unable to see any pier.

I'll turn back, he told himself. It wasn't his fault that Jack hadn't given him proper directions to find that damn port.

He turned around and began walking back, lost in thought. John had considered running away from Grand Island countless times the moment Begon had given him that mission. However, it was impossible to leave the cursed island. The autumnal storms hadn't abated yet, and he'd heard that Begon had forbidden his men from transporting him anywhere aboard their ships. He was trying to keep his balance when he tripped over something hard.

"Damn, Long Arm!"

John managed to catch himself at the last moment, and then he saw a disagreeable-looking man before him. "What are you doing here?" he asked Raff.

"I'm on my way to find Jack... For you to be here, you probably had the same objective until you decided to make a run for it."

"I didn't run away! I couldn't find that stupid old port."

"Follow me," Raff said in a disgruntled tone and started walking.

"What are *you* doing here?" John asked, eyes narrowing.

"Haven't you heard the news? I'll be coming with you on the trip." Raff stopped short and turned back to him.

John cursed his fate. He didn't want to spend days on a ship with a man who would constantly talk about the Queen and Elliot. "Why do you want to join us?"

"The fishermen who disappeared were my friends. I want to know what happened to them! Besides, Jack will need a second captain."

"We don't need a second captain. The water in the sea north of Knightdorn isn't so deep. We can drop anchor when Jack is asleep."

Raff scoffed. "Maybe the strong storms will diminish in a few days, but nobody knows whether they'll return or if the sea will stay wild until the middle of winter. No anchor would be able to hold a ship at this time of year. You've forgotten life at sea, Long Arm," he said with a hint of sarcasm. "Besides, the islet we're looking for is far north, and the waters there are deeper than you think."

Jon sighed. "I can't believe that there are men who'd ask to travel there..." he said, raising his palms.

"We're not all cowardly like you."

John snorted contemptuously. "Better a coward and alive than brave and dead."

Raff ignored him, moving further away. John took a deep breath and followed him as daylight faded from the sky. They walked for hours as the wind got stronger.

"Where's the damned port?" John called to Raff, who was ahead of him.

"Shut up and walk."

John cursed inwardly as the cold began to freeze his body under his woollen clothes. *Damned Begon. The Leader of the Ice Islands ought to have thanked me for never giving him the letter Syrella had written on Sophie's behalf.* The Ice Islands would be better off without fighting, and yet, Begon had punished him...

"Open your eyes, idiot!"

John raised his head and saw that Raff had turned left. He looked towards the shore and saw a pier, a ship tied up to it. *At last.* They'd walked so far that it would soon be dark, making his return to the small town on the Grand Island difficult.

John quickened his pace, unintentionally kicking large rocks. The small hill they walked along was hard and dry, full of boulders and stones. His feet ached through his boots. A little later, he saw the ship by the abandoned pier clearly, and the man standing next to it.

"I thought you'd never get here!" Jack stood with his arms crossed.

"One might say that this place isn't close to the town," John huffed.

"Even our women moan less than you, Long Arm!" Jack snapped.

"Why did you bring us here? Did you want us to admire your infamous ship before the trip?" John asked, annoyed.

"Stop talking and follow me."

Jack walked onto the pier and climbed a wooden plank that reached the ship's deck. John followed carefully with Raff close on his heels. A moment later, he stepped onto the deck and saw Jack heading for the large cabin below the captain's helm.

"What do you want to show us?" John asked.

"Would you rather I tell you or show you?" shouted the one-eyed man.

"Where do we have to go?"

"To the lower deck of the ship." Jack grabbed a torch hanging outside the large cabin. The firelight fell on the thin piece of cloth that covered his one eye.

Jack entered the large cabin while John and Raff followed in silence. They went to the left corner of the room and climbed down a wooden ladder, which led to the ship's lowest deck. Jack passed by some cabin doors until they found themselves behind some strange objects with nozzles stuck into round openings in the hull of the ship.

"Now you are looking at the deadliest weapon ever made," Jack said.

John smiled, thinking the man in front of him had lost his mind. "What are these pipes?"

Jack's face was inscrutable. "When you understand, it'll wipe that smile off your face, idiot."

John looked at the strange pipes once again. Their base had been driven into the ship's wood. "Do you intend to spray water at whoever attacked the fishermen?" John said playfully.

"As the years go by, you become more and more idiotic, Long Arm."

"What do these pipes do?" Raff asked.

"They go as far as the hold where there's a contraption I invented myself," Jack responded. "I made a liquid that is the deadliest the world has ever seen... Anyone who attacks us will rue the day they tried." Jack's lone eye shone brightly against the torchlight.

"What does this liquid do?" John took a step closer.

"It's the most flammable thing I've ever seen. Whatever comes into contact with it immediately catches fire—even water."

"Water?" John repeated, his brow furrowing.

"Yes, Liquid Fire ignites when it comes into contact with water."

"How is that possible? What's this liquid made of?" John asked, doubting the one-eyed man's words.

Jack frowned. "That's a secret. No one but me knows how to make this liquid, and no one will."

"Why?" Raff asked.

"Because it's very dangerous. If anyone finds out how it's made, it may be used against us one day. I wouldn't want to see pirates or Walter Thorn with Liquid Fire on their ships."

"If this liquid is as flammable as you say, how come it doesn't burn the pipes?" John wasn't convinced.

"These pipes are made of copper. It's the only material I found which can withstand the Liquid Fire."

Raff brought his hand to his chin. "And you intend to hurl it at anyone who attacks us?" he asked.

Jack nodded. "Begon doesn't want to send an army to Mermainthor. He isn't sure who's attacking the fishermen and doesn't want a fight with Walter's men until he's certain. If we sail with a lot of ships, the northerners may fear that we want a naval battle and attack us. We're alone on this trip, and I want us to be ready to face enemy ships. Whoever attacks us will regret it."

"How did you discover this liquid?" Raff eyed Jack.

"I'd been trying to make a new weapon for a long time. I wanted something that could stop even a dozen enemy ships, and I finally succeeded."

"Even if all you say is true, we have to be careful," John said. "No one has used this weapon before. If this liquid falls onto our ship by mistake, we will be the ones who will be burnt."

"That's why I called you here," Jack said. "If we're attacked, I'll run to the hold and fill the cauldron that feeds the pipes with Liquid Fire while Raff takes the helm. You'll be in command here." He glanced at John. "You and the sailors will see to it that we get our enemies. I wanted you to know before we set sail, as you will have to practise handling the pipes."

John wasn't sure he was happy about everything he'd heard. He knew full well that all new weapons that had been invented had killed many of those who had been first to use them. If the liquid was as deadly as Jack insisted it was, he wasn't sure he wanted it on their ship. "The sailors must also be trained with me," he said.

"I don't want anyone else to know a thing about this until we leave the Grand Island. You can train a few once we set sail. I think the storms will die down in about ten days," Jack responded.

"Who else knows?" Raff asked.

"Only Begon."

"Did Begon not want to know the secret formula for the production of this liquid?" John crossed his arms.

"No. He agrees that it's best if I am the only one who knows for the time being. I'll make sure we have enough of it by the time we set off on our journey."

"I'm sure that we'll find out whatever happened to the fishermen with you as captain. I'm pleased with everything I heard today," Raff said, smiling.

Jack nodded sharply.

"I'm not that happy!" John snapped. "I don't know if this weapon is all you say it is... Nevertheless, if it is, we have to be very careful, and I hope we find answers without getting into a battle."

"I'll be waiting for you here at the break of dawn. I want to see how well the pipes work," Jack told him.

John would rather have spent his morning in a brothel, but he couldn't refuse. "Time to go back to my inn then," he muttered.

"You're lucky you have gold in your pockets from the Queen and Syrella Endor... Otherwise, you'd be sleeping in some stable," Raff said in a dismissive tone.

"Even before I got this gold, I used to spend my nights in the best inns in Iovbridge with the most beautiful whores by my side."

"Liar! With what gold?" Raff spat.

"There are always easy jobs for an ex-bounty hunter... "

"Who would hire a coward like you?"

"Every foolish lord offers a reward for the men who owe him. Those jobs pay well, and you don't need to be brave to do them."

"And what do you need?"

"Something you never had, Raff. Brains."

John laughed, gave a theatrical bow and left the ship as fast as he could.

The Reckless Ruler

Syrella's voice grew hoarse as she finished her account under the gaze of many eyes. Moonlight poured through the windows of the Great Hall, covering those present with a silvery sheen. "The emissary will give our men time to reach Vylor without Velhisya losing her life," she added, feeling a newfound optimism that night.

"I understand you want to save your niece, Your Majesty. However, I'm still not convinced that this journey will be safe for our soldiers," Sadon Burns said. He was the only one present who had found the courage to speak up.

Syrella took note of his silk clothing as she made herself more comfortable in her seat, trying to curb her rage. "The decision has been made, Lord Burns. I summoned you here to tell you about the arrival of the envoy from Vylor, not to discuss the plan again."

"This is all good news. We planned to send an army, not knowing whether Velhisya was alive. Now, we are certain that the Governor's niece is safe, and we have ensured that she will remain so until our armies reach Hale's land," Jahon said, unwaveringly.

Syrella felt satisfied upon hearing his words and looked at Sadon once more.

"I know the decision has been made," said the flabby, aged lord. "However, I'm afraid that the key the young Brau showed us won't be of any help and the siege will be bloody... I'm sure Liher Hale will look into the conditions that allowed Selwyn to escape and will replace the lock to the secret passage."

"I disagree." Aleron's countenance was serene, yet his voice rang out loud and clear in the Great Hall. "From what I've heard about this man, I'm now certain that he's arrogant and vicious. Nevertheless, he doesn't sound smart, and his vanity will keep him from thinking we're about to attack him. He knows that Syrella and Sophie have been weakened after so many battles against Walter and that another is brewing."

"All of that may be true, but you're missing something, my lord," Sadon said, turning to the elwyn. "Nobody expected us to win a battle against Walter. The fact that we've faced his men twice and are still alive has probably surprised the whole kingdom. Liher has always wanted to find himself in the favour of the winner, and our victories have shown him that we aren't weak. Knowing all this, he might fear an attack from us and decide to be on the defensive."

"Do you think Liher would imprison an emissary from Walter's camp, Lord Burns?" Aleron asked.

The lord took on a puzzled look. "No," Sadon said after a moment.

"Exactly. This is your proof that Liher is terrified of Walter, though he isn't at all afraid of Syrella and Sophie," Aleron said. "The fact that we're still alive shows that we aren't as weak as most thought, but no one believes that we'll win the war eventually. Liher is trying to take advantage of the time before we're destroyed to get gold. He knows we're going to die soon, or else he wouldn't dare ask for all of Elmor's gold for one woman..."

Sadon opened his mouth and then shut it. Aleron's words had disarmed him.

"I agree with Aleron. No one in the whole kingdom would expect us to attack his city..." Lord Sygar Reis said.

"I also agree," said Richard Lamont, a captain of Iovbridge.

Syrella was pleased that most of her noblemen agreed with her decisions, and even Sophie's councillors hadn't expressed any doubts. She prayed they would succeed, and it was one of the few times in her life she invoked the God of Souls. For a moment, Edmund, the high priest of

Elmor, came to mind. The elderly high priest was now sick and weak and no longer came to their council meetings. For years, Edmund had been trying to convince her about the powers of their god-protector but to no avail. Unlike most people in the kingdom, Syrella had never believed in the gods. However, she knew that a ruler had to honour the gods to win over the dedication of the common people, so she showed them her reverence. Most people close to her knew she didn't harbour much respect for the *all-powerful* beings worshipped in Knightdorn. Nevertheless, something had changed recently. A piece of her now believed more in the power of the God of Souls. Edmund had told her that their god wouldn't allow the death of her niece, and Syrella had felt that to be true. Velhisya had to return home alive, and she hoped that Liher Hale hadn't harmed her.

"So be it." Sadon's voice broke the silence. "Us lords have given you our men, Your Majesty. These men belong to you, and the lords of Elmor will be forever grateful to you for allowing them to command their soldiers without paying taxes though they left their castles and moved to Wirskworth," he added with a bow.

"Very well," Syrella said. "It's time this council ended."

"I wanted to ask you a question, Lady Endor," Richard Lamont said.

"Speak freely, my lord."

"Have you had any news about Walter since his last defeat?"

Syrella had so devoted herself to saving Velhisya that she often forgot that they were expecting another attack on Wirskworth. "No. The only news I've heard was what Solor, the lord who escaped from Aquarine, told us," she replied.

"Exactly," Richard said with a nod. "No one can be sure why Walter chose to attack Aquarine, and I suspect he's furious about the death of his men on your land. I think he's up to something. He knows he can't lose again. I fear his attack will be devastating, and we aren't well-prepared... We've been discussing setting free Velhisya Endor for days, but this won't save us from Thorn."

Syrella recalled everything Sophie had told her about Richard—pessimistic and suggestive. "Richard the Fiend" was his nickname, according to the Queen. "We know there may be wyverns on Thorn's side. We've agreed that the elwyn and elves will help us fortify Wirskworth as best we can," she said and noted an ornate knife strapped to Richard's belt.

"Walter always catches his enemies off guard. I'm afraid there's a lot we don't know... And... And I shudder at the thought that the Queen, Peter, and Elliot might fall into a trap in Kerth." Richard took a step towards her. A pegasus was sewn onto his green jerkin.

"I believe Sophie will return to Elmor with the Emperor's men, Lord Lamont. Odin Mud has wanted to gain a foothold in Knightdorn for years, and with Thorn on the throne, he'll never succeed. He needs Sophie. As for Walter, we can't do anything more but posit assumptions... It wouldn't be wise to waste our time searching for his plans. We'll be as well-prepared as we can," Syrella told him.

"Walter has the largest army and the largest fleet in Knightdorn. We simply have to be prepared for anything," Sygar said with a false smile that reflected his pessimism.

"His fleet is of no use in Wirskworth. If he intended to lay siege to Iovbridge, he could use the men from Tahos and attack from the Scarlet Sea. In Wirskworth, he can only fight us with his infantry and his wyverns, and we'll manage to deal with them," Aleron added, taking the floor again. The elwyn's blue cloak shone under the faint light of the torches.

She was about to ask those present to leave again when a thought sprung to mind. "Thorn no longer has that many men," she said.

"After his two defeats, his forces have been greatly diminished. However, he has more than us." Linaria, who had crossed her arms in front of her chest, spoke for the first time.

Syrella's gaze went to the long sword hanging from her daughter's belt as her thoughts raced. "If we could force him to fight on two fronts, I think he'd lose…"

"On two fronts? What do you mean, Your Majesty?" Jahon asked, and Linaria seemed just as bewildered.

"You said that no one in the kingdom would anticipate our attack. Iovbridge could be laid siege to from the sea."

"And so?" Jahon pressed.

"If a fleet attacked Iovbridge while Walter lay siege to Wirskworth, Thorn would be forced to rush to Isisdor. He wouldn't let himself lose the throne now that he's become King. That would be very humiliating for him."

"We don't have a fleet, Your Majesty." Jahon looked at her as if she'd lost her mind. "If you're hoping the Ice Islands will help us, I'm certain they won't."

"I don't care about the Ice Islands. However, Tahos has no men. Its ships would easily fall into the hands of whoever marched their army there."

"That goes for every one of Walter's allies. All the soldiers are on Thorn's side. Are you suggesting that we attack all the territories that are against us because they have no army?" Sadon asked, his voice dripping with sarcasm. Syrella shot him a threatening look.

"Tahos has a fleet, and it will fall more easily than any other city in the kingdom…" Syrella said.

"And how are we going to send an army to Tahos?" Selwyn took a step forward.

"There's no one guarding the northern or the central regions. Even though Walter travelled to Aquarine a few days ago, logic suggests he will regroup in Iovbridge. My men could march on Tahos once they've saved Velhisya and take its fleet." Syrella felt the God of Souls had sent her both clarity of thought and power.

"Will our few men free Velhisya and then march on to Tahos to conquer it?" Sadon asked.

"Our small number of soldiers is still more than Tahos has. They have none!" Syrella insisted.

"Your Majesty, allow me to disagree with this plan," Jahon said as he stood before her, his face reddening. "Our men don't know how to sail ships or command a fleet. If they march on Tahos, no one will be left here to face Walter's siege!"

"Even half our men could take Tahos! The rest can return here once Velhisya has been freed. Do you remember how Walter took Tahos? If we do what he did, it will be easy to—"

"Lady Endor!" Aleron's voice echoed through the Hall, and Elmor and Iovbridge's councillors turned to the aged elwyn. "The agreement the Elder Races made with you and the Queen was to help you save your niece. If we don't get into Goldtown quietly, we will lay siege to it for three days. If we pass through its gates, we'll try to hand over its leadership to Lothar Hale, asking him for an alliance that will bring us even more men. Nothing more!"

Syrella was upset. "Aler—"

"We cannot march on to Tahos! We cannot lay siege to other cities while waiting for an enemy attack. We have too few soldiers, and Walter will attack with the wyverns and Orhyn's Shadow drenched on every one of his men's blades if our information is correct," the elwyn told her firmly.

"I agree. This is no time for recklessness, and what was agreed with the Queen must be abided by," Thorold said, standing dressed in black.

"I agree with Aleron," Richard told her. "We have a lot to deal with. It's crazy to talk about an attack on Tahos."

Syrella felt she had to surrender to what the advisors were saying. "Very well. The soldiers will start for Vylor at first light. Nothing more than we've agreed upon will be done."

Many people nodded curtly in agreement.

"There's one more thing," Selwyn said.

Syrella felt a hint of irritation. The council meeting had lasted longer than she'd wanted. "What's troubling you, Lord Brau?"

Selwyn frowned. "As soon as Vylor's emissary returns to Liher, he'll find out that Elmor's soldiers will be marching to his land. We can't carry that much gold without guards. He might fear an army, albeit a small one, approaching his city, and he might increase the watches in Goldtown."

"You were the one who prompted me to send the emissary back!" Syrella exclaimed.

"Of course. I wanted to be sure that Velhisya would stay alive. Nevertheless, we may lose the element of surprise."

"A man like Walter may well be careful, however, from what I've heard about Lord Hale, I doubt he'll increase his watches," Aleron told him. "He isn't expecting us to attack him, and a few dozen men guarding Elmor's gold isn't a threat to his city. I've agreed with the generals that we'll approach quietly and along the paths near the Lonely Mountain. Those parts are deserted, with no traders or mercenaries roaming their paths, and our scouts will see to it that nobody notices us until we reach Goldtown. The small forest west of the city will give us good cover, so we can approach it without being seen. About five hundred men will travel with carts along the main road that leads to Goldtown so that Liher may be informed of our approach. He won't find out about the rest of our army. If we succeed in quietly setting Velhisya free, he won't dare pursue us. We have twice as many men. It would be foolish of him to attack us in the open. I think there's no better plan, given the circumstances."

"I agree with Aleron," Syrella said, rising from her seat. "This council is over."

"Your Majesty!" A guard entered the hall. It was the man who had informed her of the emissary from Vylor arriving that same morning.

"What's the matter?" Syrella asked.

"Governor Borin Ballard."

Syrella seldom heard that name even though the former Governor of Ballar lived in her city lately. "What about him?"

"He's dead—died in his sleep. My men informed me a moment ago."

Borin was old and weak, but the news shocked her. Gasps filled the hall as those present exchanged uneasy glances, murmuring in disbelief. "I'll see to it that a ceremony is held in his name immediately, and his men will have to swear allegiance to me and the Queen," Syrella said after a few moments of silence.

"Ballard's captains tried to assassinate the Queen a few months ago. We have to be careful. Walter had his men around Borin," Richard told her.

"I know!" Syrella snapped. "However, those who remained followed the Queen here without incident. I believe that those of Ballard's men who were supporters of Walter have been exposed, and the rest will fight on our side. I'll speak to them at first light. You are excused."

"Very well." Richard bowed slightly, and others did the same.

Syrella glanced at her daughters. "Linaria, Merhya."

Her daughters exchanged looks with each other and remained standing until everyone else had left the hall.

"You know what you have to do," Syrella said as soon as they were alone.

"Are you sure?" Linaria's gaze revealed doubt.

Syrella raised her hand and pushed her hair back. "Yes." It was the first time in days that she felt she'd made the right decisions, and she wouldn't fail. She may not have believed much in the gods before, but now she could feel the mighty power of the God of Souls rising within her.

Deadly Sins

Velhisya half-opened her eyes and jumped back in terror to find a strange figure standing before her. She gasped in fear, her heart pounding. She tried to get up, but her legs wouldn't support her, and she fell to the ground. She turned to look at the figure, but there was no one there.

It was only a dream, she thought. The man staring at her had a face that resembled a lion's, but his body was human. *Damn.* Many times, her dreams were strange and inexplicable.

"Are you alright?" came a familiar whisper.

Velhisya looked at the wall of her cell and crawled towards it, her knees scraping on the stone floor. "I had a nightmare," she muttered to Matt. She felt lucky he was in the cell next to hers, so she didn't feel so alone. Velhisya wondered what he looked like. It was strange that she had been conversing with him for so long yet hadn't the faintest idea of his appearance.

"Was it worse than real life itself?"

The question surprised her. "I don't know," she said and leaned her back against the wall. "Your father is a merchant from Kerth who sold goods to the Mercenaries. I imagine he had quite a bit of gold. Was your life that bad?"

Matt didn't speak for a few moments. "Gold doesn't always bring happiness. Your aunt is the Ruler of Elmor. I imagine you grew up with riches few in the kingdom have seen. Were you happy?"

Velhisya felt sad. "No."

"What made you unhappy?"

She didn't know if she wanted to answer. "It's complicated. My life has been stranger than anyone else's in the world."

"I have a lot of time," Matt said softly.

Velhisya didn't want to speak any longer, but Matt sounded desperate for conversation. She knew that by talking to him, she'd help him overcome his fear.

"My parents died when I was young, and the last time I saw my mother was when I was just a baby. I grew up far away from her, and in my city, many whispered malicious rumours about me and my family," she said after a while.

"Why did you move away from your mother?" Matt asked.

"It would have been very difficult to stay in the place she lived. It was inhospitable for my father and me."

"Didn't she want to come to Elmor?"

"She couldn't." Velhisya felt a weight in her stomach talking about it.

"Where did your mother live? Why couldn't she just leave?"

Velhisya sighed wearily. "In the Mountains of—" She choked for a moment. "In the Mountains of the Forgotten World."

Silence hung in the air for a moment, and Velhisya heard Matt draw his breath in the darkness.

"I remember some stories my mother used to tell me when I was a child. Many years ago, men had imprisoned several ancient races in those mountains. That story scared me... I couldn't stay in a mountain forever," Matt said.

"Unfortunately, it's not just a story..." The image of her mother appeared in her mind once more, as it had over the past few days.

"What do you mean?" Matt spoke in a low voice. "Are the stories about men commanding winged horses true? Did these men imprison some races in the mountains?"

"Yes. My mother was an elwyn," she said softly.

"I didn't think elwyn still existed! I've never heard of a person with an elwyn mother before!" There was admiration in Matt's voice.

"I don't think there *is* anyone else. The rumours about me and my mother are known throughout Knightdorn, yet few believe them."

"How did your father meet your mother? How did he end up in the Mountains of the Forgotten World?"

"He always wanted to travel the world—to see every corner of it. My aunt told him not to go to those mountains... No one knew whether the legends were true. If they were, Syrella feared those races could be hostile to humans." A smile formed on Velhisya's lips as she reminisced about her father telling her that. "My father paid no heed to the dangers and travelled to the Mountains of the Forgotten World. He told me that he fell in love with my mother the moment he saw her. He wanted to stay with her forever, but it would have been impossible for a human to survive in such a place. So, as soon as I was born, he left and returned to Elmor with me."

"What is this prison made by the men with the winged horses?" Matt went on eagerly.

"It's not exactly a prison... There was an invisible magic that wouldn't let the elwyn leave."

"Magic? I've never heard of such magic before," Matt said.

"I wish it had never existed," Velhisya told him, her mind racing through Lothar's words to her. Elliot had freed the Elder Races, and the elwyn had fought for her aunt while the giants had sided with Thorn. She didn't know whether all of it was true, but the image of Elliot filled her with warmth every time he came to mind.

"Doesn't it exist anymore?" Matt asked.

"That's what the rumours say, but I'm not sure."

"How do you know your mother is dead when you haven't seen her in years?" Matt said.

"I know," Velhisya mumbled. She didn't want to talk about it; it was too painful.

"I'm sorry." Matt's voice seemed to be coming from nearby, as if he had his face pressed against the wall.

"All the years I spent growing up in Elmor, I heard a lot about my mother... People thought her race was cursed and dirty, and they believed she'd bewitched my father so that he'd fall in love with her. Some, like the high priest of Wirskworth, suggested that even I might be cursed and that the gods might punish Elmor if I remained on his land. Others thought that it was all just nonsense and false rumours."

"Most people are idiots... Nevertheless, there's one thing that makes you lucky."

Velhisya didn't know what he meant. "What's that?" she asked.

"Your parents loved you, and how you talk about Syrella Endor shows that you hold her in high esteem. I believe she also treated you with respect."

She felt a trace of peace within her. "That's true," she said, looking at the dark surroundings. "Don't your parents love you?"

Matt remained silent, the sound of his breathing filling the empty silence. "My father hates me."

Velhisya frowned. *Poor Matt.* "Why?"

"Because I am who I am." His voice sounded hesitant.

"I don't know what you mean, but after all we've said, I'm sure you're a good and honourable man. I hope that one day your father will realise that he's made a mistake," Velhisya said, trying to give him hope.

A guffaw sounded from behind the wall. "That will never happen. My father will die ashamed of me."

"But why? You're his son. What could you have done to have shamed him so deeply?" Velhisya was now curious to know more. She could hear Matt's breath quicken.

"When I was still a boy, I discovered I was different. I found out that..." He stopped mid-sentence.

"No matter what you say, I won't judge you, Matt," Velhisya said gently.

Matt didn't speak for a few moments. "I found out I liked other boys."

There was shame in his voice. "I spoke to my mother about it, and she didn't care. She told me she'd love me forever, but my father mustn't know, and neither must anyone else." A sob came from behind the wall, and Velhisya wished she could hug him.

"One day, my father and his brother found me with another man in a city stable and threatened to castrate me. They told me that I would disgrace them, that I didn't deserve to live with the shame I'd brought upon them."

Rage boiled over inside Velhisya. "Your father is a—a... fool!" Her voice echoed through the dungeons, and she hoped the guards hadn't heard her.

"Maybe my father's right..." Matt went on. "In Kerth, men like me are mocked just like eunuchs. I've heard that before Odin became emperor, there was no punishment for those like me. But Odin changed every-thing, and he's spread the word that scum like me must be punished. My actions belong to what he has called *deadly sins*. My father didn't want to endure such shame."

Velhisya wanted to touch him and hug him, but she couldn't. She put her hands on the wall that separated them and touched its cold surface. "There are many men like you in Knightdorn, and no one has punished them in years. Odin is a fool, just like your father. There's no need to be ashamed, Matt. The only people who should be ashamed are those who spend their lives killing and pillaging without giving a damn about anyone but themselves."

"You remind me of my mother... I wish I still had her." His sobs grew louder.

"What happened to her?"

"She got sick a few years ago. My father became even crueller after her death. He never accepted that his only son was..."

Velhisya now heard only sobbing. "Your father is making a mistake. I hope he realises this one day."

Matt's breathing sounded heavy. "My father will be happy if I die.

Only then will he stop fearing the shame I may bring him. I'm sure he was happy when he found out I got caught. Not only will he not pay for me, but he'll be relieved when the Mercenaries kill me," he said between sobs.

Velhisya didn't know what to say to calm him down. "You're his son. Now that you're in danger, I believe he'll find love for you within him once more."

Matt sniffed. "You still have hope within you, Velhisya. Mine died a long time ago."

Silence fell over the dungeons, and Velhisya once again felt like a stranger. She couldn't believe she belonged to such a brutal and violent world—a world hostile to anything different.

"If Liher Hale's men realise what I am, they'll torture me before they kill me," Matt whispered, his voice cracking.

Velhisya knew that the last cell in the dungeon contained a torture chair—the one they had tied Selwyn to. Lothar had told her about that cell, but she hoped they wouldn't torture Matt.

"They won't find out. No one will tell them anything," she said, trying to give him strength.

"Many a time I wish I'd never been born. That would have been best for everyone..."

Velhisya wished she could break down the wall that separated them and wrap her arms around him to show him that there were people who weren't like his father. "I wish I could change things, Matt—change everything."

"Maybe you can..." he said. "The stories about the races that were held captive in those mountains, the stories about the elwyn, said that those creatures were endowed with magic. Maybe there is magic inside you, and if there is, you can use it for good."

Velhisya smiled. That would be too good to be true. Then, the image of Liher burning at her touch came back to her. "If ever I find magic inside of me, I swear I'll use it to help all those who have suffered as much as you have."

"When I was a child, I believed in magic," Matt told her. "I believed it existed and that it was the answer to all my suffering. Maybe some ancient magic could make people stop killing and torturing, stop hunting everything different. Then one day, I heard that Odin Mud was on the hunt for a strange race of people who lived in an isolated forest in Kerth. He'd spread the word that these people had stolen the powers of the gods and wanted to destroy the world. Many said this race and their magic were dangerous, but I believed they would save me from my fears."

Velhisya hadn't heard about that before. "What happened to this race?"

"Odin killed them all, even their children. That's when I stopped hoping."

Velhisya hated the Emperor more than she'd ever hated before. With Odin and Walter ruling the two continents, no creature would ever escape pain and death.

"I hope that if you ever find magic within you, it's the strongest magic there's ever been." Matt's voice snapped her out of her thoughts. "I hope you will be the one to make me hope again."

The Unexpected Meeting

S elwyn walked behind the gate of Wirskworth, watching the builders
hard at work as the morning sun rose. The wyvern's attack a few
weeks ago had destroyed many parts of the city, and he wondered about
the might of the creature. Wirskworth's gate was the strongest he'd ever
seen, and its broken parts made him shudder at the thought of what
dozens of these monsters would do to the city.

He'd spent quite some time surveying the work, but he felt unable to
help. He knew next to nothing about the construction and fortification
of a city, and he had no idea how they could fight wyverns. He looked at
the landscape beyond Wirskworth. For a moment, he saw in his mind's
eye a huge army about to attack, and the thought terrified him. He may
have overcome his fears, but he couldn't stop worrying about those he
loved. His father, his mother, Elliot, and many others would fight in the
last battle, and he was sure that countless lives would be lost, no matter
who won.

"You look troubled..."

He turned to his right and saw a slight woman with brown hair tied
up in a bun and eyes the colour of blood. She wore a jerkin that matched
the shade of her eyes.

"Good morning, Alysia. I'm just watching the construction work," he
said. He didn't want to reveal that he had little knowledge of stonema-
sonry. "Everything looks great."

"I'd wager you don't know much about walls and fortifications,"
Alysia replied as if reading his thoughts.

"No, I don't know much," Selwyn admitted, crossing his arms.

"Can you see that turret?" She raised her right hand, pointing it out to him.

Selwyn spotted a building in the west and noticed some elves standing at its entrance. "Yes," he said.

"Turrets like that one are perfect for aiming at wyverns with the light from our swords. However, there are few windows around the tower, and they're small. We need to make more and bigger ones since the more light that hits the wyverns, the better."

"Does the light of your swords make them retreat?" Selwyn asked.

"Sometimes. At first, they try to avoid it by turning in the air, but if many beams hit their body over and over, they can't stand the pain and fly away."

Selwyn had heard of the light's effects on wyverns. "I hope we succeed," he said, imagining an invisible monster attacking the tower.

"Fear not. We elves have faced these creatures before," Alysia said, not taking her eyes off him.

"I don't fear for my life—not anymore."

"Then what is it that scares you? You seem worried..." Her red gaze was well-meaning.

A sigh escaped his lips. "I'm worried that if we're defeated, a lot of people I love will die."

Alysia frowned. "The fear of loss often leads one down a dark path. We can't stand in the way of fate, but we can do our best to survive and protect those we love."

Wise words... "You're right," he said after a few moments.

"When you found yourself Liher Hale's captive, were you afraid you'd die?"

Selwyn didn't immediately answer. "At first, yes. But a little later, my fear left me once and for all."

Alysia watched him closely, as if trying to discover all his hidden secrets. "What made you overcome your fear?"

"Were I to die, I'd meet up with my brothers again."

Alysia smiled. "That's a peaceful thought. No one knows what awaits us in the realms of the dead, but I'm sure there's something for everyone there. Fear not for your loved ones. The Light of Life will be with them in whatever world they find themselves in."

It was Selwyn's turn to smile. "The Light of Life, countless gods, legends and creatures. What is one to believe in?"

"Believe in whatever gives you fortitude, Selwyn Brau." With these words, Alysia nodded and started walking away.

"I'd like to ask you something." Selwyn raised his voice over the sound of the workers, and the elf turned to him again. "Elliot confided in me that you and Alaric helped him become a better warrior."

"He told you the truth."

"Train me, too," Selwyn blurted.

Alysia scratched her chin. "Do you think that will protect those you love?"

"I don't know, but it'll give me strength. I was never very good with a sword. I want to do the best I can to help."

She frowned. "You have a pure soul, Selwyn Brau. Meet me outside Moonstone's main gate just after dusk."

<hr>

Selwyn brought the goblet to his lips and took a few sips of beer. He glanced around at the people drinking and laughing in the corners of the small building, then took a few more sips. He really liked the Three Arrows. The tavern had the best beer he'd ever had in his life, so he visited it as soon as it turned dark. He didn't usually go to taverns in Iovbridge. Too many people knew his identity in the royal capital and rushed to speak to him when he sought a few moments of peace. However, in Wirskworth, he wasn't that well known, and he hadn't seen people from Iovbridge frequenting the place.

Selwyn carried on drinking, lost in thought. The practice with Alysia a few hours ago was the hardest thing he'd ever done, and had left his body stiff. The woman was incomparably quick, and when her sword was flooded with red light, there was no way he could fend it off. *How did Elliot manage to face her and Alaric at the same time? Damn...* He knew that no matter how much he practised, he would never be that good.

He noticed two men dressed in long black cloaks whispering in a corner. For a moment, he thought of the traitor living in Wirskworth—Walter's spy who had been close to Syrella for years. He'd wondered about this man's identity, but neither he nor his father had any answers.

He took another sip of beer and set his cup down on the wooden table. Its contents seemed black in the dark atmosphere of the tavern. Another black liquid found its way into his mind. At the last council, Aleron had said that Walter would drench his men's weapons with Orhyn Shadow. That filled him with pessimism, but he was in the only city that had the poison's antidote. He'd also heard that the light in the swords of the elwyn and elves could heal wounds infected by Orhyn Shadow.

"How come such a handsome young man as yourself is drinking alone?"

Selwyn turned suddenly and saw a young woman with lively blue eyes and red hair standing opposite him. She was wearing a brown dress made from animal hide.

"I like being alone," he said with a smile.

"Then, I'll leave you to yourself."

"No, you may sit," he told her hastily.

The woman threw him a smile. "I haven't seen many women in this place," Selwyn said, remembering only drunken men snickering and laughing at the Three Arrows.

"This tavern belongs to my father. I work here a few days every month. Now and then, my father lets me take a little break," the woman told him. "What's your name?"

"Selwyn."

"Just Selwyn?"

He looked at her suspiciously while the woman seemed to read his eyes. "Your clothes are made of expensive silk, Selwyn. I'd wager you're a lord."

"Selwyn Brau," he said with a smile. *She is smart.*

"Are you the son of Queen Sophie's officer?" Her eyes opened wide as Selwyn nodded. "Men like you don't frequent our tavern, Lord Brau. There are fancier inns and taverns in the city."

"I like this place." Selwyn took a few more sips of his drink.

"Would you like another beer? That'll be on me."

"What's your name?"

"Ida."

He liked her smile and almond-shaped eyes, and her voice sounded like a joyful melody. "I'll have another beer if you keep me company," he told her, grinning.

Ida smiled and rose from her seat. As she walked towards the counter in the centre of the tavern, she momentarily turned to him and gave him another look.

"I never expected to find a lord from Iovbridge here."

Selwyn saw a portly man in black clothes and a broad smile approaching him. Sadon Burns, Syrella Endor's councillor, stood before him. "This place has the best ale in Wirskworth," Selwyn replied.

Sadon chuckled. "Without a doubt," he said, his aged face contorting as he laughed. "It's also perfect for lords who want to drink on their own, away from the rest of the noblemen in the city."

"Is that why you're here, my lord?" Selwyn asked.

Sadon didn't lose his smile. "I could use a solitary night in the company of a glass of the most divine ale."

Selwyn raised his cup.

"I found many of the words you've spoken in our council meetings over the last few days commendable," Sadon continued.

"When I arrived in the city with Elliot, you didn't seem to appreciate my words."

Sadon frowned. "It was hard to digest the fact that Walter would attack the city. However, I often make mistakes... Now, I believe you could become a valuable councillor."

"I'd rather become a valuable warrior."

Sadon watched him. "All men who strive to be the best soldiers forget the most basic truth."

"What's that?" asked Selwyn.

"Intellect is more powerful than skill in battle. Learn to use your brain, and you'll discover that it can prove to be much more powerful than your sword."

Selwyn met the lord's gaze for a moment until Ida pushed her way through to them, holding two big goblets.

"Enjoy your evening, Lord Brau," Sadon muttered. He nodded curtly and walked away.

Selwyn saw him walking towards the men with the long black cloaks that he'd noticed earlier. *He doesn't seem to be looking for solitude,* he thought.

"So, how do you want to spend the rest of the night?" Ida's voice made him turn to her. She was biting her lip and leaning against the table.

Selwyn forgot about Sadon and looked into her playful eyes. Every time she spoke, a feeling of lust rose within him. He picked up the cup she'd brought him and slugged down its contents.

"Do you think your father would allow you to leave for a while? How about we go for a walk around the city?"

"I'm sure he will," Ida said with a coy smile, stretching her arms above her head before lowering them gracefully. "Shall we?"

The Fugitives of the Snow

"What's that?" John was left open-mouthed and wide-eyed. He took a closer look at the copper pipe at the front of the deck. Its opening had the appearance of a lion, and its base was nailed to the wooden floor.

"I thought you'd find it useful," Jack said with a smile.

"When did you make this?"

"I've been working day and night over the last three days!" Jack snapped.

Damn you. John wondered where he found such zest at his age.

"If you'd come more often, you would have seen what I was preparing earlier..." the man said pointedly.

John looked at him in dismay. He'd only been on this ship one other time since he'd found out about the Liquid Fire, and he didn't like to remember it.

"I asked you to come every day..." Jack seemed irritated now.

"This thing is too dangerous!" John remembered the thick green-ish-yellow liquid he'd seen spewing from the copper pipes four days earlier. He'd thrown just a little of it into the sea, and the waters had filled up with flames, while smoke had risen into the air. John recalled the noise that accompanied it. It sounded like a crack of lightning.

"That's why you have to come here every day. This is the only way you'll learn to use the pipes as best you can. If we need to throw Liquid Fire, we have to be ready."

John walked over to the new pipe jutting out from the bow of the ship and looked at it carefully. "Go downstairs and get everything ready," he said.

Jack nodded and hurried away. John looked up at the sky. Luckily, it wasn't very windy that day, so he didn't have to worry about the liquid blowing back onto him. The sun began to set, and then the wind would usually pick up. However, they couldn't pour the damn liquid into the sea during the day without risking being seen.

John examined the pipe and saw two small iron rods just above its base. One looked familiar. He'd seen it on the rest of the pipes at the bottom of the ship. When he pulled the rod downwards, the Liquid Fire shot out, but he had no idea what the second rod in the centre of the strange contraption was. He caught it with his right hand and swung it to the right. The lion's head at the mouth of the pipe swung in the same direction.

Damn. Jack is clever. The rest of the pipes only threw the liquid in one direction, but the one in front of him was even more intricate.

A metallic sound reached his ears. Jack was tapping the end of the copper pipe in the ship's hold to signal that the Liquid Fire was in place. His heartbeat quickened. The one-eyed man had advised him to wait a moment when given the cue so that the liquid could diffuse through the pipe and be ready to be ejected under pressure. Sweat rolled down his forehead, and he swung the one iron rod at the base of the pipe, driving the lion's head dead centre. His hands were shaking as he brought the second rod down abruptly. A thick liquid spewed out with tremendous force in front of the ship. John heard sounds like thunder, and moments later, he turned the rod back to its original position.

He felt his face go red. He let go of the pipe and ran to the edge of the deck, wanting to see what had happened. He'd ejected more liquid than he'd intended. His eyes widened at the sight. The sea around them seemed to have split in two, and large flames burned on its surface. *What the hell?!* The waves swept the flames towards the bow. "JACK!" he yelled, feeling panicked. No one answered, and then the flames engulfed the front of the pier. *How is that possible?* Even the stone seemed to be melting.

"What happened?" He turned to see Jack come out of the large cabin, running towards him.

"I poured out too much," John said.

Jack ran to the bow and looked down. "Follow me. Quick!"

John followed him, wondering where they were going. Jack made his way to the wooden plank that led to the pier and strode across it.

"Where are you going?"

"Shut up and follow me!"

John cursed to himself as Jack ran towards the part of the pier that had been engulfed in flames.

"Help me!"

John didn't understand until he saw a handful of large sacks near the pier. Jack grabbed one from the bottom, and John tried to help him. The sack was immovable.

"What's in it?"

"Move closer to the flames."

The air filled with smoke as they moved clumsily, stumbling towards the flames that burned across the stone surface.

"Aim for the base of the fire!" Jack shouted. "I'll count to three. One, two, three!"

John put all his strength into it, and they threw the sack into the middle of the flames. He saw it burst onto the ground and something that looked like dust scattered everywhere. The fire went out with a roar. John looked closer and then he understood.

Sand.

"We can't throw these sacks that far," he said, looking at the flames in the sea. They were nearing the ship. "They're too heavy."

"Grab a barrel!" Jack shouted.

"A barrel?" John repeated.

"There!" Jack pointed to a spot a short distance away from the sacks and sprinted towards it, panting.

John followed him in bewilderment, and soon after, he saw about a dozen barrels scattered around.

"These are lighter." Jack grabbed a small barrel to his left and ran to the part of the pier closest to the bow of the ship.

John cursed his luck, and he also picked up a barrel. It was heavy but not as heavy as the sacks. His legs creaked under the weight as he carried it.

"I don't know what's in this barrel, but if we throw it into the sea, it won't break," he said as he neared Jack.

"Open the top and throw it into the fire. It'll ravage the wood."

Jack removed the cap from the barrel he was holding and threw it with all his might at the flames in the sea. It landed in the water with a loud splash.

"We won't be able to put the fire out!" John shouted, feeling panicked at the sight of the flames.

"Throw the barrel!" Jack told him.

John lowered the barrel onto the ground, removed the lid and lifted it again. Grunting, he hurled it at the bow. The splash reached his ears, and he stood watching the fire burning the front of the ship. To his surprise, the flames began to shrink until they were lost in the sea's water.

"Didn't I tell you to be careful, damn you!" Jack looked furious, his face red and sweaty.

"I didn't do it on purpose! What was inside the barrel?"

"Do you want to burn my ship?" They were lucky the vessel appeared unharmed.

John turned to him, enraged. "The liquid was ejected with much more pressure this time. I couldn't have expected what happened! If you don't want my help, find someone else to do the job!"

Jack looked away, and John heard his shallow breathing.

"What was in the barrel?" he asked again.

Jack didn't speak. After a while, he turned to face John, his eyes narrowing as if his anger were eating away at him from the inside. "Vinegar," he said abruptly.

"I won't travel with you, even if Begon kills me, unless you fill your ship with vinegar and sand. We have to be prepared in case we need to put this thing out!" he said, pointing to the place in the sea that had been enveloped in flames earlier on.

Jack sized him up for a few moments and then nodded stiffly. Satisfied, John put his hands on his hips and then suddenly felt something bite the back of his neck. He turned round sharply and saw a white bird flying over his head.

What the hell?! He knew the bird, and a letter was tied to its leg.

<hr />

John drained the wine in his cup in one swig and made himself more comfortable in his chair. Elliot's letter had caught him off guard. He'd often told himself that the boy had forgotten him, but it turned out he was wrong. Elliot had sent his hawk to find him, bringing him news.

Wherever you are, I hope you're well, John.

The last sentence in the letter nested in his head. John moved onto the wine from the second cup on his table, Elliot's words lingering in his head. The boy had written to him about the loss of Eleanor, the freeing of the Elder Races, and the plight of Selwyn at the hands of Liher Hale. John was relieved that the younger Brau had survived, while the letter confirmed everything Begon had told him a few days before. The strangest thing was that Elliot hadn't asked him anything about his mission. John had expected to read questions about whether he'd succeeded in persuading Begon to help Sophie, questions about whether he would hasten to the Queen's side in the upcoming battle. However, he'd made a mistake. Elliot hadn't asked anything in the least, and he knew why.

He assumed I didn't want to fight. He didn't want to put me in a spot; he just wanted to know if I was all right, he thought. John felt such remorse. He knew that if he were in Elliot's position, he would have been furious. Yet, that boy had once again shown John his strength of character and principles. John was sure that if he replied by asking about the battle, showing him that he wanted to fight by his side, Elliot would welcome him with open arms, even if he found out about his choices in the Ice Islands. However, Elliot wouldn't ask him to fight again unless he told him that he wanted to beforehand.

You have to do it! his conscience told him. Still, he knew that courage didn't reside in his soul. He hadn't found it before, and he certainly wouldn't do so now. Elliot had to manage without him.

He carried on drinking his wine, lost in thought. Elliot had told him that he was in the Western Empire and that the Queen had agreed to marry the Emperor's son in an attempt to gain new allies. The plan was to return to Wirskworth with the men from Kerth as quickly as they could for the last battle against Thorn.

An ambitious and dangerous plan. Odin Mud isn't a virtuous man. John doubted the motives of both the Emperor and his son.

He set his cup down on the table and tried to put Elliot out of his mind. He'd think about what he'd write in reply later. The soles of his feet hurt; the day had proven to be more tiring than expected. The image of the fire nearing Jack's ship found its way into his head, and he felt an urge to drink more. He had to get those terrifying memories out of his mind.

He raised his cup to the man behind the counter in the middle of the tavern, and the man nodded angrily. It was just as well John had won that bet and had been drinking for free at the Dolphin the last few days. He put the cup down and covered his face with the palms of his hands. He'd tried countless times to find a way to avoid the journey north of Knightdorn. He would give anything to convince Begon to relieve him of this mission, but no matter how much he racked his mind, deep down, he knew he wouldn't change the man's mind. John was truly afraid of the trip because he was sure that Walter's northern allies were the ones attacking Begon's fishermen. He may not have known why, but there was no other possible explanation.

Walter's men could even be killing the fishermen from the Ice Islands just for fun. The northerners were known to often attack anyone who hadn't sided with their king, and it didn't take many men to sink a few fishermen's boats.

John lowered his hands and looked at the small crowd inside the Dolphin. His assumptions were both logical and worrying at the same time. He shuddered at the thought of what would happen if Thorn's allies were to attack them. He didn't want to fight, and the Liquid Fire scared him. He knew that the weapon could certainly cause problems for their enemies, but it was also dangerous to them.

"I'd say there's a lot that's troubling you, Long Arm."

He saw two women sitting at a table a little further away from his. "Who are you? How come you know my name?" he asked.

"Everyone knows your name on this island by now. You're the Queen's emissary who withheld information to stay in our land away from the war. Many call you 'The Coward,'" the older woman told him. She wore a green dress and was frowning. Beside her, a younger girl who looked like she was her daughter brought her cup to her lips, glaring daggers at him.

"I don't give a damn!" John snapped and went back to his drink, wanting to be left alone.

"Judging by the look on your face, the weight of your guilty conscience is unbearable."

"Leave me alone," John said angrily, not looking at her.

"You even concealed the fact that a descendant of Thomas Egercoll is alive, fighting by the Queen's side."

"You should be grateful for what I did." John turned back to face her. "If I'd told Begon the news before Sophie's battle with Walter, and he'd taken the Ice Islands to war, your land would have been filled with death... If nothing else, the Queen will be facing Thorn again soon, and your leader told me that he doesn't intend to fight. He also told me that he wouldn't have done so in the previous battle either. The information I hid from him wouldn't have changed a thing."

The woman stared at him in silence. "Begon doesn't know where and when the last battle will be fought. There's no information, and that makes his decisions more difficult. Nevertheless, if you'd told him everything you were supposed to when you arrived, we might have persuaded him to fight in Elmor."

John studied her more carefully. Now he was certain that the woman was close to the Leader of the Ice Islands. "If that's true, I did you a favour. You wouldn't want the death a battle against Walter would bring to your land..."

The woman rose from her chair suddenly. "Walter has spread death across my land already, Long Arm! I'll fight to avenge myself until my very last breath!"

John frowned. "Who are you?"

She took a few steps towards him. "An advisor to the Leader of the Ice Islands. However, I have been known for years as Delia Barlow, wife of Aghyr Barlow and mother of Giren and Lora Barlow." Her eyes fell upon the young woman next to her.

John's mouth went dry. "Are you Aghyr's wife?" he asked.

"I'm the wife of a dead man, Long Arm. I'm a woman who made it out of Tahos in a boat trying to save her children. A woman who lost her son while trying to escape and whose little boy saw his father die and was enslaved by a tyrant for years. I'll never forget that day... I still remember my people being slain by the arrows of the enemy's men as they fell wildly into their boats. I remember death's shadow reaching for me, too."

Impossible... "How did you survive?"

Delia's face was expressionless. "Just as Walter's men tried to sink my boat, it began to snow. The snow made them lose sight of us, and so I was saved. My boat managed to reach the Ice Islands through storms that few people have survived... Those of us who were spared decided to live here, and years later, I found out that Thorn's allies used to mock us for having run away. They called us 'the Fugitives of the Snow' and considered us of such little importance that they never bothered to look for us."

Delia took two more steps towards him. "I lost everything, but the gods granted me life so that I could take revenge. If cowards like you cease to exist, I may get my revenge one day."

Delia stepped even closer, her voice like ice. "I'm sure you know... Walter will never stop until he dominates every land on this continent. You won't be able to run forever. Tell me, John, do you have the courage to face what's coming?"

Two Daggers

S yrella looked at the Temple of the God of Souls, feeling a twinge of fear. The city's craftsmen hadn't yet been able to repair it after the wyvern's attack. She walked up the steps leading to the raised portico in front of the grand building's door while a handful of guards and two men of the Sharp Swords made a way through the crowd for her. The morning sun was warm and bright for the first time in days as if it, too, wanted to witness what was to come.

She climbed the stairs and glanced at the crowd that had gathered at the temple that morning. Thousands of people had come to bid Borin Ballard a final goodbye. Syrella knew that the Ruler of Ballar wasn't particularly popular in her land, but he was a supporter of the Queen—a supporter of the Egercolls. Her people knew that not many honourable governors remained in the kingdom and had decided to honour Borin on his journey to the realms of the dead.

Syrella had wanted to perform the ceremony sooner, but Thorold had asked to examine Borin's body for poisons, which had taken seven whole days. The Master had found nothing strange in the Governor's body and declared that he had died of natural causes.

Syrella walked up to the portico with the statue of the God of Souls in its centre. It was still cut in half after the wyvern's attack. She hoped her stonemasons would replace it quickly. The sight filled her with pessimism. A little past the statue, she saw figures sitting in a few dozen chairs, and in the centre of the portico stood a stone table laden with straw. Syrella sauntered past the table and headed for the seats. The

Queen and Elmor's councillors sat waiting for the ceremony to begin while Jahon stood behind them. Syrella sat in a chair between Sadon Burns and Sygar Reis. She would have preferred her daughters to have been there, but they had left with her army the week before, bound for Liher Hale. She lifted her gaze and looked straight at the crowd. The air was quiet even though so many people were around the city temple.

Time passed before a few guards came up the stairs, carrying a wooden structure with a body lying atop it. The guards went up to the portico and proceeded to the stone table where they slowly placed Borin's body. Syrella had suggested that his body be buried in the temple's crypts along with Endor's ancestors, but the people of Ballar had told her that Borin had requested that his body be purified by fire.

A man dressed in black approached the lifeless body, touched his head, and said a few words. Syrella didn't know the priest well. He was the one who would soon take Edmund's place, as the High Priest was now very ill. Thorold had told her he didn't have much time left.

The priest raised his voice so everyone could hear. "God of Souls, take this man into your arms and take care of him in the realms of the dead," he said.

A guard held a lit torch out to the priest. The man took it and placed it on the straw beside Borin's body. The flames rose towards the sky like golden spirits. Syrella watched the man's body burn and hoped that if she died, she too would have such an end—an honourable end. Nevertheless, she knew that if Walter took her city, he would dismember the bodies of his enemies and put their heads on spikes as a meal for the crows. The image made her stomach churn.

She tossed those thoughts away since they were meaningless. The flames continued to burn on the stone table, and Syrella thought of Borin's aged and frail countenance. The man had lost all will to live the moment he'd found out about his sons' deaths, and strangely, his death gave her hope.

May you meet your sons and never be parted again, my friend.

Syrella had spent decades believing that there was nothing after death. Many priests had spoken to her about the eternal existence of the spirit, but their words seemed nonsense to her. However, as the years passed, much of what she believed had changed. Now, the idea of some form of existence after death gave her hope. Syrella wanted to meet up with her siblings, her parents, and even her dead husband again. She thought that if she ever met the son of Sadon Burns in the realms of the dead, she'd have the opportunity to tell him how sorry she was about everything that had happened.

The fire had begun to die down, and a few clouds of smoke rose into the bright sky. *Those aren't clouds. They're Borin's soul, now free from care and pain.* A tear rolled down her cheek. She remembered how far off death seemed to her young self, but now she could feel that the end wasn't that far away. She had now lived almost fifty years, and every moment she had left in this world was precious. She was more determined than ever to accomplish everything she wanted to.

"Your Majesty."

Syrella turned to the right and saw a guard she hadn't noticed before approaching her. "What's the matter?" she asked.

"It's High Priest Edmund," he told her.

"What's wrong with him?"

"He's in great pain, Your Majesty. He asked Thorold to give him a few drops of the Green Gold. However, he wishes to speak to you before he goes."

Syrella closed her eyes and let out a weary sigh. Even without war and battles, death kept making an appearance. She leaned to her left, towards Sadon Burns, who was sitting next to her. "I have to go. Stay here on my behalf until the ceremony is over," she whispered.

She stood and followed the guard. She knew the crowd would wonder why she was leaving before the flames died down completely, but she couldn't help it. She walked towards the steps that led to the square surrounding the temple, followed by the guards and the two men of the

Sharp Swords.

"Has something happened, Your Majesty?" a guard asked her.

"There's simply a matter that requires my attention," she replied hastily, and the guard nodded. She'd explain why she'd left before the fire burning Borin's lifeless body was extinguished later; she didn't want to cause a commotion while everyone was saying goodbye to the former ruler of Ballar.

Syrella stepped down from the portico and moved through the crowd. She bet that almost all of Elmor's people were watching the ceremony. The guards continued to make way for her until they turned into a deserted alley. Syrella quickened her pace as she and her escorts made their way to the entrance of Moonstone. Out of the corner of her eye, she saw a couple of white birds flying low over the city. The sun might have been shining in the sky that morning, but she knew that when the flocks flew low, it was an omen that the rain wouldn't be far off.

The castle of Endor looked imposing as they neared, and there wasn't a soul in the alleyways. Syrella felt glad that her people had hastened to pay their last respects to Borin, yet the thought of what she'd see in the place where she was going darkened her soul. She didn't want to see yet another man just before he died; she couldn't stand any more death in her life.

When Syrella and her guards arrived at the main entrance to Moonstone, the guards at the gate immediately stepped aside to let her into the castle. She may have lived in Moonstone all her life, but she still admired it every time she crossed its threshold. Moonstone had a high ceiling and large square windows and was adorned with moonstones in every corner. She'd always liked the precious stone that could only be found in the mountain mines in the bowels of which her city had been built.

Syrella and her guards traversed the castle until they reached a dark corridor. She eventually stopped in front of a wooden door.

"Stay here," she told the men and stepped into the Hall.

The candlelight in the room was dim, and a man was wringing a wet cloth over the head of an aged figure who lay in bed with his eyes closed. Syrella had suggested that her healers take care of Edmund, but he'd asked for Thorold, saying the Master knew more than anyone else.

She walked over to the two men, and Edmund's eyes widened within their worn sockets.

"How are you?" Syrella asked.

"I've been better, Your Majesty. Thank you for coming to see me," Edmund rasped.

"Of course. I heard you want to drink the Green Gold?"

The man's lips quivered. "Yes... I can't take this torture anymore. My time has come."

"What can I do for you?" Syrella said, feeling sorrow.

"I don't want you to ever forget the power of our god," the man said softly.

Damn. Even now, on his deathbed, his thoughts are fixed on the god he serves. "I won't forg—"

"Listen to me." The man cut her short. "I know that you have seen a saviour in the face of the son of Thomas Egercoll. A skilled warrior who even managed to set the Elder Races free. Nevertheless, Elliot is still just a boy and will never have a power equal to that of the God of Souls."

"What are you trying to tell me?"

"I swore my allegiance to you, and I want to give you my last piece of advice... If you want to defeat your enemies and punish those who've wronged you, don't follow all the words of one man. Only our god can see the future and tell you the truth; only our god holds the answer to every affliction you bear. Remember these words," the man groaned in pain as he got his last sentence out.

"I think it's time you rest, Edmund," Thorold said.

"I know you want to get the Governor out of here quickly because you find my words foolish!" the High Priest snapped at the Master.

Thorold shook his head. "I may not believe so much in the powers of the gods, but every man has the right to say whatever he thinks, especially in his last moments. I hope your god will reward your faith once you meet him. However, as time goes on, the pain will increase."

Edmund was about to say something when a rattling noise escaped his throat. Thorold brought an earthen pot to his mouth, and the old man spat blood into it. He turned to Syrella once more.

"Remember my words."

Syrella nodded. "I hope you find peace, Edmund."

The man lowered his head wearily, and Syrella turned to leave the room just as Thorold held up a vial filled with a green liquid. She quickly left the chamber.

"Are you all right, Your Majesty?" asked one of the guards waiting for her outside in the hall.

"Yes," Syrella said curtly and didn't speak for a few moments.

She remembered Edmund shouting his opinions when she was still a little girl. Syrella had disliked him in the past. Edmund irritated many lords, councillors, and commanders with his unwavering adoration and exaltation of the gods. In addition, he had asked that Velhisya be thrown into a river when she was still a baby since he feared that if she was cursed, it could have brought punishment from the God of Souls to their land. She remembered the High Priest's fear and humble apologies when her brother had threatened to cut his throat. Edmund wasn't a well-liked priest. However, the helpless look of a man reduced to such a weakened state saddened her. Life had its way of constantly reminding her how weak humans were.

"I've been looking everywhere for you!" Jahon's voice reached her, and she saw him running towards her.

"How did you find me?" Syrella asked as he approached her.

"I heard you came here to talk to Edmund," he said.

"What's the matter?"

"I need to talk to you alone. Immediately!"

"Why?" Her general wore an impatient look on his face. "Leave us," Syrella told the guards.

The guards and the two men of the Sharp Swords left them.

"What's so urgent?" Syrella asked Jahon once they were alone.

"Borin's ceremony ended a while ago, and as I was walking away from the temple, a guard spoke to me—a lad I didn't know."

"And?"

"He told me he was standing watch the night that man—Walter's informant—left Wirskworth, only to return a little while later when Thorn was on our land."

Syrella felt herself flush. "Did he see his face?"

Jahon nodded. "He told me that his watch wasn't near the pass that led out of the city. However, as he walked down a deserted alley, he saw a man in a long cloak walking hurriedly, his face bruised. He stopped him and asked him where he was going, and the man told him to go back to his watch and forget that he'd seen him."

"Did he recognise him?"

"He told me he knew who he was but wouldn't reveal it to anyone but you."

Syrella was speechless. "Why didn't he say anything all this time?"

"This lad was truly petrified, and he told me that the man he saw was powerful in Elmor. He also said he hadn't heard anyone had snuck into the city when he met him. But soon after, he found out from the other guards that earlier that same night, an intruder had entered Wirskworth, and everyone suspected that the same man had managed to leave the city earlier. At first, the lad didn't believe the intruder they sought was the lord he'd seen. After a few days, he thought about reporting it but didn't know to whom. He feared accusing such a powerful man since it could have resulted in harsh punishment. He also told me that he has felt that he is being followed since the day of the incident."

Damn! Maybe luck will smile on me for once, and I'll find that traitor. "I have to talk to him straight away."

"He's in your chamber. That's the safest place."

Syrella started running, and Jahon followed. They passed through corridors with bated breath, her heart pounding with agitation. Time seemed to stand still until Syrella saw the door to her chamber. She ran as fast as she could and pushed it open. She stopped, her hands shaking as Jahon smacked into her.

"What the Hell?!" he exclaimed, confronted by a horrific sight.

A headless body was strewn on the floor of the chamber, the head resting on her bed. Syrella took a few steps towards the head and looked at it, feeling like she was about to throw up. Two silver daggers had been stuck into the lad's dead eyes, and a stream of blood flowed into his gaping mouth.

The Emperor's Reception

E lliot sat on the bed in his cabin, and his stomach hurt. Ten whole days had gone by since the moment they'd set off on their trip, and he still couldn't get used to the ship's rocking. He grabbed the bucket next to his bed, ready to vomit again. Elliot stared at the bottom of the bucket until he closed his eyes to calm down. He had to overcome the feeling of dizziness plaguing him. For a moment, he saw Long Arm laughing in his mind. He wondered how John had decided to become a pirate. It still seemed inexplicable to him how some people wanted to spend their lives at sea.

He set the bucket on the wooden floor and got off the bed. Dawn approached, and sunlight gently illuminated his cabin through a small window. It was the first day of their journey that the sky wasn't full of clouds.

We've been at sea quite a long time, he thought.

He remembered the captain saying that if the wind helped them, they would reach their destination in about ten days, but if they sailed into storms, their journey would take more than two weeks. Elliot had heard that the sea wasn't too rough on their journey, so it wouldn't be long before they reached their destination. He didn't want to imagine the nausea he would suffer if they were constantly caught in big storms. The thought of standing on firm ground again made him smile. Nonetheless, he knew there were countless dangers in the place they were going to. Everything he'd heard indicated that Odin Mud was a man without honour, and he had only sided with them out of self-interest. Sophie had shared her thoughts with him during their trip, and he had a bad premonition about the wedding that was to follow.

"Odin is opportunistic. He dreams of conquering the whole world one day, and this marriage can help him achieve that. Otherwise, he wouldn't give us a single man. If one day he doesn't need us, he'll kill us all, just like he did with the rest of the rulers of Kerth."

Elliot pondered Sophie's words. He'd already found out that Odin was ruthless; he hadn't hesitated to organise a feast and assassinate the rest of the leaders on his continent. The rumour had spread as far as Knightdorn that Odin's scheme rendered him the only ruler in his land. His act was stark proof of who he really was. However, his conceitedness gave them some advantages. If he were a cowardly fool, he would certainly have fought on Walter's side, but his arrogance and desire to extend his rule over another continent kept him from an alliance with Thorn. Men like Odin were never satisfied with second place in the hierarchy, so they didn't ally with other tyrants who had the same aspirations as themselves.

We have to be careful. If Odin wants to kill us, there isn't much we can do to stave him off.

They only had three hundred men while more than forty thousand were under the Emperor's command. Elliot, Sophie, and Peter had agreed not to reveal anything about the wyverns rumoured to be under Walter's command in the letter to Odin, and they had also withheld everything about the Elder Races. They all believed that the news wouldn't have reached Kerth yet and that the people of this continent had their own legends and traditions. They were sure the Emperor and his councillors would have considered it nonsense. Sophie wanted to speak to Odin in person about the winged monsters they had to face, while Elliot dreaded this conversation. He feared the wyverns might make Odin change his mind and decide to stay out of the battle in Iovbridge if he were convinced of their existence. Then, they would leave Kerth empty-handed unless the Emperor decided to kill them for wasting his time.

A knock on the door brought him back to the present. He took two steps towards the door and opened it.

"We're nearing Mirth," Peter said, scowling. He was dressed in a black cloak and green jerkin.

Elliot grabbed the Sword of Light from the floor and sheathed it at his belt. He left the cabin and went to where Peter was waiting for him. He seemed recovered from the injury he had sustained a few days ago. They climbed the stairs to the great cabin and found themselves outside on deck. The wind wasn't that strong that day, but the rocking of the ship brought on his nausea again. Elliot walked to the bow with Peter. The Queen's men were stationed on deck, looking ahead. Elliot followed their gazes and saw the city in the distance, which seemed to grow larger.

Let's see what awaits us there...

Elliot passed by some sailors tying ropes near the ship's sails and tried to get a better look at the approaching land. There was a harbour, and he wished they would reach its walls as quickly as possible.

"If nothing else, the city looks beautiful," came a voice from behind him.

Sophie stood a few steps away, wearing a lilac dress with a tiara adorning her hair. Her eyes looked even more blue in the sunlight. Elliot couldn't help but admire her beauty.

"You look splendid, Your Majesty," Peter said.

"Soon I'll be meeting my future husband. I must look my best."

The tone of her voice revealed her displeasure, but the look on her face showed her determination to play her part as best she could.

The ship approached the harbour of Kerth's capital against the wind, and Elliot touched the hilt of his sword. He hoped he wouldn't have to use his weapon in Kerth. He gazed at the view while another worrying thought took root within him. Odin knew nothing about him. Sophie and Syrella had told him that the Emperor had never held Thomas Egercoll in high esteem, so his having a son wouldn't matter. Even so, Althalos' reputation had spread throughout the world, and a man trained by his old Master would be highly regarded even in Kerth. They'd decided to reveal the truth as soon as they appeared before Odin since they all felt sure that the Emperor wouldn't believe a word if he didn't see Elliot's abilities with his own eyes. Elliot was tired of demonstrating what he could do with his sword, but if the reputation of a man trained by Althalos now fighting at the Queen's side gave them leverage with Odin, he would have to.

Sophie stood next to him, watching the ship approach the harbour. *All the news may not have reached the Emperor's ears, but he must have heard something,* Elliot thought. It seemed logical, yet there was no reason to torture himself. They would soon know.

The ship sailed into the harbour, and he saw the sailors running fast to throw ropes to a couple of men standing on a large pier. Elliot was taking in the sight when something else caught his attention. Hundreds of soldiers were heading down to their ship with long spears, while some held a banner with a familiar emblem. The emblem displayed a red sun against a white background, but its rays didn't have pointed ends that looked like spears like the one of the Guardians of Stonegate.

The soldiers stopped before the ship and moved to the side to create an opening. A man emerged from their ranks. Odin Mud was dressed in a tunic made of gold cloth, and wore a crown with rubies that shone in the morning light. He neared the pier, and Elliot saw two figures following him.

"Stay close behind," the Queen whispered and quickly moved to the planks connecting their ship to the pier.

Elliot and Peter followed her while the rest of the soldiers formed a line behind them. Sophie stepped off the ship, and as soon as Elliot's feet touched firm ground, he felt as if he'd been reborn. They approached the smiling Emperor. Odin Mud was a thin man with thick white hair, small blue eyes, and pearly white skin. He opened his arms in an attempt to welcome Sophie.

"I didn't think you'd ever come to my land, Your Majesty! I'm glad to finally meet you in person," he said.

Rings with multi-coloured rubies adorned his fingers. Elliot knew that Odin addressing Sophie as "Her Majesty" was positive, but he doubted he meant it.

"Good morning, Lord Odin. The truth is, I don't know how to address you, as no one in my land has ever held the title of Emperor," Sophie said with a slight bow.

The man smiled. "You can just call me Odin. These things are of no importance. Soon you'll be my daughter, too." Every word sounded pretentious. "This is your future husband, my son Marin, and next to him is Edmee, my daughter."

"Pleased to meet you, my Prince," Sophie said with a bow. She turned to Edmee. "And you, my Princess."

Marin walked towards Sophie. His face was kind and youthful. He had long black hair and dark eyes. The Prince bowed before Sophie, his white cloak touching the cobbled ground. *Is he as cunning as his father?* Elliot wondered as he studied Marin.

"It's an honour to meet you, Your Majesty, and it's an even greater honour that you travelled here so that our wedding can take place in my land. I'll make sure you don't regret it. I'll escort you immediately to your quarters so you can rest after your journey," he said, looking straight into her eyes.

"Thank you very much, my Prince," Sophie said.

Edmee neared the Queen. The woman seemed younger than her brother, and her attire differed from that of Marin and Odin. Edmee was armoured, and her red hair flowed behind her white cloak. Elliot wagered that she thirsted for blood just like Syrella's daughters. *We need to be cautious with this woman.*

"It'll be your duty to take good care of such a beautiful bride, brother," Edmee said and bowed to Sophie.

"You need to rest, Your Majesty," the Emperor said. "We've announced that the wedding will take place in ten days. Until the feast, you and your future husband's attendance will be required in many places. Our people must see the Queen of Knightdorn—the future wife of their Prince—with their own eyes. I'll ensure your wedding is the grandest this continent has ever seen!"

"That's very kind of you, my lord," Sophie said. "However, before that, I'd like to talk." Her voice had come out stiffly on the last words.

"You've had a long journey, Your Majesty. Take this day to rest, and we'll talk tomorrow morning. My men and my son will escort you and your soldiers to your quarters. We've prepared a sumptuous meal for you."

"Thank you, my lord," Sophie said. "I'd like to introduce Peter Brau and Elliot, two of my best warriors but also my most trusted advisors."

Elliot bowed sharply, and so did Peter.

"I didn't expect to see you on my land, Elliot." The Emperor looked at him with obvious curiosity.

"I didn't expect you would take any interest in me, my lord," Elliot said.

A wide grin distorted Odin's face. "Anyone would be interested in a man like you... A man trained by Althalos Baudry. The Queen may have omitted to mention your full name, but I'm pleased to have you in my land, Elliot Egercoll."

The Invisible Enemy

S yrella watched the flames smoulder in the hearth, a tide of rage
churning within her. The fire warmed her body, and a small table
with four chairs stood before her. She sat on a comfortable bench at one
end of the room. The image of the headless corpse, the daggers stuck into
the youth's lifeless eyes, hadn't left her mind for the past two nights. She
should have realised earlier that Walter's rat was a powerful man in her
city.

How have I not caught on all these years? she thought for the umpteenth
time. She'd ruled since she was only fifteen, and the years in power had
blinded her. She'd never believed that one of her noblemen would side
with a Thorn. She remembered her dismay when she'd found out that
William of the Sharp Swords was loyal to Walter.

*"William lost his father and brother in the Battle of the Forked River.
I'm sure that was when he began to hate you and wanted revenge. He never
forgave you for your decisions in that battle,"* Jahon had told her some time
ago.

*"If he'd hated me, he could have just left Elmor and have sworn alle-
giance to some other ruler—someone more virtuous than Walter, the man
responsible for the deaths of his relatives."*

*"William was a man of war. He knew that soldiers kill their enemies in
battle. I'm sure he didn't blame Walter but you for your mistakes."*

Syrella remembered her rage about the fact that a man in her guard
had betrayed her. Nevertheless, she hadn't dared to imagine that there
were other rats in Elmor. A few days after William's death, Walter Thorn

had arrived on her land. At that moment, weeks ago, she had realised yet another traitor was in her midst.

"Whoever this man may be, he's very powerful in Wirskworth," Jahon had told her the first time they'd heard about the stranger who had intruded into the city just as Walter was at its gates about to lay siege.

Syrella had been watching her councillors and the powerful noblemen in Wirskworth, but nothing that would incriminate one of them had reached her ears. As she'd told Sophie and Jahon countless times, the traitor had heard they were suspicious and was on guard.

"There may be more than one," the Queen had said.

"I don't think so. I can't be sure, but I can't imagine that Thorn could have succeeded in getting to other men from my council," she'd responded.

Syrella sighed angrily as the two daggers in the lad's eyes came back to her. A murder in her chamber indicated that whoever was the rat was watching them closely—all of them.

The traitor may even know about my relationship with Jahon. She wondered who the man who knew so much and hated her so much could be. *If he knows about Jahon and me, why hasn't he spread the word? He knows we're looking for him... He knows that if he did, his identity might be revealed.* No doubt if a man on her council talked to her about her illicit relationship with a sense of certainty, then Syrella would have suspected he was the spy. *He doesn't care about what I did with Jahon. All he wants is to stay close to me until Walter destroys me.*

Syrella covered her face with her hands and, after a moment, glanced at the lit fireplace in front of her. She continued staring at the flames until the door to the chamber suddenly swung open. Three figures stepped through its threshold. Jahon and Selwyn stood in front of her, with an elven woman behind them.

"Has the traitor been found?" Selwyn asked. He wore a blue jerkin, his hands balled into fists at his sides.

"If I'd tracked him down, his head would have been hung on a spike outside the city temple," Syrella told him. "I called you here to draw your attention to something. Walter's informant knows everything that goes on in my city. We must be careful, and anything important should not leave this room. We'll discuss things here, just the four of us."

"Thank you for this honour, Lady Syrella. I didn't expect you to trust me enough to allow me to be present during your secret councils," Alysia said.

Syrella frowned. "Elliot and Aleron trust you, and I trust their judgement," she said.

"Elliot warned of a man of Thorn's in your inner circle for some time, but I never expected something like this... How did he get into your quarters and kill a guard?" Selwyn had gone red.

"At that time, there weren't guards in my quarters, which makes me certain that the informant is watching us."

"Why would someone be watching me? I only arrived here a few days ago." Alysia grimaced. Syrella got up from her seat and approached the three. "I don't know who the informant is watching. I believe he has his men around me and Jahon, and I suspect he has been following the movements of all the important people in the city." She turned to Selwyn. "You're the son of Sophie's most trusted officer, and you"—she looked to Alysia—"you're responsible for the fortification of the city. In addition, you know the weak points of the wyverns, which will be Thorn's main weapon in the last battle."

"Do you believe that someone will try to harm me?" Alysia asked, and Syrella nodded. "So be it. Let them try." Her red eyes shone brightly as she said those last words.

"You must be careful—you never know when they might attack you," Jahon said. "You and Selwyn mustn't walk alone in the city when it's dark. If someone wants to assault you, I'd wager he'd do so at night."

"Even better," Alysia retorted.

Syrella couldn't believe that the elf was so courageous. She felt admiration for Alysia. "I know you aren't cowards," she said, looking at Selwyn and Alysia. "Nevertheless, nothing untoward must happen to us until my army returns from Vylor. We'll be careful. I can order guards to escort you wherever you go."

"I don't think that's a good idea. That will turn us into targets," Selwyn told her.

"I agree." Jahon seemed to be mulling things over, his hands hidden beneath his long cloak.

"I like walking in the city at night, however, I promise you I'll be careful," Selwyn said. "I wonder whether that young man—the guard who was found murdered—had divulged what he'd seen to anyone."

Syrella sighed deeply. "I don't think so. He was afraid they might kill him if he dared speak."

"I tried to get some information discreetly, but none of the guards seemed to know anything," Jahon said.

"I hope you didn't disobey me and reveal what happened to anyone!" Syrella said. "I don't want the few men left in Wirskworth to be terror-stricken while we prepare for battle against Walter! I don't want anyone to know that Thorn has informa—"

"I'm not an idiot! I spread the word that he died of a strange disease," Jahon cut in. "I tried to find things out discreetly. Only I and Thorold who examined the corpse know the truth, besides those in this room."

Syrella felt satisfied hearing his words. "Be careful," she said once again. "If anything suspicious reaches your ears, I want to know about it immediately."

Her gaze went to the flames in the great hearth once more. She wished her daughters and Velhisya were in Moonstone. She felt very lonely, and the image of the severed head on her bed made her nauseous at night.

"There's something I've been thinking about," Alysia said softly.

Syrella sat back down on the wooden bench and looked at her, clasping her hands together.

"Whoever this man may be, he cannot watch over you and all your loyal followers alone. He has accomplices, which means others who stand against you are in the city."

Syrella and Jahon had thought about that. "I know..." Syrella said, feeling that familiar anger. "These words may make me sound vain, but I believe that most of the accomplices of this traitor don't know what they're doing. I think he's asked them to watch us for our safety, and none of them share his aspirations."

"What makes you think that?" Alysia asked.

"People are devoted to me in Elmor. Even after my defeat at the Forked River, the people wanted me as their ruler. If the traitor had made his intentions known, the news would have reached my ears. He may have convinced some men that I should be removed, but there can't be many of them. As I said before, I'm guessing most of his men don't know what's going on," Syrella said.

"Then, perhaps we should spread the word that there's a traitor in the city. This will alert those who don't know the truth, and then we'll find out the identity of this—"

"No," Syrella said.

Alysia seemed puzzled. "Why not?"

"I agree with Alysia," Selwyn said, touching the hilt of the sword hanging from his belt. "The only reason we should hide what we know is that we mustn't make the traitor suspect we are onto him. Since he decided to reveal that he's been following us by assassinating the guard, it means he knows that we know. We have nothing to lose."

Syrella frowned. "If what happened had occurred when my army was in the city, I'd agree with you, Lord Brau. I'd decided to keep an eye on several suspects, hoping the traitor would make a mistake. I wanted everything I knew to remain a secret. Of course, after what happened in my chamber, things have changed..."

"Then why not—"

"I don't want such a commotion in the city while my army is marching on Vylor," Syrella snapped.

"Why?" Selwyn insisted.

"I have very few men in Wirskworth! I'm here alone, fortifying the city, waiting for Thorn. I'm vulnerable without my army. I may assume that the traitor has few men who are loyal to him, but I cannot risk it. I'm willing to spread the news as soon as my daughters return with my entire army."

"I agree. There aren't many of us guarding the Governor. We don't need a witch-hunt right now," Jahon told him.

Alysia looked deep in thought, and Syrella could see the trouble in her eyes. "I think that's why the traitor made such a risky move and killed that guard in your quarters. If your army were in the city, he may have run away without doing anything. He feels confident, and that's what scares me... He believes that you won't hunt him down now by spreading the news, and even if you did, he knows you cannot hurt him," the elf said.

"He may simply believe that you'll never discover who he is. His conceitedness may have blinded him," Selwyn added.

"We can continue this discussion all night without finding any answers. Thank you for sharing your thoughts with me, but for now, there's nothing more we can do but be careful," Syrella said. "Let's all go back to our quarters, and we'll talk again at first light."

Selwyn and Alysia nodded and left the room, while Jahon remained.

"I didn't want to talk in front of them," he said once they were alone. "However, I fear for your safety. Much of what was said is disturbing. The traitor may try to get you out of the way now that the army is away. He'll find no better opportunity than this."

"Walter won't want to treacherously kill any more of his ruler enemies. He did that before with Aymer Asselin and everyone still whispers that he failed to truly win that battle. He wants to kill the last of his enemies with a display of power... The traitor only wants information to ensure Walter's victory—nothing more."

"I thought everything that's happened would have taught you that you can never be sure of anything. A few days ago, Walter tried to get Borin Ballard out of the way in Iovbridge."

Syrella's gaze wandered into space. "Borin was insignificant, and everyone knew it. Walter won't do that to Sophie and me, his two strongest rivals."

"I hope you're right. I'll increase your guard." With these words, Jahon left the room.

Syrella stared into space, the soft crackle of the flames the only sound in the chamber. She had given everything for her land, even the lives of people from her own House, yet someone had dared to betray her.

Whoever you are, I'll catch you! I swear I'll catch you! And then the rats will devour your lifeless head.

Blood and Betrayal

Peter made himself comfortable on his bed and glanced out of the window. The building he was in was one of the most beautiful he'd ever seen, and the moon in the night sky had a strange, red hue. Years ago, Peter had heard that there were two moons in the world and that only one was visible from the land of Knightdorn. He hadn't believed it but it turned out he was wrong. Before coming to his room, he'd seen one moon in the west and another in the north. The one in the west was the most beautiful he'd ever seen. It was huge, and its colour was reminiscent of blood.

He tried to stretch but felt pain everywhere. His wound from the ship had healed, but his body was exhausted. He and Elliot had agreed that one of them would always guard Sophie. Elliot had urged him to get some sleep, saying that he would spend the night outside the Queen's chamber with a few other guards. Peter was grateful for that. He was older now, and journeys and hardship were difficult for him. He moved slowly and heard his back creak. Peter stood up and shuffled towards the window. The stars seemed to form a circle around the red moon, and he marvelled at the view his chamber afforded him.

Peter closed his eyes, exhaustion setting in. He knew that even on that night, his fatigue wouldn't be enough to plunge him into the world of dreams. His thoughts were like thorns biting into his flesh.

You need to talk to Sophie—and tell her the truth for once and for all. His conscience told him that repeatedly, but he hadn't yet found the courage to do so, despite the passage of many years.

He looked out the window again, and his gaze fell upon the roofs of the flat, stone houses. There were wooden belvederes with straw roofs on most of them. The houses of Mirth were square and seemed more spacious than those of the common people in Knightdorn. Peter tore himself away from the window. He had to finally find the courage to confess the truth to the Queen so that he could get some reprieve from his mental torture.

He sat down on the bed. The mattress was one of the most comfortable he'd ever lain on. The Emperor had an abundance of gold—every corner of his palace was decorated with gold, and even the windows of the ornate building were encased in multi-coloured rubies.

It makes sense he's so rich, seeing that everything on the continent belongs to him...

Kerth hadn't been plagued by war, as thousands of its people had left to seek their fortune in Knightdorn centuries ago. Peter had heard that no major wars had occurred on the continent since then. Three noble houses exerted power over Kerth's three largest cities for centuries until Odin got the other leaders out of the way at a feast and named himself Emperor. Peter found Odin cunning and bloodthirsty, but he couldn't deny that his plan had given him what he desired without unending battles and death.

Peter remembered hearing an old legend that said that before the First Kings left Kerth for Knightdorn, war was a way of life in this land. *Wherever power-hungry nobles set foot, they leave nothing but destruction...*

He recalled the events of that morning. Odin had seemed delighted by Sophie's arrival, and his son appeared content to behold his bride-to-be. If nothing else, the Queen was endowed with a unique beauty.

Is everything going to turn out all right?

As much as he tried to be optimistic, he felt afraid. Odin had tried to marry his son to Sophie before, and her refusal had shown him that the Queen didn't really want the marriage. The fact that she'd agreed to marry his son now that she'd lost her palace exposed her motives to the Emperor. Most marriages in the kingdom may have been purely for convenience, but Peter had heard how conceited Odin was and was sure that Sophie's decision had vexed him over the years. The Emperor was only using them to achieve his goals, and if one day he didn't need them, he would have no qualms about burning them alive.

Odin may be devious, but he owes Sophie nothing. You were the one who swore allegiance to her and was too much of a coward to tell her the truth, a voice whispered inside his head. He could no longer stand thinking about such things. One day, they would drive him insane. He tried to chase them away in vain. The image of the Queen as a child suddenly flashed into his mind.

"How will I rule the entire kingdom? I haven't even seen all its cities," nine-year-old Sophie had said, petrified.

"Your councillors and I will help you make the right decisions. As the years go by, you will learn everything you need to succeed," he'd told her, trying to encourage her.

Then, a memory of Althalos Baudry standing in front of him, looking grim, appeared.

"I want you to support Sophie for Thomas' office."

"Have you lost your mind?" Peter couldn't comprehend that an innocent little girl was supposed to protect the kingdom from a man like Walter.

"A leader full of love and compassion for his people will always have allies who believe in him, no matter how powerful his enemies are."

Peter had nothing to say in reply, and the aged Master had hurried off. Then, he'd searched for the strength to stop him and tell him the truth—to confess that he couldn't be by Sophie's side since he'd already betrayed her House, but he hadn't succeeded.

Peter knew he deserved to suffer for all he'd done, so the gods had punished him. His two sons, his blood, had paid the price for him, and Selwyn's future was uncertain as the last battle against Walter approached. He'd spent countless nights wondering whether he could have prevented his sons' deaths, but he couldn't find any answers. A part of him blamed Syrella Endor for what had happened, yet he knew that, in truth, his sons' fate wasn't her fault. Peter relived the past over and over again. He could still see Doran and Sindel bleeding on the ground as his men shouted at him to run, trying to pull him away.

Peter thought back to that battle years ago. Kelanger's wall was thick and tall, and the men of Oldlands were adept at protecting their city from sieges. Walter wanted that army. He knew that if he added it to his forces, he'd become invincible, and he'd decided to take Oldlands from Aymer Asselin even if it cost him thousands of soldiers. The Queen had immediately agreed to help the birthplace of Alice Asselin, her aunt, and Peter had summoned all of Iovbridge's allies. Borin Ballard had responded immediately, but Syrella Endor didn't want to fight. The news that had come from her was that Oldlands was too far from her supply lines.

Peter felt angry thinking about her decision. Even though time had passed, he found it difficult to forgive her, especially since he knew the real reason she didn't want to help Oldlands. Syrella blamed Aymer for not sending his army to help King Thomas Egercoll in the Battle of Aquarine. Aymer was closer to the battle than any of the king's allies, but he'd delayed sending his men, and Thomas was slaughtered as a result.

Peter had spoken to Sophie as soon as he'd heard the news. He'd told her it might not be wise to march an army into Kelanger without Elmor's help. However, the Queen and the whole council had objected to his words. Aymer was one of the Crown's most loyal and valuable allies, with a strong army. At the same time, Sophie felt that Walter's attack on the capital of Oldlands would be a fatal mistake since Thorn would lose with the help of the Royal Army.

Peter had obeyed. He, along with thousands of Iovbridge and Ballar's men, had travelled to Oldlands, and after a few days, he had felt more hopeful than ever. Everything pointed to the fact that Walter wouldn't easily pass through the gates of Kelanger and would also have to face the Royal Army in the open. Thorn had organised his men masterfully and managed to ward off Peter's attacks, but it looked like he would lose the battle until the tide turned.

Peter still remembered the screams waking him inside Ronhian, the old castle of the House of Huster, where he and his men had camped. They'd been attacked in the middle of the night, and the enemy soldiers were too many to count. Peter couldn't understand what had happened, and he'd seen the arrows piercing his sons' bodies as they ran to escape. Countless men breathed their last in that place—so many that he could still hear their screams in his nightmares. Borin Ballard's sons had also died during that attack.

A day later, Peter found out that Aymer had been assassinated in his sleep and Ricard Karford had joined forces with Walter, sending both Oldland's and Walter's soldiers to wipe out the Royal Army. Peter never revealed his betrayal of her House to Sophie, and he had paid the price with his blood.

He got off the bed again and kicked the wall opposite him. His scream was loud in the empty chamber, and he feared a guard would rush in to see what had happened. The pain in his right foot was excruciating, and he hoped he hadn't broken a toe. Peter was worn out. He would have given anything to be able to take his sons' place in the realms of the dead to be freed from this torment, but he couldn't.

I need to help the Queen defeat Walter. Even if I never tell her what I did, if Thorn is defeated, my sons will be avenged, he repeated to himself, but no death and no revenge would bring Doran and Sindel back.

Peter turned back to his bed once more, lay down and watched the red moon shining among the stars. He stared at it for hours until his eyelids grew heavy, and he felt his body being carried away by a strong wind that took him to another world, away from care and suffering.

270

The Knights of Faith

Sophie watched the eyes of the Emperor light up while a little further off, Marin and Edmee seemed perturbed. Odin was seated on a raised throne, clothed in purple silk, and the Prince wore a green jerkin and white cloak. Edmee was armoured with two gold clasps in the shape of the sun fastening her cloak. Sophie crossed her legs. She was seated near a wooden table next to Elliot and Peter, while across the way from her sat her future husband and his sister.

Sophie's gaze wandered around the room they were in. The walls were covered with elaborate depictions of strange symbols, and a huge picture of Odin was on the ceiling. The artists in the city had gone to great lengths to paint him accurately. Sophie remembered the faces of the gods staring down at her from the ceiling of the Royal Hall, but Odin had a large ego. It was obvious that the Emperor felt he was a god, and he'd chosen an image of himself to adorn the ceiling of his Great Hall.

"I've heard many legends about the Elder Races and the wyverns. I always thought these creatures existed centuries ago and had since disappeared. Even so, I never ruled out that it all could have been just tales. People enjoy stories about strange creatures," Edmee said, her armour glinting in the rays of the sun filtering through the windows of the majestic hall.

"These legends are real, and these creatures exist even today. As I said, the Elder Races fought with us in Wirskworth just days ago, and a wyvern attacked us," Sophie said. She recalled having had countless discussions about the war over the years, but this was one of the most difficult she remembered.

Odin frowned. "If I understand correctly, giants also belong to the Elder Races. Nevertheless, they chose to fight for Walter."

Sophie saw he was scratching his chin. "That's true," she admitted. "The giants couldn't bring themselves to forgive the House of Egercoll for everything they'd been through all these years."

"If my memory serves me well, Walter's mother was an Eger—"

"That's immaterial." Elliot cut the Emperor off, and Odin turned to face him with a look that revealed both surprise and rage. Sophie wagered the man wasn't used to being interrupted. "Walter dedicated his life to destroying their House and this is what imbued him with respect and standing in the eyes of the giants."

"I wonder about one thing... How did you manage to break the curse?" Edmee's wide eyes turned to Elliot.

Sophie watched her cousin lower his gaze in silence. "None of that matters," Elliot said after a moment.

Edmee continued staring at him, a furrow forming in the middle of her forehead.

"I agree with Elliot," Sophie said. "The only thing that matters is what we will face next. Are you with us or not?"

Odin looked on with a blank expression, as if he was trying to come to a decision.

"We'll defeat Walter, and together we'll bring peace to Knightdorn," came a voice. Marin looked at her with an expression that showed he was willing to do whatever it took for her. However, the Emperor didn't seem pleased with his son's words. Sophie swore that Odin looked despondent listening to him.

"You said these creatures—the elwyn and the elves—can take on the wyverns?" Odin asked. Sophie nodded. "Wirskworth is one of the most powerful cities in Knightdorn, and all you're missing is more soldiers?"

"Exactly," Sophie replied. "With a few thousand more men behind the walls of Wirskworth, we will defeat Thorn and retake Iovbridge."

The Emperor remained silent.

"Let's hope the elwyn and the elves can defeat those winged monsters. Judging from everything you've told us, even forty thousand men won't find it easy to take on the wyverns," Edmee said.

"The elves faced hundreds of wyverns when they fought the giants in the Black Death Age. Even if all the wyverns stand against us, there will only be a few dozen," Elliot told her.

"Even so, the elwyn and the elves have been decimated, too, if I've understood correctly what Sophie has told us," the Princess replied.

She knows far more about war than Marin... That doesn't bode well for us. Sophie expected more from her future husband. "I saw the elwyn and the elves with my own eyes defeat a wyvern without even being behind the walls of Wirskworth. As we speak, they are fortifying the city, and I'm sure they'll be able to deal with these monsters," she said.

"I agree," Peter said for the first time since the conversation began.

"I thought you wanted your son to become King in Knightdorn..." Marin rose from his seat abruptly. "With our men, it'll be easy to defeat Walter and bring peace to that continent."

"Have you ever been in a battle, Marin?" Odin's voice was honey-sweet and full of sarcasm.

"No, Father," the young Prince replied, his eyes widening with determination.

"I may never have been to Knightdorn, but I've been trading with its land for years and have heard many things. Walter Thorn is one of the greatest warriors and commanders the world has ever known. We must be careful, or the only realm you'll conquer will be that of the dead..." Odin said.

Marin's face flushed, and Sophie looked closely at the Prince for a moment. He seemed sincere, with no complex secret plans being harboured in his thoughts, yet he was too daring and perhaps naive. Edmee and the Emperor seemed to have a clearer understanding that even with all the armies in the world, Walter wouldn't easily lose the war.

"I paid careful attention to all that was said, Father. I may have never been on the battlefield, but I know my bride and I cannot rule in Knightdorn without defeating Walter Thorn. I believe the Queen hasn't lied to us. If anything, she wants to defeat Walter more than we do, and if she doesn't prepare us for what we have to face, we'll all die. If we're careful, I believe we can succeed. Otherwise, order your men to remain in Kerth and call off the wedding. I don't think the Queen will agree to marry me unless we help her regain her crown." Marin seemed to have mustered up all his courage to say these words.

Sophie glanced at Odin. "Don't take this the wrong way, my lord. Naturally, marriage to Prince Marin is the greatest honour, but I cannot abandon my people and live on this continent." She had been careful in her choice of words. Everyone knew she'd accepted the marriage because she needed Kerth's men, yet she had to appear to be grateful for her future husband.

The Emperor rose from his high seat and walked towards her. He approached her slowly, a smile appearing on his lips as he stopped in front of her. "I think if we're careful, we can succeed. My men will help you defeat Walter. Edmee and my most loyal generals will hold councils with Elliot and Peter to better prepare for battle. However, you and Marin must give the people of Kerth what they desire."

"And what might that be, my lord?" Sophie asked, filled with joy that Odin's men would fight by her side.

"The magic of a royal wedding!" Odin's eyes glinted. "My people will travel from every town and village in Kerth to see you! All of them want to admire the Queen who will unite Kerth and Knightdorn. I want you to start going around the city. All I want my people to talk about for the next few days is your beauty and your splendid dresses. A royal wedding ignites the interest of ordinary people. I don't want my people to fear the war... If they find out what we're up against—if they fear that Walter and his monsters might one day attack our land—it'll sow discord in the city. Such a thing cannot happen."

"No one has more power than you in Kerth. I'd wager that no amount of discord can harm you, Lord Mud," Elliot said, his voice exuding confidence.

"Perhaps... Even so, if you'd ruled for as long as I have, you'd know that discord breeds enemies. All those who want to see you die but dare not do anything about it seize such opportunities, and I never give my enemies opportunities," Odin said.

Elliot smiled.

"Very well, my lord. Elliot and Peter will talk with your generals and Marin, and I will do as you wish," she said. *This damn wedding is going to delay us...*

The Emperor's face lit up with joy. "Wonderful. My servants will show you some dresses and jewels that you might like to wear."

Sophie nodded curtly.

"I have another question," Elliot said, and Odin turned to face him. "When we arrived, how did you know who I was?"

The man smiled smugly. "News of an apprentice of Althalos travels quickly, my lad."

"Of course. But how did you recognise me?"

"The Queen said your name... I imagined no other Elliot would have travelled with her to be present at her wedding—you're her cousin." The Emperor opened his arms wide.

"I've never seen an apprentice of Althalos on the battlefield with my own eyes. If I'm to come up against Walter, I'd like to see whether the rumours about his apprentices are true," Edmee scoffed.

Sophie watched as Elliot took a stance that radiated arrogance—one she detested. She may have had a soft spot for her cousin, but she never liked it when he adopted that conceited look.

"I'll make sure that you see all that you wish to with your very own eyes, my Princess," Elliot replied with a smile.

Elliot looked out at Mirth from a tall tower. The Red Palace was full of high turrets from which the beautiful view of the capital city of Kerth could be admired. The ornate building where the Emperor lived looked more like a castle than a palace. Undoubtedly, it was one of the most opulent buildings he'd ever seen, and he'd heard that the golden dome at the top took on a red hue under sunlight, giving it its name.

The sun began to set, giving way to the moon. He'd expected the place to be cold during winter since it was much further north than Elmor. However, Mirth was warm, and the dry trees along its length indicated that winter and rain weren't frequent. A maid had told him that there was even a desert in the southern part of the continent. He remembered Althalos explaining what a desert was, but the Master had told him such places no longer existed in Knightdorn.

Kerth must be very hot in spring and summer.

"I've always loved seeing the city from up here since I was a child."

Elliot turned to see Marin approaching him, wearing a light blue jerkin and black pants.

"Will you miss this place if you become King of Knightdorn?" Elliot asked.

The man laughed. "I don't think so."

Marin's indifference about leaving his homeland surprised Elliot. "Why not?" He asked.

"This is a beautiful place. However, I've always wanted to live far..." he trailed off. "Some things don't suit me here."

"Do you want to get away from your father?"

Marin's lips parted. "Sometimes, I disagree with his decisions," he mumbled after a while.

"I realised that this morning," Elliot told him. "People with power and authority often find it difficult to listen."

Marin frowned. "My father has prevailed over all of Kerth... For centuries, three Houses ruled the cities, and he managed to conquer them all, bringing glory to our House like none of our ancestors ever had. He managed to become Emperor. So, yes... It's hard to get him to listen."

"It's strange that glory is synonymous with killing in this world." Elliot knew he'd overdone it. He shouldn't have insulted the father of Sophie's future husband. It could jeopardise everything they were trying to achieve.

To his surprise, Marin laughed. "I agree. However, the other two rulers of this continent would have also gladly got my father out of the way if they'd had the chance. Odin did what he did without war, and his rule brought stability and peace to our land for a long period."

"You may be right. Have any people opposed your father's rule since he became Emperor?" Elliot asked.

"Of course..."

"What does he do about them?"

Marin's face darkened for a few moments. "My father punishes those who threaten the peace of Kerth severely," he said, looking nervous.

If nothing else, it's a cunning excuse to kill anyone who opposes him. "Do you agree with his actions?" Elliot asked.

"Not always... I know a ruler must stand in the way of anything that might threaten his sovereignty, but my father made a few mistakes. He should never have punished those knights in that manner."

Elliot was surprised. "Knights? Does the order of knighthood exist in your land?"

Marin seemed angry at himself for speaking his thoughts out loud. "These knights weren't like those of Knightdorn," he said, shaking his head.

"What do you mean?"

"The knights in your land used to be men of war, and I heard that some years ago, the title was only conferred on the most skilled warriors who were the guards of Knightdorn's rulers. The newly chosen knights were richly rewarded with gold and land."

"That's true," Elliot replied.

"In this land, great warriors are called Faris, but this title gives them nothing more than a modicum of prestige. Some Faris protected leaders in Kerth, but not always. No ruler has bestowed the old title of 'knight' upon his skilled warriors for centuries here."

"And what were those knights who were punished?"

Marin sighed and glanced at the city. "They named themselves knights. Most of them were Faris and were worshippers of our god, the God of Justice. They never had wives or children and were sworn to uphold only one cause—to administer justice. They believed my father's rulership was unfair but needed gold to achieve their goals. So, they started selling their services to various lords for gold. They also assisted noblemen in trade between the cities of Kerth."

"How did they assist in trading?" Elliot asked.

"Many rich people don't want to travel through the desert to get to Gorin, and many places near Sauris are dangerous. Poverty-stricken villagers attack merchants and emissaries carrying gold. As I said, most of the Knights of Faith were Faris, and their skill with the sword allowed them to transport gold to other cities of Kerth for a reward. They ended up amassing a fortune and also enjoyed the support of several noblemen since they were of help to them." Marin paused. "At first, my father found their endeavours useful. He would never waste his men doing such dirty work for the noblemen. But when he realised that the Knights of Faith secretly wanted to change a lot in Kerth and limit his power, he decided to destroy them."

Elliot listened to everything carefully. "What did they want to change?"

Marin sighed wearily. "They believed that people would never find peace with a single ruler. They wanted the leadership to be shared amongst a council of many men and women chosen by the people. In addition, they wanted slavery to end in Kerth and for the villagers to have a more dignified life. Some of their demands didn't sound that unreasonable to me. I told my father to abolish slavery, just like they did years ago in Knightdorn, and to increase the payment of the villagers.

That way, he would convince his people that he was the leader they wanted—that there was no need for a council to rule the continent. But he didn't listen to me... He told me I was an idiot, and it would cost him Kerth if he did everything I said."

"Did the noblemen want the death of these knights?" Elliot asked.

"Not at first. The Knights of Faith had been helping them with much of their dirty work for a long time. However, when the noblemen heard they wanted to give the people the power to choose their leaders, they immediately asked the Emperor to destroy the knights."

"And did he succeed?"

Marin was expressionless. "Yes. He burned them alive."

Elliot knew from the moment he'd set foot on this soil that Odin Mud was just as ruthless and sadistic as Walter. The only thing he lacked was skill in battle. *We need to be really careful...*

"From what I've heard, Sophie is different from my father. I hope that with her by my side, I'll create a truly just and peaceful kingdom."

Elliot watched Marin's face. He still wasn't sure about him, but he swore the Prince was the only one in the palace who spoke truthfully.

A Shield of Power

S elwyn held his sword before his face, ready to defend himself. Alysia smiled at him and swung her sword at his feet. Selwyn made a sharp move to the right to avoid being hit. His movements were awkward, and he almost lost his balance. The woman attacked again, trying to wound his right arm. Selwyn felt the blade scrape against his flesh and let out a cry of pain.

"Damn!"

"Clear your head." Alysia's tone was even and calm.

Selwyn draped his jerkin over the tear, soaking up some of the blood gushing from the wound. Red seeped through the silk. After a while, he raised his sword again.

"Stop being afraid of my sword. Stop being afraid that you might get hurt," Alysia told him.

"Sometimes, fear is useful. If you aren't at all afraid, it's easy to throw away your life," Selwyn countered.

Alysia smiled. "Fear is useful as long as it doesn't make you cowardly."

"I'm not a coward!" Selwyn snapped, anger rising.

"Respect my sword, but don't be afraid of it." With those words, she raised her weapon in front of her face.

Selwyn did the same, and then the elf's sword came down towards his chest. He didn't have time to pull his body away, so he raised his sword, pointing it downwards trying to fend her off. The sound of steel clashing rang out, and then Alysia's blade flooded with red light. His palms burned, but he tried to bear the pain. Alysia thrust her sword at him, but he resisted. The burning grew stronger, and he felt his flesh would melt.

With a piercing cry, Selwyn kicked Alysia's right leg. She screamed in pain, and Selwyn swung his sword upwards. Alysia's weapon slipped from her hands as she stumbled backwards.

"Are you alright?" Selwyn asked, glancing down at the palm of his right hand. Despite the pain he'd felt, his skin was intact.

Alysia regained her balance and shot him an angry look. Her eyes were half closed, making her look like a cat about to pounce on an unsuspecting mouse. "I thought this was a sword fight."

"I thought anything was allowed since your sword can burn my hands! I can use some tricks, too."

Alysia smiled, but it wasn't a kind smile. She grabbed her sword from the stone ground and raised it high. Selwyn saw the sun setting in the evening sky and felt sweat dripping off his brow. He knew he'd soon regret what he had done. He raised his sword and was getting ready to defend himself again when he spotted an aged figure a few feet away from the small courtyard where they were duelling. Master Thorold watched them with an inscrutable look on his face.

"Ready?" Alysia asked, her red eyes alight.

Selwyn nodded sharply, and she ran towards him. He saw the small sword rip through the air, aimed at his right leg. He jumped to the left, avoiding the blade, and then his opponent went for his stomach. Selwyn raised his sword and parried her blade, trying to swing at the elf's shoulder. Alysia ducked under his weapon gracefully, and she prepared to attack again.

Damn! Her small shape made it difficult for him.

Alysia attacked his lower limbs over and over, and he tried to dodge the steel blade by hopping back. His breaths grew short. Alysia attempted to wound his arm again, but he dodged the swing of her sword as the woman brought her blade down onto his thigh. Selwyn parried, and the two swords clashed in front of his left leg. Suddenly, Alysia's blade filled with light, and he felt the flesh on his palm burning again. Selwyn tried to kick her again.

"Not this time."

Alysia lifted her leg, dodging the sword's swing and drawing her own blade upwards. Selwyn stumbled backwards, and the illuminated weapon came for his neck. He pulled away as fast as he could, and her sword changed course and came down towards his ribs. He gripped the hilt of his weapon with both hands and parried the brightly-lit blade. The burning under his palms grew hotter, and Alysia looked determinedly at him. She pushed her weapon towards him, and he felt ready to lay down his sword and surrender.

"NO!" Selwyn mustered all his strength and deflected Alysia's sword to the left, then immediately tried to wound her in the shoulder. Alysia dodged the swing of his blade and cut his right leg. Selwyn lost his balance and fell onto her, dragging her down with him. The sword slipped from her hand, losing its red light as they crashed to the ground.

"Get off me!" she snapped.

Selwyn got off her and sat on the ground, stretching out his right leg. The cut was deep, and it was oozing blood. When he'd started his practice with Alysia, he'd felt lucky that her height didn't allow her to hurt his head, but he'd discovered he was wrong. His arms and legs were now full of wounds, and he knew that in a real single combat, Alysia wouldn't need to aim at his head but could finish him off by cutting his throat.

"I think that's enough for today," he said wearily.

She looked at him disapprovingly. "If you're wounded in battle, will you ask the enemy to stop so that you can rest?"

"No. But if you continue to hurt me like this, I foresee not being able to fight the enemy."

Alysia got up slowly and extended her hand to him. Selwyn took it and stood up with a smile. He admired Alysia. She had the courage and determination he'd seen in only a few men over the years.

"How did you manage to endure the burning of the Light so long?"

she asked.

"I was wondering about that, too," came a voice, and Selwyn turned to the left.

Thorold approached, his aged eyes reflecting his obvious interest. Selwyn felt strange; he wasn't used to the apparent admiration he discerned in the words of those around him.

"I was in a lot of pain, but I wanted to give it my all. I wanted to get better," he said.

"Is your lust to kill your enemies that great?" Thorold asked.

"No. All I want is to protect my loved ones."

Thorold's blurry eyes opened wide, and he scratched his chin. "I've never wanted to train anyone after Walter attacked the City of Heavens years ago... However, you're different, Selwyn Brau," he said after a while.

Selwyn could have sworn that the Master was mocking him. "Really?"

Thorold looked skyward. "There are very few who want to fight to protect. Most men of war seek wealth, power, and revenge, and fail to see the most important virtue of a warrior. The thirst to become a shield for those you love is a powerful force few can perceive. I'll help you achieve what you seek."

Selwyn thought he'd heard wrong. "I thought Grand Masters only trained young boys. I'm rather old now."

Thorold started laughing. "Age, like ability, is more insignificant than the nocturnal walks of ants compared to what I've just told you. Let me know when your next practice is."

With that, the Master walked away, and Alysia raised her sword. "We're not done yet, Selwyn," she said.

Selwyn watched the Master for a few moments, puzzled by his words. After a while, he sighed wearily and raised his sword for another duel.

<hr />

Selwyn walked with a sense of eagerness; nighttime was now his favourite time of day. Several times, he'd caught himself waiting for it to go dark so that he could walk down the quiet streets of Wirskworth and enjoy some ale or wine in one of the city's inns. Over the past few days, his eagerness had grown as his training with Alysia wore him out.

He continued through deserted alleys, bound for the Three Arrows. The people of Wirskworth rushed home as soon as night fell. Word that Walter would attack their land again made them fearful and reluctant to go out after dusk. Selwyn looked around carefully since, after his recent conversations with Syrella, he knew he had to be alert when walking alone at night. The death of the man in the Governor's chamber had made him quite agitated lately.

As if damned Walter and his conspirator in Wirskworth weren't enough, now we have to deal with Liher, too... Selwyn thought.

It had been ten days since Linaria and Merhya had left the city with Syrella and the Queen's army, and he often wondered whether they would make it back with Velhisya alive.

The plan will work—they'll succeed. He wished that were true. He didn't even want to contemplate what would happen if their men failed. He also felt uneasy about his father's fate. He hoped he and Sophie would return to Knightdorn with another alliance, but word of the Emperor's character didn't fill him with optimism. *Odin needs us to achieve what he desires.*

Selwyn tried to push away his concerns. His arm and leg had been wounded by Alysia's blade, and his entire body ached from practice. He deserved a few moments of peace without torturing his mind. He tried to think of something joyful, and then the image of a woman with red hair made him smile. If Ida was at the Three Arrows today, he was sure to have a wonderful night.

He took in the crescent moon shining faintly through a small cloud. The roofs of the houses obscured its lower half, but he could still make it out in the night sky. For a moment, he imagined himself walking through the city with Ida at his side, gazing at the moon, and then shortly after, lying next to her naked body. He liked her smart conversation, her red hair, and even her voice enchanted him. He'd met countless noble women in his time, but they all seemed vain and spoiled, seeking only riches and feasts. Ida wasn't like that. She was always smiling, and her words made him feel good.

You've changed, he heard a familiar whisper in his head.

Ever since his brothers had died, his life had been steeped in fear, and now, just before the battle that could signal their destruction, he could put his worry behind him; he could put his hardships aside for a while to think about a beautiful woman. Nevertheless, a fear within him remained and wouldn't ever fade. No matter what he did, he couldn't help but feel concerned about the fate of everyone he loved.

Thorold chose to train you for all that you feel—for who you are. His conscience was both true and strange. Selwyn hadn't even dared to imagine that one day a Grand Master would take him on as his apprentice. He'd never had any special talent in battle, and his cowardice over the years was another reason that prevented him from becoming a good warrior. However, things had changed. Thorold hadn't chosen to train any other man in years but him.

Why me? He couldn't find any other answers than the ones he already knew. A peaceful warmth spread through his chest. Alysia, Thorold, Elliot, there were so many who wanted to help him. He couldn't remember ever having felt as important his whole life before.

A woman's voice brought him out of his reverie. He looked around, searching for the owner of the voice. Selwyn walked hurriedly down the alleys, and he scanned the doors of the houses along his way. He couldn't see anything, and the voice had hushed. He took a few more steps and then suddenly stopped.

"Help!"

He started to run, looking all around as new voices reached his ears.

"Help, help!"

The voices seemed to belong to children. Selwyn searched for the source of the sound, and then he stopped abruptly in front of a dark alley. Two figures were lying on the cobbled ground. "What's the matter?" he asked.

"They're stealing our weapons!" said a girl's voice.

Selwyn ran towards the figures and saw three men inside a small building. Their arms were full of swords and axes, and they were trying to carry as many weapons as they could.

"What are you doing here?" he asked the men and glanced at the fallen figures—a boy and girl who looked like siblings. Rage bubbled up inside him.

"Mind your own business!" one of the men said.

Selwyn drew his sword. "I'm one of the Queen's soldiers and a loyal councillor of Syrella Endor. If you don't put those weapons down and leave now, you'll regret it."

The three men started laughing. "The Queen and the Governor's men left for Vylor and Kerth. No soldiers of Sophie Delamere remain in the city," one of them shot back. "Word gets round in Wirskworth."

"So, attack me then," Selwyn said, raising his sword.

The three men dropped what they were holding, keeping one weapon each. One held an axe, the others two swords.

"Walk away and forget you saw anything!" one of the thieves shouted.

"You'll steal from this place over my dead body!" Selwyn said.

The man with the axe cried out and brought his weapon down at Selwyn. He avoided the blow and thrust his sword into the man's neck. The man fell to the ground, groaning as blood spurted from his throat. His companions looked at Selwyn fearfully, and they dropped their swords and scurried away.

"Cowards!" shouted the girl who'd got up off the ground. She tried to pick up the little boy next to her. Her hair was tied in a bun, and her cheeks flushed with fear.

"I didn't expect there to be men who would steal with such audacity in Wirskworth," Selwyn said. Soon after, he wiped his sword on his cloak and sheathed it.

The fallen man let out a gasp and then lay still on the ground.

"Damn..." Selwyn hadn't meant to kill, but he'd panicked when he saw the axe coming down at him. A sob made him turn back to the two children standing a few feet away. "Are you alright?"

"Yes," the girl replied and hugged the boy tightly. He shook with fear. "My brother is afraid of fighting."

Selwyn walked over to them and bent down towards the frightened boy. "No one will hurt you." The little boy nodded briefly and grabbed his sister's woollen dress. "Where are your parents?"

"They're travelling to Vylor with the Governor's army," the girl said. She looked to be around twelve years old.

"Even your mother?" Selwyn asked quizzically.

"Our mother is a great warrior. She wanted to help save the Governor's niece and left me behind to take care of our home."

"Are your parents blacksmiths?" Selwyn asked, looking at the small building. A large cloth had fallen in its interior. The thieves had torn it in an attempt to enter and take what they could.

"Yes... This is our store, and we live upstairs on the top floor," the girl mumbled.

"Take your brother upstairs, and I'll inform the Governor. Syrella won't allow such a thing to happen again."

The girl didn't seem convinced. "There aren't any guards left in the city. The only ones left are guarding the Governor and the gates, so the thieves just keep attacking stalls, homes, and shops every night, and there's no one to help us."

Selwyn sighed angrily. He hadn't heard about this before. "I didn't think there were men in Wirskworth who would take advantage of the situation and start stealing. I thought allegiance to the Ruler of Elmor wouldn't allow for something like that."

"In every part of the world, there are men who would give up any loyalty for a little gold," the girl shot back.

Selwyn was speechless. "Go to your bed, and I'll see what I can do," he said after a while.

The two children picked up the fallen weapons and hurried into the building. Selwyn saw them disappear inside and climb a spiral staircase. A while later, he took one look at the lifeless body and let out a heavy sigh. He had to talk to Syrella. He had no idea what was really going on in the city when he'd started his walk that night. He felt guilty that those kids had witnessed a murder, and he had to find someone to remove the body. Selwyn remained for a few moments, and some words came to mind. If nothing else, the girl had reminded him of a truth he was accustomed to forgetting.

Unfortunately, there will always be people ready to give up their loyalty for a little gold.

A Ship for a Life

V elhisya tried to sleep but couldn't. Her body was stiff, and she couldn't get comfortable on the ice-cold floor. She glanced at the wall separating her cell from Matt's and wondered if he was sleeping. She hadn't a clue whether it was day or night, but something told her that dusk had fallen and a beautiful moon had appeared in the night sky. She liked dreaming of the nightscape and the beautiful rays that bathed the trees at dusk. The images gave her hope that she would perhaps come out of the dungeons alive one day.

Velhisya knew it was a miracle Liher hadn't killed her. After what had happened in that chamber, she was sure that the Ruler of Vylor wouldn't spare her life. Nevertheless, Lothar had confided that the news of her aunt's victory had got the Governor thinking. Now, Walter had been defeated twice, and if he wasn't careful with his final attack, he could lose his life. The balance of power had changed, and the whole kingdom was wondering who would prevail. Liher was cunning. He wouldn't risk killing Syrella Endor's niece until he saw what the final outcome was.

She tried to get a little more comfortable on the cell floor, and Elliot found his way into her mind. If the rumours were true, he had managed to break the curse that had imprisoned the Elder Races—the curse that had robbed her of her mother. She wished it had happened years earlier. She'd have given everything to have had the chance to see her mother, even just once. Velhisya was eager to meet the remaining elwyn to learn as much as she could about her mother—and herself. Perhaps the elwyn could explain how her touch had burned Liher. While most of the news

Lothar had brought her was hopeful, some things terrified her.

The giants had taken Walter's side, and the wyverns had attacked Wirskworth. She hoped they might just be rumours, but deep down, she knew they were true. Her father had told her that giants hated the Egercolls and that if they were set free, it was more than likely that they would fight for Walter. One more story nestled in her thoughts. Her father had also told her everything that was being said in the kingdom about the giant man of the Trinity of Death—Anrai. A giant had raped his mother to take revenge on humans, and that woman had given birth to a boy who was half giant and half human. She and Anrai were the only creatures with the blood of two races coursing through their veins and yet, they had taken different paths for their lives.

Velhisya sighed deeply. Walter might not have been expected to lose two battles, but even so, it would be difficult for them to beat him. Thorn had more men, and giants and wyverns fought by his side. Velhisya knew that the elwyn and elves could deal with the giants riding their winged beasts, however, her aunt and her allies would have to be very careful in order to win the war.

Lothar had also told her that some men had heard Walter had attacked Aquarine, leaving only part of his army to fight in Wirskworth during the last battle. *Strange.* It stood to reason that that rumour must have been true as well. If Walter had been on the battlefield and her aunt had won, he would have been dead, and word would have spread throughout the kingdom like wildfire.

Footsteps came from the entrance to the dungeons. Velhisya wondered who they belonged to, and then she heard a menacing voice.

"Wake up, you scumbag."

Her heart pounded while sweat coated her fingers. The cell door next to hers banged open, and Matt's scream echoed through the dungeons. "What do you want from me?" he cried.

"Your father didn't pay a thing, and the time has come for you to be punished for everything he stole from us."

"No, no, please! I beg you!"

"Our ruler has given us free rein to do whatever we want with you... What do you say, guys?"

"I'd say cut his dick off and put him on a spike," came a new voice.

"He's a handsome boy," another man spoke up. "I'd like to fuck him before we start cutting his parts off."

"You've always been a pervert, Tim," said the first man with a sound of disgust.

"Leave him alone!" Velhisya got up and rushed to the iron bars of her cell door. She tried to see what was happening in the cell next to hers. Three men entered the passage, their faces illuminated by the dim light of the torches.

"You'd better shut your mouth, otherwise, you'll meet a worse fate than him," one of the men said. He was tall with big shoulders and small eyes.

"I don't think so. Liher wants me for himself—you wouldn't dare touch me." She felt disgusted uttering those words.

The man walked over to her cell door and stuck his face in front of hers between the bars. "You're lucky. Don't push your luck though because one day Liher might stop caring about you, and then you'll become the whore of the City Guard."

Velhisya raised her hand and smacked him on the nose. The man grunted in pain and staggered backwards.

"I'll kill you, you whore!"

" Open this gate, and we'll see who kills whom!" Velhisya screamed.

One of the two guards who had been watching the scene grabbed the battered man by the shoulder. "We have clear instructions. We mustn't touch her."

"You'll regret what you did. Mark my words," said the tall man.

"You're the only one who'll regret it. If you mess with Matt, one day I'll get out of here and take your head off!" Velhisya felt rage welling up inside her.

A smile formed on the tall man's lips. "I didn't think you'd care so much about this piece of shit... I may not be able to hurt you, but I can do whatever I want to him, and you'll hear it all."

"ONE DAY I'LL KILL YOU!"

The guard laughed. "You won't do anything! You're just a whore in a cell." He turned to one of his two companions. "Fuck him, then cut off his dick, and throw it into her cell," he said.

"No, no, please!" It was apparent from Matt's tone of voice that he was crying. "I'm sure my father will pay up. He just needs a little time to find your gold."

"Your father is rich! If he'd wanted to, he would have paid us already. Since he loves his gold more than his son, so be it."

The three men re-entered Matt's cell, and Velhisya pulled the steel bars with all her strength. She'd never be able to bend them, but she had to do something. "Stop!" she screamed and heard the men's laughter.

"What's going on here?"

Lothar's voice brought her relief. "Help!" Velhisya cried.

The voices in the cell next to hers hushed, and quick footsteps echoed off the walls. "What are you doing?" Lothar shouted, and Velhisya tried to see what was happening, sticking her face against the bars.

"This wretch's father owes us gold, and the Governor has given us permission to punish him."

"Don't let them touch him!" Velhisya cried, unable to see the men.

"Do you take orders from this whore, Lothar?"

"Watch what you say, Tim. Don't forget that to you, I'm Lord Hale."

"What are you doing in the cells?" Tim asked.

"I don't report to you. Get out of here!"

"You have no right to stand in the way of this man's punishment."

"I'll pay his father's debts!" Velhisya said.

"Put a rag in her mouth!" came a loud voice. "A woman shouldn't dare speak to us like that!"

"Get out of here, and I'll discuss this prisoner's punishment with my brother." Lothar's voice rang out loudly.

"But—"

"Another word, and you'll die."

Silence took over until Velhisya heard the cell gate next to hers closing. The men in the corridor hurried to the dungeon exit. Soon after, Lothar stood in front of her cell and met her gaze.

"You can't save anyone in this place but yourself," he said.

"He's a good person... They mustn't hurt him. It's his father who owes them gold, not him—"

"That makes no difference!" Lothar cut her short. "I've already tried to help you and Selwyn. I can't save anyone else."

"If I ever get out of here, I'll pay his debt."

"Listen to me." Lothar's voice was commanding. "A messenger has returned from Elmor with news I never expected to hear."

"Did Liher send another messenger to Syrella?" Lothar nodded. "I'd have thought he'd meet with the same fate as the previous one."

"Me too," Lothar snapped. "However, the emissary returned, saying that Syrella had agreed to give all the gold of her land, even that of her noblemen, to get you back."

"What?" She knew her aunt loved her, but that seemed absurd.

"I know... It's unbelievable that she agreed to such a thing to save you."

Velhisya tried to process the information. "So, will your brother let me go?"

"If the gold gets here in about ten days, yes."

"I don't believe it," Velhisya muttered to herself.

"You may finally manage to get out of here safely but take care not to provoke the guards for a few more days."

Velhisya clasped her hands together. "Liher will get so much gold. He'll become one of the richest men in Knightdorn. I don't think it will cost him anything to free Matt, too." Her gaze drifted to the wall.

Lothar brought his face close to hers, the bars the only barrier between them, and Velhisya felt his hot breath. "I told you before, you can't save anyone but yourself. Your aunt has already promised us all her gold. There's nothing more you can give."

"If your brother frees him, I'll see that Syrella gives him one of Elmor's ships." Velhisya glanced at the wall that separated their cells. Matt had stopped crying, and nothing could be heard from his cell.

Lothar took a step back, his eyes wide with surprise. "He's a stranger! Are you really considering making a deal on your aunt's behalf—handing over a ship—while Syrella is giving up all her gold for you?"

"Yes!"

"You are the strangest woman I've ever met."

"I know. Convey my words to Liher."

"I doubt your aunt will pay a debt for an agreement she didn't make herself," Lothar said.

"She will. The fact that she agreed to give up all her gold for me shows how much she values me. She will honour an agreement I've made on her behalf."

Lothar studied her for a few moments. "Stay away from trouble!" he roared and turned to leave.

"I've always wondered how you seem to appear the very moment I need you..." Velhisya said, sure that he was watching her.

The man stopped abruptly and turned back to her. "Be careful, because I don't know whether I'll appear the next time," he said, walking away.

His footsteps faded away, and Velhisya became lost in her thoughts. She couldn't believe her aunt had agreed to sacrifice all her gold for her. She bet the lords of Elmor were furious.

"Why do you care about me so much?" Matt's voice brought her out of her thoughts.

"Not everyone is terrible. Not everyone is like your father," she told him in a low voice.

"The man was right... I'm just a stranger," Matt said.

"I may not have known you for long. But you're important to me."

"Why?" the man asked.

Velhisya stared off into space. "I spent the most difficult moments of my life with you. I can't help but care about the only person with me in these cells. Without you, everything would be far worse."

"Can you do me a favour?"

"Whatever you want."

"Touch my hand."

Velhisya hadn't expected to hear those words. She walked to the end of her cell and saw the fingers of a hand jutting out of the gate of the cell next door. She reached her hand out through the bars and stretched as far as she could. Her fingers touched Matt's, and a sense of endearment flooded her heart. It was the first time in days that she had touched a human who didn't want to hurt her.

"Even if I die, fate has given me a gift in this life. It was an honour to meet you, Velhisya Endor."

The Arena of Warriors

E lliot walked around some stalls along a main street in Mirth, which were filled with spices and perfumes. The day was sunny, and birds flew overhead, singing pleasantly. Countless people were browsing the wares, and most of them were smiling. The people of Mirth seemed happy, much more so than those Elliot had seen in the cities of Knightdorn. They hadn't spent the last few years of their lives amongst battles and war.

As he continued walking, he recalled his conversation with Marin. The people of Mirth may have seemed happy, but those who lived in the countryside away from the cities had a difficult life. As if that weren't enough, slavery still existed on this continent while its ruler sometimes seemed just like Walter. Elliot would never have agreed to the alliance if there had been another way. Unfortunately, Odin was their only hope.

Marin seems to be a man of honour. Yet Elliot still wasn't certain that he could trust him. *Undoubtedly, the Prince is unsuited to wars and battles,* he thought. *Perhaps Marin would one day be a compassionate leader, but he has no hope of ever defeating a man like Walter on the battlefield... The Emperor also seems to have no idea about battles and war, even though he is cunning.* Edmee was the only one with the blood of a warrior coursing through her veins. Elliot had see-n Odin looking at his daughter with admiration and affection, which wasn't the case with his son. Edmee had something the Emperor lacked, and Odin seemed to appreciate her more than Marin.

Marin may be cunning, too. Perhaps he just knows how to hide his true motives. Time will tell.

Elliot heard voices and saw people running. "What has happened?" he asked a man next to him.

"It's the Queen of Knightdorn! She's coming to the square with our Prince!" he told him, hurriedly.

Elliot watched the excited crowd trying to reach the square and walked to the right, wanting to see the splendid sight as well. The people around him seemed ecstatic. He stopped behind a wall of figures trying to stretch their necks as far as they could to see better.

"Look! She's gorgeous!" someone in the crowd shouted.

From afar, Elliot saw Sophie in a light blue dress walking up to a square adorned by a statue in its centre. The sunlight glistened on the jewels along her sleeves, making her arms sparkle. Her brown hair flowed softly over her shoulders. She was indeed beautiful, and Marin seemed very happy by her side. The Prince was dressed in a purple cloak and black leather trousers. Golden clasps fastened his cloak over his golden jerkin.

"If there is a Goddess of Beauty, she has most certainly granted her powers to this Queen!" came another voice.

Elliot grew tired of watching the new royal couple parade amongst the masses. He was fortunate that Kerth's generals hadn't asked for council meetings today, and Peter had taken over the command of the Queen's guard that morning. Thus, he had time to wander around the city. Apprehension overcame him. Perhaps he should have also been guarding Sophie as she moved through the crowds. However, he'd agreed to split shifts with Peter, so that one of them was always at the Queen's side along with a few dozen guards.

The Queen will be safe.

Elliot turned and gently pushed past the people behind him, trying to get away, when Marin's voice reached his ears.

"The Queen of Knightdorn and I will bring peace to both continents of the world. Trade will flourish and the people of Mirth will never be faced with famine or war ever again after this marriage," the Prince said.

Elliot was trying to make his way through the cheering crowds when the thought of a huge wyvern attacking the capital of Kerth struck him. Unfortunately, if they lost the battle against Walter, the people of this place had no idea what awaited them.

The crowd was suffocating, but after a while he managed to escape and find himself in a deserted alley. Some merchants gathered their wares as the townspeople rushed to the square. He'd heard that Kerth traded with many regions of Knightdorn, such as Vylor and Elmor. Mynlands was the region where most of the trade between Knightdorn and Kerth took place. It was under Walter's rulership and closer to Mirth than most of Knightdorn. That scared Elliot, but the Emperor had assured Sophie that he didn't care whether Mynlands stopped trading with him when they found out he was going to fight against Walter. After all, if they won, a lot would change soon.

Elliot left the square. He and Peter had told Odin it would be best if the marriage remained a secret until they defeated Walter. They didn't want Thorn to expect Kerth's involvement in the battle. However, the Emperor had insisted that Sophie receive adoration and adulation in his land, fostering devotion for her so that his men would be eager to fight for her. Elliot wasn't sure he believed him. His instinct told him that Odin revelled in banquets and feasts, and the fact that he'd succeeded in having his son wed the Queen of Knightdorn was an achievement he wanted to let the whole city know about. The Emperor had also told them it would be impossible to keep Kerth's involvement in the battle secret. Sooner or later, the merchants would spread the word about their alliance, though this wouldn't happen soon as storms were obstructing any sea voyages.

Even if the news reached Walter, he wouldn't be able to do much. The violent storms and tempests wouldn't allow for a naval battle, and Kerth was too far away from his supply units. In addition, Thorn didn't know whether they had elwyn and elves with them and wouldn't attack with his wyverns without an army. The final battle would be fought in Elmor, and that meant the news of the wedding wouldn't change much, except that Walter would be better prepared for battle.

He won't win, Elliot thought as he walked through the empty alleys. With Kerth's men at their side, it would be the first time they'd have more soldiers than the enemy. Walter was going to lose the battle, and something told him that Thorn would be overestimating the powers of his wyverns with dire consequences.

The sound of clashing swords brought him out of his thoughts. Elliot searched for the source of the sound and found himself in front of a huge, round building. It had countless seats built along its length around a dirt field. Elliot walked towards the interior of the strange building and saw two men fighting in the centre of the dirt field. He approached them silently, and his gaze fell upon an ornate seat in the middle of more seats on the north side of the building. A red cloth shielded it from the sun while a figure stood in front of it. He looked a little closer; it was Odin Mud.

"I've been waiting for the moment I'd see you here, apprentice of Althalos."

Elliot turned in surprise and saw Edmee looking at him with a smile. She was standing next to the duellists, who were fighting furiously. "What is this place?" he asked.

"Mirth's arena."

"Arena?" Elliot repeated.

She nodded sharply. "Don't you have such places in Knightdorn?" she asked.

"Maybe... But if there are any, I've never seen them."

"This is where the Tournament of the Faris takes place."

Elliot didn't understand. "What is this tournament?"

"Some of our greatest warriors fight each other, and the winner gains glory and gold. My father has taken some of the winners into his personal guard."

"Interesting... In Knightdorn, there are the knights' tournaments, which usually take place on horseback, but I have never come across such a place as this," Elliot said, taking in the arena.

"The Tournament of the Faris is the most well-known celebration in this land. Probably the second most important event this year, after my brother's wedding..." There was a hint of sarcasm in Edmee's voice.

Elliot looked closely at her white cloak and glittering armour. A long sword hung from her belt. "I bet a woman like you hates weddings and feasts."

"That would be a correct assumption."

"Nevertheless, marriages make for strong alliances."

"Naturally. My father came by a powerful alliance when he wed my mother, and he managed to become Emperor even though she died."

"What did she die of?" Elliot asked.

"She got sick." Her expression darkened, clearly unwilling to discuss it further.

"I'm so sorry," he said.

A scream rang through the air. Elliot suddenly turned around to see a duellist slump to the ground as his opponent prepared to drive his sword into his chest.

"Stop!" came Odin's voice.

"Why are they fighting?" Elliot asked.

Edmee frowned. "For practice. However, my father doesn't want any killing before the tournament."

Damn... "In the knights' tournaments, the knights who fight don't often die," Elliot told her.

Edmee stood expressionless. "At the Tournament of the Faris, the Emperor decides who has fought bravely and, despite their defeat, deserves to have their life spared."

Elliot was speechless. He supposed that Edmee realised that he thought her father was unscrupulous.

"The duellists consider it an honour to die in this tournament," the Princess said after a while.

"When will it take place again?"

"It usually happens in the spring, but I don't think my father will organise one until the war with Walter is over."

"Wise decision," Elliot said.

"My father adores these tournaments. He even enjoys watching duellists practise sometimes." She gestured to where he stood. "How about we try?"

A smile formed on her lips, her brown eyes shining. He didn't know why, but he appreciated her courage. "Are you curious to know whether you can defeat an apprentice of Althalos?"

"Yes," Edmee said without batting an eyelash.

"Would you say you're ready for something like that?" The days when he felt arrogance rising within him were over. Nevertheless, Elliot knew that people expected great warriors to be vain and had decided to play the part. He had to earn their respect so that they would obey his orders in the upcoming battle.

"I think you'll lose your smugness after our duel," Edmee said. "Most men in Kerth wouldn't dare challenge me out of fear that they might lose one of their limbs."

"Very well."

Edmee gestured with her head and walked into the centre of the arena, with Elliot close behind. A short while later, they reached the spot where the two men had previously fought. Now, both stood a little further away, staring fixedly in their direction. "I never thought you'd agree to fight against a woman," came Odin's voice.

Elliot glanced in his direction. "The Princess says that no one in this land dares to fight her without fearing they might lose their limbs. That sounded like an interesting challenge."

The Emperor smiled and folded his arms. He seemed interested in the spectacle that was to follow.

"In the arena, you can only have one weapon and one shield; armour and arrows aren't allowed," Edmee said, loosening her steel breastplate.

The steel fell to the ground, and she removed her pauldrons.

"I don't need a shield," Elliot said as he watched her remove her armour.

"Neither do I," she responded and drew the sword hanging from her belt. It was a magnificent weapon, with a single ruby set in its hilt and a gleaming blade.

Elliot's eyes widened. He'd already seen many swords like it and was now able to distinguish between them. "That is one of the Seven Swords!" he exclaimed.

Edmee seemed to have not been expecting these words. "How do you know?"

Elliot frowned. *How did she get one of those*? "You're holding one of the weapons the Elder Races made for the Egercolls, and many here don't even believe in the existence of elwyn and elves."

"Only fools don't believe in the existence of the Elder Races. If you've ever held a sword like this, you know that no man could forge anything like it. No blacksmith has been able to discover the metal from which this blade is made."

"It's called Aznarin, and it only exists in Knightdorn," Elliot said and drew the Sword of Light from his belt.

Edmee looked at the rubies in the hilt of his sword. "This is another of the Seven Swords!" she said, enthusiastically.

"It's the Sword of Light."

Edmee brought her sword up in front of her face, ready for battle. "Let's see how the Sword of Light will fare against the Blade of Silence."

Elliot remembered hearing that name from Althalos. He didn't have time to think as Edmee's sword came at him with great speed. Elliot sprang back and raised his blade, parrying the blow. The two swords remained locked together, and his face approached Edmee's.

This woman has a lot of strength. He swung his sword sharply and tried to cut her in the leg, but Edmee dodged and aimed at his shoulder. Elliot countered with the hilt, gripped his weapon with both hands, and tried to wound her right arm. His blade tore through the Princess' leather jerkin, and she screamed.

"I don't fight to kill. It's just a duel for training," he said, watching her redden with anger.

"You should have thought about that before you cut me."

Edmee charged at him and brought her blade down towards his head. Elliot raised his sword to parry, but just before the blade touched his, she changed the direction of her weapon and tried to get his right elbow. Elliot used the hilt of his sword as fast as he could and hit her in the face. Edmee staggered and fell to the dirt, her weapon slipping from her hand as blood ran from her lips.

"I didn't mean to hit you," Elliot said and ran to her side, knowing that the last attack he'd received had been very dangerous.

He leaned towards Edmee, trying to see if she was all right, but she suddenly raised her hand and threw dirt into his eyes. Elliot stumbled back in surprise as the sword slipped from his hand. He tried to clear his stinging eyes. He heard her yell, and rubbing his eyes, he saw her charging at him. Her body crashed into his, and they both hit the ground hard. Edmee punched him in the face, and he felt the sharp pain in his chin. Then, she elbowed him in the stomach.

Elliot didn't want to hit her. He saw her raise her fist again and moved his right hand to his boot. Edmee's scream pierced his ears as her fist slammed into the ground, a dagger at her neck.

"This duel has come to an end," Elliot said.

"A dagger?" Edmee looked at the steel against her neck. "I thought you heard that only one weapon is allowed."

"I tried to help you, and you threw dirt at me. You're not the only one who knows how to play dirty."

"Of course." Edmee raised her hand with lightning speed, and her dagger found its way to his throat.

Elliot felt the cold steel on his neck and wondered if she would try to kill him. Then, Edmee let her dagger fall. "This was the best duel of my life,' she said, offering him her hand.

Elliot let out a sigh of relief and lowered his dagger when another sound reached his ears. The Emperor was looking in their direction, clapping more passionately than ever.

A Virtuous Man

Sophie removed her earrings and sat in the chair in her chamber. She was looking at the ornate mirror in front of her. She'd never seen a mirror so big. The frame was adorned with strange symbols, and the image of herself at its centre appeared clearer than she'd seen before. The mirrors in Knightdorn were much smaller, and her reflection always seemed dim on their surfaces. This mirror was truly magnificent, and she had no idea what it was made of.

She looked at her face for a few moments. Her eyes were bright, and her brown hair was fluffed up and well-styled. She hadn't imagined she would go on a tour of Kerth prior to the wedding, alongside a man she'd met only a few days before. Bert's image crept into her thoughts; she would have given anything to have been able to marry him and travel the world at his side just before their wedding. Her eyes watered, and a sigh escaped her lips. Life was so unfair.

Sophie took off the rings and bracelets that adorned her hands and wrists. She couldn't recall ever having worn so many diamonds. The Emperor had ordered his servants to take her to a room full of dresses and jewels. She had to admit that even as Queen of Knightdorn, she'd never seen such beautiful clothes. Sophie knew that Odin had almost all the wealth of the continent in his hands, and his taste was particularly expensive. A maid had told her that the Emperor had spent a lot of time searching for the best tailors and the most skilled men in jewellery making. In her kingdom, people looked for the best builders and blacksmiths, while Kerth's ruler desired the most elaborate trinkets to adorn his body.

The day's events flashed before her eyes. She'd traversed the countless streets and squares of Mirth in a beautiful carriage as the people of the city rushed to see her up close. The wedding was taking place in approximately eight days, and Odin had requested that much be done before the ceremony. Over the next two days, she and Marin would watch some troubadours play a type of music that was popular in Kerth while also handing out gifts to the masses that were expected to gather in the city's largest square. Odin wanted them to give away flowers and various woven rugs emblazoned with the emblem of the Western Empire and the pegasus of the Egercolls. Soon they'd have to visit some villages with the same purpose. People had to feel that the alliance would improve their lives.

Her eyes flicked back to the mirror again, and she noticed the emblem of the Western Empire at the top—a sun. She'd seen white banners with a blood-stained sun at their centre in every corner of the city. The emblem belonged to an ancient house of Kerth, the House of Colsmith. She had heard the stories about the House being wiped out in a rebellion hundreds of years ago. Now there was no one left with that name, and rumour had it that the descendants of that House were the Asselins and the Karfords, known to many in Knightdorn as the "Twin Enemies." Odin had given the ancient coat of arms of Mirth to his entire empire, even though the emblem of the Muds was different. Sophie bet that a man as vainglorious as Odin would wish to adorn every bit of his land with his sigil. However, the people of Kerth adored the emblem of the Colsmiths as much as they adored the God of Justice.

Does the God of Justice agree with the way justice is served in this place?

Elliot had confided in her that her husband-to-be had told him about the Knights of Faith. He was horrified by everything he'd heard, but she knew full well how many leaders at risk of losing their power acted. She expected nothing less from a ruler like Odin. Elliot had also told her that slavery hadn't been abolished in Kerth, but she was already aware of that. It was one of the reasons she had loathed the idea of being wedded to the Emperor's son ever since she'd heard of this proposal. Unfortunately, they could do nothing about it, and already there were enough things they needed to accomplish. However, Odin's power over his land had some benefits for her. From what she'd heard, there were no particularly powerful councils in Kerth other than a handful of wealthy nobles who bowed down faithfully to Odin's wishes, so the only one she had to convince of her plans was the Emperor himself.

She heard a knock on her door and turned.

"May I come in?" came a familiar voice.

She hadn't anticipated Marin visiting her at such a late hour. *Fuck...* She was sure the young Prince was after her body; she'd seen him devouring her with his eyes all day long. Sophie didn't have the strength or resolve to sleep with him yet. She shuffled through the luxurious chamber and, heart pounding, opened the door.

"Good evening, my Prince."

"May I come in?" he asked again, his voice smooth. Dressed elegantly in silk, his red vest stood out. His face wore a good-natured expression.

Sophie stepped aside, and Marin entered the room. The door closed with a thud and their gazes met.

"Don't be afraid. I'm not here for what you think," he told her.

Sophie panicked. She didn't want her expression to betray her feelings. "I don't understand what you mean, my Prince. I'm glad to see you."

He walked across the room and sat in a chair next to a wooden table. "I want to talk."

I don't believe the only thing you want is to talk... Sophie took a seat in the chair opposite him.

"I may have never been to Knightdorn, but stories have travelled to this continent. I know you took the throne when you were still a child and had a man by your side who stood by you until his death."

"I don't want to talk about that." Sophie shivered. After Bert's death, she barely spoke about him, not even with Eleanor.

"For me, marriage isn't only of military importance. My father acquired a powerful alliance by marrying my mother, but they wed out of love. I always hoped the same would happen to me," the Prince said.

Someone loved Odin? Sophie weighed his words carefully. "I hoped for the same for myself, too," she said.

"I know. That explains why you never wed all these years... You only wanted to marry a man you loved, and when your councillors opposed the marriage, you remained alone. The war didn't allow you to ignore your council."

"Why do you want us to talk about this?" Sophie asked. She didn't understand—the idea that the Prince simply wanted to sleep with her was less painful than talking about Bert.

"I know you never wanted to marry me, and everything I've heard about you shows that you don't particularly admire men like my father. Nevertheless, I have always been searching for a woman like you." His expression was soft and sincere, and his eyes reflected a quiet honesty that seemed to strip away any pretence.

Sophie frowned. "Why? You don't know anything about me."

Marin smiled. "I know enough. Rumour has it that you've always tried to be honest and fair, however hard that may have been. For you, marriage is more than an alliance. What I want to say is that I'd truly like to win your heart, Sophie Delamere."

"My Prince—"

"Stop being afraid! We all know why you suddenly asked for this marriage... The last battle for Knightdorn is near and without our men, you'll lose everything you have fought for your whole life. You need us, and a marriage is a trivial thing compared to the death of all your people. However, I don't just want to win the war at your side; I want to win you over, too. I want you to be happy by my side."

Sophie didn't know if it was just a ploy, but the look on Marin's face seemed genuine. Marin wasn't as naive as she'd thought. "You're a good man, my Prince." Marin smiled. "I wonder how come you haven't married yet. I'm sure any woman would love to marry the Prince of

Kerth."

Marin's eyes clouded over for a moment. "My father wanted to build a very strong alliance through the marriage of his first-born son. No woman in Kerth would give him the alliance he desired."

"I understand," Sophie said and meant it. "But have you ever loved as I loved Bert?" She never thought she'd be asking such a question.

Marin's expression was cryptic. "Once," the man muttered after a while with sadness in his voice.

"What happened?" Sophie asked.

"She died..."

"How?"

A strange smile formed on the man's lips. "I see what you meant a moment ago when you said you 'didn't want to talk about it'..."

"I don't mean to pressure you, my Prince."

Marin sighed. "The woman I loved wasn't from the nobility. One day, thieves tried to rob her home, and she and her brother resisted. Both died." He looked away.

She felt a deep sadness; she couldn't bear the thought of anyone enduring the same pain she had after Bert's death. "I'm sorry..."

"My father would never have allowed me to wed Esme. It was wrong of me to have got her mixed up in this."

"You're not to blame for her death."

"I'd tried to make sure no one found out about us, but there were rumours. Perhaps the robbers knew and believed they'd find plenty of gold in her house." Marin looked like he was close to tears.

"It's not your fault," Sophie insisted. "I know what it means to feel that you're to blame for the death of your loved ones."

His brown eyes turned to her. "I thought that when my mother died, that would have been the worst thing that could ever happen to me, but Esme's death was even more..." He stopped mid-sentence.

"I heard your mother fell ill years ago," Sophie said, feeling affection for the man in front of her.

Marin nodded. "My father loved her very much. When she died, he changed—he became colder. I think that the day my mother left, seventeen years ago, the Emperor of Kerth was born. Father made it his life's purpose to dominate the continent, and two years after her death, he succeeded."

"Do you remember your mother?" Sophie asked.

He stared past her. "I was still a boy when she died, but I do have memories of her. She was always smiling, and every person in Kerth remembers her as the most loving lady who ever lived on this soil." Marin sniffed and looked at her. "Do you remember your parents?"

"Yes… Unfortunately, I remember everyone Walter Thorn's taken from me." Her thoughts went to Eleanor, and a sharp pain moved across her chest.

"I'm sorry," Marin muttered. "I can't believe that man is your cousin."

"Nor can I," Sophie admitted.

"I can't imagine fighting my whole life against a relative. I'm fortunate to have Edmee in my life."

Sophie smiled. "I used to wish I had siblings," she said. "I wished I had a brother or sister who would take the burden of the throne instead of me. However, fate only gave me a girl that I considered my sister, and Walter killed her a few days ago." Sophie had decided she wouldn't speak about any of it again. All that mattered was achieving her goals and getting her revenge. However, Marin had managed to unleash her pain.

"Who was she?" the Prince asked.

Sophie sighed. "Bert's little sister."

Marin rose from his chair and touched her gently on the shoulder. "In eight days the wedding will take place, and then we'll sail to Knightdorn to kill Walter Thorn once and for all. I know you want us to set sail for Elmor as soon as possible, but just be patient." The Prince leaned over and kissed her gently on the cheek. "Good night, Your Majesty."

Marin headed for the chamber door while Sophie watched him leave. When he reached the door, he stopped and gave her another look. "I'll never ask you to sleep with me unless you truly want to," he said and walked out the door, smiling at her one last time.

The Buried Secret

J ohn looked at the sea from the ship's bow and let out an indignant
sigh. The wind whipped his face furiously. The storms had hardly
abated, and despite his objections, Jack had decided to set off on their
journey that day. The waves had picked up as soon as they'd got out of
Merynhor, the harbour of the Grand Island. He felt nauseous, and the
wine he'd drunk the night before certainly wasn't helping.

John spotted the man he was searching for among the sailors, just a
few feet away. "Jack!" he called.

The one-eyed man turned and strode towards him. "What is it?"

"I hope there's sand in the ship somewhere, as agreed."

Jack snorted contemptuously. "Come here."

They walked along the front part of the deck until they reached the
end of the ship. Jack leaned against the wood framing the deck and
looked down. John tried to follow his gaze and saw a strange sack hanging
in front of the bow. He didn't recall seeing the sack the last time he'd seen
the ship, and when he'd gone on deck a few hours ago, he'd been so sleepy
that he hadn't noticed anything at all.

"What is that?" he asked.

"Sand. There are three sacks in front of the ship, two in the back and
three more on the sides. See those ropes?"

John followed the man's finger pointing to the pipe for the Liquid Fire
with the carved lion in its mouth. Three thick ropes were tied to its base.

"If you cut these ropes, the sacks will fall into the sea. I have other
sandbags and barrels of vinegar in the hold."

"Great," John said, relieved.

"Don't worry, my ship can't catch fire now."

"I hope so... No doubt these sacks will help if a fire comes close," John said.

"There's one more thing." Jack smiled. "I mixed vinegar with other liquids and doused the ship's hull a few days ago. My experiments have shown that it will be impossible for it to catch fire with this precaution."

Once again John mused over how resourceful Jack was. "I hope the storms don't end up killing us instead of the Liquid Fire," he snapped.

"You're getting old, my friend. In the past, you weren't so difficult and grouchy." With these words, Jack walked away.

John watched the other sailors working until the ship suddenly rocked, and he almost lost his balance. *Goddamn sea!*

It had only been a short while since they'd left Merynhor, and the waves had grown stronger. Some fishermen on the Grand Island had told him that it would take weeks for the storms to subside completely, but they believed they could now take their vessels out to sea. John disagreed. He knew full well that the storms considered tolerable by the men of the Ice Islands were quite dangerous for other men.

John held onto the ship's railing and tried to walk towards the large cabin when something caught his attention. Raff was in the captain's place at the helm with a big smile. He and Jack had agreed they would both command the ship on their voyage.

Fool, he thought, eyeing him. *Only a fool would have volunteered for this mission.* This trip might be our last, and he's laughing like an idiot.

John had a premonition about the voyage. Something told him that everything would go wrong, and that luck wouldn't be on his side. He'd tempted fate more times than he could count, and it was likely that at some point he wouldn't be so lucky. No one constantly putting his head on the block could get away unscathed.

I'm the fool. I should have tried harder to get away! He blamed himself, but deep down he knew he wouldn't have found anyone to quietly get him off the Grand Island. The men of that land were loyal and devoted to their leader and wouldn't disobey his orders for any amount of gold. Fate had betrayed him. He'd left Elliot and everyone who respected him on their own to escape the war, and now he was on a ship with some hot-headed sailors, looking for an island in the northernmost part of the world—an island from which some of the best captains hadn't returned alive.

For a moment, he thought about Elliot's hawk and wondered whether he would make the same decisions if he went back in time. He wasn't sure... *Giren Barlow's wife and daughter escaped the storms and arrows in a small boat. I may come out of this adventure unharmed, too. However, no one can escape Walter and his wyvern.* He'd mulled over that thought many times, but he couldn't deny that Elliot had accomplished things that most people wouldn't even dare to dream of. *Elliot didn't win those battles alone. Perhaps he'd just had luck on his side, and Althalos had also helped him with his plans.* Try as he might, John knew he'd never believe what his conscience was telling him. Elliot was special.

John headed towards the cabin, putting Thomas Egercoll's son out of his mind. Now, he was on a dangerous mission. He no longer had the luxury of dwelling on his regrets; he had to be careful.

"Where are you headed, Long Arm?" Raff called to him from afar as he turned the helm.

"For my cabin," John told him.

"You don't have a cabin... You'll sleep in the hold along with the other sailors."

"I'll sleep in the cabin where I left my things, and you can try to get me out of there."

Raff turned red with anger. "You're here to pay your debt to our leader. This is your punishment!"

"Just being here is my duty. Begon never mentioned working on the ship or sleeping in the hold. If nothing else, I'm still an emissary of the Queen..." he said, hoping to annoy him.

Raff looked like he was about to let go of the wheel and pounce on him, but John ignored him and strode into the ship.

———◄0►———

John took a few steps onto the deck and gazed at the moon shining in the clear night sky. The sea had calmed down and the rocking of the ship didn't make him as dizzy. He'd spent several hours in one of the cabins, trying to rest from all the drinking he'd done the night before on the Grand Island. His conscience told him he shouldn't have drank as much before setting off on the journey, but if this adventure was to be his last, he owed it to himself to spend the night in an inn as he wanted.

John watched the few sailors working on deck and looked over to where the captain stood. Jack was scowling as he looked fixedly ahead. John climbed a few steps to the elevated area from which the one-eyed man commanded the ship.

"I'll make sure I sleep during the day and stay awake at night," John told him.

Jack turned to him with a frown. "Why?"

"I don't want to see Raff's ugly mug... If he's captain in the mornings, I don't want to be here."

Jack shook his head disapprovingly. "Raff couldn't care less about you. He just hates Walter Thorn. We all know that regardless of the treaty, Walter considers us trash, and he didn't fight against us because he didn't want to waste his time on a few isolated islands. Ever since that ally of his, Eric Stone took over the leadership of Tahryn, the men from Tahos have treated us shamefully, and stopped trading with us except for when it suits them."

"You can trade with other regions," John said.

"Of course, but Tahos was always where we sold most of our wares since it's fairly close to the Ice Islands. We now do business with other merchants, but they have to travel all the way to Stormy Bay to meet us."

315

"That's better than a battle with Walter."

"I think that's why Raff hates you so much, Long Arm. Because you're a coward. Why are you so afraid of that man?"

"I've seen a lot that I never want to see again in this life."

Jack snorted. "You've seen a lot? I heard you met Aghyr Barlow's wife and daughter. That woman lost everything. She saw her city being destroyed and her people being slaughtered. She even saw her son become a slave, and even now she prays to the gods that she might be given the opportunity to take revenge."

John was irritated by being called a coward, but he didn't let it bother him. After all, he had known he was one his whole life. "We aren't all the same."

"And that's why Raff likes Delia Barlow and not you. If anything, you deprived many of the hope of getting revenge on Thorn when you hid Sophie Delamere's message from Begon."

"Even if Begon had decided to fight, how many would have died to get their revenge on Walter?"

Jack gazed at him disapprovingly, his expression shadowed under the moonlight. "So, the solution is to let Thorn become the tyrant of Knightdorn to save our lives? If everyone thought like that, we'd have to hand over everything to him to survive."

"I just don't want to fight. I don't want to see any more fighting and death."

"I often wonder what happened to you. What made you run from place to place all your life, not wanting to commit to anyone? Have you ever felt excited about fighting for something worthwhile?" John remained silent and looked at the moon again. "You don't have to tell me... I know the answ—"

"Once," John told him.

Jack momentarily let go of the helm and turned sharply towards him.

"There was a time when I loved a woman. I had decided to leave the life of a bounty hunter behind me and live with her. I had never thought

I would ever do something like that, but... but..."

"I never thought there might be someone who'd make you lose your mind, Long Arm! What happened?"

John's heartbeat quickened. "Walter had just taken over the rulership of Gaeldeath at the time, and this woman had killed the son of one of the lords loyal to him when he'd tried to rape her. Thorn wanted to murder her, but she belonged to the City Guard and many opposed killing her. Walter didn't want discord at a time when he'd banished his father, so he decided to punish her by sending her to find a knight who had run away. The soldiers of Gaeldeath forced me to help her. You see, I was the most famous bounty hunter in the north back then. If I had refused, they would have killed me, so I decided to help."

"Why didn't you run away?" Jack asked.

John sighed deeply. "Had I left the north I couldn't be a bounty hunter anymore. They didn't hire men like me in the South, and I loved that life. Along the way, many things changed. Our decisions brought us face-to-face with Walter's soldiers, and we ended up fighting to save ourselves. You see, this knight was quite important, and Thorn had moved Heaven and Earth to have his head."

Jack looked at him strangely, trying to connect the dots, until his eye opened wide. "Were you there? Were you there when they found the Knight of the Moon?"

John nodded without a word. He'd never told anyone about it and had erased those images from his memory over the years. "After what I saw that day, I'll never fight again. I'd rather run, and if the whole world is prey to the whims of a single tyrant, I'll find some isolated village and spend the rest of my life there. A village that will never attract the attention of any ruler."

An emotion rarely seen on Jack's face—compassion—flickered across his features. "What was the woman's name?" he asked.

"Nemesis," Her image flashed in his mind, and a sharp pain gripped his chest. John didn't want to talk any longer. He turned his back on Jack and left. He stopped at the far end of the ship and looked at the moon, tears rolling down his cheeks. It was one of the rare times he'd cried in seventeen years.

The Locket of Creation

Elliot took a bite of cheese and devoured it greedily. He was famished, and the food in Mirth was truly tasty. Several other people around the table in the Red Palace's Great Hall ate in silence. Sophie looked pensive, sitting at Marin's side while the Emperor was eating a chicken leg. Elliot carried on eating cheese and bread until his gaze fell upon Edmee. She brought a cup of wine to her lips, her eyes fixed on him as she sat there in her armour. He avoided her gaze, looking towards the other end of the room. He'd already caught himself looking at her, however, he didn't want her to notice. Edmee was brave, confident and beautiful. He knew he liked her even if he didn't want to admit it to himself.

"Lord Brau hasn't graced us with his presence today," the Emperor remarked.

"He told me he likes exploring the city, so he chose to walk through the markets near the harbour this morning," Sophie said.

"It's a nice day to walk around," Marin added.

"If I recall correctly, you and your fiancée will be watching the minstrels in the Square of Justice, this afternoon," Odin said. Marin nodded in agreement. "Wonderful! Something tells me it will be quite a spectacle."

"I didn't know the big city square was called the Square of Justice," Sophie said, bringing a few grapes to her mouth.

"Trust me, it's a fitting name," Odin replied. Elliot watched him chewing greedily as if he hadn't eaten in days.

"Why?" Sophie's expression revealed her eagerness.

The Emperor took a few more bites and tossed the bone onto his plate. "Because that's where the justice of our god is meted out."

"To whom?"

Odin looked her in the eye. "To all those who break the law."

"So, that's where the Emperor's justice is carried out. I don't think the God of Justice ever executed anyone in that square," Elliot said, watching as Odin, clad in gold, turned angrily towards him. Sophie also shot him a pointed look.

"Our god gave me the power to become emperor, otherwise I would never have succeeded. Since he wanted me to rule over Kerth, that means he agrees with my decisions. I often feel his wisdom in my thoughts. In Kerth people know that what I do is the will of our god."

Elliot took a few sips of water, while Edmee fixed her eyes upon him again. He had to hold back what he wanted to say since he didn't want to jeopardise the alliance they needed.

"If I remember correctly, we're going to be handing out some woven cloths as gifts to the citizens tomorrow morning," Marin said, changing the subject.

"No," the Emperor said sharply. "Things have changed. You'd better visit some villages outside the city tomorrow. The villagers are eager to meet the Queen of Knightdorn."

"What has changed?" Marin asked.

"Nothing that demands your attention." Odin didn't seem to want to say anything more. Then, the Emperor turned to Elliot. "It would be wise for you and Peter to follow the Queen to those places. Most of the villagers are good people, but some of them are violent. The more security in place to protect the Queen, the better."

"Of course," Elliot responded. "Lord Peter and I had decided to split our watches. However, we can do double shifts for a few days."

The Emperor seemed satisfied with his words. "No one will harm Sophie on my land. Still, the more protection, the better."

Elliot suspected that Odin wanted to get them out of the city the next day, but he didn't know why. Marin frowned.

"You caught the boy you were looking for," Marin said. "That's why you change—"

"Silence!" the Emperor shouted, and the Prince shut his mouth immediately.

All eyes were fixed on Odin. *What's going on in the city tomorrow? Why do they want us out of here?* Elliot thought, his worry growing.

"Pardon me," Odin said softly a few moments later and took a few sips of wine.

"I'd like to talk to you after dinner," Marin said.

A smile formed on Odin's lips. "In a few days, you'll wed a woman the whole kingdom would want as their bride. Soon after, we'll set sail to beat Walter Thorn. You have enough to do already, Marin. Let me take on the responsibilities of ruling over Kerth."

Marin lowered his head without responding.

"To peace," Odin said and raised his glass. The others followed him. "Soon we'll conquer Knightdorn, and no one will bring war to the world again." Odin's gaze shifted to Elliot. "The truth is, I didn't expect Althalos to have been alive all this time. Under everyone's nose, he trained a boy to conquer the kingdom alongside Sophie."

"Althalos didn't train me to conquer Knightdorn but to protect it from a tyrant. He knew that only with Sophie on the throne would there be true peace. I'm fighting for the Queen because, with her, the people of my land will be safe," Elliot retorted.

"Wise and virtuous words," Odin said and sipped his wine. "Nevertheless, no one wants a kingdom only to protect its people. The lure of power always permeates the souls of men."

Elliot made himself more comfortable in his seat. "Not everyone's."

The Emperor laughed. "You're young. One day you'll understand what I mean. Nonetheless, the motive is of no concern. Only with a single ruler can a place find true peace, no matter why he wanted to gain power in the first place."

"Then, even with Walter on the throne of Knightdorn there will be peace," Elliot said.

"Perhaps, yes. Nevertheless, you and the Queen want power over that land. You think your peace will be better than Walter's," said the Emperor without losing his smile.

"No place with a leader like Walter will ever find peace. Power in the hands of one man alone isn't enough to bring about peace," Elliot insisted.

"And what is needed?" Odin asked.

"A good leader." Elliot's tone of voice was pointed, and he was sure the Emperor had noticed. Sophie shot him another pointed look.

"Nobody is good for everybody. Goodness is relative," Odin replied in his honey-sweet tone.

Elliot didn't reply, but the Emperor's eyes were still fixed on him.

"My mother always wanted to protect people, and I want the same. If we take Knightdorn, I'll do what I can to protect its people from battles and death," Marin rejoined.

The Emperor's look was filled with reproval, his gaze sharp and full of silent judgement. "Kill your enemies quickly, and the rest will fall in place. Your mother was innocent, and innocence won't keep you on the throne." His voice cracked as he talked about his dead wife.

Elliot took a few more sips of water and felt a drop of optimism in his heart. He wasn't yet sure whether he was right, but his instinct told him that Marin was much more than they could have expected for the throne of Knightdorn.

Elliot walked through the Red Palace, deep in thought. He felt tired but couldn't sleep. He'd considered offering to take Peter's place in the evening watch outside the Queen's quarters, but if he did, he'd be exhausted the next morning. *I must sleep.* He knew the journey to the villages would be more tiring than the jaunts to the squares of Mirth. *Why doesn't the Emperor want us here tomorrow morning?*

If he'd asked around, he may have found out more, but there was so much on his mind that he'd neglected to do so. Elliot couldn't imagine what Odin didn't want to reveal, but he knew he had to let it go. All that mattered was for the wedding to take place and for them to return to Elmor as soon as possible. He may have liked Marin, but it didn't prevent him from feeling uneasy about Sophie as long as they were in the Emperor's land.

He felt it was time he returned to his room when he saw the open entrance to the Great Hall. He went in and looked around. Whenever he was in that hall, he thought of Odin's vanity painted on the ceiling. The Emperor-god—that's what they called him in Mirth. Suddenly, a flash of light caught his attention. Elliot saw a half-open door at the far end of the hall to the right of the elevated throne. He'd seen the door before, but this was the first time it had been open. He walked towards it, curious to see what was in there.

His footsteps echoed in the hall, and he pushed the door, hearing it scrape against the floor. Candles flickered dimly in the room, casting faint light on the stone tomb standing at its centre. Elliot walked up to it and touched its surface. A woman's face was engraved on its head, and he immediately realised who it was. The rumours that the Emperor had loved his wife were true; Odin had placed her tomb right next to the Great Hall so that they could rule the land of Kerth together.

Elliot took a closer look at the room and thought his eyes were playing tricks on him. On one of the walls, there was a sword resting on two small wooden stands. It wasn't Edmee's sword but another of the Seven Swords.

There are two of these swords in Kerth? How?

He was about to approach it when a small table in the other corner of the room with a silver platter in its centre caught his attention. On the table was an object that seemed to glow.

Elliot forgot about the sword and walked towards the small table. He stopped short and looked at the object—a locket. He was sure Odin's guards wouldn't be happy if they caught him rummaging around in the room, but he couldn't help himself. It was as if the jewel beckoned to be touched. He reached out, and his fingers touched the cold object. Elliot picked up the locket and brought it closer.

It's beautiful. It was a green diamond, and something seemed to glow within it. He leaned in for a closer look and was startled by what he saw. He'd heard of lockets that opened and something could be put inside, but he'd never seen one up close.

He tried to get a better look inside. A small opening had been dug into the centre, which had a green tint. On impulse, he tried to open it but failed. *Strange.* Elliot lifted the object higher and tried to get a better look at its interior under the dim candlelight. He peered at it for a few moments and suddenly felt himself being enveloped in a dark vortex.

Elliot tried to throw the object away and draw his sword, but his hands were stuck to the locket. Now, he couldn't see a thing. He struggled to free himself when a huge figure appeared before him, intangible and holding a sceptre in its hands.

"You'll never win, brother. None of your powers will survive in my world." The sceptre in the figure's hands flashed like lightning, and a black shadow appeared in front of it.

"This world belongs to me."

Elliot felt like his heart would stop. The second voice had come from the shadow. He tried to free his hands again, and again everything went dark. Just as he was certain he was about to die, a voice echoed in his head.

"You have to believe..."

"Believe in what?" Elliot asked, more frightened than ever before.

"In whatever matters."

"Elliot!"

His hands suddenly came unstuck from the locket, and it fell to the ground.

"Elliot?"

He was back in the palace, and a familiar voice was calling his name. He turned towards the entrance and saw Edmee looking at him in fear. It was the first time he'd seen her in a purple silk dress instead of her steel breastplate.

"Are you alright?" she asked.

"Yes," he said, though he was soaked in sweat.

"You seemed to be babbling. You'd better not touch that locket again... My father doesn't like his things being tampered with."

Elliot didn't want to handle it again. Nevertheless, he reached out and picked it up off the ground. To his relief, nothing happened. He placed it back on the silver platter.

"What is this locket?" he asked.

Edmee approached him. "The Locket of Creation." Elliot gave her a look that he knew betrayed his confusion. "There are countless legends surrounding it. Some think a god inserted a powerful force inside it—the force that created our world. But no one has ever been able to open it."

"Its interior is empty. Someone has opened it," Elliot said.

Edmee raised her hands as if to say she had no idea. "Some think that in the past it opened for the chosen one, and he took its contents. Others are sure that's all just nonsense. However, no one can deny that it's beautiful."

"Where did your father find it?"

"Years ago, a sailor travelled to some unknown islands south of Kerth and returned with it. He offered it to my father as a gift, as he believed that this jewel was only fit for the hands of the Emperor-god. Since then, some have recognised it and told us it is the Locket of Creation of the ancient legends, but no one can be certain. Undoubtedly, the fact that no one can open it is strange."

"We can break it."

"My father would kill anyone who destroyed such a beautiful jewel. My mother wore it round her neck for years." Edmee frowned. "Did you see something when you touched it? You seemed to be raving... No one else has ever reacted that way just by holding it."

"No," Elliot lied. *What was that I saw? Whose voice was that?*

She looked at him suspiciously. "What are you doing here?" she asked after a while.

"I couldn't sleep... I was walking in the palace and saw this open door. My curiosity got the better of me."

Edmee was expressionless. "My father doesn't allow anyone in here. I'll do you the favour of not telling him."

Elliot stepped closer to her. "Thank you," he said. "It wasn't my intention to go through your father's things."

"I won't protect you if I catch you again," Edmee said.

Elliot nodded. "Only this time... I deserve a gift since I beat you in battle."

Their faces were close, and she took another step closer. "You would have won if you hadn't tried to be noble so as not to hit me. One day, your nobility will cost you your life."

Their lips were now very close, and then two starry blue eyes came into his mind. Elliot turned his face away. "You're right; it's time to go."

Edmee didn't speak, and he walked towards the door that led back to the Great Hall. He heard Edmee following him until the Princess came up beside him. "Are you afraid of women, Elliot Egercoll?"

He stopped and saw her gazing at him intensely. "No."

"You should be," she said without blinking.

Elliot felt attracted to her. He liked her courage and how she looked at him, yet even though he knew he might never see Velhisya again, he couldn't get her out of his mind. "Why does your father want us out of the city tomorrow?" he asked.

Edmee seemed surprised. "You can ask him yourself."

"I'm asking you."

"It must be strange to find yourself in a place where you don't trust anyone," Edmee said and stood silent for a while. "There's nothing to learn—nothing of importance to you. I wonder why you care what happens here?"

"I could find out by asking around, but I want you to be the one to tell me."

Edmee frowned, disarmed by his words. "Why?"

Elliot smiled. He knew his feelings might be a mistake but believed in them. "Because I trust you and think you trust me, too. You and your brother are the only ones I trust in this strange city."

The Child of Promise

Sophie stared at her reflection in the huge mirror as the maid brushed her hair. The morning was beautiful, with the sun's rays bathing the chamber in golden light. For a moment, her eyes fell on her right wrist. The cuts she had made on her arm some time ago had healed, and she hadn't felt the urge to do herself harm over the last few days. It was as if her thoughts were so deeply entrenched in her plan that Eleanor's loss had sunk into a remote corner of her mind. Her soul had found a little peace since she had focused on her goals.

"You look beautiful, Your Majesty," the maid said.

"I would trade my troubles for my beauty in a heartbeat," Sophie told her.

"What troubles can a beautiful Queen like you have?"

Sophie saw herself smiling in the centre of the mirror. A woman like the one who brushed her hair could never understand the weight she bore. Ordinary people looked at her and her peers in envy, yet they were lucky that they neither knew nor would they ever know the truth. Rulership wasn't what they thought it was.

That *isn't true for everyone. The Emperor seems to bask in the glory and power of rulership, said* a voice in her head. Perhaps some were destined to have a beautiful life, whether or not they ruled. Maybe she was the one who was doomed to live in pain and death. However, there had been a few welcome surprises lately that had caught her off guard. Her future husband was a good man, and that had soothed her heart more and more over the last few days.

You may have lost Eleanor and Bert, but the gods sent you Elliot and Marin. She didn't want to be ungrateful. Elliot was a good lad and seemed determined to even give up his life for her while Marin seemed to really want to make her happy. Nevertheless, she still had her reservations about the Prince of Kerth. After everything she'd experienced in her life, it wasn't easy for her to trust anyone.

A knock sounded from the chamber door.

"Your Majesty. I have to speak with you urgently!" came Elliot's concerned voice.

Sophie felt worried. "Come in," she said.

Elliot entered the chamber and approached her. "I thought I'd find Peter watching your quarters with the guards," he said, his blue jerkin crumpled. His concern scared her.

"He left a moment ago to prepare for our departure," Sophie replied.

Elliot nodded. "I heard some news I want to share with you."

"Go ahead.". Elliot glanced at the maid, and Sophie turned to her. "Could you leave us alone for a few minutes?" The woman curtsied and walked towards the exit. "Well?" Sophie asked when they were alone.

"I was walking through the palace last night and ran into Edmee."

Sophie raised an eyebrow. "I heard you fought against her the other day and now you just happened to find her in the middle of the night? You'd think we might have to prepare for another wedding."

"Listen to me! She told me why the Emperor wanted us to leave the city today."

"Why is that?" Sophie feared something really bad had happened.

"Odin has been hunting a clan that lived near a forest for years. Edmee told me that this place is called the Forest of Magic and that many claim that the centaurs lived there before they left for Knightdorn."

"So?"

"There are rumours that while the centaurs lived there, some villagers chose to leave their land and stay with them. These humans became their most loyal companions and in turn, the centaurs tried to give them some of their magic."

Sophie got out of her seat, irritated. "I think the Princess has made you lose your senses. Have you come here to talk to me about silly legends? I've been hearing stories about people with magical powers since I was five, yet I've not met even one such person. Why would the Emperor want to send us away because of a legend from the time when the centaurs lived in Kerth?"

Elliot frowned. "The descendants of these humans stayed in the Forest of Magic up until today. When Odin took power, a few of his loyal lord allies tried to force them to plough the forest and harvest the crops for the ruler of Kerth. They refused, and the Emperor's men attacked them…"

I don't understand what he is telling me… "And?" she asked.

"Edmee told me that these people could control fire and water with their minds while some of them could even tame the rain and the wind. The soldiers who attacked them came to a tragic end, and since then Odin has hunted this clan down until he killed them all."

"After the story you told me about the knights that were burnt alive, this doesn't surprise me. I still don't understand what this has to do with—"

"There's only one boy from this clan left—a boy who watched all the people he loved die. Odin's men have captured him and plan to execute him in the big city square tonight. The Emperor didn't want us to see this."

Sophie exhaled heavily. "We already know a lot about him. I didn't think he'd care whether or not we heard about another execution."

"Now, he knows quite enough about us, too. For days, we've been talking about saving Knightdorn from a tyrant like Walter. Odin assumed that we wouldn't be pleased to see a child executed. I believe he doesn't want to risk the marriage with such a spectacle," Elliot told her.

"He knows I need this marriage. An execution wouldn't make me back away, and even if we weren't here, we might have heard the news," Sophie said. She hated what she had heard, but she had no choice.

"You may need this marriage, but he knows it wouldn't be wise for you to be hating every minute of the ceremony I'm sure he expected we might find out what happened, but then he would have come up with dozens of excuses. It's one thing to hear the news and another to have the opportunity to see a child being executed with your own eyes. The whole city will be gathering in the square to see the last boy of the sect of heretics who stole the powers of the gods."

"Stole the powers of the gods?" Sophie repeated.

"The Emperor and his priests spread that rumour."

"So, they think this boy has special powers like the rest of his now-dead clan?"

"Edmee told me he can control the rain. They'd been looking for him for a long time before they caught him."

"If he has such a mighty power, why doesn't he use it to kill Odin himself?"

Elliot shrugged.

Sophie crossed her arms. "I realise we've allied ourselves with a vicious man, but we knew the truth about him beforehand. I don't know what you want of me. To annul the marriage for a boy? How many boys will die if Walter beats us?" Sophie wished she could leave the continent immediately, but Odin was their last hope. *Poor child...*

"Talk to Marin! He may be able to change his father's mind."

"Have you seen how Odin talks to him? He'd never pay heed to Marin."

Elliot was about to say something when a knock thumped on the chamber door.

"May I come in, Your Majesty?" came Marin's voice.

"You lose nothing by trying," Elliot told her in a whisper.

Sophie heard his pleading. "Okay. However, nothing will change. I advise you to prepare for our departure." Then, she raised her voice and said, "Come in."

The door opened and to her surprise, Marin and the Emperor entered her quarters.

"My goodness! You look divine, my dear. I'd bet a pile of gold that the people in those villages will be dazzled by your beauty," Odin said in a cheerful voice. He wore a dark red jerkin and a gold cloak, his fingers studded with multicoloured ruby rings.

Sophie curtsied lightly. *What does Odin want here?*

"Are you ready to protect your Queen, Lord Egercoll?" The Emperor's eyes darted to Elliot.

"Always," he replied.

"Excellent! It's a beautiful day. Mirth would have been boring today. You'll love the beautiful scenery on the way."

"I'm sure that's why you didn't want us to stay in the city today, my lord," Elliot said in a voice full of sarcasm, and Sophie gave him a sharp look.

"What do you mean?" Odin's face had lost its benevolence.

"Nothing," Elliot replied with a bow, but Sophie felt the damage had been done.

Odin reddened with rage and turned to his son. "Did you talk?"

Marin didn't seem to be afraid, but his expression betrayed his bewilderment. "No," he said sharply.

The Emperor looked at the Prince and then at Elliot.

"It doesn't matter how we found out," Elliot said, and Sophie prayed he'd restrain himself. It would be suicide to sacrifice the alliance now.

"You're right. It doesn't matter how you found out but that you *did* find out. I wanted you to be spared something like this just before your wedding, my dear," Odin said, looking Sophie in the eye.

"I appreciate your kindness, my lord." Sophie had not once done him the favour of addressing him as "Your Majesty. "

"I imagined that if you were in the city, the news would have brought you to the square and an execution wouldn't be a pretty sight for a queen."

"Perhaps you could spare that child's life, Emperor," Elliot said.

Odin looked furious. Sophie imagined that if those words had been spoken by one of his own people, harsh punishment would have followed. No one questioned the Emperor's decisions in Kerth.

"That *boy* has powers you can't even imagine. If he were near me, he would be able to throw a bolt of lightning at my head," Odin responded.

"And why didn't he?" Elliot asked.

"He may have tried. I remember endless storms these last summers, but no one can do me any harm in my palace. If, however, I hadn't hunted down this clan—If there were more of them—they would have killed us all." Odin spoke more to himself than to the others.

"Now, you have won, my lord. This boy is the only one left. If his whole clan hasn't harmed you, he won't manage to. Grant him his life," Elliot insisted.

The Emperor sniggered. "If I hadn't found the weak spot of those damned heretics, they would have killed me. I'm not going to spare the life of that monster! One day he'll grow up, have children, and his kind will threaten everything I've built."

"If you let him live, he may never want to hurt you."

"I've told you before, Lord Egercoll, you're new to the world."

"What was the weak spot of these people?" Sophie asked.

"Grief..." Odin said flatly.

"What do you mean?" The man's answer puzzled her.

"A few years ago, I caught one of those monsters. One who could control fire. However, he couldn't create it, only control it, so I locked him in a room without candles or torches. My men and I interrogated him for days until he broke."

Sophie didn't even dare to imagine the torture that man had endured.

"He told us that the power within them was somehow unified. When one of them died, their power was disturbed, and grief made them unable to use their abilities. I had long been afraid to attack their forest, but when I found out about all of this, I knew what to do. A handful of archers killed some of them from afar, so their power was disrupted.

After that, they were unable to attack my soldiers. Since then, I've been trying to kill those that have remained before their power revives." The Emperor seemed pensive, as if he wanted to put that threat out of his mind.

Sophie wasn't sure if she believed all of this.

"Perhaps if you hadn't bothered them, those people may never have harmed you," Elliot said, raising his voice.

"I think Althalos made you a warrior because he knew you would become a weak ruler had you taken your father's throne! A clan of a few hundred people with such powers would inevitably have used their powers to gain control."

Elliot remained silent in the face of the insult, while Sophie felt as if another Walter Thorn stood before her. He alone would sacrifice an entire race out of fear if he knew it had the power to overthrow him.

"I wasn't going to tell you any of this since the leadership of Kerth is my responsibility alone. However, since we will be joining our Houses, perhaps it's good after all that you know what I've had to face to ensure peace. Not only giants and wyverns can destroy us in this world." Odin's eyes had locked on hers, and Sophie felt an urge to spit in his face.

"I was wondering how you caught the child. He evaded us for a long time." Marin's voice was steady, but Sophie discerned a slight tremor. She could tell her future husband was furious about his father's decision no matter how hard he tried to conceal it.

"He was caught in a small village near that damned forest. Every time my men found his trail, fog covered everything. The prisoner who had confessed said that only this monster had such a power. His clan called this child the 'Child of Promise'."

"And why did he let you catch him? If he controls the rain and can create fog, he could escape being caught forever," Elliot said.

"I told you about their weak spot. The boy is all that's left of his clan. I guess, in the end, grief killed his power," Odin declared callously.

"Or maybe it's all just silly rumours and legends of a few bored drunks," Elliot said.

"Don't question my judgement again, lad. I know full well how to differentiate between legends that are foolish and those that are not." The Emperor's eyes narrowed.

Sophie knew the conversation should have ended a long time ago. "So be it. We must depart," she said, looking at Elliot and then at Marin.

"Wouldn't you like to see this boy's powers with your own eyes before you kill him? From your words, it seems everything you know about him is just the testimony of others," Elliot continued and took a step towards Odin.

The Emperor had recovered his familiar smile. "The truth is, yes—others have spoken of his powers. But it would be far too dangerous to let him use them."

Sophie secretly admired her cousin. She remembered him saying a few days ago that every vain and cowardly man tried to destroy a power he couldn't have. Nevertheless, such men always wanted to catch a glimpse of that which they would never acquire. Odin wanted to see, but he was afraid.

"If you execute the boy, you might see his powers with your own eyes. He might bring about a thunderstorm and lightning might strike in our direction," Marin said.

"I'm not a fool!" Odin spat. "They'll force him to drink an herb that induces sleep before he comes out of the dungeons to be hanged. He's lucky he won't feel the anxiety of death. I would kill him with poison if I didn't want my people to see the end of the heretics!"

"The Princess confided in me that the battles of the Faris are worshipped in this land. Organise a tournament in honour of the Queen for the upcoming wedding, and put this boy in the arena," Elliot said, and Sophie swore Elliot had lost his mind.

"Are you mad?" Odin raised his voice. "If he gets the chance, he might—"

"If we see that he's using his famed powers, you can order archers to be on hand to kill him," Elliot interrupted.

"It' would be very dangerous," Marin said.

"I know, but it'll be our last chance to see a human using such a gift with our own eyes," Elliot insisted. "If he does use it in the arena, the spectacle will be amazing."

Odin remained silent for a while, and Sophie couldn't help but admire her cousin—Elliot had wormed his way into the Emperor's mind and whetted his appetite.

"So be it," Odin said softly after a while. "This spectacle might be remembered for a long time by my people. If the boy uses his powers and then dies at the hands of my guards, I'll go down in history as the man who managed to defeat those who stole the powers of the gods." Odin's face shone at the thought of fame and glory.

"If everything we know is true, we won't see a thing. His grief over losing his clan must have destroyed the boy's powers. That's how we were able to capture him," Marin said.

"Or it was all just rumours. I know nothing of this clan, but I know that the fear of death awakens one's deepest instincts. In any case, even if he uses his supposed powers, the boy will die," Elliot told him.

"Leave for your journey, and I'll arrange the tournament in two days," Odin said. He turned and left. Marin glanced at his father and hurriedly followed him.

"Why did you do that?" Sophie asked when she was finally alone with Elliot. "Now this poor boy will die duelling in an arena!"

Her cousin looked at her resolutely. "Or he'll kill that vile Emperor and escape. Then you and Marin might bring true peace to this world."

Rats on the Rampage

O ver the last few days, Selwyn had forgotten the carefree feeling he
usually felt every evening as he strolled through the city's alleys.
After the incident with the thieves and the man in the Governor's chamber, he felt Wirskworth wasn't as safe as he'd thought. A few days ago,
he'd have sworn that the common people were loyal to Syrella Endor,
but he'd forgotten that gold always had a way of buying loyalty. The
Governor hadn't seemed surprised when he'd told her the news.

*"In these times, without a proper guard around the city, the lure of theft
is greater than ever,"* Syrella had told him.

*"We must protect the weak. Those children could have died alone since
their parents have gone to save Velhisya!"* Selwyn had said.

*"I'll ask the guards to set more watches, but I can't expect much. We don't
have enough men."*

Selwyn walked in search of a place where he could have his evening
drink, but in reality, he wanted to keep watch over the city alleys after
everything that had happened. He knew Syrella would have preferred
it if he stayed safe in his room at night, but something compelled him
to help the guards. The last three days his hand was constantly on the
hilt of his sword when he wandered around at night, and he felt better
prepared to face potential thieves than ever before. His training with
Alysia had improved his skills, and Thorold's advice during practice had
helped him.

Why did he want to train me? he thought for the umpteenth time. He
had no answers, but he wondered why he felt so troubled by the reason

Thorold had chosen him as his apprentice.

You don't consider yourself worthy, an inner voice told him. Never in his life had he expected a Grand Master to waste time training him.

"The thirst to become a shield for those you love is a powerful force few can perceive." The words the Master had said to him circled in his mind, and he hoped he could truly succeed in protecting his loved ones. He couldn't bear to lose anyone else.

Selwyn looked up at the cloudy night sky as he walked and saw smoke rising from several chimneys. He was walking near some Wirskworth manor houses and then passed in front of a building with many people inside. It was a fancy tavern frequented mostly by lords and prostitutes in search of clientele.

A loud sound made him turn round abruptly, and his sword came out of its sheath, but he stopped. "What are you doing there?" he asked.

A boy had fallen to the ground a few feet away, staring up at him in fear.

He is following me...

With a sudden movement, the boy got up and ran. Selwyn followed. *He might work for the traitor we are looking for.* The boy turned down an alleyway, and Selwyn felt out of breath.

"I order you to stop!"

The boy ignored him and ran faster. Selwyn sheathed his sword and, despite being in pain from training, kept sprinting as fast as he could. He reached out his hand, and his fingers touched the boy's woollen jerkin. Selwyn pulled hard on the garment, and the boy lost his balance, falling to the ground.

"Are you following me?" he asked, raising his voice.

The boy didn't lift his head, afraid to face Selwyn. His short trousers had torn, and his leg oozed blood.

"Who sent you?" He didn't want to threaten a child with a sword, but he wouldn't hesitate to do so if it was necessary. Whoever was using the boy had to be the traitor they were looking for.

"Don't hurt me," the child pleaded.

"Tell me who sent you, and I won't."

"I can't. If I do, I'll die, and so will my family."

"Has someone threatened to kill you and your parents if you don't watch me?"

The boy nodded.

Damn—this man watches us all the time! We need to catch this cunt.

"Tell me who it is, and I'll protect you from him."

He heard a loud thud and felt intense pain in his head. The boy got up and darted away. Selwyn clutched his head. His fingers were coated in blood. He turned around slowly, trying to stand upright, and saw another boy running away. He looked down and saw the object that had hit him. A stone painted red with his blood. He took a few dazed and unsteady steps in an attempt to get back to the tavern.

"Help. Help!" He didn't know whether he'd spoken but could have sworn he'd heard his voice.

Selwyn took a few more steps until he felt the world slipping from under his feet. He crumpled to the ground, and before he was enveloped in darkness, he saw a figure bend over him.

Selwyn felt like his head was about to split.

"Will he be all right?"

The voice sounded familiar, but he had difficulty recognising who it belonged to. He tried to open his eyes, but he couldn't. His eyelids were heavy, and he felt as if an invisible force was holding down his body.

"I think he's coming round."

The other voice was familiar, too. He made another attempt to lift his eyelids, and light blinded him.

"Take it easy. You're going to be fine."

He adjusted to the light and saw Thorold standing beside Syrella, both looking at him expectantly.

"What happened?" the Governor asked him.

His head was suddenly intensely itchy, and Selwyn moved to scratch his skin.

"No." Thorold grabbed his arm. "I've dabbed on an herbal potion. I know it makes you itch, but you have to let it take effect."

Selwyn couldn't stand the itch. He tried to distract himself.

"Who attacked you?" Syrella asked again.

He slowly raised his head off the hard mattress he was lying on and looked at the Governor. "I was walking through the city, near the manor houses beside the temple. Then, I heard a sound and saw a child who had stumbled a few feet away. When he saw me looking at him, he ran away."

"A child?" Syrella frowned.

"Yes... A boy."

"Very clever. A boy doesn't draw anyone's attention," a voice said, and Selwyn lifted his head a little more. In the back of the room stood Jahon, looking austere.

"And did the boy attack you?" Syrella spoke again.

Selwyn shook his head and felt a sharp pain at the back of his scalp. "I ran after him in an attempt to catch him, and I did. I asked him who told him to follow me, and he said that if he talked, he and his family would die. I told him I'd protect him, and then a stone hit me on the head... I had just enough time to see another boy running away before I passed out," he said, feeling dizzy.

Syrella let out an angry cry. "I'm going to find that traitor and feed him his balls!" she shouted.

"Do you think he—"

"Of course! Who else would have any reason to be watching us? He knows Selwyn has been by my side all this time. I'll uncover this cunt, and when Elmor sees his punishment, no one will ever betray me again."

"How?" Jahon asked.

"What do you mean, *how*?"

"How will you uncover him?"

Syrella half-closed her eyes. "He's one of my most loyal lords. I've thought about it dozens of times. Only they knew about the plan in the Battle of the Forked River with time enough to send the news to Walter. I thought my lords might have opened their mouths and told someone else the secret, but after what happened in my chamber, I know whoever is behind all of this is a very powerful noble."

Selwyn felt very tired.

"We're talking about a dozen men. It won't be that difficult to discover who it is," Syrella added.

"Then why haven't we already done so?" Jahon snapped.

"I can't do it now. However, just before the final battle against Walter, I'll tell my loyal lords about a plan... a bold plan. And then, I'll watch them to see who will try to send the news to Thorn," Syrella told him.

"Whoever the traitor is, he knows that we're looking for him, and he's taking good care to protect himself. He won't send Walter any news this time. He'll assume he's being watched," Jahon responded.

"He may send news with someone else. He may use a boy like the one who was following me," Selwyn said.

"No one is getting out of my city this time! Whoever dares to try, I'll catch them."

Despite the headache clouding his vision, Selwyn could see the rage on Syrella's face.

"What matters is winning the battle, not finding the traitor," Thorold told them.

Syrella gave him a venomous look. "This man is responsible for the death of my brother, my nephew, even my husband! I won't rest until I kill him. Even if Walter wins, I have to punish this bastard!"

"Anger is never helpful counsel," Thorold said softly. "No matter how much harm this traitor has done, he wasn't the one who killed your loved ones on the battlefield. Walter has spread death across the kingdom, and if we don't defeat him, he'll continue to do so."

Syrella opened her mouth to say something but closed it again. She had found no answer to Thorold's words. Selwyn glanced around the small room. There were a few shelves here and there and a handful of candles lit up the dark space. "That Sadon Burns has always seemed—" he began.

"He's not the traitor." Syrella cut him off.

Selwyn wasn't convinced. "How can you be so sure?"

The Governor frowned. "I've thought about it many times. I know he's obnoxious, even more so lately, but his son—my dead husband—was on the battlefield at the Forked River. I don't believe he would have sent Walter to kill his only son."

"He may not have expected his son to be in the battle." Selwyn's head hurt progressively more as he spoke.

"I don't think so, but we'll find out the truth soon enough."

"Lord Brau needs to rest," Thorold said.

"It'll be impossible to rest with this damned itch." Selwyn didn't know how he'd restrain himself. He wanted to scratch his flesh so hard that it'd bleed even more than it had bled when the stone hit him.

"I'll give you another herb so you can sleep," the Master responded.

"We'll talk in the morning," Syrella said curtly, heading towards the door.

"What are we going to do about the boys who are following us? The city is full of spies." Selwyn raised his voice.

Syrella stopped short. "We must be careful until I catch the traitor. I already have enough spies close to my loyal lords. However, if an informant finds himself at your mercy again, don't be chivalrous. Hold your blade to his neck and bring him to me, no matter how young he may be."

The Governor left the room with Jahon close behind, and the Master worked on making something on a small table.

"Here we are," Thorold said, holding out his hand with a small wooden mug in it.

Selwyn took it and drained its contents. The taste of the liquid was awful, but he immediately felt a nebulous darkness envelop him. He tried to remember the boys' faces, but his memories were blurred.

"You did well not to hurt that boy. Now rest."

He saw Thorold's aged eyes looking at him, and as he laid his head back against the hard mattress, the void swallowed him.

The Promise

Velhisya watched the rat sniffing around the corners of her cell. She suspected it was looking for food, but it wouldn't succeed in finding a single crumb. The food they brought her was so sparse she never left any of it. The little creature stuck its head into a corner and sniffed the ground. Most people were afraid of vermin, and rats in particular, yet she found the strange creatures vulnerable and helpless. They were constantly scampering around, foraging for food from people's leftovers and rarely bothered anyone. She'd heard stories of men being bitten by rats, but she was sure that those fools must have tried to harm the tiny creatures.

The cell was dark and quiet, and a gentle snore reached her ears. Matt had fallen asleep, but she couldn't sleep. She kept mulling over the news Lothar had brought her. It felt like days had passed since she'd last seen him, but she didn't know how many. Judging from the amount of food they had brought her, it must have been about three.

Velhisya couldn't believe her aunt had decided to give up all of Elmor's wealth for her. Tears streamed down her cheeks every time she thought of Syrella's face. Her aunt had loved her as her daughter, and that made her feel special. She may have felt lonely countless times in her life, but in truth, she wasn't alone. She had people who loved her, and that filled her with joy. She knew full well that countless men and women had come into the world without anyone ever caring about them.

She continued watching the rat, which had started approaching her, sniffing ground. Walter Thorn came to mind. If the news Lothar had told her was true, Walter wouldn't rest until he killed every person in Elmor. His men had been defeated twice in the region of Endor—the only two defeats they'd suffered in all these years. Velhisya knew that the third battle wouldn't end in retreat. The victor would rule the kingdom and the blood of the vanquished would stain Elmor's soil.

We'll beat Thorn; we'll succeed!

She'd fight in the final battle, and no one would stop her. She hoped that the elves and elwyn would help her learn to illuminate her sword with the power of Light and that then she could become valuable in battle. Ever since she was still a child, she'd tried to fill her mother's sword with light, but to no avail. Someone had to teach her how to keep the Light in the sword, and the elwyn were the only ones who could help her.

My Light may be weak. If it is, no one will be able to help me. The thought frightened her. After almost twenty years in the world, she'd discovered that she did not possess most of the elwyn powers, which meant that the Light within her wasn't strong. Perhaps she'd never be able to fight with a brightly lit sword like her mother. *If I'm so weak, how was what happened in Liher's chamber possible?* She had no answers, but she hoped the elwyn would be able to explain.

The rat scurried quickly towards her and neared her hand. She didn't want to pet it. Rats sometimes attacked if people tried to touch them. The small creature sniffed her fingers and lifted its eyes to look at her.

"If only I had some crumbs," she whispered.

The creature bent its head to the side as if it were trying to understand her words.

"Can't you leave these dungeons? If you leave the city, you'll always find fruit in the countryside."

The rat continued watching her, and she felt silly speaking to it. Nevertheless, the companionship of the tiny creature was comforting. The rat sat still for a while, then turned and ran towards a corner of the cell. Its tail swished back and forth as it sniffed the ground, and then a loud snore came from the cell next to hers. She was pleased that Matt had managed to sleep that day. Velhisya recalled his sobbing and heavy breathing most nights they'd spent in the dungeon. She wished she could help him and tell him that everything would be alright, but she was powerless to do so. She couldn't relieve him of his troubles, and this made her feel immense sorrow.

I will save him. The idea she'd had a few days ago was all that could help the unfortunate man, and she didn't think Liher would refuse. A ship was worth far more than any gold the merchant owed his men, and by killing Matt, they wouldn't gain a thing. *Syrella will be furious.*

Her aunt was stripping every lord of Elmor of all their wealth just before the final battle against Walter. That decision would undoubtedly bring great discord to Wirskworth, yet Syrella had risked it to save her. It wasn't right to force her aunt to also give up one of her ships. However, Velhisya knew that in a few days, everything would be resolved. They would either all die, or they'd win, and then she was sure that Syrella would hasten to get her gold back from Liher. She was also sure her aunt wouldn't give away all her gold. No one could know how much Elmor's wealth amounted to. Liher was no fool. He'd almost certainly calculated approximately how much gold there might be in one of the richest areas of the kingdom. But Syrella would keep some back, too, without anyone knowing.

Liher won't care about my aunt keeping some gold back. He'll get so much gold that he'll become one of the richest rulers in the kingdom. The very idea that he would gain all that wealth infuriated her. She shouldn't make her aunt squander a ship after all that, but she couldn't abandon Matt. *If we win the war, we'll get everything back,* she told herself.

But there was another problem. She was certain that Syrella wouldn't travel all the way to Elmor, and so she would have to request that a ship be delivered to Liher when she returned to Wirskworth. She feared the Governor of Vylor wouldn't agree to release Matt without guarantees, and she didn't want to leave her fellow prisoner here for so long.

"What are you doing here, my lord?" a voice said.

"I want to speak to the prisoner." The familiar voice of Lothar echoed in the dungeons.

Velhisya felt momentary unease and got up abruptly. Why had he come to see her? Perhaps her aunt had changed her mind. Each step Lothar took made her heart beat faster until the man stood in front of her cell.

"Good evening."

"What's wrong?" she said, looking the man in the eyes.

"My brother has agreed to spare the life of your fellow prisoner. Nevertheless, he wants guarantees that he'll get the ship you've promised," he responded.

It was as if the gods had heard her thoughts and had sent Lothar to her. "I have to speak to my aunt. Liher will get the ship as soon as I explain it to her."

"I'm pretty sure Syrella Endor won't be travelling to Vylor. Her men will deliver the gold. You'll have to return to Elmor to ask her to give my brother the ship."

"That's true," Velhisya confessed.

"Liher will keep the prisoner here until he gets his reward. He won't agree—"

"I want him released the moment I'm released," Velhisya interjected.

"He won't do that. He won't agree to freeing this man until he gets his ship."

Everything she had been frightened might happen had done so.. "No! My aunt will be giving him all of Elmor's gold! I think that's enough for me and one more man. In a few days, as soon as I get to Wirskworth, I'll see to it that he gets the ship, too."

"He won't—"

"If he doesn't agree, the deal is off. His men will lose their gold!" Velhisya knew she wasn't in a strong bargaining position. Nevertheless, gold was everything in Vylor and Liher's men would pressure him into accepting the offer in the hope that they would get their payment.

"I'll try to talk to him again, but I don't think he'll agree." Lothar frowned.

"I think his men will convince him to take the risk. A ship is worth far more than a man, and my aunt will pay her debt if I talk to her."

Matt's snoring sounded loud, and Lothar scratched his chin. "Do you really think so? Will she give up a ship for a strange man because you made a promise on her behalf? It'll have cost her a lot to save your life already."

"She'll do it!" Velhisya insisted. She knew Syrella might disregard the promise, but she'd try to convince her. After all, if they defeated Walter, they would get the ship back along with Elmor's gold, having killed Liher first.

"I want to tell you another thing." Lothar lowered his gaze and reached his hand through the bars of the cell gate as if to give her something.

Velhisya walked to the gate, feeling pain in her muscles, and put her fingers under his. Two cold objects landed in her palm. Velhisya lifted her hand and saw two rusty keys. "What are—"

Lothar immediately motioned for her to be quiet. Then, he brought his face as close to the cell bars as he could. "If my brother changes his mind and wants to kill you, I'll let you know, and then, you'll escape," he said in a whisper.

Velhisya couldn't believe her ears. "I don't want you to risk your life—"

"Be quiet!" the man whispered, and she fell silent.

"I believe Liher won't harm you, however my brother has always been unpredictable. If he changes his mind, I want you to leave here. I'll be somewhere far away from the castle when you do so. I don't want anyone to be able to prove that I helped you. I'll make sure there are no guards for a while, and that way you'll be able to find the passage to the other end of the dungeons. It's between two torches along the bigger wall." He pointed to the right in an attempt to explain where the secret exit was to be found.

"I thought that after Selwyn's escape, your brother always had his men in the dungeons and that you wouldn't be able to free me."

"If he tries to kill you, I'll find a way to remove his guards."

Velhisya felt touched. "Thank you, Lothar. I don't understand why you've done so much for me, but thank you."

He nodded curtly. "I want to tell you something I told Selwyn, too," he whispered. "If you ever decide to take revenge on my brother, I want you to swear that you won't punish the people of Vylor."

"I swear. I hope that one day you'll be the Governor of this land," Velhisya said.

Lothar didn't speak, but a smile formed on his lips. "I wouldn't want my brother to die, but his actions will have consequences. No one escapes fate," he said. "I'll talk to him about your promise of a ship. I'll do what I can."

A thought crept into Velhisya's mind. "If Liher changes his mind and decides to kill me, what will happen to Matt if I escape? Can I also open his cell with these keys?"

Lothar motioned for her to lower her voice. "No. The one key is for your cell and the other for the secret passage. The entrance to the tunnel is one with the wall, so feel around until you find the keyhole. If you need to escape, close the gate behind you, and as soon as you reach the other end of the tunnel, search for the keyhole again. The same key opens both doors to the secret passage."

"And what will become of Matt?"

Lothar sighed. "If it comes to that, I can do nothing more for him. I don't want the men of the city getting angry with me... I'm sure many will be suspicious of me when you escape, and if I free Matt as well, word may go round that I don't care about anyone in Vylor—neither the men of my land nor my brother. I don't want to lose my reputation. This place needs me."

Velhisya tried to think of something, but there were no other options.

Lothar had already done so much for her.

"Let's hope it doesn't come to that. We'll speak soon." With that, Lothar began to move away from the cell.

"Lothar."

The man turned abruptly and seemed bewildered that she'd called out to him so loudly.

"Thank you. Thank you for everything."

The Knight and the Faris

E lliot saw the warriors waiting in the arena. There were no more than twenty, but their faces seemed determined. None of them wore steel breastplates or helmets, and they carried all kinds of weapons—spears, axes, swords, and shields. Bows were the only weapons that were prohibited.

He glanced to his right and saw the Emperor in a golden robe, rubbing his hands together in satisfaction. He seemed eager for the spectacle that was to come. Edmee and Marin sat on either side of their father, while Sophie was placed between her future husband and Elliot. A beautiful tiara adorned the Queen's head, but her blue eyes looked worried.

"I have a bad feeling about this," Peter whispered.

Elliot cast a look at the frowning man to his left. It was obvious that the Lord of the Knights didn't share in the Emperor's joy.

"I wonder where the boy is," Peter went on.

Elliot wondered the same thing. He looked repeatedly at the warriors, searching for the boy with *magical* powers—the boy who inspired fear in the Emperor for the prosperity of his land. Jeering rang in his ears, and he saw the people sitting around the arena rise from their stone seats. The sun's rays fell on their bodies as they yelled, eager for the fighting to begin. Elliot was grateful that a cloth canopy shielded him from the sun. Odin had made elaborate seats for himself and his guests, and the shade above made it easier to see the arena.

Elliot felt a knot tighten in his chest. He hoped the boy truly did possess magical powers and that he could escape from that place unscathed.

The thought of watching a child being slaughtered was unbearable. Perhaps he had been a fool to convince Odin to organise a tournament in honour of the Queen.

Grief kills their powers, the Emperor's words alarmed him. The child had witnessed the death of his entire clan. If the rumours were true, grief wouldn't allow him to fight for his life, and if he died, Elliot would feel guilt eating away at his flesh.

Even if you had said nothing, the boy would have been hanged, his conscience was right, but even so, if they had executed the child in the city square, it wouldn't have been his fault.

I gave him a chance to fight for his life! He was going to die anyway. He couldn't set his mind at ease.

The crowd's jeering grew louder, and then he saw two men enter the arena with a small figure standing between them. Elliot looked a little closer, and his breath caught in his throat. The boy was very young—a child—and the guards accompanying him had their swords in their hands. The jeering continued unabated, and the boy, with the two guards, approached the rest of the Faris at the end of the arena. Elliot saw dozens of archers along the length of the seats pull the arrows from their quivers and nock their bows, ready to release. The Emperor had given clear orders. If the boy used his supposed powers, he'd die immediately.

He saw movement out of the corner of his eye and turned to Odin, who had risen from his seat.

"You know the rules!" the Emperor shouted. "Two men at a time will duel until only one survives. Whoever wins all the battles will have glory and honour few in this world have known conferred upon them!"

The first two duellists walked towards the centre of the arena. Neither of them held a shield, and one of them was very large in stature. They faced each other and raised their weapons. The man holding the sword was of slight build, while his opponent held a large hammer. Elliot didn't like hammers and axes, nor did he like spears. He'd always believed that swords were the most effective weapons.

The match began, and the smaller duellist struck first, bringing his sword down. His opponent dodged swiftly. A moment later, the hammer was raised, swinging towards the swordsman's skull. He darted aside, and the clang of metal against the ground echoed through the arena. The sword sliced through the air, but the larger duellist lifted his hammer just in time to deflect the blow. Elliot was impressed by the skill of the two Faris. The men seemed to know how to handle their weapons well. His fear for the little boy grew.

The sword tore through the air repeatedly, forcing the burly man with the hammer to step back, watching for an opening to wield his heavy weapon. *This is why I don't like hammers...* The sword aimed at the duellist's feet, and he deflected with the base of the hammer. The slight man stumbled and lost his balance, and then the hammer rose into the air and came down towards the ground heavily.

A panicked scream echoed through the arena as the head of the man who had been holding the sword was shattered.

"Magnificent!" Odin's voice rang out. Thousands of people began clapping as the man with the hammer bowed deeply and raised one hand, joyous of his victory.

"Let the next two duellists come in!" cried the Emperor.

A few men in tattered clothes rushed to pick up the body of the dead duellist while two more Faris advanced along the length of the arena, headed for its centre. One carried a shield and sword, while the other was carrying only an axe.

Poor choice. Axes are difficult weapons to handle, and the shield gives the man with the sword an advantage. The men prepared for the duel, and the sound of the crowd died down. *How sick can people be?* He'd never imagined that death and fighting would become entertainment for people. Of course, the tournaments of Knightdorn had all sorts of contests, too, but the knights rarely died at those celebrations. The aim was to make a show of the most skilled warrior, not the death of his opponent.

The man with the axe attacked with ferocity, each blow forcing his opponent to raise his shield and driving him farther back. *Come on...* Elliot wanted to yell at him to raise the shield, create an opening, and stab his opponent in the stomach.

The axe kept tearing through the air, and the man with the sword seemed to have grown tired. Suddenly, the blade in the man's hands jerked sharply, tearing into his opponent's shoulder, but the duellist with the axe brought his weapon down again with a cry. The shield slipped from the man's hand, and he tried to retaliate with his sword, but it was too late. The axe tore into his shoulder, and he fell to the ground in agony. The victor raised his left hand in the air, and the crowd cheered. A moment later, he looked at the Emperor as if expecting to hear something from him—Odin brought his right hand to his neck, and he dragged his finger in front of his throat. The fighter raised his axe and slit his opponent's throat.

Elliot shuddered at the sight while the crowd roared with excitement. He was certain Odin wouldn't let any losers leave the arena alive. The slaves once again rushed in to collect the body of the dead duellist, and two more Faris strode into the centre of the arena, each holding only a sword. They raised their weapons in readiness to attack, and he hoped both were skilled fighters. The majority of the Faris may have been capable warriors, but the last man who had lost his life hadn't known how to use his weapon properly.

The single combat began, but Elliot kept his eye on the boy at the far end of the arena. The child watched the duel from a distance, unmoving. A scream shook the air, and he saw the head of one of the two duellists severed from his body. Elliot didn't want to watch any more. He glanced at the people around him, trying not to look back at the arena. Sophie and Marin were scowling while Edmee scratched her chin in thought. Odin Mud and a few of his lord-allies who were sitting a little further away were the only ones who seemed to be enjoying the spectacle.

"I'd like to leave," Peter whispered in his ear.

"Me too. However, we can't leave. It's a 'celebration' for the upcoming wedding, and we're here for the Queen's protection," Elliot murmured. He and Peter may not have been wearing armour like the countless guards around them, but they were still the commanders of Sophie's guard.

Peter nodded sharply and turned his gaze to the arena, a dejected look in his eyes, while Elliot buried his face in his hands. He didn't want to see another death whose only purpose was to entertain the people of Mirth.

Time passed, and Elliot didn't look at the arena again. He could tell what was happening from the crowd—their cheering, broken by stretches of silence, marked each round. He knew the boy would be the last to face his first opponent, and as the moment drew near, he wished he could stop time. The cheering swelled again, and he cast a fleeting glance across the arena. Many spots near the centre were stained blood-red, and the slaves who collected the bodies were now carrying the lifeless carcass of a man, his throat still spewing blood.

I don't want to see any more. I don't want to see any more, Elliot told himself again, looking at the stony ground between his feet. He may have seen countless men die in battle, but this was different. The Faris weren't dying for a cause, only to entertain the crowd and gain glory and gold. *Aleron would vomit if he saw this.* Elliot even pitied the slaves who ran to collect the bodies from the arena.

He kept his eyes down, trying to ignore the impulse to look up when the cheering erupted around him until he felt a pinch on his right elbow. He lifted his head and found Sophie's blue eyes staring at him in fear. Then, he saw the little boy walking towards the centre along with another duellist.

You must win... You must use your powers! He couldn't explain why he now believed wholeheartedly that the boy had special abilities. Perhaps, because it was his only hope of living. Elliot's breath caught in his throat—the boy held a small sword awkwardly, and it was clear he had no idea how to use it. His opponent raised a long spear.

"He won't manage to win many battles. He won't even manage to win one," Sophie whispered.

Elliot's stomach turned. The boy had to win two battles, and then there would only be five duellists left. The Emperor would send the most skilled amongst them to the final duel while the remaining four would fight two more battles. To win, a duellist had to win at best three battles, and at worst five.

The man raised his spear, and the boy took a step back. *Use the rain! Use the clouds and the wind!* Elliot hoped to see a bolt of lightning strike the Emperor's head even though he, Sophie, and Peter were very close to Odin.

The man with the spear yelled and brought his weapon down against the boy's side. Elliot thought his heart had stopped. The boy jumped to the left, avoiding the blow, immediately throwing his sword away and starting to run. *No...*

"Perhaps it was all just rumour after all... I may have killed this clan for nothing. Their tricks misled my men, and I wasted so much time chasing after them," came the Emperor's voice.

"Or grief prevents the boy from fighting," Marin said.

"No amount of grief can defeat the fear of death," Odin replied.

The boy ran towards the arena's exit, and a handful of guards blocked his path as his opponent chased him frantically.

"No!" Elliot got up from his seat and ran towards the centre of the arena, pushing aside whoever got in his way. He could hear people swearing as he jumped over the stone steps and got to the side of the arena.

"What are you doing?" an archer asked him, aiming at the boy.

Elliot ignored him and jumped into the arena. His legs ached as the soles of his feet hit the ground.

"Elliot, come back!" He heard Sophie's voice over the din. The crowd's jeers died down as if the spectacle had astonished them all.

The boy ran to the left, and the duellist readied to throw his spear. Elliot sprinted as fast as he could until he reached the boy and pushed him down with all his might just as the spear passed between them. He lifted his head and saw the child looking at him with yellow eyes. He had never seen eyes like that before.

"Stay behind me."

The duellist charged towards him, his fists raised. Elliot drew the Sword of Light in one swift move and slashed his throat. There were angry outcries, and Odin's voice resounded like thunder.

"How dare you kill my duellists! Do you want me to have you executed?"

Elliot looked up to where the Emperor sat. He could see his enraged face; his deed may have cost them the alliance that would have saved their people's lives.

"This tournament is being held in honour of the Queen, who hoped to see some of the ablest men in the world duelling. I'm sure that the murder of a defenceless boy wouldn't bring Her Majesty any joy," Elliot yelled back.

"Get out of the arena immediately if you value your life!" Odin screamed.

"This boy is not what you all thought he was! There's no reason for him to die, and I can offer the crowd a spectacle they've never seen before."

"What kind of spectacle?" Odin shouted, raising his fists.

"However many duellists are left will duel with me all at once—all of them against me. If I win, this boy will be set free."

"Get back here!" Sophie rose to her feet. She seemed desperate to stop him from ruining everything.

"NO!" Elliot shouted. "No one can deny that it would be a unique sight... A knight without armour against nine Faris."

The crowd began to roar more furiously than ever.

"FIGHT, FIGHT, FIGHT!"

The Emperor raised his hand, and the shouting died down. "I thought you came all this way to protect your Queen, but if you want to die in an arena, I have no objection. FIGHT!"

Nine men ran from one end of the arena towards him, yelling while the crowd roared, too. An axe came down hard, aimed at his head, and he evaded it as the Sword of Light pierced his opponent's chest. He saw three more swords come towards him and spun. The weapons cut through the air, and he raised his own, ready to strike, when he saw an axe pointing at his chest. Elliot ducked, and the axe cut into the neck of one of his opponents.

"Come on", Elliot beckoned, now looking at seven men surrounding him.

The burly Faris holding the hammer ran at him. Elliot darted to the side, and the weapon hit the ground. He was about to kill his enemy when a sword came at his shoulder. He ducked again, then got up with a leap, flipping his sword around. The roar of the crowd blanketed everything while the three men who had charged at him from behind fell to the ground, their throats spewing blood.

Elliot saw three swords and a hammer coming at his head and stepped back quickly. One of his enemies tried to hit him in the neck with his shield, but he evaded the blow and cut the man's arm. The shield fell to the ground, and Elliot picked it up, deflecting two swords. The hammer aimed for his feet, and Elliot leapt to the left. Then, he brought the sword up alongside the shield and jumped on two of his enemies. The men were startled and fell to the ground. Elliot also lost his balance and his weapons fell out of his hands.

He saw the hammer coming at him again. He spun across the ground, scrambled to his feet, and grabbed his blade and shield. Charging towards the fallen men still struggling to rise, Elliot's sword tore through the air, stabbing them in the neck. Then another man stepped in front of him. Elliot drove his sword into the man's chest and turned—just in time to see his final opponent raising his hammer high. He dodged to the side again, but his boot struck something hard, and he lost his balance. The sword and shield slipped from his hands once more, and he looked up to see the burly man lifting the hammer for another strike.

Elliot saw the stone that had caused his fall and lowered his eyes, waiting for death. The hammer was about to come down on him when his opponent let out a scream. The boy with the yellow eyes had stuck a sword into the back of his opponent's right leg.

Elliot leapt as fast as he could, grabbed his sword off the ground, and stuck it into the duellist's belly. The hammer slipped out of the burly man's hands and fell behind his back. He kneeled before Elliot, his lips turning red with blood. Elliot stood tall as his opponent collapsed to the ground. Sweat ran down his forehead, and the blade of the Sword of Light gleamed crimson—but his eyes darted towards Odin, whose face was a storm of rage and surprise. The crowd's cheering rang in his ears, and then he saw a creature in the sky. A white hawk flew above his head, and a small letter appeared to be tied to its leg.

Secret Betrayal

Peter knocked on the door of Sophie's chamber. "May I come in, Your Majesty?" His heart thumped so strongly that he feared it would burst through his chest.

"Come in."

Peter pushed open the door and stepped inside the chamber. The flames of a few candles gave off a dim light as the Queen sat in a chair behind a wooden table. He crossed the chamber quickly until he stood before her. Sophie was dressed in a lilac robe, her hair tousled. Two small dark circles had formed under her eyes. "I thought Elliot was supposed to be standing guard outside my chamber today with the other soldiers. I had planned to speak to him about his exploits earlier…"

"I told him I wanted to be here tonight," Peter said.

"After what happened in that damned arena, perhaps he needs some rest," Sophie shot back, still looking both shocked and irritated by what she had witnessed that day.

"Undoubtedly, that was a spectacle I'll never forget," Peter admitted.

"None of us will ever forget it! Elliot put everything at risk. I fear Odin may not forgive this insult and may call the wedding off…"

Peter searched for a way to change the subject; he wanted to get everything off his chest, but he couldn't find the courage to do so. "The Emperor wants this marriage; he won't back down now. The spectacle the people of Mirth witnessed today will never be forgotten in this land."

"Perhaps. However, Elliot is foolish. He risked everything for a boy! What if he'd lost his life? What if Odin decides that our differences in leadership are irreconcilable? One of my knights left his post and risked his life for a random boy."

"Elliot doesn't govern any part of Knightdorn," Peter said softly.

"No, but he's close to me, and everyone suspects I take his counsel seriously," Sophie said, her fingers tightening around the armrest. "A foolish councillor gives a bad impression of my choices and of my merit as a leader. I should punish him, to prove I don't tolerate such behaviour."

Peter frowned. "Elliot is still just a boy. No matter how well he knows how to wield his sword, it takes experience and maturity to make the right decisions, and we all know he's still green. The Emperor won't judge you for his actions, nor will he throw away the opportunity to make his son king. We all saw you yelling at Elliot to stop."

"He wouldn't listen to me!" There was annoyance in Sophie's voice.

"That's true, but he saved a boy in an act of self-sacrifice and bravery." Peter admired Elliot for what he'd done.

Sophie sighed. "I'm happy that unfortunate child wasn't slaughtered before my eyes. Nevertheless, I heard Odin imprisoned him again, and I bet he won't let him get away, even if he didn't seem to have any *strange powers*. Elliot may have risked his life for nothing... If he'd died, we'd have lost our most capable warrior, and I'd have had to face Walter even more alone."

"You're right, Your Majesty. But I'm sure that his act wasn't intended to offend you. He just couldn't bear to see that boy fighting for his life and his hot-headed self got the better of him," Peter explained.

"Althalos should have taught him to be more...more..."

"Wise."

"Exactly!" Sophie said.

"Perhaps, but in all my years, I've never seen such a brave act with my own eyes before."

Sophie stared at the ceiling for a few moments. "I agree. Bravery and foolishness sometimes go hand in hand. Elliot has the power to go down in history as the man who overthrew one of the greatest tyrants the world has ever seen. And yet, he risked his life for one single soul."

"If all knights were as honourable as Elliot, then no children would ever die in war."

The Queen fell silent as she listened to his words.

"What's done is done. The marriage will take place and soon we'll set sail for Knightdorn, and that boy will have the end that fate has in store for him," Peter added.

Sophie was expressionless. "I hope Elliot doesn't make any more rash decisions until the wedding..." she said, but her voice had lost its angry tone. Peter swore that no matter what she said about Elliot, deep down, she admired his deeds.

"Why are you here?" Sophie asked suddenly. "Did you want to talk about this morning's events?"

Peter hesitated, and out of the corner of his eye, he saw the red moon through one of the chamber windows. "Well, I..."

"I'm exhausted," Sophie said. "If there's something you want to tell me, please do so without humming and hawing. I never thought a wedding could be even more exhausting than war."

Peter mustered all his courage. "As I said before, what I saw today was..." he was so afraid to utter what he really wanted to say.

"Peter—"

"Today, I saw an act that few men would have the courage to perform. And then, I realised what a coward I've been all these years. How unworthy I was and still am."

Sophie straightened in her chair. "What do you mean? What nonsense is this? Just because you didn't risk your life for some boy, you're unwor—"

"I betrayed you and your House, Your Majesty," he interjected. "I have tried to find the courage to tell you for years, but I've been a coward—a man without honour. I was afraid to speak the truth. You've been through so much, I just couldn't... I didn't want to cause you any more pain."

Sophie's mouth was half-open. She rose from her chair and stood in front of Peter. She looked at him as if she were seeing him for the first time. "What do you mean?"

"Before your uncle became king, he took me into his ranks when I left George Thorn and departed from Iovbridge. I'd fought beside the First King in a couple of battles, and when I saw George's true face, I decided to leave the royal capital and fight for Thomas Egercoll."

"I know," Sophie said hastily.

"I helped your uncle overthrow George, and he gave me a lordly title and a general's seat on his council."

"I know all that! How did you betray me and my House?" Sophie demanded the truth, and Peter was sure his end was near.

"I was always loyal to your uncle, and eighteen years after George's defeat, I wanted to fight against Walter. When Thomas was about to leave for Ballar, he ordered me to stay behind. He wanted some men to look after Queen Alice and Emma Egercoll in Iovbridge, and I obeyed. One night before the King set out for Ramerstorm, I heard the knights and the Lord of the Knights talking in the Palace of the Dawn. They said that Thomas would die soon and that they would help their true lord defeat the king."

"Did you know that the royal knights were plotting with Walter?" Sophie seemed unable to take it all in.

Peter nodded abruptly, and tears flooded his eyes. He looked away from her face and down at his boots, his tears falling on the chamber floor. "I thought about talking to Thomas right away and telling him everything, but I was afraid. I thought that if Walter had his men that deep in Iovbridge, there would be others, and Thomas would have no chance of winning. Selwyn was only three years old, and my other two sons were still boys. I feared that if I spoke up, Walter's men would kill my family—I lost my nerve!" Tears poured from his eyes.

"The King departed from Iovbridge, and I prayed he'd defeat Walter. Then, I would have told him what I'd done and begged him for forgiveness. But he never returned, and the treachery of the knights was revealed. Guilt ate at my body like a rodent. I couldn't believe that Thomas was dead and that a Thorn would take over again. Nevertheless, I never found the courage to tell Queen Alice and Althalos the truth—that if I hadn't been a coward, Thomas might have been alive. When the Grand Master left and asked me to support you in the succession of Thomas, I swore that I'd give my life to you, even if I died." Peter took a breath and tried to hold back his tears.

"I kept my word and never lost my nerve again. I've tried to make amends for my actions and my betrayal of your House. When my sons died, I believed the gods were laughing at me. I had betrayed Thomas to protect them, and a few years later, Walter's men took them away from me. I know that no matter what's happened since, I haven't done enough for my betrayal to be forgiven. I've tried countless times over the years to tell you the truth, but I've never found the strength." He gathered what courage he had left and looked up. Sophie's eyes were wet with tears, too.

"What made you tell me all of this today?" she asked almost in a whisper.

Peter wiped his eyes on his sleeve. "I saw a lad run to fight to save a child, risking his life to do the right thing, while everyone else sat idly by and watched the spectacle. I couldn't bear my shame after all I saw this morning. If Elliot had the courage to fight nine men to save a single boy, then how unworthy, miserable, and weak must I be, having never found the courage to tell you about my betrayal all these years?"

He expected Sophie to call the guards and order them to arrest him. He expected her to ask Odin to execute him in the Square of Justice, but the Queen's hand touched his shoulder gently.

"You're a good and honest man, Peter. I know that you must have suffered, having to carry this burden all these years."

"I'm sorry. I'm so sorry," Peter whispered.

"I may have done the same. I, too, may have been afraid for Eleanor and Bert and my family. None of us has ever made all the right decisions, and you have given your all to protect me all these years—to help me do the right thing. I have made mistakes, too. When I killed those prisoners who were at my mercy, you were the only one who insisted I do what Althalos would have done if he were in my place. You may have made a mistake, but you've been loyal to me and my House for many, many years."

Peter sobbed. "I deserve to be punished. I deserved to lose my sons," he said between gulps of air.

"No," Sophie said. "I can't be sure what my uncle would have done, but I believe he would have done what I'm about to do now."

Peter looked into her blue eyes, speechless.

"I forgive you. On behalf of the House of Egercoll, I forgive you and thank you for the loyalty and devotion you've shown me all these years. Your family and your House will always have my respect. May you find peace and live the remaining years of your life free of guilt."

Peter knelt before her. For the first time in decades, the weight on his chest was removed. He felt as if he could fly, now that he was free of the guilt that had poisoned his body. "I'll fight by your side until I die, my Queen."

The Shadow of a Man

Elliot looked at the empty seats in the arena and sighed heavily. In his mind's eye, he saw the duellists coming towards him again and again, brandishing their weapons. He saw the hammer rise, ready to crush his skull. He couldn't believe he was alive. *Althalos would have been furious if he'd seen me risking Knightdorn's salvation for a boy,* he thought. *However, Althalos believed that knights should be the epitome of honour and bravery. What honour is there in a man who stands by as a helpless child is murdered before him?*

Elliot took a few steps towards the centre of the arena, gazing at the stone seats. He stopped and glanced up at the night sky. A red moon shone in the west while a yellow one glowed in the north. Elliot hadn't spoken to anyone after the fight. He'd stood up, walked towards the exit of the arena, and the guards had allowed him to leave with Hurwig following close behind. Then, he'd run to his room and spent the rest of the day there until the time had come for him to stand guard outside the Queen's quarters. Elliot had wanted to avoid doing so since he knew that Sophie would be quick to yell at him for what he'd done. Still, he'd strapped his sword to his belt and had hastened to her chamber. However, as soon as he'd arrived there, Peter had asked to take his place that night. Elliot was relieved and had hurried out of the palace as quickly as he could.

A sharp rustle of wings made him turn, and he saw Hurwig flying a few feet above his head. He was glad that his hawk had returned, but John's letter had left him with mixed feelings. His former companion was safe, but the Ice Islands wouldn't fight for Sophie. Furthermore, Long Arm had decided to stay on the northern Islands of Knightdorn, away from the war.

You are Knightdorn's greatest hope of overthrowing Walter Thorn, but I can offer you nothing in battle. I've tried to help you as best I could, but I think it would now be best for me to stay here. I hope you don't hate me for not deciding to return to your side. I hope you defeat Walter alongside Sophie and don't ever forget what I told you. Whatever happens, don't make any hot-headed decisions!

Elliot wasn't angry. He'd known for some time that John didn't want to risk his life alongside the Queen, but he felt a great emptiness within him. Morys and Eleanor were dead, and Long Arm had decided not to return. Selwyn was all he had left of their company, and that hurt him. Furthermore, John was valuable. He may have had many vices, but he knew how to read people well, and his views were often wiser than those of countless councillors in Knightdorn. Deep down, he felt responsible that Long Arm had decided not to return. Elliot had sworn to protect his companions, yet two of them had died, and Selwyn had suffered torture at the hands of Liher Hale. Elliot had failed, and John knew that if he returned, there was a good chance he'd lose his life in battle.

"If you knew this world, you would know that no one can protect anyone." John's words at their first meeting found their way into his memory. Long Arm was right, and Elliot had been too young to understand everything he'd told him. *He may change his mind, but I can't hope for such a thing.* No one knew whether John would ever return to his side. *At least he's alive.* That thought brought him joy, and for a moment, a smile formed on his lips as he thought of the last phrase John had written to him. *"Whatever happens, don't make any hot-headed decisions!"* He wondered about the scolding John would have given him if he'd seen what he'd done a few hours earlier.

Elliot took another look around the arena and remembered Odin staring at him angrily from the ornate seat. He wondered if his actions had cost them their alliance with the Emperor, but he believed that was unlikely. Odin wouldn't throw everything away over a duel, but Elliot's actions had undeniably shown disrespect towards him, and the Emperor dealt harshly with those who disgraced him.

I couldn't just let a helpless boy die! he said to himself once again. No matter how much he'd angered Odin, he knew that if he could go back in time, he would do exactly the same.

Where is the boy now? Elliot had no idea what had happened once he'd won the duel and left the arena. He remembered asking Odin to release the boy if he won, however, he didn't know whether the Emperor had kept his end of the bargain.

I must speak to Marin. He would do so at first light; they all needed some rest after all that had happened that day.

Elliot walked around the arena, the only sounds that broke the silence being those that Hurwig made. His eyes wandered to the two moons again and again until two starry blue eyes appeared in his thoughts. He'd tried not to think too much about Velhisya since whenever he did, his body went numb, and he had to focus on the place where he was. Elliot was well aware that the plan to save her was fraught with danger, and he had no idea whether Syrella and Sophie's army had made it to Vylor. He hoped with all his heart that Velhisya was safe— and that she hadn't been tortured by Liher.

Damn it! There were so few of them, and they were fighting so many. He cast another look at the white hawk and thought he should send him to Syrella as soon as possible. *News of Velhisya's rescue may not have reached Wirskworth yet... It will take some time before our armies return from Vylor since most of the men are on foot.* Elliot preferred to send Hurwig to Aleron since the elwyn would be able to tell them more about the events in the land of Liher Hale. However, he and Sophie had promised Syrella that they would send her news a few days after their arrival in Mirth. *I must discuss this matter with Sophie.* He may have wanted to avoid the Queen's scolding about what he'd done in the arena, but this was important. Suddenly, Hurwig flew towards him and landed on his right shoulder.

"Beautiful hawk," came a voice.

Elliot turned back, and Hurwig leapt into the air, spreading his wings. Edmee stood behind him, dressed in woollen clothing, a long sword hanging from her belt. "What are you doing here?" he asked her.

"I was wondering the same about you," said the Princess. She didn't seem angry at him for what he'd done a few hours before.

"I wanted to walk."

"In the place you almost died?"

"Yes," Elliot said sharply.

"My father isn't pleased about what you did," Edmee responded.

"I'm sure... However, I couldn't watch a little boy being murdered."

"What you did today is the most foolish, yet bravest thing I've ever witnessed."

"I did the right thing," Elliot said boldly.

"And had you died, you would have left your Queen to face Walter alone," Edmee shot back.

"She wouldn't have been alone. I'm only one man."

Edmee frowned. "Walter is only one man. You have been trained by Althalos, and you know Sophie needs you." Elliot could tell by her tone that she thought his deed was reckless.

"I know my place is by Sophie's side!" His eyes locked onto hers. "Althalos trained me to save Knightdorn, and I risked everything for a boy. However, for years, my Master drummed into me that a knight must protect the weak and not sit back in the face of their torture! I would have been disgusted with myself if I'd watched a poor child being slaughtered without doing anything!"

"No one else cared about that boy," Edmee said.

"Maybe you're all crazy then. I never thought I'd see men giving their lives to provide a spectacle for a mob. I never thought I'd see a country watch a child die and do nothing." He'd tried to hold back his words but to no avail.

Edmee approached him slowly. "Or maybe *you're* the one who is mad, risking your life and neglecting to consider your true purpose."

"Maybe." Elliot pulled his gaze away from her. "What happened to the boy?" he asked after a moment.

"Father is keeping him in a cell. However, I heard him say he'll release him soon, in keeping with your agreement."

Elliot was enraged. "And why didn't he release him immediately? He agreed that he would if I won the duel."

Edmee crossed her arms. "You have to admit, a lot happened today. My father was furious. I'm sure he'll do it soon. I don't think any of us believes that the boy has strange powers any longer."

"And yet, his whole clan died because of some foolish rumours." Elliot knew he had to watch his tongue. He'd done enough already, risking their alliance with Kerth over and over. *Stop being hotheaded!* Long Arm's words came back to him.

"We can't know whether all the rumours were false. My father talked it over with some of his councillors a moment ago, and they told him that several of our soldiers were burned alive or drowned while hunting down this clan."

"These people may have attacked your soldiers cleverly. The fact that they drowned and burned them isn't proof that they could control water and fire," Elliot shot, annoyed.

Edmee's expression was grim. "Or some of them had strange powers, but not this boy. I can't be certain, not having seen any of it with my own eyes."

Elliot thought of the boy's yellow eyes—he had never seen anything like them before. Fear welled up inside of him. "If the Emperor still believes this clan possesses magical powers, he'll kill the boy. He'll assume that if he grows up and has children, he may pass on the powers of his clan, even if he doesn't possess them himself."

Edmee fell silent. "Why do you care so much about this boy?" she asked after a moment. "If you continue to oppose my father, and he chooses to go back on his agreement with the Queen, how many boys will Walter kill in a few days?"

Her words reminded him of those he expected Sophie to say to him. He raised his eyes to the sky, avoiding an answer.

Edmee walked up and stood before him. "I believe my father will set the boy free... Several people, including Marin, insisted that it would be brutal for this child to die after what we saw today. He'll set him free and spread the word that, despite his clan's attacks on our men, he's being merciful."

Elliot was afraid. The Emperor was capable of disregarding everyone and doing as he pleased. Instinct told him that the boy was still in danger.

"Are you really so honourable and brave, or are you hiding something, Elliot Egercoll?" Edmee's voice was a whisper.

"Saving a child shouldn't be mistaken for bravery."

"Your honour may one day be the end of you."

He'd tired of hearing those words. "So be it," he said, not looking at the Princess.

She brought her hands to his face and gently turned it towards her. "I'm sure I'll never meet a man like you again."

Elliot was about to answer when Edmee pulled his face to hers and kissed him passionately. It was as if all his cares had flown away as he tasted her lips, but an invisible voice told him to stop. Elliot pulled his head away gently, and his gaze met Edmee's.

"You're a good woman, my Princess. You deserve a man who would give anything for you. I'm but the shadow of a man doomed to spend his whole life in war and death. I can't give you what you deserve."

Elliot kissed her gently on the cheek and walked away, feeling stranger than ever before.

The Deserted Island

J ohn shivered. The moon appeared in the cloudy sky, yellow and full, and a few birds flew past. He looked at the view stretching beyond the deck but couldn't make out any land. The wind had picked up halfway through the trip, and the small island they sought remained hidden from sight. John let out a weary sigh. Jack had told him the island should appear on the horizon that day, but he must have made a mistake.

Damn. I've spent five long days on this confounded ship and would give anything to return to the Grand Island. But we might never go back. He turned and glanced at the one-eyed man commanding the ship. Raff had left the helm to rest a few moments earlier, so John had hurried up on deck. He preferred to spend time there when Raff was away. He looked out onto the vast blue sea again, and his thoughts drifted to what he'd confided to Jack a few days ago. He hadn't spoken of Nemesis in decades and had tried to bury those memories as deeply as he could.

If Nemesis could see me, she'd hate me. His life was filled with wine and whores; he cared for nothing and no one and was at the same time a coward. Nevertheless, John had no regrets. He hadn't wanted to waste his life for a kingdom or a ruler. *Nemesis would never have stood by if she had seen what Walter had done.* Nemesis may have come from Gaeldeath, and the thought of fighting her homeland might have gone against her principles—but she was honourable. Before her death, Walter hadn't committed most of his heinous crimes, and he was sure that if Nemesis had seen his acts, she would have opposed him without hesitation.

It doesn't matter what Nemesis would do. Everyone makes their own choices. John had chosen not to fight for anyone or anything.

He moved closer to the mast and thought about the letter he'd written to Elliot a few days earlier. He wondered how the lad would feel when he read his words. Would he be angry with him? John had often felt sad at the loss of Morys and Eleanor, and now he believed he'd have been happier by Elliot and Selwyn's side than on the Ice Islands. The two lads respected him, which wasn't true of anyone on the cursed northern islands. Nevertheless, that wasn't enough to make him fight Walter.

You chose to leave Elliot to escape the war, and you'll die on a tiny island in the middle of nowhere! You're a fool! his conscience shouted at him. He'd imagined dying many times in his life, but he hadn't expected it to come so futilely. He would rather die trying to steal gold or have his heart stop beating after countless hours in a brothel rather than on the sea.

John stole another look at the water. The sea was darkening with the fading light, and he began to walk towards Jack. The man's eye landed on John as he climbed the stairs that led to the helm.

"I'm in no mood to listen to your whining about our not finding the island yet," the man barked.

"If we don't find it, are we going to go back?" John asked.

Jack took on a despondent look. "If we never find it, then at some point we'll be forced to turn back... But I won't give up the fight so quickly."

"It must be nearby. You told me that we'd need about five days with this wind."

"That's what I thought. With a headwind, it would have taken us weeks, but now we must be close."

"You made a mistake. Have you ever seen this island before?" John wondered why he hadn't asked the question earlier.

"No."

John panicked. "Perhaps it doesn't even exist!"

Now, Jack looked angry. "A number of our fishermen have been fishing near its shores for quite some time, you fool. I knew some of the men who went missing."

"Perhaps the waves covered it up. There have been great swells for days."

Jack let go of the helm and turned towards him. "No matter how much nonsense you say, I'm not turning back. Do you understand?"

"Very well..." John said, disregarding his angry look. "I hope we don't find ourselves up against ships from Mynlands."

"I, on the other hand, would be glad to shoot Liquid Fire at some of those bastards!"

"Captain!" Jack and John looked in the direction of the deck. "Land on the horizon!"

John saw nothing. "What's that idiot saying?"

"You're the idiot. To the northeast."

John looked in that direction, and then he understood. A small piece of land loomed in the distance. Jack turned the helm sharply, and the ship changed course, swaying to the dance of the waves.

"Wake all the men and tell them to come on deck!" Jack shouted to one of the sailors who rushed to carry out his commands. He turned to John. "You told me you showed two men how to operate the pipes at the bottom of the ship."

"Yes."

"Find them and tell them to be ready. Then, go to the pipe on deck and be ready, too."

John turned abruptly and climbed down the stairs, his heart thumping loudly. *The end may be drawing near*, he thought, but there was no point in thinking about it. Sailors filled the deck as they came out of the large cabin—John saw two short, stocky men talking in one of the corners.

"Mark, Robb, go to the pipes and be ready to fire if we're attacked," he told them.

The two men turned to him. "Do you believe we might be attacked? I don't see anyone," Robb said, taking a step forward.

"I don't know. Nevertheless, we must be ready."

The two men nodded sharply and left hurriedly while John took another look in Jack's direction. Raff approached the captain and took the helm while the one-eyed man headed for the edge of the deck, trying to get a better look at the island they were approaching.

John rushed towards him, pushing aside anyone in front of him. The men were uneasy, he could see the fear on their faces. He got to Jack's side and looked at the island, which seemed to be getting bigger.

"Found it at a bad hour. It'll be night soon," John said. "This island is very small."

"Be ready!" Jack spat at him. "The fishermen always said it was small. This must be it." He squinted in an attempt to see better.

They neared the island, and the wind picked up as they approached the shore. The ship rocked frantically, and John's stomach churned. He feared he was about to vomit, but he had to stay focused. The north wind drove them towards the shore at high speed, and John made his way to the pipe. The lion's mouth was ready to spew Liquid Fire, and his sweaty hands gripped the steel bars at its centre.

"I don't see anything near the island. It seems deserted," one of the sailors a few feet away said.

John agreed; there wasn't a thing there. *Did the fishermen perhaps get lost in some other place we haven't found yet?* He let go of the pipe and moved to the edge of the deck. He could make out a few trees on the dry surface of the island, but there was nothing else.

"What's that?" Jack yelled.

John saw something strange. Near the shoreline of the island, the sea seemed to be foaming. He tried to get a better look and then he knew—it was a whirlpool. His palms began to sweat.

"John! Get ready to fire!"

Jack ran towards the large cabin as fast as he could, and John was sure he'd lost his mind. "Liquid Fire won't save us from the whirlpool!" he shouted.

"It's not a whirlpool. Raff, try to avoid it!" Jack yelled.

John snarled. "What do you mean it's not—" Jack entered the large cabin. "What does he mean it's not a whirlpool?" he asked a sailor next to him.

"I have no idea."

John glanced at Raff, who tried to turn the ship to avoid the vortex, but it was pulling them closer. The sailors ran in all directions, panic-stricken, and John marched towards the pipe that launched the Liquid Fire and prepared to meet his death. For a moment, he felt the urge to laugh. Begon and his men thought their fishermen might have been attacked by the northern regions of Knightdorn, yet they had been killed by a whirlpool. He never expected his end to be at the bottom of the sea.

He glanced back at Raff, still fighting to steer the ship, but it was hopeless now—there was nothing anyone could do.

John watched as a man threw himself into the sea.

"No! Tom!" a voice cried out.

"If we jump, maybe we can still survive!" someone else yelled.

"Do you think you can survive by swimming away from a whirlpool that's dragging in a whole ship?" *How could people be so foolish?!*

The vortex was within breathing distance, and John readied himself to be pulled to the bottom of the sea. John swallowed hard, and then he heard a sound from the pipe. Jack was giving him the signal that the Liquid Fire was ready. *Fire won't save us, you idiot!*

Suddenly, a loud thunderclap rumbled overhead, and he saw two jets of liquid shooting out towards the sea. Mark and Robb had shot the Liquid Fire from the lower deck of the ship but had missed the whirlpool as their pipes could not move left and right. John decided to obey the orders, too, and he aimed the pipe slowly at the vortex directly in front of the ship.

How ridiculous that this will be my last act. John forcefully lowered the metal at the base of the pipe and saw a jet of greenish-yellow liquid shoot into the middle of the whirlpool. Its surface filled with flames. He stopped breathing for a moment and readied himself for death. Then, he saw the vortex dissipate as the ship changed course abruptly, turning to the right. The wind caught the sails and drove them swiftly towards the shore.

"Drop anchor!" Raff shouted.

"Where did the whirlpool go?" John asked the sailors running around him, but no one paid him any attention. The large cabin door opened, and Jack came on deck, out of breath.

"Jack! What's going on?" John asked.

The captain rushed to his side. "You got them real good," he said.

"Who?" John asked as several men untied the ropes that released the anchor.

"There are never any whirlpools so close to land. That wasn't a whirlpool."

"What was it?"

The ship jolted so hard that they all collapsed onto the wooden floor. John struggled to get up and reached his hand out to Jack.

"What was that?" came Raff's howl as John ran to one end of the ship and looked to sea. Creatures were in the water, and the Liquid Fire was burning their bodies.

"Mermaids!" Jack cried as he stood behind him. "They've never attacked our men before. I'd heard from my father that only fire can harm them."

John saw a mermaid throw herself against the ship's hull and felt the deck jolt again. He could now see several mermaids near the bow—some engulfed in flames, screaming, while others tried desperately to help those in distress.

"We mustn't kill them," John said.

"What do you mean? If we don't, they'll kill us," Jack insisted.

"Do you think I got all of them with the Liquid Fire? Those who remained unscathed are trying to help those that are dying! Soon, they'll kill us all unless we help those who are getting burnt." The ship lurched again just as John finished what he was saying.

"Whatever we do, they'll kill us! I'll burn them all."

John ignored Jack and ran towards his pipe. As soon as he reached it, he drew the sword from his belt and turned to the two thick ropes tied to its base—the ones that would release the sandbags hanging in front of the bow.

"Don't do it!" Jack shouted, but John ignored him and brought his sword down, slashing the ropes. The ship lurched harder than ever. John lost his balance, and the sword slipped from his hand. He tried to hold on to something, but his body was dragged across the deck along with dozens of men. An elbow struck him in the nose, and he groaned as blood soaked his lips. He made another attempt to get up, and then a sound like thunder shook the air. The ship came to a sudden halt, and John and the rest of the men crashed into the end of the deck. He thought his head would burst from pain when he heard a voice.

"Get ashore!"

John staggered to his feet and tried to get his bearings. The ship had run aground on the shore. He hoped its hull hadn't been destroyed.

"Come quickly!"

He searched for the source of the voice and then saw figures on the shore. Men in ragged clothes waving their arms frantically, trying to signal to them. John turned to the sea and searched for the burning mermaids. He could no longer discern any creatures wrapped in flames through the sand mixing with the dark blue of the waves.

"Run for land! They'll rip the ship apart!"

Jack stood a few feet away from him, and then the ship jolted again.

"Run!" several voices all shouted at once. John ran as fast as he could and jumped ashore, praying he'd escape death once more.

The Agreement

"Come closer. Getaway from the sea!"

John was hurt all over, but he kept on running, drawing closer to the men who were shouting frantically. Around him, the rest of the sailors were running chaotically as well. He reached them and fell onto his knees, trying to catch his breath.

"George! I didn't expect to find you here! I thought you were dead."

John raised his head and saw Jack a few feet away, looking at the unfamiliar men as if he couldn't believe his eyes.

"We're the only ones who survived. We were attacked by the damn mermaids, too..." George said. He was a stout man with grey hair and a beard. John bet he was over fifty years old. "When they hit our ship, some of us were thrown overboard. Luckily, the jolt pushed us close to shore, and we managed to swim to land."

"You've been missing from the Ice Islands for weeks. How have you managed to survive on this deserted island without food and water?" Raff asked as he approached.

"We've been lucky. Only five of us survived, and the sea washed ashore some of the food that was in our ship's hold. We've survived on that and caught fish with a few spears from the wrecked ships we found in the sea. As for water, the island is full of ponds that fill up with rain."

"Has no one else survived?" Raff asked.

George looked sad. "No."

"Why are the mermaids attacking us?" Jack asked George.

"I don't know... Good thing these lads survived with me because I'd

379

have gone crazy if I'd been stranded alone on this island for weeks," George said.

John saw four young men behind him as he got up off the ground with difficulty. "Didn't the mermaids try to attack you on the island?" he asked, straightening his back.

"No," George replied. "We saw them looking at us from the shoreline a few times, and we prepared for battle, but they were unable to get too far out of the water. When we fish with spears, we always watch out that none are near us."

"Mermaids become weak on land. That's why they don't attack you here. When water touches their bodies, they're almost invincible. Only fire can hurt them in the water," Jack said.

"How come you know so much about mermaids?" John asked.

"My father taught me," the one-eyed man said.

"What was that fire that set the sea aflame? I've never seen anything like it before," one of the lads behind George said.

"My own invention, it saved our lives," Jack told them.

"And what about those sacks you dropped into the water? The mermaids seemed to be burning, but they disappeared when those sacks fell." George looked bewildered.

"Sand. It's the only thing that puts out Liquid Fire. Long Arm wanted to be kind and save the mermaids that attacked us!" Jack turned on him angrily.

"I saved your lives, you idiot!" John was angry too.

"Those you saved were the damn mermaids that have been killing our men all along!"

"You're a fool! We wouldn't have been able to burn them all. It would have been impossible. Most of the unscathed ones were trying to save those that were burning and left our ship alone momentarily. After a while, they would have killed us all to avenge themselves if we hadn't helped them."

"I don't know who you are, but I don't understand your plan," George said, looking John in the eye. "Do you believe that now that you tried to save those who were burning—when it was your ship that set them on fire—that they will let you leave here alive? Before you know it, they'll have ripped the ship apart. Even if we tried to use it, they'd kill us all at sea."

"I thought that if I helped them, they'd let us go. They have no reason to kill us," John responded.

"They had no reason to kill all the men of the Ice Islands who have died in these waters, but they did," Jack added.

John remembered the mermaid that had spoken to him. "*They took our sisters.*" He wondered why he hadn't told anyone about it. "They may have thought the men of the Ice Islands meant them harm, so they attacked first. My actions proved that we didn't want to kill them, only that we wished to survive."

"You're free to take the ship and set sail for Grand Island then. I'm sure they'll let you sail off safe and sound." Jack's voice dripped with sarcasm.

"If you'd kept trying to kill them, we definitely wouldn't have stood a chance!" John insisted.

"And nor do we have a chance now!"

"Our only hope was for them to realise that we don't want them dead!"

Jack growled something unintelligible.

"We have to run to the ship and get all the food we can," Raff said.

"No. It's too dangerous, especially at night." George said.

"We can't stay on this damned island forever!" Jack shouted.

John looked around. The moon hung bright in the sky, casting its pale light over the island cloaked in darkness. The ground was scattered with rocks and stones, and in places, patches of damp grass clung to the earth.

"I don't know how we can get out of here," George said.

"Unless the mermaids allow us to, it will be impossible. I also have no idea what condition the ship is in, and I just hope the jars of Liquid Fire haven't broken in the hold." Jack looked uneasy at the thought of spending the rest of his life on the island. He shook out his bad leg nervously, his lips becoming a thin line.

"Look." One of the sailors pointed to the south. John turned, his joints creaking, and he gasped. A few dozen mermaids had appeared on the shore, their tails in the water as they watched them from afar.

It's the only way. John started walking towards them, determined.

"What are you doing, you fool?!" Jack cried.

"I'm going to talk to them."

"Why?"

"They haven't broken up our ship yet, and only they can allow us to leave."

"They don't speak the Human Tongue!" Jack said. John ignored him and carried on walking. "Don't go near them. They might even kill you from afar by throwing a stone at you."

"Even so, I'll be doing you a favour. I don't think you take any particular pleasure in my company!" John shouted back and neared the shoreline. He could see the mermaids more clearly in the dim moonlight. Their eyes were fixed on him. One of them seemed taller than the rest and wore a necklace made of pearls. John couldn't help but admire their beautiful faces, which seemed to have been sculpted by an artist, while the scales below their waists looked green with a hint of purple.

"Why are you attacking the ships of the Ice Islands?" he shouted as soon as he was a few feet away from them.

The creatures stared at him silently, and he felt foolish for having shouted. Perhaps none of them spoke the Human Tongue. Suddenly, the tallest mermaid crawled towards him, sea water lapping at her tail. Her breasts were pure white, and she looked at him with suspicion.

"What was that fire that didn't go out in the water?" Her accent was odd. It sounded like a snake hissing with a human lilt, yet John understood her words.

"We discovered this fire a short while ago. Water cannot stop it," he said.

"Did you build this weapon to kill me and my sisters?"

"No! We were afraid of being attacked by ships from the northern regions, and we built this weapon to use against them. We didn't want to kill you; we were just trying to save our lives when you attacked us," John replied.

The mermaid looked at him as if she was seeing a human for the first time. "Why did you throw the sand into the sea?" she asked after a while.

John felt something approach him from behind and turned in fear. Jack, Raff, and several other men marched towards him. "So that your sisters wouldn't get burned. We didn't want to kill you—we just wanted to survive," John said.

"You're a strange human."

"Why?"

"Humans have never shown mermaids any respect."

"The First King of Mynlands admired you. He made a mermaid the coat of arms of his House and his kingdom," he said.

"Hundreds of years ago." The mermaid's accent was so strange that it made him cringe. "Nowadays, humans hate us."

John remembered the words of the mermaid he had seen not long ago. "Not everyone. The men of the Ice Islands have never wanted to harm your kind! Why are you attacking them?"

The mermaid didn't speak, mulling things over.

"You say humans hate you, yet you killed our men without us ever harming you! You hate us and have robbed countless families of their men!" Jack snapped.

The mermaid seemed to get angry, and her voice grew louder. "Humans killed three of my sisters!" John feared that Jack's outburst would cost them dearly. "I've been looking for them for years. I thought they wanted to live away from us, to see other seas and oceans, but they never returned. We looked all over the world for them but couldn't find them."

"Why do you believe humans harmed them?" John asked.

"Humans can't do any harm to mermaids in the water!" Jack shouted.

"That's what I thought, too," the mermaid said, the words coming out in a hiss. "I thought my sisters had died from something we didn't understand, and I believed I'd never find any answers. Then, a few months ago, I was swimming near a ship and heard humans talking…"

"What were they saying?" John thought he knew what she'd say next, before she even uttered the words.

"They were wondering what their lord had done with the mermaids he'd captured."

"Did they have an emblem on their sails?" came Raff's voice.

The mermaid glanced at the moon. "I didn't look. My rage was immense, and my sisters and I destroyed their ship—along with the five others that sailed beside it. I wanted to catch those men and force them to tell me how they managed to imprison my sisters, but they all drowned."

"Where was this ship sailing?" Jack asked.

"A little more to the west of here."

"They must have been from Mynlands! Our fishermen have never sailed further west than this island," Jack said.

"I don't know where they were from! After their deaths, my sisters and I tried to stop many ships and interrogate their sailors, but it's hard to catch your kind without drowning you. Thereafter, we decided you deserved to die and attacked any ship we found in the Sea of Shadows. The men from Mynlands are now afraid to sail in our waters. They only cast their nets close to the shores of their land. However, we don't go any shallower; we fear they might have some way of capturing us. We don't know whether they caught our missing sisters." Another mermaid on the left hissed something unintelligible. "My sister says that this fire you cast may have captured our sisters," the tall mermaid added.

"This fire can only kill. You said the men you heard were wondering what their leader had done with the mermaids he'd captured. So, I assume they took them alive," John said, though he couldn't imagine how someone had managed to do such a thing.

"Why did you attack our men? Our ships have never sailed further west than this island," Raff said.

"One of my sisters told me there were ships with men on board coming to this place often. We thought maybe it could have been you who took our sisters. We didn't know who the lord was who had taken them captive."

"You killed our men for nothing! We didn't attack your sisters. We paid for sins that were not ours!" Jack was furious.

The mermaid raised her hand angrily. "And who should have paid for my sisters, human?"

"Those who were to blame!"

"I don't know who was to blame! You declared war on our race, and I declared war on yours."

"I should have filled the sea with fire until I had killed you all!" Jack shouted.

John saw the mermaid's face harden, and then she spoke in an unknown language. The rest of the mermaids began to hiss loudly. There were too many of them to handle.

"If you don't restrain yourself, we'll never get off this island," John told him.

Jack glared at him. "Mermaids protect their own kind. They know that if they attack us, they'll win but they'll suffer losses away from the water. They won't risk having any of their sisters die."

"You're right, human. I won't risk my sisters for you. You'll die of hunger sooner or later on this island," the tall mermaid said.

"You disgusting mons—"

"Shut up!" John snarled. Jack looked as though he was about to tackle him, but to his surprise, he didn't speak.

John turned back to the mermaid. "I'm sorry about your sisters, but we weren't the ones who hurt them. Humans harmed your race, and you killed innocent men to get revenge. If we continue to attack each other, thousands of us will die."

"You'll pay—"

"Listen to me!" John didn't expect he'd find the courage to interrupt her. "This weapon—this fire that burns on the sea—is something this man invented." He pointed to Jack. "If you carry on attacking humans, others will use it, too, and they'll burn you alive. If you want to catch those to blame for what has happened, you need allies."

"Allies?" The mermaid's eyes narrowed. "Will you help us find those responsible?"

"Yes! I was the one who dropped the sand into the water. I'm the one who saved you. I don't want your death."

"Your ship dropped the fire!"

"To save our lives! Not because we wanted you dead! If you let us go back. If you stop harming the men of the Ice Islands, I'll help you."

"How?"

John wished his idea would work. "I'll search until I find out who caught your sisters, and when I do, I'll tell you."

The mermaid laughed. "You may never find out!"

"Perhaps... But you and your sisters will never know the truth. Those secrets never reach the ears of the sailors who roam the seas. I'm sure the men you heard would have known very little even if you had caught them alive. I have a better chance of finding the man responsible on land and discovering what really happened."

"I won't help the creatures who killed my brothers for no reason!" Jack cried.

"The mermaids will make up for that! They'll allow the men of the Ice Islands to fish in these waters and protect them if they are ever seen being attacked by northern soldiers or pirates. In this way, they'll make amends for the unfair deaths they brought to pass on the Ice Islands," John said.

"I won't protect humans!" the mermaid shouted.

"I won't help you find those who killed our sis—"

"QUIET!" John shouted. "If you decide to fight each other, countless creatures will die. Humans hurt mermaids, and the Ice Islands must understand their pain and forgive them for their attacks!" He looked at Jack. "But the mermaids must also see that they've taken innocent lives.

We need to stop this cycle. Let us become allies. And if we can, we'll help you find those truly responsible for taking your sisters," he added, looking at the tall mermaid.

No one spoke for a moment, and only the sound of the waves filled the silence. The tall mermaid seemed to be trying to make up her mind.

"Even if I agree, I'm not the Leader of the Ice Islands. Begon has to agree to this accord," Jack said.

"Begon will listen to our words. I think Long Arm is right." John couldn't believe that those words had come out of Raff's mouth. "We need each other. I think the mermaids will never find out the truth without help. If the Ice Islands are ever attacked, they cannot easily defeat any enemy. With Walter on the throne, we need allies," Raff continued.

John looked at Jack and then the mermaid.

"If I accept the agreement, we'll protect you only if you're attacked. I won't fight so that you can gain land and kingdoms. If one day you find out who took our sisters, this man will have to bring me proof. You won't deceive me into attacking your enemies!"

She glanced at John. "Why do you want me to bring you the proof?"

"I saw you when you ran to cut the ropes and throw the sand. I trust no one but you. I'll make a pact with no one else."

Sweat broke out across John's forehead. *I will never return to this fucking island!*

"Agreed. If we find out who caught the three mermaids, this man will bring you the proof," Jack said suddenly.

The mermaid watched John for a few moments and then crawled in his direction, holding out her hand. John wanted to say no, but he'd never leave the island without the agreement. He took a step closer to the mermaid and took her hand. Her skin was very soft.

"How will I know which ships sailing in the Sea of Shadows belong to the humans of the Ice Islands?" she asked.

"Our ships have this emblem on their sails," Jack said, pointing to the iceberg symbol on their ship's mast by the shore.

"We'll allow you to return to your land and to fish near this island," the mermaid said and let go of John's hand. Then, she turned to her sisters and said something in their strange language. The rest of the mermaids dove into the sea, and their leader followed until they all disappeared.

"You have more talents than you think, Long Arm," Raff said, breaking the silence. "Let's rest up. We'll set sail at first light—if the ship's still intact..."

Jack looked at John as if he too couldn't believe he'd just succeeded in making an agreement with the mermaids. John turned his gaze to the moon, unsettled by everything that had happened. He knew he would never find the man who had taken the mermaids and that he would never return to the island. Yet only one thought swirled in his mind. *It must be my destiny to live forever.*

The Brave Prince

Elliot walked through Mirth, gazing up at the stars sprinkled through the sky. The red moon was very bright that night, as if its surface had been soaked in blood. He thought about the kiss Edmee had given him the night before. He hadn't been prepared for it.

He turned down a deserted alley and continued looking vacantly at the city, lost in thought. He'd realised that the Princess had been eyeing him for several days, but he hadn't expected her to make such a move. Her kiss had filled him with desire, yet something had stopped him from going further. Elliot knew full well that he might never see Velhisya again, but her eyes kept appearing in his mind. He couldn't, for the life of him, get her out of his mind. The more he thought about her, the more he realised how much he admired her.

Velhisya may not have been a warrior, but she was courageous. She'd also never kept the truth about her mother's race a secret, proving she felt proud about who she truly was and had shrugged off the foolish rumours that had accompanied her throughout her life. Elliot believed he might live to be a ripe old age, and even then, Velhisya would be on his mind, forbidding him from loving any other woman.

He kept walking until he found himself in the Square of Justice. There was no one there at that hour, and the moonlight illuminated the statue of the god-protector of Kerth. The God of Justice stood grim and resolute at the centre of the elevated square, a sceptre-like object clutched in his right hand. Elliot stood a few feet away from the statue. He couldn't fathom how the people in this land believed their god endowed the

Emperor with wisdom.

We're lucky Odin's children are better than he is.

Marin was honest and just, and Edmee was graced with courage. Nevertheless, Elliot had found that the Princess rarely objected to her father, and she didn't like it when people questioned his judgement. However, he swore Edmee's true nature was virtuous. Elliot remembered the city's lords and Odin looking ecstatically at the spectacle of the little boy running from the duellist who chased after him, but Edmee wasn't happy. He'd seen her pursing her lips and looking away as if she wished she could leave the arena.

She loves her father and turns a blind eye to his brutal nature.

Elliot imagined that a murderous father was a curse to any virtuous son or daughter. Edmee was devoted to Odin and tried to justify his actions. Thanks to him, she'd become the Princess of the Western Empire. Nonetheless, Elliot believed that, unlike her father, she wanted to win all her battles fairly, proving her superiority. He knew full well that every man in the kingdom would have wanted a determined, brave, beautiful princess like her. However, he felt his heart belonged elsewhere.

"Edmee has lived for twenty-five summers. How many have you lived for? Seventeen? She's too old for you," Sophie had told him one day when she'd seen him stealing glances at her over dinner.

"I don't care about age. Besides, I'm not interested in the Princess."

"Of course," Sophie had replied with sarcasm in her voice.

Elliot realised he'd been standing in the square for a while and walked back to the Red Palace. Peter might have been assigned to the Queen for the evening watch, but Elliot was the one who had to take over the morning watch, and he needed to be rested. He traversed a few empty streets until he saw a man standing in his way. He passed by him, walking hurriedly.

"Damn merchants. You can't get a little cheese anywhere without paying a fortune!"

Elliot smiled as he heard the man talking to himself. It was strange that he would be so angry with the merchants at such a late hour. The Red Palace came into view. Though it was one of the most ornate buildings he'd ever seen, it never brought him any joy to behold it. He remembered hearing how the villagers outside the cities of Kerth lived a hard life of poverty while Odin had built a palace full of gold just for himself.

Vain and spiteful. He thought once more of the Emperor.

Elliot neared the entrance to the palace when Selwyn and John came to mind. He was glad they were both alive, even though Long Arm's decision wasn't what he'd hoped for. Elliot had thought of trying to make John change his mind, but he'd decided against it; he wouldn't force anyone to fight for him ever again.

Morys and Eleanor died for me, and Velhisya may be dead, too. He tried to push those thoughts away. The death of his companions filled him with pain and guilt. He didn't even want to contemplate the idea that Velhisya might have travelled to the realms of the dead. *At least Morys and Eleanor are together now,* he told himself, trying to find a little solace.

Elliot climbed the steps to the palace entrance, knowing he had to put the death of his loved ones out of his mind; otherwise, he wouldn't be able to sleep. He tried to think of something joyful but to no avail. Poisonous thoughts swamped his mind, and even Reynald Karford came to him. The former Guardian Commander of Stonegate was a man who had made many mistakes in his life. Nevertheless, he had repented, and Elliot's plans were to blame for his death, too.

He walked through the palace door and tried to get his bearings, looking for the way that led to his chamber. He'd spent days in the Western Empire but still got confused in the giant palace. Elliot looked around when he heard a voice coming from the entrance of the building.

"Hurry up."

He turned back and saw a few soldiers with their swords raised while three young lads walked hunched over in front of them.

"What's going on?" Elliot asked the guards with the raised swords.

"These peasants were charmed by the idea of a rebellion and attacked us when we asked them to work harder in the fields," one of the guards said.

"My father worked himself to death. If we work any harder, we'll all die," said one of the prisoners, who was tall and skinny.

"Shut your mouth." The guard kicked the young villager.

"Why do you want them to work even harder? The Emperor already has ample gold."

"We're only following the Emperor's orders," the first guard replied.

"What punishment awaits these men?" Elliot asked.

"Death."

"Death?" Elliot couldn't believe his ears.

"The decisions of the Emperor are decisions of our god. These men attacked us in defiance of our ruler. We don't spare the lives of men who…"

"This lad lost his father who was trying to cultivate the land for the sake of the…"

"Step aside. You have no jurisdiction here!" the guard snarled, his face reddening with rage as his two companions raised their swords threateningly.

Elliot had never felt so great an impulse to kill before. *Hatred torments the soul of a creature*, Aleron's voice echoed in his mind.

"Very well," he said and stepped aside.

"Please, my lord! Help us. We don't deserve to die,' said one of the captive villagers.

Elliot touched the hilt of the Sword of Light. The lad was about his age. *You've already put Sophie in a tough spot with what you did in the arena. If you attack Odin's men, the alliance will be off, and everything we've tried so hard to build will be destroyed.* The lad began to cry, and Elliot let go of the hilt, unable to help.

"I wish the Knights of Faith had killed you all. I hope the Emperor dies and the crows eat his eyes!" yelled another captive peasant standing beside the one crying.

Elliot wished with all his heart that the young man's words would come true. Odin Mud deserved to die, and so did Walter. One of the guards raised his sword and stabbed the peasant in the leg. "I intended to kill you quickly, painlessly. After these words, you'll all suffer."

Elliot's hand tightened on the hilt of his sword again. *The people of Knightdorn are relying on this alliance*, the voice of his conscience wouldn't allow him to give the prisoners a swift death. *Our kingdom will be worse off with a man like Odin Mud!* A new voice shouted in his mind. Nevertheless, the Emperor would have no jurisdiction over Knightdorn, and Marin seemed better than his father.

Elliot decided there was nothing he could do and headed for his chamber quickly. He no longer felt sleepy. What he'd witnessed had angered him, and he was sure he wouldn't be able to sleep. He passed through a few dark corridors until he got to his chamber. He entered the chamber, and his eyes fell on the table beside the window. The servants had left some fruit and cheese on a platter, and a handful of candles cast light on the room. His stomach growled, and he went to the food when he heard a knock on the chamber door.

"What the hell?" He swore under his breath and opened the door abruptly. Marin stood before him as white as a sheet. "What's wrong?" Elliot asked.

Marin motioned for him to close the door, and Elliot obeyed. "I've been looking for you for quite a while. One of my men told me you'd just returned," the Prince said.

"Do you have your men following me?" Elliot asked.

"No. But today I asked two of them to look for you. I had to speak to you."

"What's going on?"

"The boy." Marin's eyes were fearful, and Elliot realised something bad had happened.

"Is he dead?" he asked.

The Prince was unexpressive. "Not yet. However, my father has ordered his men to kill him at first light. I heard that he doesn't want to risk sparing his life. Even though he has no special powers, he fears that if he grows up one day and—"

"And has children, his children might have powers and destroy his House," Elliot continued.

"Exactly."

"I was sure Odin would make that decision. Yesterday, I told Edmee that the Emperor wouldn't spare the boy's life."

"I'm sorry, Elliot. I never intended for any of this to happen. I tried to reason with him, to explain that our House gained power not to murder children but to bring peace."

"With your father as ruler of this land, there will never be peace except for the powerful." Elliot knew better than to push too far.

"That's not true. When there were three rulers in Kerth, there was always the fear of war, which could have cost thousands of lives."

Elliot couldn't help himself and opened his mouth again. "I don't think anything has changed for the common people. The merchants, the lords, and those with a little gold can have a better life... Nevertheless, there are slaves and peasants dying from overworking, and entire clans are being murdered because their nonexistent powers are considered dangerous! I'm sure that this clan had no power; that was just the pretext for Odin to attack them because they refused to cultivate their land for his benefit!"

"Elliot—"

"I'm sorry, Marin, but this isn't peace. A short while ago, I saw soldiers dragging peasants to the palace to execute them. These men were emaciated and weak from working too hard. One of them said his father had died trying to work as hard as he could... When they resisted the guards' orders, they were beaten and brought here to be tortured before being killed!" Elliot had lost control, and he knew that if the Prince told his father what he'd just uttered, their alliance would be dead.

Maris's face was clouded with sorrow. "I'm truly sorry, Elliot. My father has always believed that if a ruler doesn't show his might, it'll be just a matter of time before he loses everything to various usurpers. He thinks that by punishing every rebel, fear will prevent anyone else from rebelling against him."

"He's wrong. Fear and oppression bring enmity, and enmity brings war. The Knights of Faith won't be the last to try to overthrow Odin."

Marin crossed his arms, frowning. "I have opposed my father countless times, but I don't have the power to change his decisions. If I ever rule Knightdorn alongside Sophie, I won't treat its people so brutally."

Elliot tried to regain his composure. *I made a mistake in saying so much in front of the Prince.* "Why did you want to talk to me in the middle of the night? You could have told me the news at first light. In any case, there's nothing more I can do for the boy."

Marin took a step towards him. "Do you trust me?"

Elliot couldn't tell whether the question was a trap. "Yes," he said after a while, though he had his reservations.

"I trust you, too. After what you did in the arena, you are one of the few men I trust. Few have honour as you do."

"You wanted to find me to tell me—"

Marin stretched his hand out and opened his fist. A key lay in the palm of his hand.

"What's that?"

"The key to the boy's cell."

"Why are you giving it to me?"

"Outside your chamber, a city guard's uniform is hidden. I heard about the peasants who attacked my father's men and were brought here to be punished. We'll go to the dungeons together, and I'll ask the guards to show me the cell of these captive peasants. I'll ask them to escort me there so that I can kill the rebels, and I'll insist that I need every guard for protection. When there is no one in the corridor, you'll release the boy and climb a winding staircase. When you reach the end of it, you'll turn left, and you'll find yourself in the palace backyard. Once there, you'll let the boy run away. The harbour is near there, and beside the pier, there's a cave that leads out of the city to land inhabited by some peasants. They'll protect the boy; a child who has run away from the Emperor will find refuge with the villagers."

Elliot's eyes widened, and his mouth felt dry. "If I'm caught, your father will kill both me and Sophie."

"I won't let him do you any harm!"

"There's nothing you can do to protect us."

Marin sighed wearily. "It's your choice. Do you want to free the boy?"

Elliot stayed silent for a bit. "What will happen to those peasants?"

"We can't save them all, my friend."

Elliot sighed, disheartened. "Those peasants may already be dead... Then your plan will fail."

"I doubt it. Our men take pleasure in torturing prisoners before they kill them."

"If your father finds out that you were in the cells at the time of the escape, he'll suspect that you had something to do with it. He'll punish you!"

Marin smiled. "But he'll have no proof! I'll have witnesses that I wasn't anywhere near the boy's cell. He may speculate about me or the boy's powers, but he won't be able to prove anything."

Elliot wanted to say no, but a moment from his training came to mind. *"A knight is the shield of the weak,"* Althalos had told him long ago.

If I'm caught, Sophie and the people of Knightdorn will meet a tragic death. What's better, to be a shield for them or just for a boy? Elliot couldn't decide. He felt like the voices in his head would drive him mad.

"I won't let them catch you," Marin insisted.

"Why do you want to save the boy?"

"After what you did in the arena, I can't get my head around the idea that we are going to murder this innocent child whose entire clan we've killed!" The Prince had raised his voice.

"Then why didn't you try to protect the rest of this—"

"I did try, Elliot! Perhaps I could have done more, but I was a coward," Marin told him.

"And now you've become brave?"

"Thanks to you..."

"What do you mean?"

"I saw you risk the salvation of your land to save a child, jumping into an arena to fight ten men! We all should have rushed to help that boy, but only you dared to."

"I was reckless. Don't become like—"

"You were brave, and I wish I'd met you sooner. Maybe I would have been braver a long time ago. You're seventeen years old, and I'm thirty. You have a courage I didn't dare imagine existed in the world."

"I don't want to risk Sophie's life," Elliot said.

"Trust me—we won't get caught! If they do catch us, I also have a lot to lose. I'm taking a risk. You might say it was all my idea, and everyone will know it would've been impossible for you to find a guard's uniform or even the way to the dungeons without someone from the palace. I'll fall from grace for years, and my father, even if he doesn't kill me, may imprison me."

Everything inside Elliot told him that he should refuse. "Alright," he blurted.

"Hurry. We don't have much time."

Marin headed for the door, and Elliot left the chamber with him. The Prince stopped in front of a large pillar, behind which hung a decorative deer hide stretched across the wall like a tapestry. Marin approached the mounted trophy and pulled it aside, and a stone ledge revealed itself. There rested a white cloak, a jerkin, and black trousers.

"Get dressed," Marin said, tossing the clothes at Elliot.

Elliot began changing quickly.

"Give me your clothes," the Prince said and immediately put them behind the mounted animal.

"Why didn't you bring this uniform to my chamber?"

'I didn't know if you trusted me. If you'd told me you had no confidence in me, I wouldn't have mentioned this plan. Keep your head down as we walk. If we run into any guards, I don't want them to recognise you."

Elliot nodded, and they walked fast. The torches nailed to the walls illuminated their path as they crossed parts of the palace Elliot had never seen before. After a bit, they found themselves next to a spiral stone staircase.

"As soon as you free the boy and get back here, run to the left. The palace yard is a few feet away." Marin pointed to a spot in the distance, and Elliot made out a door. He nodded sharply, and they started down the winding staircase until they reached the bottom. The lower level had none of the grandeur of the rest of the palace. There was little light, and everything was damp, with cobwebs hanging on every wall. The floor looked slimy. Elliot followed Marin until there was a shout, and the Prince grabbed him by the shoulder.

"The boy is in the last cell on the left. Stay here," he whispered, handing him the key to the cell before moving on. Elliot hid in a dark recess between two walls.

"Good evening," Marin said in a clipped voice.

"My Prince! What are you doing in such a place?" came a voice.

"I heard you caught some villagers who had attacked you."

"That's true, my Prince. These cunts dared to say that the Knights of Faith should have overthrown the Emperor."

"Have you killed them?" Marin asked

"Not yet. Pip is torturing them," the other man said.

"I want to kill those bastards myself. However, I'd like you all to escort me for protection."

"Of course, my Prince. We intended torturing them a while longer, but who are we to disobey your command?"

"Let's go then," Marin said, and footsteps echoed through the air.

Elliot waited a few moments before leaving his hiding place, walking silently. After a while, he stopped and looked around—there was no one to be seen. He continued moving through the dungeon, trying to find the boy's cell.

Marin said it was the last one at the end of the corridor. Elliot couldn't see inside the cells—the thick metal doors and brick walls blocked his view. He reached the end of the corridor and saw the door of the last cell. He slipped the key into the keyhole as quietly as he could and pulled the door open with a gentle motion. Torchlight lit up the interior of the cell, and he saw a small figure curled up in the corner. Elliot walked over to the boy and touched him on the shoulder. The boy jumped up, startled from his sleep.

"Come quickly. We don't have much time."

The boy seemed to recognise him. "No." His voice had a strange accent.

"What do you mean no? Do you want to die?"

The boy nodded. "Everyone I loved is dead. My parents, my friends—everyone. I no longer want to live."

Elliot leaned over and touched his knee. "I used to think the same way. My mother died in childbirth, and my father was murdered before I was born. I even lost my twin sister, having spent years apart from her. For years, I wished I'd never been born and that I would die; I couldn't get over losing my parents. My friends also died because of me... They tried to help me, and it cost them their lives. Your loved ones wouldn't want you to die in this cell. Live a good life, and that way you'll take revenge on those who tried to kill you. We don't have much time. We must leave now, or you will die in this place!" Elliot doubted he had convinced the boy, but he hoped he had.

"What's your name?" asked the boy.

"Elliot. Yours?"

"Rain."

"As in rain?"

The boy nodded, and his yellow eyes stared up at him. A few moments later, the child tried to get to his feet. Elliot caught him by the arm and lifted him firmly. "Let's go," he said quietly.

They left the cell and moved quickly towards the winding staircase. Just before they reached it, pained cries echoed through the dungeon. He wanted to help the unfortunate villagers, but he couldn't. They reached the ladder and began to climb up it. Elliot's lungs burned as he stepped onto the last rung and turned left. Rain followed, holding his hand, and he prayed he'd find the exit to the courtyard quickly. There were more torches, and he caught sight of a wooden door at the end of the corridor. Elliot ran towards it and opened it in one motion. The icy air whipped his face while the courtyard seemed deserted.

"Let's go! Hurry," he said and ran with Rain at his side.

They crossed a courtyard filled with countless colourful shrubs and came to a cobbled path leading downhill. Elliot prayed that the harbour would appear soon as the two bright moons in the sky lit their way. Sweat coated his brow. In the distance, he saw a few ships and fishing boats sailing into the large marina. Fortunately, no one was there at such a late hour. He searched for the cave that Marin had said was near the harbour, and then he saw the moonlight fall on a large rock which had an opening in the middle.

"See that cave?" Elliot asked. The boy nodded. "It leads to a village outside the city. Run down its length, and when you get to the village, knock on the villagers' doors. Someone will help you."

"Why did you save me?" Rain asked, his yellow eyes narrowing.

"My Master wanted me to be an honourable knight who would protect the weak. You did nothing wrong. No child deserves to be murdered in an arena. Now run!"

"Goodbye, Elliot," Rain said and ran with all his might.

Elliot watched him cross the pier quickly and head uphill towards the cave until he was out of sight. *May you find good fortune, Rain.*

Fear and Loneliness

Syrella sat back in her chair, arms folded, irritated by Jahon's words. The Great Hall of Moonstone grew darker as the sun slowly set in the sky outside the castle.

"We're doing the best we can," Jahon said, reading the look in her eyes.

"Then your best isn't good enough!" Syrella glowered.

Jahon looked angry. "We have very few men! Even if they all take turns on watch without sleeping, there aren't enough to guard the entire city! The thieves have caught on, and I'm sure they're colluding with each other so that they rob remote parts of Wirskworth at the same time. We can neither catch them all nor protect every merchant and blacksmith."

"Have you managed to catch anyone?"

"Our men have tried to arrest a dozen of them."

"What do you mean *they've tried*?"

The man sighed. "They resist, and the guards are forced to kill them."

"All of them? You are fools!" Syrella snarled.

Jahon reddened. "They know that if we catch them, we'll torture them until they betray their accomplices, so they resist. The guards have no choice when they are attacked with knives and metal bars. They also use lookouts, and when they see the guards approaching, they shout and hurl stones."

"Damn! We can't find Walter's damned spy, and anarchy has descended upon my city... I always thought the people of this land were loyal to me, but as soon as I was left without an army, Wirskworth filled up with thieves."

"Most people are truly loyal to you. Fifty or a hundred thieves don't represent the majority of the city folk."

"Tell the guards to be careful. We need to catch some of the thieves alive and find out who their accomplices are. I suspect that they all belong to the same ring. If we catch one, we'll uncover the whole gang." Jahon nodded curtly. "Did you find out anything more about the boys that attacked Selwyn?"

The man's scowl showed he hadn't been able to find out anything at all. "No. I've told the men of the Sharp Swords to watch out for strange boys who might be following them, but none of them have noticed anything suspicious. Thorold, Selwyn, and Alysia have told me they have seen no one following them the last few days."

"I doubt that is the case... After the attack on Selwyn, I'm sure he's still being followed. Try and find out as much as you can."

Jahon nodded and began walking away, his long yellow-black cloak brushing the ground. Just before leaving, he turned back to face her.

"I've ordered the men of the Sharp Swords to guard you at all times until the army returns. Now, only one rests while four are always on guard. I will also be on your watch as soon as night falls." With that, he walked out of the Hall.

Syrella felt protected as she listened to him. She knew that it was difficult for anyone to harm her in her city, even without the presence of her army. *William of the Sharp Swords could perhaps kill me, although it wouldn't be easy.* She was never guarded by a single man unless it was Jahon. There were often also other soldiers around her apart from her personal guard.

She glanced towards the entrance of the Great Hall and saw a yellow and black cloak in front of the open door. Her guards must have been exhausted from all the watches. William may have proven himself a traitor, but Syrella trusted the rest of the men in her guard. These soldiers had begged to become members of the Sharp Swords and had been at her side for many years. Daw was the last one who had joined her personal guard, taking William's place, but she and Jahon had known him to be dedicated for a decade.

"Lady Syrella, may I speak with you?" Selwyn entered the room dressed in a purple cloak and a woollen jerkin.

"What is it, Lord Brau?" she asked.

"I wanted to ask you if your men have found any of those boys who attacked me," he said. The man seemed to have recovered from the attack a few days ago.

Syrella wished she had better news. "Unfortunately, not. We have few soldiers and they're trying to deal with the thieves in the city, and the watches for my personal protection are also exhausting them."

"I hope the army returns soon," he said, his features revealing his eagerness.

"So do I," Syrella told him, praying that her daughters and niece were well. The fact that she had no idea of the goings-on in Vylor irritated and scared her at the same time.

"Perhaps I can help protect you, too," Selwyn said.

Syrella looked into his eyes, feeling grateful. "You're very kind, Lord Brau. A trustworthy man like yourself, who I hear is being trained by a Grand Master, would be very useful in my guard. Nevertheless, you're a guest in this city, and I want you to remain safe. Try to become as skilled as you can be before the final battle with Walter."

Selwyn bowed sharply.

"Jahon told me you haven't been aware of anyone following you again."

"That's correct."

"After the incident, the informants are being careful... How is your head?"

"Fine. Thorold told me that the stone could have done much greater damage."

"Avoid going out into the city at night and be careful. If you see anything unusual again, don't hesitate to use your sword," Syrella said.

"I don't want to kill children," Selwyn told her.

"It's better than you dying. Of course, it would be ideal if you brought me an informant."

Selwyn nodded. "Have you had any letters from Elliot or Sophie?"

He'd asked her the same question countless times. "No. With so much wind, Elliot's hawk will need quite some time to get here from Kerth. Elliot also told me that he would wait a while before sending me news; he was sure that the Emperor would welcome them with open arms, but that after a few days in Kerth, he'd show his true intent. I trust we'll soon have news from him."

"You're right, my lady. I'm sorry to trouble you with my questions," Selwyn said.

"I know you fear for your father. However, we all need to be patient."

Selwyn bowed deeply. "I hope you have a good evening, my lady."

"You, too, Lord Brau. I will inform you if anything of importance reaches my ears."

Selwyn bowed again and left the room, leaving her lost in thought. Syrella felt very much alone in Wirskworth the past few days. She missed her daughters, Velhisya, and even Sophie. Trying to fortify a city that would soon be attacked by a huge army and wyverns was a difficult and lonely task. Sometimes, she wished she'd forbidden Velhisya from rushing to Vylor to save Selwyn. If she hadn't made that mistake, the Royal Army and her own would have been here, and her daughters and her niece wouldn't have been in danger. Her decision to go to Selwyn's rescue had cost her too much. The younger Brau may be a good lad, but she wasn't sure that if she could go back in time, she would make the same choices again.

Syrella hoped Velhisya hadn't been tortured by the Mercenaries. A young, beautiful woman like her should never have found herself in such a place. She'd imagined Liher molesting her niece countless times and hoped those disgusting thoughts hadn't become reality. Syrella felt her stomach turn every time she thought of Velhisya, and she blamed herself for everything that had happened.

I shouldn't have allowed her to leave! She felt the need to chastise herself. *Velhisya wanted this mission—she wanted to fight. She couldn't stand idly by when Elliot and his companions were trying to accomplish so much! If I'd kept her in the city, she would have hated me. People who feel imprisoned rebel and make risky decisions when they're angry.*

Her conscience repeated the words Sophie had told her. For some time now, Velhisya had felt Syrella was holding her back, but this mission was terribly dangerous. She should have tasked her with something else. Her niece may have admired Elliot and his companions, but half of them had died trying to make it.

We can't beat Walter without taking risks... Elliot's companions had displayed inestimable courage. Still, she couldn't bear the thought that everyone she loved might die, even if it was for a good cause.

"Soon, Walter will attack us. Nothing is more dangerous than that. If you'd continued keeping Velhisya imprisoned in the city, she would have done something reckless in battle, and then she might have been killed. Liher Hale is less dangerous than Walter," Sophie had said.

The words kept going round in her head, but whatever she was thinking, she was sure that given the chance, she would never let her niece go to Vylor again. Syrella had never been particularly devoted to the gods, but now she prayed every day, pleading for her daughters and Velhisya to return safely.

She pushed her hair back and tried to clear her head. *How does Sophie feel about her new husband?* The thought often tormented her. Syrella knew full well that Odin was vicious and not to be trusted, yet a part of her hoped his son was different. *Children are rarely better than their parents.*

She felt pity for the Queen. She knew that even if the Prince of Kerth was a good husband, Sophie wouldn't be spared misery. The Queen had loved only Bert, and it wouldn't be easy for any man to unlock her heart again. Syrella felt the Queen's pain for days before she left for the Western

Empire; she remembered feeling that way herself throughout her life. Sermor Burns wasn't a bad man, but he wasn't the husband she wanted at her side.

If we win the battle, Sophie will get the Prince out of the way. She won't be able to bear the torment of being married to him, nor will she ever stop fearing that Marin might try to murder her and seize the throne. Syrella would help Sophie rid herself of Odin and her husband if she asked her to, and she was sure they would succeed.

Her thoughts drifted until Jahon came to mind. Syrella had been harsh with him over the past few days and hadn't allowed him to come to her chamber. The truth was she missed him, but without her army, she was vulnerable and couldn't bear the weight of their secret as well. Weariness overwhelmed her body and she rose from her seat. She headed for her quarters, hoping she'd be able to sleep peacefully without the face of the man with two daggers in his eyes haunting her dreams.

The Lesson of the Hales

V elhisya paced up and down her cell, anxiety taking root within her. She hadn't slept in days. Each time they brought her food, she'd made a mental note, tracking the passing time. It had been several days since Liher's emissary had returned from Elmor, and if her calculations were correct, her aunt's gold would soon arrive in Goldtown—along with her long-awaited chance to escape. The thought filled her with anticipation but also with anxiety about whether everything would go well or not. She tightened her fingers around the keys Lothar had given her, and her skin chafed against the metal. Thinking about it, she couldn't believe that Lothar had risked so much for her. No matter how many years she lived, she would owe him her eternal gratitude.

Velhisya sighed heavily. *Liher may go back on the agreement. My aunt may go back on her word. And what will become of Matt then?* These thoughts haunted her. She didn't want to leave Matt behind, but she knew that Liher Hale was a sadist. It seemed strange to her that he would let her go without torturing or molesting her.

Liher is scared, she told herself once more. *He's scared after what happened in the chamber. He won't risk touching me and setting me free will provide him with untold riches.* Velhisya imagined the Governor of Vylor spending her aunt's gold on whores and wine, and she seethed with hatred. That man had to die; if they survived Walter, she would take Elmor's army and attack Goldtown.

"Are you awake?" came Matt's voice.

Velhisya took a few steps closer to the wall between their cells. "Yes," she said quietly.

"I've been listening to your footsteps for a while now. Having trouble sleeping?"

"Yes," Velhisya admitted.

"Why? I would have thought you'd be happy now that you've found out that your aunt will set you free."

"Liher is unpredictable. Now that the time for me to leave is drawing near, I'm afraid he will try to do me harm."

"The men here live for gold only. Liher won't risk touching you since he's about to get such great treasure."

"He may rape me and then send me back to my aunt, taking all the gold," Velhisya said.

"I don't think so. I'm sure Syrella Endor made it clear that if they touch you, they won't get a thing. Liher won't take that chance," Matt told her.

Velhisya disagreed. *My aunt would pay to save me even if they raped or tortured me, and the Governor of Vylor knows it. The only reason Liher hasn't tried to touch me again is because he's scared.*

"Soon, you'll be leaving this cell. Try to get some sleep," Matt said again.

"I don't want to leave you behind, Matt. I hope they'll set you free, too."

"Don't worry about me. You did what you could. Nobody has ever offered to give a ship for me." Matt's voice was apathetic, as if he no longer cared about what would happen to him. "My own father didn't give the gold he owed to save me..."

"He may be searching to find all the gold that Liher's men are asking for," Velhisya said in an attempt to make him feel better.

Matt's laugh echoed in the dungeons. "My father has enough gold, certainly more than he owes these men. He chose to leave me here. This solved all his problems."

"That's not true. I can't believe that—"

"I know my father. I don't believe he expected that these men would keep me hostage, but I'm sure that he was pleased when he got the news. He always feared the shame I might bring upon his name."

"Even if he feared you might embarrass him, I don't think he wants you dead, Matt!"

She heard his heavy breathing through the wall. "You have a pure soul. I know a woman like you can't understand how a man like my father thinks." She heard shuffling in the next cell as Matt got up. "If my father had wanted me alive, he would have paid the gold days ago. He decided to keep his wealth and rid himself of the fear of my secret. Perhaps if my mother had lived, he would have paid for her sake since she would never have left me to die."

Velhisya searched for the right words that would relieve him of the grief that coloured his every word, but she found nothing to say.

"If I'm happy about one thing, it is that I will meet her soon. Her and Luk, too."

"Who is Luk?" Velhisya couldn't remember hearing that name before.

Matt remained silent for a few moments. "He was a young villager who lived near Mirth. Many villagers revolt against the hard work the Emperor of Kerth subjects them to, but the villages near Mirth have fewer men who are willing to cause trouble. It'd be foolish to revolt, being so close to the capital of the Empire," he said, sniffing before continuing. "Luk was the first man that... " His voice faltered.

"I understand," Velhisya said. "What happened to him?"

"When my father caught us together in a barn, he told Luk that he'd kill him if he ever came near me again. Terrified, Luk fled and never returned to Mirth. I secretly took one of my father's horses and set off in search of him, but when I met him, he told me to leave. He feared that my father might pay men to do him harm. Luk was the only son in his family, and his parents needed him. I left disheartened but decided to find him again and talk to him. I loved him very much."

"And did you find him?" Velhisya asked.

"He found me. A day later, he came to Mirth and apologised. He wanted me in his life, too. I told him that I would see him again in a few days and... " Matt struggled to continue. "When I went to his village some days later, they told me he was dead."

"How?"

"The Emperor's guards behaved cruelly to some of the villagers. There was an argument, and the soldiers drew their swords. Luk tried to help, and they killed him. They left his head on a spike to remind the villagers what would happen to them if they didn't obey their orders." Tears welled up in Velhisya's eyes. "I couldn't protect him. I couldn't do anything."

"I'm so sorry, Matt. Odin Mud and his men remind me of everything we've witnessed in Knightdorn over the past few years. Walter and his soldiers are just as vicious and without any honour."

"I spent a long time crying, thinking about what I'd witnessed. I'd seen the head of the man I loved on a spike... My mother was the only one who managed to calm me down. She said that Luk was now somewhere far away where no one could hurt him and that he was happy. No one would harm his soul again. My mother always had a gift for giving me hope until I lost her, too. Now I have no one but a father who is ashamed of me."

"You have me, Matt. In Elmor, you'll get a fresh start. You may have had a hard time, but surrounded by better people, you'll have a beautiful life."

She heard the sound of footsteps echoing in the dungeons. She hoped it was Lothar; every time he came to the cells, he gave her hope. "Be quiet," she whispered to Matt and clutched the two keys in her palm, her heart pounding in her chest until four men stood in front of her cell. None of them was who she'd been expecting to see.

"Good evening, my dear lady," Liher said, his eyes glinting.

Velhisya felt a chill of fear as she saw him. She remembered the faces of the three men behind the Governor. They were the ones Matt's father owed, the guards who had tried to torture him a few days ago.

"My scouts have informed me that about two thousand of your aunt's men are approaching the city with wagons. They'll soon arrive to give me their gold!" Liher exclaimed.

"Did you come here to inform me that I'll soon be set free?" Velhisya asked.

The man's smile widened even more. "The truth is, I never thought our farewell would be like this. It's better than I'd ever dared to dream of."

Velhisya felt a surge of hatred listening to him. She longed to break free from her cell and shatter every bone in his body. She couldn't remember ever feeling such an urge to torture before. "Fate plays strange games. You expected to rape a woman. Yet you failed to do so, passed out, and now you've ended up with gold."

In the dim light of the dungeons, she could see Liher's face flush with anger. Lothar had told her to be careful. She shouldn't tempt fate until she was out of the city, and she hoped Liher would accept the offer of a ship in exchange for Matt's life.

"I may not have lain with you, my dear, but as you said, I'm going to be rich. In a few days, Walter will take Elmor, and then I'm sure you'll become the slave of his men for a long time. I dare say your aunt's decision to give me all her gold will be bad for your future. If you'd remained with me, your life would have been far more beautiful than the one that awaits you."

Velhisya took a step closer to the door and clenched her fists. "No one can choose their own fate," she said.

"Of course not!"

"Is that what you came all the way out here to tell me?"

He shook his head. "Unless I've been misinformed, you want to offer a ship to save the man in the next cell. My brother has informed me that you will ask Syrella to honour this agreement once you return to Elmor."

"It's true," Velhisya said sharply. "My aunt will listen to me; she will honour an agreement I've made on her behalf."

"And when do you think the ship will be delivered to me?"

"In less than a month. As soon as I return to Wirskworth, I'll speak to Syrella, and your ship will sail for Silver Bay. The sailors will deliver it to you. A ship is worth far more gold than this prisoner's father owes. You can sell it, and with the gold you get, you can pay these guards and keep the rest."

"A generous offer. I accept," Liher said with a grin. He nodded curtly to the three men. "You heard the lady. You won't lose your gold."

With those words, the Governor turned and took a few steps with his men close behind him. Velhisya felt the weight in her chest lift.

"However, my lady, I didn't come here just for this agreement but to also teach you a lesson." Liher's voice echoed in her cell.

Velhisya heard the door to the next cell open and stuck her face to the bars. "Don't hurt him!" She felt that her heart would stop as cold sweat poured down her forehead.

"It was an honour to meet you, Velhisya Endor." Matt's voice was cut off with a thud.

"NO! YOU'LL DIE. I SWEAR THAT ONE DAY I'LL BE SMILING OVER YOUR DEAD BODY, LIHER HALE!"

"Did you think you were going to trick me?" Liher asked. "Did you think my thirst for wealth would blind me and that I wouldn't see your trap? Only a fool would give a ship for a stranger, and Syrella Endor has never been a fool. This is your lesson... Now, you will forever remember that an Endor will never deceive a Hale. You're lucky your body won't rot in these dungeons along with that of this bastard." His laughter echoed in her ears.

"YOU'LL DIE. I SWEAR YOU WILL DIE!"

"You and all the people of your House are the only ones who will die, Lady Endor, and I'll spend the rest of my life squandering your gold."

The Talents of a Leader

John watched the sunrise from the ship's deck, feeling exhausted. They'd left the desert island a day ago, and he couldn't believe he was returning to Grand Island alive. Their journey back would take a long time since the wind was blowing in the opposite direction. John couldn't wait to lay on a bed and have a carefree night. The ship's hull had sustained significant damage from everything that had happened, but they managed to push it out to sea. Using a few wooden planks, they succeeded in climbing back onto its deck

"*The ship is fine; there's no sturdier ship than mine,*" Jack had told him the day before.

"*The hull has taken quite a hit from when it landed on the island's shore. If the swells get stronger, it'll break and we'll all drown,*" John had said.

"*And what would you suggest? Staying here?*"

John had no answers, so they had set sail the next morning. *Stop being so pessimistic! You survived those mermaids, and you think you're going to die at the bottom of the sea because the ship is going to sink?* The truth was that if he died like that after all he'd been through, it would be as though fate were laughing at him.

The wind grew stronger, and he shivered under his clothes. The mermaids had reached an agreement with him, placing their trust in his hands. John still found it hard to believe all that had happened. The last few weeks of his life had been filled with so much adventure that sometimes he thought he was asleep and that soon someone would wake him up, bringing him out of his troubled dreams.

The sun poked through the clouds in the east, and John let out a weary sigh. He had spent the past few years in Iovbridge, taking on odd jobs for lords and merchants to earn gold, which he squandered on the pleasures of the flesh. His life had been dull, yet carefree until Elliot Egercoll had appeared and persuaded him to travel to the kingdom with him. John had been in a battle, had fought Walter's soldiers, and had agreed to travel as far as the Ice Islands.

Damn. He never expected to live such an adventurous life again as he neared fifty. John had thought his days would settle into a dull routine once he reached Grand Island and yet, he'd ended up sailing across rough seas and deserted islands, trying to cheat death. The strange thing was that he had succeeded, and at the same time, some creatures that didn't trust humans had decided to make a treaty with him.

John sighed again and dreamed of the inns of Grand Island. Once he set foot on land, he'd spend his nights quietly, steering clear of his habits. Now, whores and wine-filled nights in various inns irked him. What he craved was a few moments of true peace.

He got up off a wooden chair he'd brought onto the deck, his back aching as he straightened his body. He took a few steps towards the pipe to his right and touched the carved lion's head. *In the end, that damned Liquid Fire saved us.*

John may have had the good sense to help the mermaids and talk to them, but without Jack's contraption, they would all be dead. He glanced at the sea and thought of his former companions. Soon, Elliot and Selwyn would face Walter Thorn again—and the place where Thomas Egercoll's son now was held its own dangers. John had heard that Odin Mud was not to be trusted, and he was astonished that Sophie Delamere had agreed to marry his son. Elliot and Sophie were risking a lot in an attempt to gain allies, but John feared that their efforts were so reckless that they could have the opposite effect.

The Ice Islands might be able to help Elliot. However, you've never tried to convince Begon to fight. He was tired of hearing his conscience blaming him for his actions. Besides, it was too late now.

"You have more talent than I thought after all," a voice said.

John saw Raff standing a few feet away, dressed in thick woollen clothing. "What do you mean?" he asked.

"Mermaids are hostile towards humans. Throughout history, many men of the Ice Islands have experienced their aggression, and I don't recall hearing of any human making a treaty with them. I didn't think you could pull off such a thing... "

"Surprises are the elixir of life," John responded nonchalantly.

"I think I now know why Elliot Egercoll and Sophie Delamere chose you to bring their words to the Ice Islands. You have the art of persuasion, Long Arm. Of course, only when you want to. I'm sure they didn't expect you'd decide to live a life away from war as soon as you arrived in our land."

"I don't feel like listening to your accusations, Raff. Elliot sent me here, and if he wants to punish me, he knows where to find me."

"You're a lucky man, Long Arm. You've been a bounty hunter, a pirate, you've found yourself in battles and wars, and yet you've survived to this day. The gods have also endowed you with talents that few men have in this world, and yet you've chosen to live a life without giving a damn about anyone or anything... The gods gave you the gift of leadership. Even if you don't realise it, you can inspire others and convince them that they should listen to you. Yesterday, the sailors looked at you in awe. I don't know how much life you have left, but don't waste it."

John would have sworn Raff was talking about someone else. "Leadership is a curse. Lucky are those who can see how dull the role of a leader is. I don't know why you suddenly think I'm not a boorish drunk looking for opportunities to swindle people out of their gold. However, if I do have the gift of leadership, I'm smart for not having ever used it to gain power."

"A good leader can change the lives of thousands of people. It's not a dull role," Raff said with some annoyance.

John started to laugh. "To listen to the will of the mob, knowing that your every decision will displease some men and having to do things you never wanted for the sake of your people..."

"To inspire loyalty and help a land and its people thrive. To know that when you leave this world, you'll leave something better behind you."

John laughed even louder. "Leaders kill for power and exploit the weak. They leave everything worse than they find it and destroy the world all the more. There may have been two or three honest rulers over the years, and they were either murdered or sacrificed their lives to please their people."

"Begon lived a good life and at the same time helped the land—"

"Really?" John interrupted. "Trade with Knightdorn has died! He may have saved your lives with the treaty he made with Walter, but there's no longer any respect for your land. Some would argue that if he'd sided with Walter, your lives would have been better, but if he had, many would have called him dishonest because he supported a tyrant. Even when a leader wants to do the right thing, he's doomed to fail. His every decision will favour some while for others it will be a reason to become his enemy."

"You're so stubborn!"

"Why are you telling me this, Raff?" John was beginning to lose his patience. "I've lived almost fifty years and have never had a real homeland. No one is devoted to me... I'll never become a leader."

Raff smiled for the first time. "You don't need to lead an entire region, Long Arm. You can inspire a leader to fight for your cause, you can get men to devote themselves to you, you can advise kings and queens. In short, you have the gift to help and inspire, and I'm sure Elliot realised this before he sent you to our land. If you really wanted to, you could help the boy. Find him new allies and persuade rulers to fight alongside him."

"I think you should never have been a mere captain, Raff. Only priests, lords, and Masters never stop spouting as much philosophical nonsense as you do."

"What I mean to say is that—"

"I know what you mean, you fool—" John cut him off. "You want me to dazzle Begon with my ability to make an agreement with the mermaids and convince him to fight Thorn. I won't do it, but he wouldn't listen to me even if I tried."

Raff moved towards him. "If you want to convince him, you can! Talk to him more about Elliot. Make him understand that he's our only hope against Walter and that if we don't fight now, there won't be another chance."

"Why do you care so much about Walter? Even if he becomes king, he'll never bother with the Ice Islands. Do you want to fight against him because Tahos no longer has trade—"

"Sometimes, you really are a fool!" Raff snapped. "Walter is a man of war. Any man with an ounce of sense can see that it won't be enough for him to lead a kingdom and heed the wishes of the common people. That man will fight until he dies. Once he takes Knightdorn and gets rid of Sophie and Elliot, he'll attack those who didn't fight alongside him, and when he has no other enemies, he'll even take the Western Empire. He won't hesitate to even create new enemies to be at war forever. Begon's inaction will be his downfall."

"Then you talk to him, and let me enjoy this damned morning!" John cried, and some of the sailors looked in their direction.

"I can't do it!" Raff said. "You're the only one who can convince him that Elliot is our only hope and that if he dies, Walter will bring death to our land too someday."

"Begon has no regard for me," John insisted.

"If he finds out what happened, he'll change his mind."

"I've told you countless times! I don't want to put the Ice Islands at war."

"And if one day war comes—"

"I'LL GO AWAY! I've had my fill of war, Raff. I'll never live through

417

another."

Raff sighed, raising his hands in surrender. "You're costing us our only chance to fight."

"No. The decision is Begon's, not mine. Do you now see what a curse being a leader is? Your leader knows that if he doesn't fight, many will be displeased, and if he does, many will accuse him of dragging his people to their deaths for a kingdom that doesn't give a damn about them. I agree with his decision. Any decision that doesn't cause bloodshed is wise," John said.

"I hope you decide to do something with your talents before you die," Raff said, then walked away.

John growled something unintelligible. *I preferred it when everyone thought I was just a drunk.*

"He's right."

He turned to his left and saw Jack standing with his arms crossed, one eye fixed on him. The man's black cloak billowed behind him.

"How long have you been standing there?" John asked.

"Quite a while."

"Damn... Who's steering the ship?"

"I decided to leave it ungoverned for a moment. I wanted to listen in as soon as I saw you two arguing..."

"Get back to the wheel before we sink, you fool," John said.

"That woman you spoke to me about, Nemesis, she would have like—"

"I didn't tell you about her so you could use her against me!" John was furious. "No one will ever know what she wanted because she's dead! The fact that I happened to convince the mermaids not to hurt us was pure luck, and at the same time, I was an idiot! A mermaid appeared in front of me a few weeks ago on Grand Island! She told me that humans had taken her sisters, and I never told anyone about it. I should have assumed the mermaids were responsible for the fishermen not returning! It was obvious; that mermaid told me that humans would pay. You think

I have some kind of talent, but in reality, I'm a fool."

"You should have told us that a mermaid had said that to you." Jack seemed surprised. "However, what she told you wasn't enough for you to be sure that the mermaids were attacking our fishermen. I don't know if you're a fool, but you're certainly a coward."

"I'll drink to that as soon as we get to Grand Island," John retorted.

Jack headed for the wheel, but a few moments later, he stopped and frowned at John. "I too hope you do something with your talents before you die, Long Arm."

A Payment in Blood

Velhisya's tears had dried up. She'd lost all sense of time, and a tray of food lay abandoned on the floor of her cage. Two rats ate its contents, and she swore one of them was the rat which had been in her cell a few days ago. Some time earlier, Lothar had brought the tray with food, and a few guards had collected the body of the unfortunate Matt.

"*I'm sorry. I couldn't do anything,*" Lothar had told her.

"*I want to leave here. I can't stay in this cell any longer,*" she'd told him with tears in her eyes.

"*You'll be leaving soon. Liher wants the gold.*"

Velhisya had raised the keys he'd given her. "*I was ready to leave my cell and attack them when they killed Matt. I want to leave now.*"

Lothar had turned red. "*If you'd left the cell, the guards would have hit you or even worse, they would have killed you! You can't use the key now. If you needed to do so, I'd see to it that the dungeons remained unguarded for a short while. I don't want you to leave before Liher gets his gold. All of Vylor is waiting for us to get these riches. If you escaped now, everyone would be suspicious of me, and even my loyal men would go against me. I can't die. This place needs me, and it'll be difficult for them to forgive me if I cost them so much gold. Unfortunately, no loyalty to this land is enough to pass over all of Elmor's gold.*"

Velhisya couldn't recall ever having cried so much. *Liher is cunning. He never once believed that Syrella and I would keep to the agreement about the ship.* She pushed her thoughts aside. None of it mattered anymore. Matt was dead, and he would never return.

Tears rolled down her cheeks again as she tightened her grip on the two keys in her hand. Lothar had left them with her just in case, but he was certain that Liher wouldn't risk losing the wealth that was now within his grasp. Velhisya felt only loneliness and pain. A man who had hurt no one had been murdered a few feet away from her, and even his father had abandoned him.

Matt suffered all his life... It was difficult for her to comprehend living in such a cruel world—one devoid of morals, where diversity among people was neither valued nor respected. She wished she could change everything and lead humans down a new, better path.

Liher Hale's sadistic smile lingered in her memory, and she longed to see the light fade from his eyes and his face devoid of life. A strange sound brought her out of her thoughts. It sounded like something hitting a wall a few feet away from her. She gripped the bars of the cell and tried to look to the left into the dim light.

"What's that?" she heard one of the guards say.

"I don't know. It's coming from over there—that wall covers the secret passage," said another man.

Velhisya heard the sound of swords being unsheathed, and her heart started pounding. *What is going on?*

"Open the passage!" shouted the first guard.

Suddenly, there was a loud noise like a door clanging open, and shouting broke out in the dungeons.

"Run and fetch more guards!" a voice shouted, and then Velhisya heard the repeated thud of bodies falling to the ground. Footsteps approached her cell, and she pulled back in fright.

"Good evening, cousin," Linaria said, her face lighting up with a huge smile while Merhya stood beside her, grinning.

Velhisya's mouth opened. "Linaria, Merhya, thank the heavens!" Her heart fluttered. She thought so many times that she'd never see Linaria and Merhya again. She'd feared she would breathe her last in the miserable dungeon.

"We need to open this damn cell. One of the guards will have the key," Linaria said.

Merhya rushed to find the key, but Velhisya took a step towards the door of her cell and shoved one of the keys she'd been holding into the keyhole.

Linaria's eyes widened. "How did you have a key to the cell door?"

"It's a long story. I'll explain later," Velhisya exited the cell and hugged her cousins. Over their shoulders, she saw the lifeless bodies of the castle guards strewn across the floor.

"I'm so glad you're alive," Linaria said.

"Me too!" Velhisya replied and hugged her again. "How did you get here?"

"That's a long story, too," Merhya said.

Velhisya released her cousin and glanced around. There were many armoured soldiers from Elmor in the dungeons. Next to them stood an elderly man with silver-blue hair. His features seemed different to those of the rest of the soldiers.

"Who are you?" Velhisya could now see the colour of his irises. His eyes were starry blue, like hers.

"My name is Aleron. I knew your mother," the man with silver-blue hair said, moving in their direction.

Velhisya remained silent, and only one thought lingered in her mind. *Elliot truly broke the curse.*

"Time to go." Aleron turned, but Linaria grabbed him by the shoulder.

"We're not leaving yet."

"What do you mean?" The man looked puzzled.

"My mother gave me orders that I can't disregard."

"Orders?" Aleron grew angry. "The plan was clear! We managed to get to the city quietly by using the forest on its outskirts as cover, and we've freed Velhisya. The agreement was that we would leave without a fight if we didn't have to fight."

"Liher may send his army after us," Velhisya said.

"We discussed this; we have more men than he does. If he risks a battle out in the open, he'll be defeated. He can't touch us when we're far from his city, and he knows it," Aleron told her.

"I'm sorry, Aleron. Elmor's army will follow my orders, and the men of the Royal Army are free to do as they wish," Linaria said.

"What does that mean?" The elwyn raised his voice. "Syrella and Sophie swore that they wouldn't go back on our agreement, and the elwyn and elves won't kill innocent people! What are you planning to do?"

"I know you don't approve of what is about to happen and that you and your people saved our lives a few weeks ago. Nevertheless, Liher Hale should pay. A man without honour must get what he deserves, and the Endors don't pay in gold but in blood."

Screams echoed from the end of the dungeons as Velhisya saw dozens of soldiers from Elmor entering through the secret passage, pushing past those already inside.

"Have you ordered your soldiers to come through here?" Aleron's eyes widened.

"I hope this doesn't cost us our alliance with the Elder Races." Linaria's expression showed she meant what she'd said. "ATTACK!" she screamed.

Countless men carrying swords and shields ran towards the stairs leading to the ground floor of the castle.

"You!" Merhya spoke to two men. "Escort my cousin out of Goldtown until the battle is over. Take her to the woods near the city and wait there."

"No! Liher Hale is mine!" Velhisya looked her cousin in the eyes. "I want a sword."

"You've been a prisoner for weeks. You need to rest, and the soldiers will protect you. We didn't come all this way to have you lose your life in battle," Linaria said.

"If you deprive me of Liher Hale, I'll kill you!" Velhisya's eyes narrowed with rage, a fierce emotion she knew Linaria hadn't expected from her.

"Very well," the woman said and motioned to a soldier a few feet away. He gave Velhisya his sword with some reluctance.

"Your souls are steeped in hatred. The leader of this land may have committed heinous crimes, but the people of Vylor must not pay for sins that aren't theirs!" Aleron shouted above the cries of the soldiers running to the stairs.

"There are no innocent people in this land. The Mercenaries are notorious throughout the kingdom for their utter lack of honour. Nonetheless, my men will only kill Liher Hale and anyone who tries to protect him," Linaria responded.

"A battle will break out, and innocent victims always pay the price during battle. Your soldiers will disregard your orders, and they'll loot the city on the pretext that they were attacked by guards who had hastened to protect the Governor," Aleron insisted.

"If the Mercenaries don't fight back, they won't sustain any losses. The orders are clear," Linaria said again.

"Liher's brother mustn't die. He helped me more than anyone in this place," Velhisya told her, thinking of Lothar.

"We have given orders that no one is to harm Lothar Hale," Merhya said.

"Call off the attack, and let's go!" Aleron shouted, looking at Linaria.

Her brow furrowed, trying to make a decision. "I'm sorry, it's too late," she said.

In one motion, she drew her sword and ran towards the stairs with Merhya on her heels. Velhisya saw Aleron's eyes fill with disappointment and fear, but she had no more time for talk. She raised the sword and ran after her cousins. Countless men made their way up the stairs to the upper levels of the castle, and screams reached her ears. The unsuspecting guards of Goldtown Castle had come to a grim end. Velhisya followed after Linaria until they came out into the main passage. She remembered the route to the chamber where Liher had tried to rape her. His quarters had to be near that room.

I must kill Liher and make sure that Lothar is spared. She remembered her promise. She'd sworn that if one day Vylor was at her mercy, she wouldn't kill innocent people.

"This way!" she called to her cousins, and they followed her while a few men changed direction upon hearing her voice.

They went up another flight of stairs, and then the lifeless body of a man lay before her. Some soldiers from Elmor had already gone through there. Velhisya started running as fast as she could. Screams rang out from the other end of the corridor. She turned right down a passage decorated with kilims and statues, and as she walked, a woman came running towards her, shouting, while a soldier in a yellow and black cloak chased after her.

"I'll get you, you whore!"

Linaria raised her sword in front of the soldier, and the woman fled. "What do you think you're doing? I ordered you not to harm innocent people!" Linaria shouted.

The man growled something unintelligible, and Velhisya felt that Aleron's fears were about to come true.

"Have you found Liher Hale?" her cousin asked.

"Not yet," the soldier replied.

"Stop chasing maids and help us find him!" Linaria's voice was sharp.

Velhisya paced down the passage again, casting glances through the open doors of the rooms. Elmor's men seemed to be in every chamber.

"Fucking traitors! You'll all die."

She found herself in front of a splintered door. She ran inside the chamber and saw five men with raised swords. In front of them, Liher Hale wielded an ornate blade. He wore a gown and was barefoot.

Now, you will pay. "Let him go! He's mine!" Velhisya said.

"You damned whore! I should have tied you up and let my entire army fuck you in the dungeons!" His face was flushed, and spit flew out of his mouth.

Velhisya walked slowly towards him, hatred bubbling up inside her. "If you utter another word, I'll see to it that *you* become the whore of Elmor's army. Disregard my words, and you'll spend months in the company of the men of my land."

He seemed about to start cursing, but her threat made him bite back his words.

"I knew there'd come a day when you wouldn't dare utter a sound before me," Velhisya said and moved closer to him. "Throw your sword down, otherwise the whole of Elmor's Guard will fuck you." She had never imagined speaking such words, but it gave her satisfaction to see the frightened look on the once gloating man's face.

Liher threw the sword to the ground. "Take your men and leave my city. My people did nothing to Elmor."

Velhisya stood before him and felt her heart pounding, but this time, it was out of impatience and not fear. "Before I go, there is one more thing I have to do." She lowered the sword, and with a sudden movement, stuck it with all her might between the man's legs. "I told you I'd kill you!"

Blood soaked Liher's lips, and two more rivulets of red liquid ran from his nostrils. He was trying to scream, but no sound came out of his throat. The man fell to the ground, and his body began to twitch until it lay still. *That was for Matt...* she thought, seeing his lifeless body.

Velhisya turned back and glanced at Merhya and Linaria, who were watching her from the chamber entrance. "Time to go," she said.

"We should kill a few more soldiers to make sure they can't attack us once we leave the city, my lady," one of the soldiers from Elmor, wearing chain mail and a helmet said.

"Their leader is dead. No one is going to attack us," Velhisya declared.

I need to make sure Lothar is all right. Velhisya took another look at the lifeless body of the Governor. Her sword was still stuck between his legs. She took a few steps and picked up Liher's sword lying at his side. The

Golden Sword had strange symbols carved into its hilt. *This man didn't deserve one of the Seven Swords*, she thought and began to walk towards the door.

"Let's move," Linaria said.

"Not yet. I need to make sure Lothar is all right." Elmor's soldiers moved through the halls while servants and maids ran around screaming.

"Don't touch the innocent!" Linaria screamed again as a soldier from Elmor walked past her, holding a gold cup.

"We came to kill the Governor, not to punish innocent people and rob the castle!" Merhya shouted at him.

"I've been fighting for your mother, risking my life for years. I think I deserve payment!" the man with the cup said irritably.

"I order you all to retreat. Spread the word. Anyone who disobeys me will be punished." Linaria was now furious.

The soldiers obeyed unwillingly; it was obvious they wanted to loot Goldtown. They had to leave soon. Velhisya rushed down the corridor, looking into the chambers, but Lothar was nowhere to be seen. Most of the rooms had been ransacked, leaving behind broken tables, torn mattresses, and dead guards lying everywhere.

"Get off me!" One of Elmor's men had pinned a maid to the floor of a chamber and was trying to pull down his trousers.

Velhisya ran towards him, and her sword touched his neck. "Your captains have ordered you to retreat. Disobey that order, and I will feed you your balls"

The man turned to her, his cold features hardening in anger. However, he rose without a word, and the woman he had beaten pulled herself into a corner, weeping.

"Don't worry, no one will hurt you," Velhisya told her.

"Lady Endor! We've also caught the other Hale."

Velhisya heard the voices and ran back to the passage, pushing aside any man in her path. She saw a soldier throw something at Linaria's feet. Her blood froze, and an invisible knife stabbed her gut.

"No!" Lothar Hale's head lay on the floor, the unfortunate man's eyes wide open.

"I ordered you not to hurt Lothar Hale! Why did you kill him?" Linaria was seething.

"I thought you'd be happy! I was one of the first to arrive here, and the servants told me where the two Hales were," the man protested.

Velhisya couldn't contain her anger. "Damn you!" she cried.

"I ordered you not to harm Lothar Hale! I explained to you that Selwyn Brau and my mother had asked us to let him live!" Linaria snapped, full of rage.

"And are you going to punish me for it?" The soldier raised his voice. "Syrella Endor has always said that the Hales must die—all of them!"

"You had direct orders!"

"I thought it wasn't necessary to do Lothar any harm, but I didn't think it was an order to leave him unharmed!" the soldier insisted.

"I told you not to kill him, Tom!" another man from Elmor shouted.

"You'll be punished for disobeying orders!" Merhya said, enraged as well.

"Elmor is full of madness! I'll be punished for killing one of our filthy enemies!"

Velhisya felt like she was about to vomit as she looked at the severed head on the ground and raised her sword with a scream. The Golden Sword slashed the soldier's throat. He fell to the ground, making grotesque sounds as he tried to breathe.

"I order you all to retreat! If even one man so much as harms civilians or steals gold, he'll die! Leave the city immediately and spread the word to any of our soldiers you find on your way!" Velhisya's voice rang out through the corridor.

"Do as Velhisya says!" Linaria roared.

The soldiers began to retreat, and Velhisya, along with her cousins, followed them.

"The gods will curse us for this. Lothar didn't deserve such a fate. He was the leader this land needed." Velhisya was disheartened, and her eyes were wet.

"We can do nothing for him now. We have to leave before our men destroy everything in their path," Linaria said.

They continued running until they came to a place in the castle that Velhisya didn't recall seeing before. "Let's go to the dungeons—let's leave from there," Linaria said hastily.

"Linaria Endor!" came a loud voice.

Aleron ran towards them, his blue cloak billowing behind him. "You thought you could control your men... You thought they were better than Walter's... And yet, the first chance they got to be in a position of power, they proved themselves to be the same as Thorn's men!"

"I ordered a retreat!" Linaria cried.

"The decisions you, Merhya, and your mother took were foolish and vicious! You were given the opportunity to avoid battle, and you strove to have it! Every leader has the army he deserves!"

"Stop the preaching! We're leaving!" Merhya said aggressively.

"It's too late now. Come and see your handiwork, captains of Elmor!" Aleron began running through the palace, and a terrified Velhisya followed him. She heard footsteps behind her and knew that her cousins were following her. Her heart had stopped, and she hoped their men hadn't done what she feared. She saw thousands of soldiers in the castle now, some in the cloaks of Elmor and others in those of Iovbridge. The Royal Army had also thrown itself into battle, and dead servants and guards lay everywhere.

A large door came into sight, and Aleron headed towards it. Velhisya left Goldtown Castle for the first time in weeks, and the cold night air hit her face. She was wearing light clothes, and the wind chilled her body. However, the pain of the icy frost was nothing compared to the anguish of the sight before her.

Goldtown was burning to the ground, and from the elevated entrance to the castle, she could see the roofs of the houses that had been engulfed in flames. The air was thick with shrieks and pleas as countless people ran about chaotically, some to attack and others to escape death and torture.

"Look at your fine work, ladies of Elmor!" Aleron's starry blue eyes were full of pain.

"STOP THE ATTACK. RETREAT. RETREAT!" Linaria shouted.

Velhisya began shouting the same words, and Merhya ran towards the city, yelling at the men to stop.

"ALARIC!" Aleron screamed, and Velhisya saw a short man standing just a few feet away at the base of the castle steps turn towards them. "Order the elwyn and the elves to help the people of the city. If necessary, use force to stop the soldiers of Elmor and Isisdor!"

"I'll help, too!" Velhisya said, gripping the Golden Sword tighter.

"Velhisya! No! It's too dangerous!" Linaria told her.

Velhisya ignored her and ran towards the city. All around her she saw swords and axes swinging, and voices got louder.

"STOP THE ATTACK! STOP THE ATTACK. RETREAT!"

She made out a short elf trying to stop a soldier in a pegasus cloak who was struggling to hit a bloodied man. The soldier tried to kick the elf, but the short man raised a sword bathed in red light and cut him in the leg.

"I'll kill you, you damned elf!" the soldier screamed.

Merhya moved in front of the soldier. "Whoever disobeys my orders will be hanged!" she shouted.

The soldier sheathed his blade, frightened. Velhisya kept running, seeing blades with red and blue light everywhere, trying to stop the soldiers who were attacking the city.

"STOP THE ATTACK!"

Men were now sheathing their swords, and then she saw a soldier in a yellow and black cloak chasing a man who was holding a baby in his arms.

"Come back, you coward!" The soldier ran wildly. As the man tried to get away, he pushed him hard. The man fell to the ground in front of a burning house, and the baby fell out of his arms, crying.

The soldier lifted his sword, and Velhisya raised hers to shield the fallen man. The blow was so forceful that the Golden Sword slipped from her hands and clattered to the ground.

"You're about to kill a father who is trying to save his baby!" Velhisya shouted to the soldier.

"That cunt hit me!"

"The captains have ordered a retreat!"

"Stand aside!"

"I am Velhisya Endor! Dare to disobey my orders, and I'll have your head hung at the gate of Wirskworth."

The soldier stood still for a moment and then immediately sheathed his sword. "Why are you protecting these men? They used to fight for Thorn! Men like them killed our people at the Forked River."

Velhisya glared at him without responding, and the soldier walked away. "Are you alright?" she asked the fallen man who held the baby in his arms again.

"Yes. Thank you." his face had two tears above his right eyebrow.

"Find shelter. Soon, our armies will retreat from the city."

The man got up and ran away quickly with the baby in his arms.

"HELP! HELP!"

Velhisya raised the Golden Sword and turned in surprise. She couldn't understand where the woman's voice was coming from. She looked all around, her legs shaking. The woman's voice was coming from within a burning house.

"HELP!" Velhisya yelled in a panic. She didn't know what to do, and the flames were growing bigger. She tried to approach the entrance to the house and immediately felt the fire burning her skin.

"HELP!" The woman's heartbreaking pleas came again, and Velhisya began to cry, unable to help.

Someone shoved her to the side. Aleron barrelled past her like a tornado, kicking the door of the house with force. The wooden entrance fell to the ground, and the man stepped into the house amidst the flames.

Velhisya recalled her father's words about the gifts of the elwyn race, and she stood there with numb legs, staring at the shattered entrance. A few moments went by until she saw figures approaching her.

Her mouth was dry as she watched Aleron come out of the burning house, naked, with a woman and a small boy wrapped in his arms. The two humans fell to the ground coughing, and Aleron lay beside them, out of breath. For a moment, Velhisya watched the white form of the elwyn in the light cast by the flames. His flesh was untouched, and his skin glowed like pearl.

A Touch of the Wind

S ophie looked at her reflection in the mirror as she sat in a chair. Her dress was light blue with vertical seams of gold thread, and she wore a tiara full of pearls and rubies in her hair. She felt strange. She had never imagined marrying a man other than Bert, yet fate had sent her into Marin's arms. Even so, the young Prince had brought her joy over the last few days. Marin had proved to be better than she'd dared to hope.

"I've never seen a more beautiful bride," the maid who was combing her hair said, while another adorned her right hand with gold rings and bracelets.

Sophie continued looking at her face. Her hair was more well-groomed than ever before, and her blue eyes appeared refreshed. Nevertheless, she hadn't managed to sleep the night before. She was anxious about the forthcoming wedding, and as their return to Wirskworth drew closer, her dreams became more turbulent. She glanced at the sunlight creeping through the windows of the grand chamber that lit up her huge bed.

Now, I'll be spending my nights with Marin. The idea would have seemed terrifying a few weeks ago, but now the company of the virtuous Prince didn't seem so bad. She remembered Marin knocking on the door of her chamber that one night; she had been horrified at the thought of him asking her to lie with him, but the Prince had opened his heart to her and assured her he would never force her into his bed if she didn't want to.

Together with Marin and Syrella, we'll succeed. She may never have been particularly devoted to the gods, but she hoped they would help

435

them in the last battle. *Did our armies manage to set Velhisya free?* She often wondered about the fate of their men in Vylor. Elliot had told her he'd send Syrella a letter that same day, informing her of what had happened in Kerth, while Hurwig was to return with news from Elmor.

A few days ago, Elliot had asked her to send a letter to Aleron instead of to the Governor of Elmor, but Sophie had insisted that it was more important that Syrella heard from them. Elliot had been looking for a way to find out what had happened in Vylor, and Aleron would have known more than Syrella if their army hadn't yet returned to Elmor. However, they had promised the Governor that they would send a letter, and they were obliged not to break that promise. Elliot and Sophie had agreed to wait a few days until they were sure of Odin and his son's motives, but now the time had come.

Everything went according to plan, she thought. She also hoped the news they were to receive from Wirskworth would be good, too. There was so much that could have gone wrong... A failed attempt to free Velhisya, a battle in Vylor, and the death of Syrella's daughters. All of that would be enough to fill their camp with gloom and pessimism just before the battle against Walter. Sophie hoped their men had achieved their goal without spilling blood in Vylor. If they had laid siege to the region's capital, many of them would die.

Perhaps Walter has already attacked Wirskworth. Our men may have been defeated in Vylor, and Thorn may have destroyed Syrella's city. As hard as she tried, it wasn't easy to push away the negative thoughts that poisoned her mind. *Walter has suffered two defeats, and he needs time to march his men to a new battle. He won't attack so soon, and Goldtown has weak walls. The Mercenaries hadn't been expecting an attack on their city; the Royal Army, and the men from Elmor will win, even if the ploy with the key doesn't work.* She tried to find as many arguments as she could to calm herself down.

Sophie looked at her reflection in the mirror again and imagined the countless people who would be gathering around the large city square to watch the wedding. Shortly afterwards, hundreds of merchants and nobles would gather in the vast courtyards in front of the Red Palace to eat and watch the troubadours play Kerth's favourite songs.

Sophie was glad that Elliot and Peter were with her. The rest of the guards and the defenders of her personal guard who had accompanied her to Mirth were unimportant to her; she needed people she felt close to at her wedding. Anger wrapped around her insides every time she thought of Elliot. The young man had made risky decisions that had almost cost them their alliance with the Emperor. Sophie seethed with rage whenever she recalled Elliot leaping into the arena to face the Faris, all to save that boy.

"What would have happened if you'd died in that foolish fight? It was a miracle you survived!" she'd shouted at him the day after the event.

"I couldn't just stand by and watch them slaughter an innocent child."

"How many innocent children will die if we are defeated by Walter?"

"I couldn't just stand there, arms crossed, and watch that spectacle unfold!" he'd shouted and walked away.

As much as his deed had angered her, she'd admired his bravery and courage. The last boy Althalos had trained may have been reckless and headstrong, but he was a true knight of honour like those in the tales of old. Sophie had heard about the Emperor's wrath after the incident, but they were fortunate that Elliot's action hadn't cost them the alliance.

Marin had also admired what Elliot did in the arena, she thought. The news that had reached her ears two days ago had surprised her beyond belief.

"Marin helped me set Rain free," Elliot had told her.

"Rain? Who's Rain?" Sophie had asked.

"The boy..."

She'd felt anger and surprise when she heard that once again Elliot had risked the alliance, but she hadn't expected the Prince to have taken part in such a plan. That brought her joy. A man who dared to defy his father and act so boldly under his very nose was someone with true honour and courage. Sophie never imagined she would find such a husband in Kerth. Elliot had sworn her and Peter to secrecy since they were the only ones he trusted with the truth.

She sighed wearily. No matter how stubborn Elliot was, she was glad he'd set the child free, and the fact that he'd collaborated with Marin filled her with optimism. *Together we'll defeat Walter*, she thought once again.

She heard a knock on the chamber door, and a maid rushed to open it. Peter entered the room, wearing a black cloak and a dark green jerkin. He'd taken care to groom himself better than ever before.

"You look divine, Your Majesty," he pronounced, with a large smile on his face.

Sophie was happy for him. Once he'd told her his secret—the secret that had been crushing his soul for years—the man seemed to have found peace. Now, he was always optimistic in the councils with Odin's officers, and he smiled often. The Lord of the Knights had stopped smiling since he lost his sons. Sophie knew that pain would overwhelm him again soon enough, but his new demeanour brought her joy, no matter how long his happiness lasted. "You look very smart yourself, Peter."

The man bowed deeply. "I know we have much to do to defeat Thorn. Nevertheless, I think we can banish those thoughts and enjoy the day. As of tomorrow, our only concern will be the war." Sophie smiled, too, and quickly nodded in agreement. "I remember when you were just a little girl. It seems unbelievable that today is your wedding day."

Sophie didn't stop smiling. Peter was like a father to her.

"I want you to be happy. If your husband doesn't treat you—" Sophie gave him a sharp look. "Uhm, what I meant to say is that I'm sure your husband will do everything in his power to make you happy. Any man would kill for such a wise and beautiful queen."

Sophie breathed a sigh of relief. Peter often said he'd kill the Prince if he wasn't a good husband, but the Mirth maids mustn't hear that.

"I would be so happy if Eleanor were here." Sophie didn't like to think of the ill-fated girl. The pain was unbearable, and every time she brought her to mind, she felt the need to cut her wrist again. She had stopped doing that, though, trying to bury her pain.

"I'm sure she'll be proud of you, wherever she is," Peter said with a sad look in his eyes.

"If she were here, she would frown at my marrying anyone but Bert," Sophie responded, trying to regain her smile.

"Eleanor would be on your side," the Lord of the Knights said. "Where's Elliot? I expected to find him here."

"Perhaps it took him some time to get ready."

"I don't think he would care much about his wedding clothes. He seems to find all this boring."

"He may want to impress the Princess."

Peter laughed. He'd told her many times that Edmee kept looking at Elliot.

A knock came at the door, and the maid opened it. James, a defender of her personal guard, stepped into the room.

"A few dozen of the Emperor's men are outside the chamber, Your Majesty. They bring you a message from the Prince. Shall I let their captains come in?"

Sophie nodded, wondering how many of her soldiers were outside. She always had about forty guards, and another two hundred and sixty men of the Royal Army would accompany her during the wedding, along with Odin's soldiers.

Four armoured men came into the room. The sunlight shone on their steel breastplates, and large swords hung from their belts.

"What message does the Prince send me?" Sophie asked, looking at the tallest among them. He had short black hair, a thick beard and a small forehead.

The Kerth captain took another step towards her and drew his sword. Sophie jumped up off her chair, and the maids in the chamber seemed surprised.

"What do you think you're doing!" Peter unsheathed his blade, and shouting was heard outside the chamber—shouting that betrayed a battle was going on.

What is going on? Sophie thought, terrified.

The other three captains also drew their swords, and the tall man laughed. "Too bad Althalos' apprentice isn't here. I was hoping to kill him, too."

The four men raised their swords and rushed to attack, but Peter stepped in front of Sophie. He tried to deflect their swords, but there were too many to defeat. The sword slipped from the Lord of the Knights' hand, and one of the captains cut his throat. Peter gasped on the ground, holding his neck while blood stained his clothes.

"NO!" Tears streamed from Sophie's eyes.

"What are you doing?!" one of the maids in a corner shouted, huddled with the other women.

"Shut up," the captain said and turned to Sophie. "I never thought I'd have the honour of killing a queen."

The sword tore through the air, and the maids screamed frantically. Sophie grasped her neck, trying to breathe. She fell to the ground and tried to stop the bleeding streaming down her throat. Her eyes filled with tears.

"It's time we left." She heard a voice, but her vision had blurred.

Sophie struggled to get air into her lungs as she felt her limbs going limp. Everything went dim, as if a dark vortex was enveloping her, until she saw a figure waiting for her outside the black clouds. Bert smiled, younger and more handsome than ever, and his arms were wide open, ready to take her into his embrace.

———◦———

Elliot was walking near the Red Palace. The sun was hot and bright that day as if it too wanted to attend the wedding that was to follow. Sophie and Marin would become husband and wife, and then they'd finally be ready to start on their journey to Wirskworth. Elliot knew he had to dress for the wedding, but the warmth of the day had prompted him to take a walk around the city. Peter, along with another forty men, were there to protect the Queen, and Elliot didn't need much time to get ready.

He walked through the small forest he'd traversed a few days ago while trying to set Rain free. He remembered Odin's fury the moment he'd heard the news, but no one had been able to explain how the boy had disappeared. The Emperor had suspected that his son had had something to do with the escape, but the guards in the dungeons had confirmed that the young Prince was in a cell with some peasants along with countless soldiers. Marin had interrogated the "traitorous villagers" and had hastened to kill them. But, at the last moment, he'd changed his mind and had decided to have them put to death in the Square of Justice so that all might see the fate of the men who rebelled against Odin. Elliot knew that the Emperor was unsure of Marin's sincerity, but there was no proof that the Prince or anyone else had helped the boy escape.

"In the end, that boy may have had strange powers. Perhaps he used them to get away!" one of the guards had said to Odin.

"Perhaps," the Emperor had replied. *"If I ever get my hands on him again, he won't get away. I hope he doesn't cause us any problems! I should have killed that bastard and never thrown him into the damned arena."*

Elliot hoped Rain would never again find himself in Odin's clutches.

Birdsong came from the treetops, and Elliot saw a handful of birds circling the small forest. He kept walking until the harbour of Mirth appeared in the distance. His eyes fell upon the cave in the middle of the rock cliff near the edge of the pier, and Rain found his way back into his mind. He turned and headed towards the other side of the forest. He had to return to the palace since the wedding would start soon. The fresh morning air filled his lungs, and a strange rustling sound reached his ears. Elliot gazed to the left, and then it hit him—it was whispering. He knew he shouldn't eavesdrop, but suddenly, the voice grew louder.

"Do I have your word?" The voice belonged to Odin.

Elliot moved closer to the voice and saw two men through the trees. He couldn't understand why the Emperor was in the woods just before his son's wedding.

"Walter always keeps his word when it comes to his loyal allies."

"I hope so, Launus. If you betray—"

"Why would I? Neither I nor Walter will gain anything if we betray you... My King cannot govern two continents without help, and Kerth's loyalty is all thanks to you."

Launus, Elliot remembered that name. He was the Governor of Mynlands, Walter's sworn ally. Sweat ran down his temple, and an invisible hand squeezed his chest.

"I didn't expect him to send a monster to my land." There was a note of fear in Odin's voice.

"It was necessary. Walter came with two wyverns to Mynlands to tell me the agreement he wanted me to bring to your doorstep. After that, he ordered one to follow me here so that it could send him news of your decision."

"How will it send him the news?" Odin asked.

"We'll tie a letter to his toe. Walter also told me that he has ordered the wyvern to help me if I asked it to capture Elliot or Sophie."

Elliot found it difficult to breathe. *Fucking traitor*.

Odin laughed. "We have forty thousand soldiers for that purpose."

"If they try to escape and we need assistance, then I'll ask the monster to help me. Walter told me it wouldn't obey any of my orders other than to capture Elliot or Delamere," Launus explained.

"That won't be necessary. I've already dealt with that. Where is the monster?"

"It flew south of the harbour so that nobody could see it. I'll visit it soon and tie a letter to its foot."

"Very well. I hope you'll keep your prom—"

"I've already told you! Walter keeps his promises," Launus snapped, cutting him off. "Even when forced to make difficult decisions, he knows how to repay his allies."

"What do you mean?" Odin asked.

"A few weeks ago, Walter was forced to sacrifice thousands of my men. However, when he visited me a few days ago, he brought me some gold and promised that once the war was over, he'd give my House power it's never tasted before."

Elliot saw Odin's face momentarily. He seemed to have been convinced.

"I'm surprised Walter didn't come here himself to tell me everything he wanted."

Launus sniggered. "He wouldn't have come to a place with forty thousand soldiers who might have attacked him."

"You told me he has a dozen wyverns by his side!"

"Walter thought that Sophie might have been seeking an alliance with you! He didn't know whether she would be here with the elwyn and the elves. Nevertheless, even without them, an arrow would have been enough to wound him on his wyvern. You might have tried to attack him," Launus said. "He's not a fool like Sophie. He wouldn't come here without an army. Walter would have had to delay the rest of his battles too long to travel all the way here with all his men."

"So, he sent you, not caring whether you died."

"Why would you kill me? I'm just a messenger. Many would like to kill Walter, but few would like to kill me. Moreover, if you kill me without reason, Walter will be enraged, and the past has shown that the fate of those who have angered my King hasn't been the best. Are we finally in agreement?" Launus held out his hand.

Odin squeezed it. "I've already made my decision, Launus. Nevertheless, I like to ask for confirmation from my future allies," he said laughing. "With Walter, we'll rule the whole world."

Elliot walked away as quietly as he could. He had to run back to warn them.

"I didn't think you'd accept this agreement. I thought you would have preferred Delamere take the throne and then get her out the way later, conquering it all for yourself."

Odin laughed. "The Queen is weak. I'd rather she die at my hand and that I rule the world with another powerful leader. Together with Walter, we'll be invincible, and our Houses will reign for thousands of years!"

Elliot began to run, his legs aching and his lungs burning with each breath. He had to warn Sophie and Peter, hoping they could escape before it was too late. Suddenly, something struck his head, and everything went black.

———————◆———————

Elliot's body ached all over. He tried to open his eyes, but all he could see was darkness. It was cold, and his head throbbed painfully; his legs felt like axes were stuck in them. He attempted to get up, but as soon as he was on his feet, he collapsed onto the ground again.

Elliot couldn't see a thing. He put his hand on his right leg and felt his trousers torn in many places. Pain jolted his body as soon as he touched a spot behind his knee. His leg was wounded. He felt his left limb, and it too was injured in the same spot. He couldn't understand what had happened.

Sophie! We've got to get out of here. Memories came back to him. The Emperor had shaken hands with Launus Eymor.

His head felt ready to split, and then he felt around his waist. They'd taken the Sword of Light. The cell door creaked open and made him turn. The light illuminated the cell he was in, revealing a man standing before him.

"Fuck!"

Elliot knew that voice. "Marin?" The Prince approached and touched him on the shoulder. Elliot pulled away sharply. "Don't touch me! You betrayed us!" he shouted.

"I knew nothing." He saw Marin was crying.

"Where's Sophie? Where's Peter?" The man's sobs grew louder. "Tell me!"

"We don't have time for that. We have to go now!" Marin said.

"I'm not going anywhere with you."

"Listen to me!" The Prince's voice echoed through the cell. "I won't let you die in this place! Stand up and come with me, otherwise, I'll have my men take you by force."

"Where's Soph—"

"She's dead! They're all dead! My father killed them."

Elliot sat in shock as tears streamed down his face. "I failed! I failed! TRAITOR!"

"I DIDN'T BETRAY YOU! MY FATHER BETRAYED US ALL!"

"I DON'T BELIEVE YOU!"

"I DON'T CARE! WE HAVE TO LEAVE!"

"NOW YOU WANT TO SAVE ME?!"

"YES! I'M GOING TO SAVE YOU, WHETHER YOU WANT ME TO OR NOT. I LOVED SOPHIE."

"LIAR!"

Marin wiped his eyes and grabbed Elliot by his jerkin. "I can't take revenge on my own father! I can't hurt him! But you can, and if you die, no one will ever avenge what happened. You need to live! Get up!"

Elliot felt his words were truthful, but the pain was so overwhelming that he wanted to unleash his anger on someone. *I can't die... If I die too, everything will be lost.* "Where am I? How did I get here?" he asked Marin, wiping his eyes and trying to calm down.

"In the prison where the boy was. A guard saw you running and punched you in the head."

"How did you get here? Did you get someone to distract the guards again so that you could help me escape?"

"No... After what happened with that boy, my father placed twenty men down here. They cut your legs to make sure you'd be helpless. They're afraid of you."

"And how will you get me out of here?"

"I, too, have men devoted to me in this land."

Elliot sneered. "Men who would disobey the Emperor's orders?"

"Yes. They're outside this cell and have disabled the guards."

Should I believe him? "Then why didn't you use your *loyal* men to save the boy as well?"

"I wouldn't rebel against my father for a boy. However, you're our only hope against the tyranny that plagues this world. We have no more time. Let me help you get up!"

Elliot thought Marin was telling the truth, but he had difficulty believing him. After a moment, he tried to get up but pain paralysed his body. Marin caught him by the shoulder and supported him. "Let's go," the Prince told him.

Elliot limped along with Marin's help, and they left the cell. A couple of dozen men had raised their swords and had pushed the Red Palace dungeon guards up against the wall. The sight surprised him.

"Help me," Marin said, and one of the men sheathed his sword and caught Elliot by the other shoulder.

They carried on walking with difficulty until they reached the winding staircase. "If any of the guards dare follow us, they'll die!" Marin shouted.

They began to climb the stairs, and Elliot heard the Prince's loyal soldiers following them for protection. Elliot glanced behind him. About thirty men were marching with their swords raised. He was in great pain, but after a while, they managed to climb the stairs and moved towards the door leading to the forest behind the palace. Each step caused him even more pain until they finally reached the door and stepped out of the castle. The red moon lit up the sky, and the yellow one seemed dull that night.

"I failed... Sophie is dead." The pain in Elliot's body and soul tore at his insides.

"We don't have time to mourn now," Marin rasped. He and the second soldier continued to support Elliot as they moved towards the forest.

"Are you going to hide me in the caves like you did the boy?"

"No."

They'd been walking for a while, and Elliot could have sworn they were on the same path he and Rain had followed. He felt his eyes closing; he wanted to sleep, and the pain numbed his mind. Suddenly, he heard a loud roar and turned right. A wyvern raised its head above the trees several feet away from them. A jolt of panic shot through Elliot.

"Pay no attention. Move quietly," the Prince murmured.

"If it hears us, we'll all die," Elliot whispered.

"It won't hear us if we are careful."

They kept walking, and the harbour of Mirth came into sight. There was no one on the pier.

"I'm surprised Odin doesn't have guards everywhere after what happened with Rain," Elliot whispered.

"He doesn't need them... He killed all your men and the Queen. You're the only one left because he wanted to kill you in the city square. He wanted to punish you for your insolence. He also didn't consider that you might escape with wounded legs and twenty guards in the dungeons since you have no magical powers."

Elliot hated Odin—he wished he could kill him with his bare hands. They continued downhill between the tall trees for a while, and they came to a dirt road leading to one end of the pier. The two men carried him more forcefully up to the pier.

"This way," Marin said, turning right.

Elliot tried to keep going and saw the cave that Rain had run into a few days earlier a little further away. Suddenly, a loud noise like the sound of a bell rang out, and the wyvern let out a roar.

"What's that?" Elliot asked.

"The temple bells! They've discovered your escape. Hurry!" Marin said.

They kept moving and stopped by a fishing boat. Elliot saw some men on deck, men he hadn't noticed before, the intense pain numbing his senses and making him oblivious to everything else.

Marin pulled a sword from his belt and held out his hand. Elliot's mouth opened wide as he stared at the Sword of Light. "Where did you find it?" he asked, taking the sword. For a moment, he wondered why he hadn't noticed the elaborate hilt on the Prince's belt all this time.

"It doesn't matter. Take these and go!" Marin shouted and shoved two glass vials into the palm of his left hand.

"What are these?"

"Pour the yellow one onto your wounds to stop the bleeding otherwise, you'll die. The other will help you sleep."

Elliot freed himself from the arms supporting him and walked with difficulty along the plank that led onto the deck. The pain in his legs slowed him, and he stopped to face the Prince. "Your father's men will come after us."

They don't know where you're heading, and they won't be able to catch up with you. This ship has the best captain and the best sailors we have—all of them are loyal to me," Marin said hastily.

Elliot saw five men scurrying around the fishing boat. "Thank you," he said.

"I'll see you again, Elliot Egercoll."

A screech came from the sky, and Elliot saw Hurwig flying towards him. "Stay here," he told the hawk as soon as it got close. "Marin will tie a letter to your leg. Take it to Aleron and then come back to me."

"Do you want me to write a letter on your behalf?" the Prince asked.

"I don't think I'll find ink and scrolls on the ship. Write a letter to Aleron. Tell him that the Emperor has betrayed us and that everyone is dead. As soon as you're ready to send the letter, Hurwig will find you," Elliot said.

The Prince nodded curtly.

"Untie the rope!" the man standing by the helm of the small vessel cried, and Elliot walked on deck, the pain killing him.

Marin loosened the mooring lines that tied the ship to the pier, and the fishing boat moved away from land. Elliot took a few more steps and sat on the ice-cold deck. He gripped the vials tightly in the palm of his hand, feeling dead inside.

I failed. I let Sophie die... I failed at everything.

The ship left the harbour and swayed more on the open waves. Angry voices broke out. Elliot tried to stand up, leaning against one end of the ship, and noticed several men gathering on the pier. He saw a few archers raising their bows in the distance, but he knew their arrows wouldn't reach him. Elliot felt as if he was about to faint, and then he heard a roar that sounded like thunder. His breath caught in his throat, and his mouth went dry as a huge creature rose into the sky. His end had come.

The wyvern flapped its huge wings and headed for the ship. Elliot readied himself to meet all the dead people he loved when his eyes caught sight of movement. The light of the red moon shone onto the top of the cliff above the cave, and a small figure stood there, his arm stretching out. Elliot couldn't understand what the person was doing. *Rain?*

The wyvern roared once more and descended on the ship. Then, Elliot felt the wind sweeping past his body.

"What the—!" the captain cried.

Clouds and fog spread across the sky so quickly that everything went dark. The wind grew stronger, and thunderbolts crashed into the sea.

"Watch out! Hoist the sails!"

Elliot could still hear the roars of the monster over their heads, but now it could no longer see them. He tried to keep his body upright as the wind pushed their ship away from Mirth, as if it too was trying to protect them.

A Miserable Emperor

Marin walked towards the chamber where he had been told his father was, his blood boiling. Two guards stood in front of the door, and one raised his hand to stop him.

"Step aside," Marin said sharply.

"I must ask the Emperor if he'll accept visitors," the guard said.

"Step aside now!" Marin shouted.

The guard gave him a hostile look and knocked on the door. "Who is it?" came Odin's voice from within.

"The Prince."

"Let him come in."

The guard stepped aside, and Marin pushed the door open. His eyes fell upon his father sitting comfortably in a chair behind a large table. A few feet away, his sister sat. He hadn't expected to find her there. Marin took a few steps towards Odin and felt the urge to draw his sword.

"How could you?" he asked.

Odin got out of his seat. He was wearing an embroidered golden robe, and his face had gone red. "How dare you talk to me like that, you fool. You're lucky I don't want to spill my blood, otherwise, your head would have already been adorning some spike in the city square. Did you let Elliot escape? You know you'll pay dearly for this."

"You'll pay for everything you've done today! You killed my bride! You killed a queen just before her wedding!"

"I did what I had to do to secure the future of our House. Sophie Delamere was a weak woman. She would never have been able to defeat a man like Walter, and her weakness would have made her easy prey for the throne of Knightdorn for the rest of her life. If she'd ruled with a weak man like you, someone else would have taken the throne away from you even if we'd defeated Walter."

Marin couldn't accept that his father had killed his bride. He had loved Sophie. Drawing his blade, he shouted, "How dare you say such things about me! You killed my bride and still have the audacity to insult me!"

He expected his father would threaten to call the guards but to his surprise, he smiled.

"I never thought you'd have the guts to draw your sword in front of me, Marin. I always believed you were just a foolish coward. Had I known this side of you, I might have believed you could be a leader."

"Did you agree to Sophie travelling here so that you could kill her? Was that your plan from the start?" Odin didn't answer. "Speak!"

"Or what? Will you kill me?"

"You deserve to die!"

"Then do it. Raise your sword and kill your enemy. Take your fate into your own hands."

Marin wanted to do it and have his father's head thrown into the sea.

"I'd decided to have you marry Delamere and fight against Thorn by her side," Odin said suddenly. "I knew that it would be difficult for a man like Walter to ally himself with me, but Sophie needed me. After all, I was sure that with her on the throne, it would have been like me ruling both continents. If Walter lost, I would have the most soldiers in the world. However, as I got to know Sophie and the famous son of Thomas Egercoll, I couldn't help but see that they were both idiots. They didn't have the power to keep hold of a kingdom; they were foolish idealists who thought they could create a beautiful world where only peace would reign. To have peace, you need fear! You need a ruler that no one dares to rebel against."

"A tyrant... " Marin said in a voice full of sarcasm. "You may think so, but history shows that there have always been people who started rebellions against tyrants."

"And if you're smart, you know how to quash every rebellion. Nevertheless, the so-called honourable leaders have never had, nor will they ever have, any future. I've been trying to explain this to you for years, but you've never listened. That's why when Walter sent Launus to offer me an alliance, I decided to get rid of the Queen and unite my House with that of Thorn."

"To unite your House? What do you mean?" Marin asked, his sword still raised.

"Your sister will marry Walter. Soon, she'll grant him an heir, and the Houses of Mud and Thorn will lead the world for hundreds of years. Walter will never allow anyone to overthrow him, and he knows about my power over Kerth. This is the only way there will be peace in the world."

Marin glanced at his sister. He knew that look well—her brows furrowed, her lips pressed into a thin line. Edmee wasn't pleased about the marriage, nor was she happy about the way things had turned out, but she didn't dare go against her father. "When did Walter offer you an alliance?" he asked.

"At dawn, this morning... I couldn't believe it, I dare say. It was a pleasant surprise. I thought I'd been trapped into the marriage with Delamere, but the God of Justice is on my side."

"If there is a God of Justice, you'll meet with a dishonourable death."

Odin's features hardened. "Only my enemies will have a dishonourable death, just as they have always had all these years. My choices have brought our House to where it is today. I became Emperor and you a prince. Without me, you'd be nothing."

"It would have been better if I were nothing! Better than belonging to a house led without honour!"

Odin took a step towards him. "I was right not to want you on the throne of Knightdorn. You're weak—you always have been. You shame our House!"

"*You* shame our House!" Marin shouted.

"If we'd handed Elliot's head over to Walter, we would have immediately gained his loyalty, and you allowed him to escape. You forced me to keep your actions from Launus. I couldn't have the news that my own son let Thomas Egercoll's heir escape reach Walter's ears. I don't want to punish the men who decided to help you; I need every soldier on my land. However, you have only one more chance. If you dare make men disobey my orders again, you'll die. The only reason you're alive is for your mother's sake."

"If my mother were alive to see what you have become, she would have hated you. She would have been ashamed of you."

His father's face took on an almost purple hue. "I intended, even if you are unworthy, to give you Kerth when I die, but you'll get nothing from me. Edmee shall rule by Walter's side in Knightdorn, and one of their children shall take governance over my land. If you ever dare speak to me like that again, you're dead."

"Kill me, then. The only coward is you. You killed the other rulers of Kerth at a feast and Sophie Delamere on her wedding day while you were her host. You have captured nothing through battle because you would have been incapable of winning."

Odin scowled. "You're an idiot! The only reason I didn't fight was to protect my men. I didn't need to spread death to get what I wanted. I brought peace by protecting countless soldiers from war."

"And you gave your land to Walter Thorn, a man who always wanted to rule the world. Once he uses your men and kills his enemies, he'll murder you, too, at the very moment you least expect it. The only hope you had of taking the throne of Knightdorn with a ruler who wouldn't have betrayed you was by being on Sophie's side."

His father snorted. "Sophie would have killed you when she didn't need you! Her beauty blinded you!"

"Then why did you want to marry me off to her?" Marin asked, enraged.

"Because I would have killed her first. That foolish young girl thought she could trick me..."

"Sophie might have killed me, but only if she believed I wanted her out of the way. If she knew that I wouldn't betray her, she would never have murdered me. However, Walter will kill you, no matter what you do!"

"Sophie could never have defeated Walter—even with our men. Did you see that beast that's bonded to him? That wyvern is just one of the monsters fighting on his side. No one can defeat Walter. I had to ally myself with him. As for him getting me out of the way, he's never done so with any of his sworn allies, and I know how to take care of myself better than the foolish Delamere. I made the right decision. Any true leader who got to know Sophie and Elliot would immediately realise that they would have never succeeded in retaining the rulership of a kingdom."

"When I hear of your death, I shall not mourn. You deserve to die." Marin returned his sword to its sheath.

"You deserve to get nothing of all I've built!" Odin yelled.

"I want nothing from you. Whatever you've built is doomed, as are you. Walter won't be long in getting rid of you."

Edmee rose from her seat and looked at him angrily. "Don't talk to father like that!" she snapped.

"I feel sorry for you, sister. You'll spend your whole life in misery to satisfy our father's whims... Walter will treat you like trash, and if you ever talk back to him, you'll die. At least I'll now live a free man to do as I wish. No one cares anymore which woman I marry!"

"If you were a little smarter, you'd care about which woman you should marry! Then, I wouldn't have had to kill that foolish girl you cried about loving in the past," Odin said.

Marin stopped, his hands shaking. "Was it you... you kill Esme?"

"Of course! I didn't want my firstborn to marry a woman with no wealth! I didn't want a marriage that would give us nothing. I thought you'd realise that yourself, but I overestimated you. I did what had to be done. Nevertheless, you're right. I no longer care which woman you marry. The future of our House is secured, thanks to my daughter, who was always better than you."

Marin saw Edmee looking at their father in astonishment as if she'd never expected to hear those words.

"I'm disgusted by you. I wish I had another father," Marin managed to say.

"And I another son. I've sent my best captains to capture Elliot, and if you dare stand in my way again, you'll suffer," Odin said.

Marin turned and headed towards the door filled with hatred, the likes of which he'd never felt before. *My own father... He killed both women I loved.*

"At last, you know the taste of rage and hatred. You've learned what revenge feels like. All this may finally make you a worthy member of my House one day," Odin called.

Marin touched the door handle and looked back at his father. "I've never learned anything from you. You're a man who lives in misery, and you'll die in it, too."

<hr>

Marin walked towards the pier as the sun rose timidly in the sky. Kerth's harbour was deserted, and the three hundred and fifty men who accompanied him walked in silence. He saw the ship he was looking for in the distance and approached it, the wind whipping his face.

Marin glanced around as he walked, his heavy cloak billowing behind him. *I should have left years ago.* He couldn't change the past, only what would happen next. He approached the plank that led on deck. A dozen sailors were getting the ship ready for departure.

"Where are you off to, brother?" Marin turned sharply and saw Edmee standing behind his soldiers with a handful of men. "Order these men back to the city, or you'll die," she said.

"No," Marin said. He hadn't expected to see her here, but he would never again obey her orders.

Edmee drew her sword, and her men did the same. Marin watched as his soldiers also took out their blades.

"You took everything from our father. I think I deserve these men," Marin said.

"You deserve only what Father decides."

"Really? How would you have felt if he'd succeeded in killing Elliot? I noticed how you were look—"

"Shut up! I only do what Father orders!" Edmee shouted.

"And that's why you'll die miserable. If you attack me, my men will die, too, but so will yours, and I'll fight to the death. I either leave or die today."

Edmee stared at him as she walked towards him. Marin's soldiers blocked her passage. "Let her through."

The men stepped aside, and Edmee stopped in front of him. "Father never thought you'd dare disobey him again, but I knew you would. You aren't as cowardly as he thinks."

"Let me go or fight."

His sister's almond-shaped eyes bore into him with such intensity that for a moment, he thought they would scorch him. "I'll let you do as you wish, but if you leave, you should know you will no longer be my brother. If I ever see you on the battlefield, I'll show no mercy."

Marin laughed. "Goodbye then, Edmee. Onto the ship!" he called to his men, and they sheathed their swords and continued marching.

Marin was about to leave, but before he did, he took one last look at his sister. "On any other day, you wouldn't have allowed me to leave without a fight. As much as you refuse to admit it, in your heart, you know the truth, too. Don't waste your life for him." With those words he climbed aboard the ship as fast as he could, feeling free for the first time in his life.

The Ruler of the World

Walter gazed at the rising sun from the courtyard of the Palace of Dawn. The sunrise was a splash of red with hues of yellow. He was very happy that morning; he felt that whoever the real gods were, they were helping him.

He clasped the scroll Launus had written to him, feeling satisfied. Odin Mud had agreed to fight for him and his whore of a cousin was dead. Walter would have preferred to have killed her himself, proving to the entire kingdom how powerful he was, but he'd decided that it wasn't important. Everyone now knew that Elliot Egercoll was the only reason the Queen had stayed alive, and without him, she was doomed. He no longer saw the need to personally kill the Queen or Syrella Endor to show Knightdorn how powerful he was. Thomas Egercoll's son was the only one he must defeat in front of everyone, and then the House of Pegasus would die once and for all.

Sophie kept you from the throne for seventeen long years. Her death by your hand would have sent a message, his conscience told him. *Sophie gave up her throne and hid in Elmor. Everyone knew it was only a matter of time before she died, but then the last of Althalos' apprentices appeared!* Elliot was now the symbol of the rebellion against him, and he had to be killed by Walter's hand. Sophie and Syrella no longer mattered. *Perhaps I should ask Sadon to get the Scarred Queen out of the way. This might bring discord to Elmor, and Elliot would be left without any allies except for the Elder Races.*

He considered the thought for a moment but quickly realised it wasn't the best option. The assassination of Syrella might unite Elmor against him, and old Sadon wouldn't be able to convince them to side with him easily. It was possible that Elmor would rise up after the assassination of its ruler, and Walter didn't want them to thirst for revenge. Fear was preferable; he'd kill them all in battle.

He scratched his chin. Now everything was simple. He had sixteen wyverns, forty thousand new soldiers, and he was invulnerable to everything except to the Seven Swords and fire. *The boy can't stop me, and the Royal Army is without a leader.* He knew Sophie's men would fight for Syrella, but after his cousin's death, their loyalty wouldn't last long. Those men had suffered through years of war, and once they saw Walter's army in Wirskworth, it wouldn't be long before they deserted and surrendered.

A marriage brought me victory...

For days, Walter had been thinking that Odin was the only one left in the world with a large army—the only one who could tip the balance in the war. He'd assumed that Sophie would have perhaps tried to get him on her side, but he hadn't imagined that she would rush to Kerth, intent on marrying Marin Mud. Walter had flown to Mermainthor with two wyverns and had asked Launus to travel to Kerth to propose an agreement with the self-proclaimed *Emperor*. He may not have been sure whether Launus would find Sophie there, but he'd told him to be prepared for anything. He'd let a wyvern accompany him to prove to the Emperor who would win the war of Knightdorn.

The plan worked... Launus had spoken to Odin as soon as the weather had permitted him to travel to Mirth. The Emperor had murdered Sophie, and Launus had tied a letter with the news to the wyvern's toe. For a moment, he imagined the terror on Launus's face as the wyvern approached him so that he could tie the letter to its foot, and he felt the urge to laugh. Launus may have been very old, but he had proved very useful. Walter didn't have the time to travel all the way to the Western Empire with an army, and he wouldn't have risked going there alone, even with sixteen wyverns. He might be invincible, but forty thousand men might have somehow managed to capture him, and he wouldn't have taken that risk. Launus had managed to build a valuable alliance. Moreover, the Governor of Mynlands was the man who had captured the mermaids on Walter's behalf a few years ago. A scene from the past flashed through his mind.

"*You want me to capture mermaids? But they are very strong and invulnerable in water, too,*" Launus had said.

"*You're a clever man. I'm sure you'll find a way.*"

"*Why do you want to capture mermaids?*"

Walter had smiled. "*I want to study them.*"

Launus had been about to ask more questions, but Walter had looked at him in a way that ended the conversation.

Sometime later, the Governor of Mynlands had brought him three mermaids and had told him that he'd used a huge ship with steel nets to catch them. Launus had confided to him that mermaids adored crabs, and he'd thrown countless of them into a spot at the bottom of the crystal clear sea near the shores of his land. Launus' sailors had waited for days until they saw some mermaids approaching the crabs, and then the metal nets had trapped them. They'd tried hard to break the traps but hadn't succeeded before the sailors threw them ashore. Walter had wondered why the mermaids had scrambled to eat the bait that was in a metal net, and Launus had laughed when he'd expressed his puzzlement.

"*The metal lay on the seabed, and I'm sure they didn't understand why it was there. They may have thought we were experimenting with something. They didn't suppose we would try and catch them. Mermaids know that only a foolish human would mess with them. Nevertheless, I don't want to do that again. I don't want the rest of the mermaids to suspect that I captured some of them and start attacking my men. That would be disastrous.*"

Walter had agreed, and Leonhard's experiments had killed two of the captive mermaids, leaving only one. That mermaid wasn't to die; he needed her blood. *Without a doubt, Launus has been useful to me*. Walter had promised him that after Elliot's death, he would kill Odin and his daughter and appoint him Governor of Kerth while Mynlands would also remain under his command.

Elliot managed to get away again. That thought irritated him.

Launus had written to him that despite his objections, Odin had decided to kill the boy and send Walter his head. However, Elliot had escaped on a fishing boat. Walter felt odd about that news. On the one hand, if the Emperor killed the boy, it would infuriate him, but on the other hand, the idea that Elliot had escaped once again was also unnerving.

How had he managed to get away? The letter said he had broken out from the cells, but Walter knew it would have been impossible to escape without help from within the city. *Someone in Mirth helped Elliot, and it didn't reach Launus' ears*. Walter had ordered his wyvern to obey Launus if he asked for help against Elliot. He'd told the wyvern not to kill the boy, but that if he attacked Launus or tried to run away, it was to help Launus catch him. But his wyvern had failed since clouds had covered the sky and lightning had struck the beast's back. It was a wonder how the boy always managed to get away, but his luck would run out at some point.

You'll die soon, he told the image of Elliot in his mind.

"Why do you so want to overthrow the Egercolls? Your mother is an Egercoll!"

His father's words came back to him. He remembered Robert Thorn standing before him, asking for a truce—asking him to stop the war and return to Gaeldeath. That memory infuriated him. His own father had been such a coward that he'd told him he would let him keep Gaeldeath if he returned north and stopped the rebellion against Thomas Egercoll.

I took his territory from him by force, and instead of fighting for what was rightfully his, he allowed me to keep his land in exchange for Thomas' life. Robert Thorn didn't deserve to belong to his House.

Walter touched the hilt of the sword and remembered the moment he'd drawn his blade and slashed his father's head. He wished he'd had another father—a man of courage.

"I didn't think you'd be awake so early," came a voice. He turned around and saw Berta, dressed in a black gown, walking towards him. Her face wore its familiar beauty, yet something seemed to be bothering his most loyal companion.

"What's the matter?" he asked.

A furrow had formed on her forehead. "Are you eagerly anticipating meeting your future bride?"

Walter smirked. "A warrior and member of the Trinity of Death shouldn't preoccupy herself with such nonsense. Jealousy doesn't suit you, Berta." The woman got closer to him, still scowling. "You know my bride will die along with her entire House once I kill Elliot, Syrella, and each and every remaining enemy of the kingdom."

"Kill Odin and his daughter as soon as they set foot in Knightdorn and take their men," Berta said in a loud voice.

"Jealousy has blinded you," Walter told her, a note of disapproval in his voice. "I don't know how loyal Odin's soldiers are to him. If I kill him before the battle, his men may turn against me, and that will do me no good. I must kill Elliot first, and then the Emperor and his daughter will follow him to their deaths. Afterwards, all the soldiers will see how powerful I am, and there will be no other leader left to turn to—no one will dare disobey my orders."

"You're right, Your Majesty," Berta said with a bow.

Walter looked at her with a smile. "Soon, I'll rule the world, and you'll be by my side, and no one will ever get in our way again."

A Lifeless Hand

S yrella was agitated as she walked through the corridors lit by the scant light of dusk, two men of the Sharp Swords following close behind. A soldier had told her that some men from the City Guard had requested her presence in the Great Hall of Moonstone. The guards had arrested two young boys who had thrown stones at them. *These boys must be the ones who attacked Selwyn.*

Syrella could see the sun setting through the windows, and she felt a sense of satisfaction. Her plan had worked. *Now I'll find out who the traitor is*, she thought.

Syrella didn't want anyone else to know about the traitor she was looking for; enough people already knew. However, she had told the City Guard that there were boys who had thrown stones at Selwyn Brau while they were following him. She'd asked them to keep an eye out for the boys, saying that they might try to cause trouble in Wirskworth again. Syrella realised the traitor might find out she was looking for the young spies who worked for him, but she didn't care.

The boys who've been caught may not have been working for the traitor but only for some foolish thieves. Syrella had decided not to speak of the traitor she was looking for in front of the guards. She would ask the captives who they were working for, and perhaps their answers would give her what she was looking for.

She went down another corridor and found herself in front of the Great Hall. The guards stepped aside, and she walked into the Hall with the men of the Sharp Swords. The room was crowded, and a few dozen men stood before her stone seat. Two boys lay on the ground amongst them. Syrella walked over to them. Their faces were inscrutable, and the cheeks of one of them were splattered with mud.

"Where did you catch these boys?" she asked the guards.

One of them stepped forward—Syrella didn't know him. "We heard about thieves trying to steal food and armour in the city. We rushed to the scene and found three of them raiding a merchant's stall and an ironmonger's shop just a few feet apart. When we caught the thieves, these boys started throwing stones at us. We managed to stop them, but the thieves escaped. However, the boys remained in our grasp, and we brought them before you, my lady. I heard you had asked us to watch for young boys who might cause trouble."

"I gave those orders, but there was no need for two dozen guards to bring these boys to me... "

"We all escorted them to the castle because we feared their accomplices might attack us, intent on freeing them," the guard said.

Syrella glanced at the two children who hadn't looked up all the while. They looked like street urchins. "A couple of boys threw stones at a man's head a few days ago and seriously injured him. Was it you?" she asked them. Neither of the boys responded. "Crime is punished harshly in Elmor. I don't know who asked you to do what you did, but you'll pay for your actions. If you tell me everything, I'll make sure your punishment isn't so harsh." The children looked in her direction, but their lips remained tightly closed. They couldn't have been more than ten years old.

The guard who had spoken earlier drew his sword. "If we cut off their hands, they'll speak."

The boys kept lying on the ground, frozen in place.

Syrella looked at the guards. "I want one of you to run and bring Lord Brau here. He'll be able to identify the boy who was following him." She should have thought to call Selwyn earlier, but when she'd heard of the boys' capture, she'd been too alarmed to think of it. After the murder of the man in her chamber, she feared what else might happen.

One soldier marched away immediately. The guard with the raised sword took a step closer to the boys and grabbed one by the shoulder. "If you don't speak up, I'll feed you your hands." The boy looked him in the eye, remaining silent. The children seemed to have lost the will to live, so they didn't care much about their threats.

Syrella seized the guard's hand and motioned for him to step aside. Then she leaned towards the boy whose wrist the man had gripped. "Why won't you tell us who you're helping? Are you afraid his accomplices might harm you?"

To her surprise, the boy laughed. "Whatever I say, I'm dead. Me, my parents and my sister, we'll all die."

Syrella frowned. "No. I'll punish you for what you did, but you'll live, and so will your family. However, I'll kill whoever made you attack my men. No matter who he is, he won't be able to do you any harm." She was almost certain now that the children were working for the traitor she was looking for. Their fear of speaking out revealed that they knew how ruthless the man was, which he'd proven by the way he'd killed the lad in her chamber.

The boy lowered his eyes. "No one can save me," he whispered. "I've seen what he's capable of."

"What man? Who is the man who made you do what you did? Tell me his name." The boy looked up again but didn't speak. Syrella was enraged. "The lord who was attacked by a few boys like you is coming here, and if he identifies you as the ones who attacked him, I'll have no choice but to punish you. If you don't speak up, your punishment will be even harsher."

"Harsher than death?" the boy asked.

"Death isn't the worst thing, young man. Life without a tongue, eyes or limbs is much worse than death. If I were you, I wouldn't try my luck." She didn't like threatening children with such harsh punishment, but she had no choice.

"What's going on here?"

Syrella turned towards the entrance and saw Jahon approaching alongside Sadon Burns.

"The City Guard caught two boys throwing rocks at my men while they were struggling to capture some thieves. Who told you to come here?" Syrella asked the two men.

"A guard crossed our path a moment ago and said he was looking for Selwyn Brau so that he could identify the boys who attacked him," Sadon said.

Syrella had spread the word about what had happened to Selwyn without mentioning the traitor she was looking for. "That's true," she said.

Sadon and Jahon walked towards the boys, and Syrella turned to them again.

"Today you've committed a crime against Elmor and its people. As I said before, if it turns out that you're the ones who also struck Lord Brau, I'll be forced to punish you severely. I'm giving you another chance. Tell me who you're working for, and I'll make sure your punishment is as lenient as possible." Syrella leaned towards the boy who had spoken earlier. "Talk to me, and no one will harm your family."

The child fixed his eyes on hers. "You can't protect me. Even if I tell you who the man I'm working for is, he'll murder you before you can kill him," he told her.

Syrella was taken aback. "Why would you think that?"

"Because he's behind you."

Everything happened very fast. The guards drew their swords, and screams filled the hall. Syrella saw blades slicing the throats of her personal guards as the soldiers restrained her and Jahon. Then, a hand grabbed her arm, and she felt something cold press against her throat. She looked at the blade of the dagger pressed against her flesh and felt hot breath on the back of her neck.

"You can't imagine how many years I've been waiting for this moment," Sadon said.

"You?! You're Walter's traitor?" Syrella felt fear. There was no way out. She had to scream in an attempt to summon more guards.

"I'm glad your arrogance never let you see the truth."

"Why?" was the only word that escaped her lips.

"You dare to ask why? You've dishonoured my son! You've been fucking this bastard for years and even bore his daughters!" Syrella couldn't see Sadon's face, but she was certain his glare was burning into Jahon. "I saw you kissing that filth years ago and decided to help Walter kill you. Nevertheless, I hadn't imagined you would send my son to the Battle of the Forked River. I didn't think you'd kill him."

"I didn't send your son to battle! Sermor chose to go there without my knowledge, seeking glory!" Syrella cried.

"Lies!"

It was the truth, but she would never succeed in convincing Sadon. "You were the one who killed Sermor! You were the one who betrayed my plan to Walter! You wanted to take revenge on me, and your betrayal cost the life of your son, along with that of countless people from Elmor! YOU ARE A COWARDLY TRAITOR AND A FOOL, TOO!" She felt the dagger tremble against her throat. "You didn't think your son would fight... You just wanted me to fail in battle, but fate punished you. If you want to kill the one responsible for Sermor's death, take this dagger and cut your own throat."

Syrella screamed in pain as the dagger pierced her ribs. Jahon tried to rush to her side, but three swords pointed at his neck. The two boys stood frozen, staring at the spectacle on the floor.

"Shut up you whore! You're to blame for everything! You forced me to betray my land to avenge myself for what you did to my son! You gave birth to Jahon's bastards and made Sermor believe he was their father! Did you think I'd let your betrayal go unpunished? I thought of leaving the city with my loyal men and fighting for Walter, but I chose to stay here and destroy you from within—to take everything from you, just like you took it all from me!"

"I'll kill you, Burns!" Jahon cried.

Sadon laughed, and Syrella felt the pain tearing through her insides. "Why didn't you tell Sermor the truth?" she asked. "If you'd told him, he wouldn't have fought in the Forked River."

"My son never kept his mouth shut. He would have spoken, and that would have destroyed our House. You would have killed us all for fear we might seek revenge. I had to wait until the right moment, and now, after all these years, you'll be punished," Sadon said.

"You didn't tell him the truth, and it cost him his life, all for the plan you divulged to Walter! Even if you kill me, you'll never find peace for what you've done, Burns!" Syrella spat, breathing through the pain.

She felt the man's breath in her ear, and the dagger still lodged deep into her flesh. "Maybe not. However, I'll always remember your defenceless face. I was the one who created unrest in your city, the one who killed the idiot in your chamber who was about to reveal what I'd been doing, the one who had boys follow you and your men. You were foolish; you never caught on to me. As soon as I heard you were going to send our army to your niece's rescue, I made sure to keep only my loyal men here in order to kill you, and I succeeded! When you die, I'll spread word of what you have done and let it be known that you tried to kill me to hide the truth about your bastards. I'll take the rulership of Elmor. I'll kill your daughters, and this place will see peace with Walter on the throne."

"My people won't believe you. They'll never devote themselves to Walter. They'll punish you for what you've done, and my daughters will feed you your own intestines."

"We'll see about that. However, you won't be here to see what happens, my dear."

"Will you help a traitor?" Syrella shouted, looking at the rest of the soldiers. None of them spoke, and the two boys watched the scene unfold before them, seemingly stupefied. She couldn't believe her end would come like this, within her own city.

"These soldiers are dedicated to me. They won't help a ruler who has been lying all these years," Sadon told her.

Syrella looked at Jahon. He had several swords pointed at him, and he seemed desperate to do something to save her. "Mark my words, Sadon. My daughters will take revenge for what you're about to do."

Sadon laughed. "Soon their heads will adorn a city square, side by side with yours."

Syrella loathed him. She moved backwards sharply, and Sadon pulled the dagger out of her ribs and drove it into her stomach. She tasted blood on her lips and fell to the ground as another body slumped beside her. Her vision had blurred, but she saw Jahon's neck spewing blood next to her. Everything began going dark as she reached out to lay her hand over his lifeless one, the heat slowly leaving his fingers as a tear rolled down her cheek.

From Gregory Kontaxis

If you enjoyed this story, please consider leaving a review on Amazon. It would mean so much to me. And if you are on Goodreads, would you share your thoughts with friends and followers?

You can also find all of my latest writing news, a free novella of the Dance of Light series, interactive maps, and much more on my website at www.gregorykontaxis.com.

About the author

Gregory Kontaxis was born in Athens. He studied Informatics and Finance in Greece and the United Kingdom, and he has worked as a Financial Analyst in Vienna and London. He currently resides in London, where he busies himself with investment risk management and writing. *The Return of the Knights* is the first book of his pentalogy, *The Dance of Light*.

www.ingramcontent.com/pod-product-compliance
Ingram Content Group UK Ltd.
Pitfield, Milton Keynes, MK11 3LW, UK
UKHW041814060525
458268UK00002B/10